THE ZEPPELIN DECEPTION

A Stoker & Holmes Book

COLLEEN GLEASON

To everyone who was Team Mina or Team Evaline...thank you from the bottom of my heart.

London, 1890

MISS HOLMES

- IN WHICH THE END BEGINS -

The dawning of the last decade of the nineteenth century did not come—at least in my opinion—accompanied by celebration and optimism.

In fact, I regret to say, the change from the old year to the new annal of 1890 brought with it darkness, apprehension, and despair.

For the latter nine months of the year 1889, I had partnered with Miss Evaline Stoker—a young woman who, though quite different in temperament and intellectual capacity than myself, was an incredibly brave and honorable individual. We had formed this partnership at the behest of Miss Irene Adler, joining her in service to Her Royal Highness Princess Alexandra.

Those nine months had been fraught with adventure, danger, mystery, and crime-solving, as well as the burgeoning friendship between myself and Miss Stoker despite our mutual initial reluctance to work together. There had also been several members of the male gender who inserted themselves into our investigations, willy-nilly and, at times, unwelcomed.

But as the year ended and rolled into 1890, everything changed radically—and in utterly unpleasant ways.

On the day this narrative begins—specifically the seventh

of February, which imposed cold, blustery winds and tiny, unforgiving ice pellets on the city as a sort of underscore to the news I was soon to receive—I stumbled gratefully back into the house after running several imperative errands that morning.

Our housekeeper Mrs. Raskill had gone off to Cornwall to care for her niece, who'd just had her third child, leaving me to run the household on my own—which I am, of course, fully capable, though not particularly desirous, of doing. Today, that included going to market despite the inclement weather, and that was from whence I was returning.

I'd misplaced half of my favorite pair of gloves—which I needed on a day like today—and instead of protecting me from the sleet and damp, my new umbrella had ended up dumping the wet all over me due to a malfunction of one of its mechanical ribs.

This, along with the weather, had already put me in an untenable mood, but when I managed to get my dripping, freezing self inside the two-story brick residence I shared with my father, Sir Mycroft Holmes—at least when he bothered to come home—and saw that the mail had been delivered, my emotions soured further. And that was when something very like despair overtook me.

I glared at the inanimate object of my antipathy as I removed my sagging hat and tossed my soaking cloak vaguely toward the automatic closet.

There on the table, where the Eppie's Mail-Monger had sorted each item by size, was the missive I had feared and dreaded.

Please understand that *despair* is not a word often used to describe the emotions of a Holmes—whether by myself or someone else. Those of my kindred are of much stouter heart, stronger of spine, and ingenious of resource than to resort to despair.

But I confess that when I picked up the small square box

sitting atop the pile of mail, my insides shriveled. And for the first time in nearly a year, I felt utterly and completely *alone*.

Although I knew who the sender was, and what awful news it portended, I examined the package with the careful study that has made the reputation of my infamous family—not only that of my father and my uncle Sherlock, but mine as well.

The item that captured my reluctant interest was larger than the palm of my hand when I rested it there to feel its weight. A square, cardboard package of brilliant white, it had a crimson ribbon of velvet that tied it closed. A wax seal that seemed to be (and could very well have been, considering the wealth of the individual who'd sent it) made from ground pearls glittered at the seam and ensured that the ribbon had not been disturbed. A small cluster of flowers—miniature red roses of a stunning, bloodlike hue I'd never seen before, and *fresh*, in February!—were affixed to the top in an elegant sort of nosegay.

The writing on the front of the teacup-sized box was in a hand not familiar to me, but the perfect script in—Good heavens, did the ink actually carry the scent of roses in its very makeup?

Pushing a damp lock of hair from my face, I tilted the box and sniffed the pale red writing. Yes, the essence of rose emanated from the particularly large and thick dot at the end of my name—Miss Mina Holmes—on the front. A pale sprinkle of pearlescent glitter dusted the edge of that frontispiece of the cube, and had clung to the ink before it dried. This gave the script a lovely, sparkling depth.

On any other occasion, I would have been properly awed by the beauty and uniqueness of such a package, but not in this case.

I considered setting it aside and refusing to open it—after all, there were several other items in the sorted stacks of mail, including a simple, boring, small envelope with my name stamped on it that, at first glance, indicated nothing about the sender.

But, as I have mentioned previously, a Holmes is always of stout heart (although in my case, that stoutness might be less robust when entering a small, dark, enclosed location), and I knew that ignoring the package would have no effect on its contents and the event it portended.

And so I carefully removed the tiny blood-red nosegay and pried up the pearly seal, setting them both aside in order to open the lid.

It lifted easily, and before I could look inside, I heard a quiet whirring from within. To my amazement, a small cardboard block emerged from inside the box, and then another smaller one from inside that one, and another and another, until it telescoped into a sort of tower approximately eighteen inches high from the original package.

Each block was made from sturdy cardboard whose sides had been cut out in a complicated, lacy pattern and was painstakingly edged with gold paint. It looked almost like a square wedding cake with gilt edges, and as each little extension emerged, a little puff of rose fragrance was released.

I was impressed and charmed in spite of myself, and when the smallest filigree cube had emerged, the whirring changed slightly. All at once, a small roll of paper emerged like a finger from the top, and suddenly it unfurled itself, down the front of the lacy tower.

As it unrolled, the paper—which was a shimmery, pliable, vellum-like substance—unfolded two arms so that it became as wide as the original cube and the scroll cascaded down the front of the tower. Finally, the quiet mechanics ceased and the paper hung like a pearlescent banner from a miniature castle's peak, proclaiming the event that I had been dreading.

Sir Emmett Oligary
Requests your esteemed presence
At the Nuptials of his brother

Edward Lucas Oligary
&
Miss Evaline Eustacia Stoker
The First of March
In the Year of Our Lord
The Oligary Tower Penthouse
Six O'Clock in the Evening

I WAS NOT at all surprised to see the words, but I was startled by my physical reaction to them. My stomach pitched sharply downward, my eyes stung, and my heart began to beat faster.

It is actually going to happen.

In three weeks.

I supposed I'd somehow harbored hope that something would occur to change the inevitable. After all, during the last nine months, Evaline and I had managed over and over again to come forth triumphant in the endeavors we undertook.

Well, most of them.

I still smarted over the failure of the Chess Queen Enigma, wherein the devious villainess known as the Ankh had managed to steal—right from under my nose!—the secrets (if there actually were any) hidden inside a Byzantine chess table that had belonged to two powerful British queens.

I sighed and pushed the dripping hair out of my face. As cunning as it was, I couldn't look at the elegant, complicated, fragrant invitation any longer. I turned away in a whirl of skirts and abject frustration, nearly oversetting the Brolly-Warmer Deluxe.

I hadn't spoken to Evaline, nor heard anything from her, for nearly two months—since that night at The Carnelian Crow when the Ankh escaped justice yet again.

I'd sent her a note the next morning...but she never responded. And despite the fact that I'd thought to call on her several times since, something held me back from contacting her again. She clearly had no desire to be in touch with me, and I told myself I was giving her the opportunity to contend with everything that had happened at The Carnelian Crow.

Had I made a mistake, staying out of touch?

And yet I hadn't received even the whiff of a contact from her either. Apparently, she'd decided to move on with her life.

But I don't want to get married. Can't you do something? You're a Holmes!

Evaline had said that to me—in a variety of words, tones, and volumes—more times than I cared to count during our investigation of The Carnelian Crow.

But there was nothing I could do. Nor was it *my* place to do anything.

For, as much as I hated to admit it, Evaline's problem wasn't something I or anyone else could fix for her. She had to decide what to do, and then take the appropriate action.

It was Evaline's brother, Bram, who'd gotten himself and his wife into a financial fix that required—or so they told Evaline— her to marry a wealthy man. And quickly. They'd told her she had to at least become engaged before the end of the year, or they would succumb to the bill collectors and all of them would be thrown out of Grantworth House.

When she approached me for help, I merely pointed out to Evaline that she had three options: she could do as Bram and Florence wished and marry to save *them*, she could marry for *herself* when and if she chose, or she could simply decide not to marry at all and let Bram and Florence deal with their own mistakes and problems.

I even offered to allow her to live with me for a while (although, to be truthful, I wasn't certain how that would go on, for, as I've indicated previously, Evaline and I possess such different personalities that one might describe them as sand and glass).

I glowered at the fancy filigree invitation. Apparently, Evaline had made her decision.

As I continued looking at the shimmery vellum announcement, I attempted to quell the unfamiliar sense of despair. When Evaline married Ned Oligary on March first, our partnership would be over.

In effect, it was already over.

That was why I hadn't seen nor heard from her in months. And I had no intention of contacting her.

But what would I do without my partner?

Well, certainly, there were benefits to working on my own—which I had been doing over the last months, thanks to Miss Adler.

I could continue with the sorts of tasks to which she'd been setting me: discovering where one of Princess Alix's ladies-in-waiting's cat had disappeared to (in the cellar of Buckingham Palace, where the mouse population had happily been decimated), determining the origin of a particular, suspicious-looking tea leaf that had apparently found its way to Her Majesty's table (a silver needle tip that was imported from China), translating a document from Russian that possibly revealed the location of the Lost Library of Ivan the Terrible (it turned out to be a badly written love poem), and more.

Not particularly interesting or exciting cases—nor dangerous—but they were enough to keep my mind occupied.

Working alone, I didn't have to worry about Evaline doing something impetuous and getting us nearly killed—as she'd done that first night we encountered the Ankh in a secret chamber under the Thames—and several times since. She tended to rage into situations without thinking or planning... Although, I must admit, she'd slightly improved in that area over the last few months.

I sighed and realized my eyes were stinging. I blinked rapidly, annoyed with myself. A Holmes does not allow emotion to guide her actions.

Which was why I'd left Evaline alone for the last two months.

I'd made a mistake in doing so, hadn't I?

And now it was too late.

But perhaps it wasn't. Her birthday was in three days. Perhaps I could—

A violent pounding at the front door startled me out of my musings.

What on earth?

I was alone in the house, of course, and thus it fell to me to answer whoever it was that insisted on ignoring our mechanized copper and brass cog-work door knocker and using their meaty (they sounded like the size of a ham) fists—yes, plural—to attempt to gain entrance.

"Open up in there! It's Scotland Yard!"

My eyes widened, and my heart gave a funny little skip. I hadn't spoken to Inspector Ambrose Grayling since that night at The Carnelian Crow. I'd seen him once, from a distance, when I'd visited the Met with my uncle.

Once, from a distance.

Grayling had nodded at me, but hadn't made an effort to speak to me, even after...well, after everything that had happened that night at the secret club.

"One moment," I called back, stifling the niggle of despair that reared its ugly head again.

Grayling would never pound on the door in that violent, uncouth manner, and I certainly didn't recognize the demanding voice, but the fact that it would be one or more of his colleagues —and perhaps even Grayling himself—spurred me to attempt to fix my drooping hair. I frantically jammed a pin into my heavy locks—and, painfully, into my scalp—in an effort to put myself to rights, despite the fact that the hems of my frock were soaking.

"Open up!" The door heaved on its hinges beneath the onslaught of heavy fists, and I began to become alarmed.

What on earth was the matter?

Were they in search of my father on some urgent task?

Was there an emergency? If so, why didn't they say so instead of making such rude demands?

Or were they just being ham-handed (I make that jest quite purposely) and obnoxious?

I flung open the door, prepared to give whoever it was a very strident lecture. There were three men standing there—none of whom were Grayling. "Sir, your impatience and vociferous—"

"Miss Alvermina Holmes?" demanded the burly constable whose raised hand indicated he was the one who'd been attempting to pound down my door.

How *dare* he interrupt me? What a rude individual. I was going to have to speak to his superior.

"I'm Miss Holmes. I cannot understand why—"

"Miss Holmes, step out here, please." The man actually had the audacity to interrupt me a second time—and to give me an order.

"I most certainly will not—"

"Miss Holmes, I'm not going to say it again. Step out of the house and keep your hands where I can see them."

Evaline Stoker might be one of the most physically strong and capable people I know, and she might be quick to defend or attack, but at that moment, when I realized what was happening, I would have anticipated even her.

I reacted in an instant, slamming the door and bolting it in one smooth, quicksilver motion. My heart was thudding wildly.

Something was wrong. Something was very wrong.

"Alvermina Holmes, open the door immediately! The house is surrounded by constables, and there is nowhere for you to go."

Something was *definitely* very, *very* wrong.

"Open up, Miss Holmes!"

That little niggle of despair I'd been battling?

In that moment, as the situation began to sink in, it became a full-blown hurricane of shock and fear. And when I heard the next words, I went completely numb:

"Alvermina Holmes, the Metropolitan Police are placing you under arrest for the murder of Frederick Boggs."

MISS STOKER

- INVITATION FROM A MURDERER -

The day the invitations to my wedding were sent (and delivered; the Oligarys don't wait on the post) was a horrid day. And I don't just mean the weather (which was cold, sleety, and windy).

I felt as if I were Anne Boleyn, having her execution date set. There'd been no escape for her.

There was no escape for me.

The last two months had been a blur of activity. Dress fittings. Trousseau fittings. Guest lists. Invitation design. Wedding theme. Blasted *flower* choices.

And then, somewhere in there, Florence had had the idea of a masquerade ball for my eighteenth birthday. (It was partly my fault, because she'd asked me what kind of celebration I wanted. I was not in a good mood—there had been three meetings in a row about what sort of *stockings* I was going to wear under my wedding dress—so I'd made a flip comment about everyone walking around with masks on so I didn't have to talk to them. And the next thing I knew, there was going to be a masquerade ball.)

And as if the meetings and planning wasn't enough, there

were also all of the required social calls. That was so everyone could swoon over my "choice" of fiancé.

Which I despised. (The social calls, not my fiancé. Honestly, Ned was a nice enough man. It wasn't his fault I didn't want to get married.)

To make it worse, my sister-in-law Florence had been floating around as if on air since everything had been finalized. And now she had moved on to badgering me about what I was going to wear at the masquerade ball in three days' time.

(Did I care? No. No, I did not.)

And so, on the day my wedding invitations were hand-delivered all over the city, all I wanted to do was hide away and sulk.

Or to hit something. Hard enough to shatter it.

So that was what I did. I locked myself in the large, empty ballroom that I used for practicing my vampire-fighting skills. Florence didn't know about this side of me, of course. And now that I was getting married and saving him from financial ruin, Bram pretended to have forgotten about it—because, of course, once I was an Oligary, I would no longer be able to slink around on the streets at night and slay the UnDead.

Not that I had been doing that anyway, for the last two months.

Grimacing at the thought, I turned on the Sure-Step Debonair Dance-Tutor, which was supposed to be used to teach young ladies to dance. But in my case, it had been reformulated by my trainer, Siri, to help me learn to fight better.

I was so angry and upset that it took only a single, rounding blow from my leg to send the Sure-Step clattering across the room. It ended up in a heap of groaning cogs and steaming mechanics that hissed into silence.

Drat and *blast*! Now what was I going to do?

I fumed, spinning, kicking, and punching at invisible vampires and society matrons and bill collectors and floral designers until I was a sweaty, panting mess.

And just as I gave one last furious stomp, someone knocked on the chamber door.

"Miss Evaline?" It was Brentwood, our butler.

"Yes?" I limped over to the door (I'd stubbed my toe in a fit of pique) and cracked it open. There was no need for Brentwood to see that I was wearing very unfeminine clothing, and how much of a bedraggled mess my hair had become.

"There's a message come for you."

"Thanks," I said unenthusiastically. I accepted the message slipped through the small opening. Probably another invitation to *tea* or to a *fête* or to the *theater*.

"The—er—messenger is waiting your reply."

I closed the door firmly. My reply? Simple: *No thank you.*

A gust of wintry wind rattled the window, and I glared at the sleet and ugliness outside. Then I glared at the message.

Now that I was going to marry the most famous, wealthiest bachelor in the city—excluding Ned's brother Sir Emmett, of course—the invitations had poured into our house. I'd had social engagements aplenty before, and I'd avoided as many of them as possible. But they'd increased tenfold since the announcement in the *Times*, which Ned, Bram, and Florence had published *without my agreement.*

The reminder of what they'd done infuriated me every time I thought about it. But it was too late. The damage had been done. And in three weeks, I was going to be a very rich woman.

A *wife.*

Tears stung my eyes, and before I could stop myself, I pulled back my fist and punched the wall.

It went through the plaster so hard and fast that my knuckled slammed into the inside of the wall on the *other* side.

And it hurt, blast it.

Venators—vampire hunters—can be injured. We heal quickly, but we can feel the pain.

I glared at my bruised knuckles and blinked back the tears.

How could I give up my responsibility as a vampire hunter now that I was going to be a *wife*?

In my fury, I'd dropped the new message on the floor. Still frowning, I swooped down to pick it up. One of the benefits of being a Venator was that I often went without the tight stays other women wore. Thus, I could bend and twist with ease.

The thick crème packet was heavy between my fingers. I gave it a dark look. If Mina Holmes were here, she'd probably look at it and be able to tell me exactly who it was from and what they wanted—without even opening it.

Mina Holmes.

I gave the same sort of sniff she did when she didn't want to admit she was wrong about something.

I hadn't heard a thing from Mina since that night at The Carnelian Crow—the night I'd learned Pix's real identity.

The night he had been arrested.

For murder.

Mina hadn't so much as sent me a note since then. Even after the engagement announcement was published.

And I saw no reason to contact her if she ignored me. In fact, I told Florence not to bother to send her an invitation to my birthday masquerade.

I wanted to tear the message into pieces. I almost did.

And then I saw the seal on it.

Cosgrove-Pitt.

My stomach flipped.

I turned it back over. My name was written on it in a feminine hand: *Miss Evaline Stoker*.

Before I realized what I was doing, I'd removed the coppery wax seal.

Miss Stoker:
Felicitations on your upcoming nuptials.
Would you be so kind as to join me for tea today? Three o'clock at

Cosgrove Terrace.
—*Lady Isabella Cosgrove-Pitt*

I STARED at the beautiful handwriting. Then I yanked the door back open. "Brentwood!" I rushed into the hall, uncaring that I looked like a harridan. I was engaged to be married, after all. It no longer mattered what I looked like, I thought bitterly. It only mattered what I *did*—or, more accurately, *didn't* do.

"Yes, miss?" He appeared quickly, and it was a testament to his station that he didn't even wince at the sight of me.

"Is the messenger still waiting?"

"No, miss," he replied. "I took your response to be—a—er —negative."

Drat. "Send word to Cosgrove Terrace, to Lady Isabella, that I accept her invitation."

Without waiting for him to respond, I flew up the stairs to my bedchamber, calling for Pepper. It was nearly one o'clock. I hadn't a moment to waste.

Why was I so excited about this particular invitation?

Because Lady Isabella Cosgrove-Pitt was, according to Mina Holmes, the Ankh. (I supposed, after the events at The Carnelian Crow, I must agree with her. I had, after all, seen her there with my own eyes.)

The Ankh was the woman who'd nearly electrofied me to death, the woman who'd killed at least two other young ladies, the woman who'd purposely caused her own husband's death, the woman who kept getting away from me and Mina.

A first-rate criminal.

A cunning villain.

Why was she inviting me to her house?

I couldn't wait to find out.

This was the sort of thing I loved. Adventure! *Mystery.* Action. **Danger**.

"Pepper!" I shrieked, punching the two buttons on my wardrobe so fast that the revolving racks started and stopped with great, clattering jolts. A bangled peach frock fell from one of its moorings, landing in a glittery heap on the floor.

"What is it, miss?" cried my maid, bursting through the door.

"I'm going to tea!" I was pawing through the selection of wraps and gloves.

"All right, then, miss," Pepper said. But she was looking at me as if I was going mad.

I caught a glimpse of myself in the mirror and realized she might have a point. My hair was a wild mess. My eyes were bright and intense. My face was flushed from my activities.

And I hadn't been interested in any social event for months.

"Sit ye'self there, then, and let me see to your hair, Miss Evvie," Pepper said in the sort of voice one might use to a cornered, hissing cat. "And then we can talk about which frock you want to wear."

I was glad to put myself into her capable hands. She helped me out of the loose trousers and simple linen tunic I wore when practicing. Beneath, I was wearing only a short, tight chemise that kept my bosom from flopping around but allowed me to move, and a pair of knickers.

I sat down and began to relax as Pepper pulled the pins from my dark, curly hair.

Why did Lady Isabella want to see me? Her husband—before he died in December—had been the Parliamentary leader, *the* most important man in the governing body. I'd only met them (officially; not counting when Lady Isabella was acting as the Ankh) two or three times, during large parties or balls. We'd only ever exchanged a few private words—once at the funeral of Richard Dancy, and only briefly at the Roses Ball and Yule Fête —both at Cosgrove Terrace.

The answer came to me. It was obvious. I was going to be an Oligary. A member of a very powerful family in England—even more powerful than the Cosgrove-Pitts, perhaps.

So Lady Isabella wanted to be friends.

The Ankh. A criminal. A *murderer* wanted to be friends

with me?

I shook my head, and Pepper *tsked* when she lost her grip on a curl she was pinning at my crown.

Should I send word to Mina?

Maybe Mina had been invited as well.

I sneered inwardly. Mina Holmes. She hadn't even bothered to congratulate me—or berate me—on my wedding announcement.

She couldn't have failed to see it. It had been in every dratted newspaper in the city, blast my sister-in-law.

Why hadn't Mina contacted me?

Why hadn't she helped me figure a way out of this *mess*?

The anger I'd been feeling for weeks bubbled up inside me again. I curled my fists tightly and felt one of my joints creak. My fingernails left deep, bloody wounds in my palms. (Sometimes I don't know my own strength.)

I forced the thoughts away.

I would go to Lady Isabella's for tea. I'd assess the situation. If, as I suspected, Mina was there as well, I would be cool, remote, and very, *very* pleasant to her. Extremely pleasant.

And then I'd leave and that would be it.

I nodded to myself, accidentally moving my head again. This time, I was jabbed in the scalp by one of the pins. I yelped.

"Sorry, miss," Pepper said. But she didn't sound sorry at all. "Shall I fix up a bit o' weaponry for you, then, miss?" There was a gleam in her eyes.

Besides Bram, Pepper was the only one in the household who knew about my secret life. She enjoyed the challenge of outfitting me with stakes hidden on my person—in my hair, or in secret pockets of my skirts—as well as other vampire-hunting equipment. Crosses. Salted holy water. And, once, she'd even experimented with a way for me to carry a sword (useful for beheading a vampire, but not so convenient when one was trying to waltz).

I opened my mouth to say no, but then I heard Mina's exasperated voice in my head: *When are you ever going to learn to be prepared for any eventuality, Evaline?*

Right.

Well, *today*. Today was the day I was going to learn to be prepared for any eventuality.

After all, I *was* going to Lady Isabella's house—presumably the lair of the Ankh. It would be foolish of me *not* to go prepared.

"Yes, Pepper. That would be excellent."

Pepper's eyes lit up as brightly as her frizzed coppery hair. She spun and crouched, flipping up the rug that covered the secret compartment in the floor where we kept all of my vampire-hunting equipment.

I couldn't stop a wave of grief.

When I moved to Ned Oligary's house, I wouldn't have a secret hiding place like that. I wouldn't be able to bring that chest of equipment.

I wouldn't need it anymore.

❦

As MIDDY NAVIGATED my carriage up the broad, curving drive of Cosgrove Terrace—which was the name of the mansion where Lady Isabella had lived with her recently deceased husband—I couldn't help but remember the last time I'd been here.

That was the night Lord Belmont Cosgrove-Pitt had jumped to his death in the middle of their Yule Fête. He'd landed with a *splot* on the ballroom floor.

Pix had been there that night too. I'd almost missed him— he'd been dressed as a maidservant, of all things.

I coldly steered my thoughts from Pix—better known as Mr. Edison Smith.

He was in jail. For murder.

For the murder of Ned's brother's business partner, Hiram Bartholomew.

It didn't surprise me. Not really. Pix—Mr. Smith, I mean—had always been mysterious and dangerous, with an underlying aura of violence. I'd seen evidence that he could take care of himself, physically. I suppose it wasn't a stretch to imagine him killing someone.

Murder.

I'd kissed a murderer.

And now I was about to *visit* and take tea with another one.

I was *thrilled*.

As I'd expected, the massive Cosgrove Terrace was draped in the black of mourning. Two huge black banners hung from the uppermost balconies down four stories, puddling on the ground behind the bushes. Each window was covered with a sheer black drape. The banners must have been weighted on the bottom, for though the fabric danced and shivered in the wintery wind, it remained in place. A massive black velvet bow hung on the front door, with a wide ribbon striping from top to bottom behind it.

The mansion looked gloomy and forbidding in the cold, colorless day. I couldn't control a shiver.

Middy helped me down from the carriage as the sky spat sleet and snow. My sea-green skirts swirled neatly into place beneath the heavy green velvet cloak I'd worn. The fashionable over-corset I'd chosen was flexible enough that I could bend and twist. My slippers had soft but thick soles covered with something that kept them from slipping on wood or marble, and I was grateful someone had sprinkled white sand over the drive so I wouldn't ruin them in the wet. The gloves I'd chosen were of thick forest-green wool, with little cog-work frog connectors all along the back of the hand, wrist, and halfway up my arm. I loved those gloves.

Thanks to Pepper's ingenuity, I didn't clatter or clink as I made my way up the steps to the main entrance (a footman had appeared and was protecting me with a three-sided umbrella), but I was well armed.

Mina would be proud.

I soured again as the door opened for me. I didn't care what Mina Holmes thought. Or didn't think.

But I couldn't help but realize: often when we'd attended a gathering at places like Cosgrove Terrace, we'd ridden together.

Except, now, I usually attended balls and parties with Ned, in his carriage. And once in his brother's very amazing steam-car.

Oh, *drat*.

I pushed away the monstrous thought of my wedding and walked into the foyer.

"Miss Stoker, welcome. Lady Cosgrove-Pitt is expecting you."

The butler led me up the stairs to a small parlor tucked deep in the rear of the mansion. Although I'd done my share of snooping at Cosgrove Terrace—including in Lady Isabella's private office—I'd never seen this elegant room.

Although small, the chamber had been furnished with elegance and taste. It was breathtakingly lovely and exuded comfort and luxury. It was feminine without being fussy.

The divan and two armchairs were upholstered in a rich sapphire blue. I guessed you'd sink down several inches when you sat on them. The walls were covered with silken fabric—not paper—of midnight blue that shimmered gently from the gold and silver threads woven through it. The movement was subtle, and I realized there was some sort of low fan mechanism behind the wall that caused the fabric to shiver ever so slightly, always causing some delicate movement without it being distracting. It was almost like being underwater, with the constant, gentle movement.

Beads and sequins created ornate images on the fabric walls: swirling vines and flowers, a celestial sky with stars and planets, a forest with tall, graceful trees embracing a glittering pond and grasses that seemed to sway. Though the furnishings were dark, the ceiling was high, so the chamber felt cozy instead of enclosed. There were five tall, slender windows that allowed in the gray light—and today the wind tossed the black mourning banners back and forth, offering even more illumination.

A massive five-tiered chandelier in the shape of an inverted pyramid hung from the ceiling. Countless tiny gaslights flickered behind crystals and cut glass. It was so tall that the bottom layer, the narrowest, hung only three feet above the seating arrangement of two chairs and a round tea table. The light it cast was soft and patterned.

"Miss Stoker. Come in."

Lady Isabella was alone in the chamber. She rose as I stepped into the room, her taffeta skirts and petticoats rustling. Her entire ensemble was in unrelieved black, but it was trimmed and embroidered beautifully.

She was an attractive woman. Not stunning, but beautiful in her own striking way. According to the latest edition of *Kimball's British Peerage,* Lady Isabella was thirty-five. She had dark brown hair, although today it was covered by a flat lacy cap in mourning black. Her eyes were gray, a fact that Mina insisted helped Lady Isabella conceal her identity as the Ankh.

Her eyes appear to change color depending upon what she's wearing, Mina had told me—numerous times. Then droned on about how elementary it was to effect excellent yet simple disguises when one knew as much about human behavior as she did.

I gritted my teeth.

"Good afternoon, my lady," I said with a brief curtsy. I realized this was the first time I'd ever been alone with the woman— except the time she'd tried to kill me. No, actually, we hadn't been alone even then. Two of her goons had been there. I wondered what had happened to them.

She'd probably electrofied them too.

"Please, Evaline—it's Isabella." Her smile was warm. "If you'll permit my informality."

I hid my shock. For a peer to suggest that I, not titled and a much younger woman, call her by her familiar name was very unusual. Although, I suppose, when a woman has tried to murder you, what's the sense in formality?

I nodded.

"I'm so pleased you were able to accept my invitation," she continued, gesturing to the chair opposite hers. "Of course, I'm not able to be as social as I'd like at this difficult time. Thus, I'm relegated to relying on people coming to visit me. And, of course, attending your birthday masquerade on Friday would be quite inappropriate."

"Not at all," I said. I'd been right—the chair was soft, and I sank right in.

"It's so lonely now that my dear Belmont is gone," Lady Isabella went on (I just couldn't think of her as plain old Isabella). "And since it wouldn't be proper to even make social calls—for of course I must emulate Her Majesty in demonstrating grief over the loss of my dear husband—I find it even more difficult to get through the days with no one around but for the servants."

It remained unspoken but obvious that one simply didn't talk to servants. One hardly realized they were there, in fact. And yet, they were everywhere in a house like this. Chambermaids, parlourmaids, scullery maids, grooms, footmen, the housekeeper, the butler, the cook, the valet, various lady's maids to attend to Lady Isabella and her wardrobe... Cosgrove Terrace must have more than a dozen servants. She was closed off, but not the least bit alone.

We didn't have a large staff at Grantworth House anymore. Just Pepper and Mrs. Gernum and Brentwood. But when I married Ned, we'd have an army of servants.

For some reason, that made me feel prickly. I didn't want people around and underfoot all the time. I supposed Lady Isabella was used to it—she wouldn't even know the names and faces of them all, because that would fall to the housekeeper—but *I* certainly wouldn't be used to it. Could I ever be?

"Shall I ring for tea, then, Evaline? It's such a dreary, nasty day; I could use something soothing and warm." Lady Isabella smiled. "And my cook is absolutely brilliant with strawberry cream puffs."

"Yes, of course. That would be very nice." My mouth

watered. Strawberries at this time of year? Cosgrove Terrace must have a greenhouse where they grew.

"Very well." She reached an elegant hand—gloved in black, of course—out to push the button on a small device resting on the piecrust table next to her. I thought I heard a distant chime, but I couldn't be too certain. I definitely heard the wind buffeting against the mourning banners and rattling the windows. "What a dreadful day," she said, reading my mind. "Again, I'm so grateful you were able to visit, despite the weather. I know how busy you must be, and how in demand you are—socially speaking."

Even though I knew she was the Ankh, and that she'd been the one to cause her husband's death, I found it difficult to remember that as she spoke. And at the same time, she knew that *I* knew she was a murderous villain.

It was a very strange interlude.

"Oh, well, as it happened, I didn't have any engagements today." At least any that I'd wanted to fulfill. It was an invitation from a murderer that had excited me. But so far, Lady Isabella seemed bland and boring. Not at all villainous.

Was it possible Mina was wrong?

Maybe Lady Isabella had an identical twin who was actually the Ankh!

The chamber door opened and a maid—also dressed in head-to-toe black—slipped in, pushing an elegant wheeled cart. She set up our tea service, then edged the cart toward us while Lady Isabella and I waited in silence. Then the maid moved about the room adjusting the curtains and stoking the fire that blazed merrily from a corner.

Finally, she left the parlor, closing the door behind her. Lady Isabella and I were alone once more. I hoped something interesting would happen—although the teacakes looked marvelous, and I'd hate for them to be wasted. Hopefully whatever she had planned would wait until after tea.

"You must be very eager for your upcoming nuptials," she said, pressing a button on the filigree copper tea stand.

"Oh, yes, of course," I replied absently. I was watching the tea stand (and the strawberry puff cakes) with interest.

I'd never seen anything like that tea stand. Even Miss Adler didn't have one. The teapot—a tall, slender, curvy one made from ink-black china painted with dark blue flowers so as to match the chamber—sat on a round platform. Beneath, a small mechanism steamed silently, obviously keeping the pot warm. The platform was open on the sides, cut out in a filigree pattern that reminded me unpleasantly of my wedding invitations. Five flat, round disks stuck out from the tea stand on elegant curved arms, and on top of two of them rested matching blue and black teacups and saucers.

The teapot rose from the center, then slowly tilted. At the same time, the nearest cup holder lifted smoothly and silently to a position beneath the slender, elephantine spout. Steaming tea poured in a perfect stream into the cup. When Lady Isabella pushed the button again, the teapot tilted back and a different cup holder circled into place.

She handed me my tea. It smelled light and floral, and even the saucer was warm in my gloved hands.

I was just about to sip when something stopped me. I was having tea with a murderer. Maybe I should wait to see whether she drank from the same pot. I set down my cup so abruptly that it clinked against the saucer.

"Sugar? Milk?" she asked as tea streamed into the second cup.

I was enchanted, for the sugar wasn't in square cubes. It was formed in the shape of fingernail-sized roses, each tinted blue. Of course, I added three of them to my tea. They were so pretty.

As I stirred, I eyed Lady Isabella casually. I wondered if she'd add sugar to her drink. Maybe the poison was in the sugar.

Because why else was I here? Surely she meant to do *something* to me besides bore me to death with inane chatter.

Poison me. Drug me. Attempt to kill me.

If she didn't, she wasn't much of a criminal.

"Do have a strawberry puff, Evaline. And then you must tell

me all about the wedding. I'm afraid I must decline to attend—it wouldn't be seemly, of course—so I shall have to hear all about it from you. I can only imagine how lovely it's going to be." Lady Isabella's smile seemed genuine as she lifted her cup to sip. "The Oligarys have excellent taste."

Drat. I hadn't noticed whether she'd added sugar to hers.

Now I dared not drink, even though I *really* wanted to. I did pick up a cream puff, taking one on the *opposite* side of the plate —closer to her. Just in case. And then, thinking better of it when I saw that her tea plate remained empty, I set it down on my plate.

Blast it! Was I going to have to sit here all afternoon and merely *look* at this lovely tea?

"It's certainly going to be an event," I replied vaguely, picking up the thread of the conversation. To be honest, I hadn't been paying much attention to the details of the wedding. Florence and Ned and even Sir Emmett had plunged into the planning as if it were a royal wedding, mostly leaving me to my own devices. I barely knew what my dress looked like.

I eyed the three-tiered plate of pyramid-shaped biscuits. They appeared to be made from cocoa, and each was topped with a pale pink glaze that looked like a blushing snowcap on the chocolatey pyramid's pointy top. And there were also some very lacy-looking, rippling pastries that looked like artistically wrin-kled doilies. They were drizzled with a cinnamon glaze.

My stomach growled quietly. I clenched it tightly from the inside.

"It must be very exciting to be marrying into the Oligary family, especially now that Sir Emmett has just been knighted. Just think of how different your life will be." She smiled. "I had a similar experience, you know. When I married Belmont, I was only a bit older than you, and I hadn't come from a very wealthy family."

"Oh yes," I said, unable to hide my listlessness. "My life will be very different."

"I beg your pardon if I'm prying, Evaline, but you don't sound very happy about your future."

I looked at her, expecting to see that same warm, sparkling expression in her eyes. But instead there was a glint of hardness there. And one of sympathy. I opened my mouth to speak, then shut it. I wasn't about to share the whole situation with Lady Isabella.

"It's rather a shame, I think—a woman like you having to make such a sacrifice for her family."

Exactly!

"What I mean to say—if you permit my bluntness—is that your...er...activities will, by necessity, become rather restricted once you join the Oligary family."

I am well aware of that.

But I still kept my lips clamped shut. As much as I privately agreed with her, I simply couldn't do so outright.

When I didn't respond, she settled back in her chair with a sigh. "Evaline, please drink your tea. I assure you, I haven't poisoned it or anything here."

"Then why have you invited me here?" I demanded. "Are you going to electrofy me instead?"

Her eyes flared with surprise then turned a bit frosty. "Not at all, Evaline, and I must say, it's abominably rude of you to mention that whilst we are having a civilized tea."

I scoffed, but took the opportunity to pop one of the straw-berry puffs into my mouth. After all, if she wasn't poisoning me—

It was heavenly.

I nearly moaned, and it was all I could do to keep from plucking up three more and shoving them in rapid succession into my mouth.

"At any rate, Evaline, the reason I've invited you here today is simply because I have...a delicate situation. It has to do with the UnDead. And I want your help."

MISS HOLMES

- WHEREIN OUR HEROINE MAKES A
BOLD MOVE

Even as the words *the murder of Frederick Boggs* penetrated my always-keen mind, I sprang into action.

I pushed it away—any accusation of murder against me was, of course, absurd—and focused all of my efforts on speedy, efficient, and effective movements.

I didn't have time to change my entire ensemble; the way the constables were pounding on the door indicated their unwavering intention to come inside no matter *how* they must accomplish it. I calculated I had no more than five minutes before the door splintered and they were pouring into my house. Illegally, might I add.

How *dare* they accost the daughter of Sir Mycroft in such a manner? What *cheek* for them to demand custody of the special agent of Her Royal Highness, Princess Alexandra! Though I was infuriated, I couldn't spend even an instant of energy focusing on such an atrocity.

I'd fled to my bedchamber and was busy in there. My only avenue of escape was a bold exit, and I had a single chance. This must be the best—and fastest—disguise of my life.

Moments after taking what I needed of my personal effects, I dashed to the kitchen and its attached pantry, where Mrs.

Raskill kept her things. The pounding had not ceased, and as I passed by the creaking, heaving front door, I called, "Mrs. Raskill! Please don't let them in!"

The thudding became more violent after that; I could only assume they'd heard me, as I had, of course, intended.

As I busied myself in the pantry—thankful that our house-keeper kept a small mirror and a wash basin there as well—I took one more moment to cry out, "Please don't let them in, Mrs. Raskill! I'll explain everything once they're gone!" I pitched my voice loud enough to be heard, I hoped, by someone gathering around the house.

I forced myself to be methodical and efficient, despite the fact that my fingers shook a trifle and my insides were knotted tightly. Although it seemed as though time both raced past and was crawling infinitesimally slowly, it took less than the five minutes I'd allotted to turn myself from a fashionably dressed young woman into an older, thicker, more simply garbed housekeeper.

Thus, when I flung open the back door by the kitchen—the one where Mrs. Raskill not only came and went, but also tossed the contents of soup pots or dishwater—the constables standing there didn't immediately rush toward me.

"Glory me!" I cried in an elderly voice stricken with horror. Dramatically, I clutched the market bag I'd packed against Mrs. Raskill's borrowed cloak. "Mina! What on earth is happening?" I called into the house behind me. Then I turned back to the men, ducking against the spray of the horrid weather. "What are you doing here? What do you want?" My voice quavered with age and outrage—the latter emotion being quite genuine.

"Ma'am, you're going to have to step away and allow us inside. Miss Alvermina Holmes is wanted for—er—questioning in a murder case," said one of the constables, whose hat was dripping with icy precipitation. He, in contrast to the one banging on the front door, seemed at least marginally deferential.

"*Murder?*" I reared back, widening my eyes in surprise. Fortunately, the tiny specks of spirit gum I'd placed at the corners of my eyes and mouth to change their shape and create wrinkles remained in place—there had been a question as to whether they would, as I'd been working so quickly. A round pair of glasses, tinted with a soft gray, sat on my nose, making my eyes look smaller to the person in front of me. They fogged up immediately in the cold sleet. But the neat gray wig with its bun sat warm on my head, and a simple tunnel bonnet offered a bit of obstruction over my features—as well as protection from the sleet. "Why, that's impossible!"

"Sergeant! Back here!" called one of the other men.

"Ma'am, you're going to have to let us in the house to get her."

"But, glory be, she—she told me not to," I replied, edging away from the door and into the small courtyard behind our house. The gate leading to the street sagged open, thanks to the dratted Metropolitan Police. It was only a few steps away. "It'll be my job if you—"

"Do you have her?" shouted a man, splashing around from the front of the house. I tensed, for I recognized him immediately as the one in charge. The one who'd announced his intention of arresting me for murder. The one who'd nearly yanked me through the open door five minutes ago.

"She's inside, sir," replied the man to whom I'd been speaking. He shifted his feet in the slush.

If my disguise failed me now, I didn't know what I'd do.

Yes I did. I'd think of something.

"Inside? The door's open? It's not breaking in, then, right-o? Let's go!" The leader, who slipped a little in the icy muck, pushed past me and barged into the house.

"Oh dear," I said, taking another step toward the open gate and freedom. "I *do* hope she's not hiding in the *cellar* any longer. It's frightfully damp and cold down there."

"Blaketon! She's in the cellar!" shouted the constable. One of

Mr. Stoker's players at the Lyceum Theater couldn't have been more on cue.

This caused an absolute stampede of constables (had the Met really sent *six* men to arrest *me?*) into the house, and storming about—obviously looking for an entrance to the cellar...which didn't exist.

Having been thus abandoned, except by one lowly constable who looked longingly into the house, I calmly walked through the gate and onto the street.

As soon as I passed beyond the gate—which I latched responsibly behind me—my heart began to beat again. But I knew I wasn't, as one might say if one were prone to disperse clichés, out of the woods. I made my way along the street as quickly as possible, making certain to keep my posture in the form of Mrs. Raskill's—although I was moving much more quickly than she ever did (except when something like a dissected hand in my laboratory shocked her into great speed).

The unpleasant weather was both a blessing and a curse. No one was out to witness my lone figure trundling along, and the icy pellets allowed me a reason to hide my face. But it was cold and wet, not to mention slippery, and I tend to have difficulty keeping from tripping or slipping under optimal conditions, so I dared not move with too great of haste. There was a large wagon with bars on the windows—for me? How obnoxious!—parked in front of the house. I glowered at it as I crossed the street.

I couldn't help glancing toward the park where Inspector Grayling and I had once sat and conversed quite amiably, but, ignoring the pang in my heart, I made my way down the block in the opposite direction. All the while, I watched for a hackney cab—but, as is an unbreakable rule in London, there is never a hack when one is in need. And the worse the weather, the more likely that aphorism is to be true.

I sloshed along in a more upright position now that I was out of sight of my block. My feet were inside Mrs. Raskill's too-large boots, and despite the handkerchiefs I'd stuffed therein to keep them from thumping awkwardly, my toes were icy and cold from the moisture that seeped through. I would have to insist she get new boots at her earliest opportunity. The large market bag I'd packed was growing heavy, and my nose felt like a large, prominent, dripping icicle. I wiped futilely at it with Mrs. Raskill's heavy woolen glove and trudged along.

Did I have a destination in mind?

Of course I did. Several, in fact.

But as I sloshed down the street, I considered and rejected each of them in rapid succession. My father, Sir Mycroft, was secretly out of the country on important Home Office business. And of course I knew better than to go to the obvious places—Uncle Sherlock's flat or Dr. Watson's medical suite.

Grantworth House, where Miss Stoker lived, was out of the question for obvious reasons. Miss Adler no longer had an office at the British Museum, and I'd never known the direction of her personal apartments, for we most often met at parks, cafés, or in carriages in order to keep my work for the Crown secret. Nor was I going to contact my friend Dylan (for a number of reasons which will eventually become clear during this narrative, but aren't pertinent at the moment).

Regardless, any of those locations were obvious enough that even the bumblers at Scotland Yard would think to look for me there. I felt a renewed rush of outrage at the way those constables had acted.

There was only one place that made sense for me to hide—at least until I determined what was happening. The only problem was that I didn't particularly want to go there.

But I suppose when one needs a safe place to hole up, the best place to go is the hideaway of an underground criminal.

Thus, I had no choice but to head to the dirtiest, darkest, most dangerous area of London: Whitechapel.

If only I could find a dratted taxi!

MISS STOKER

- WHEREIN OUR HEROINE ENJOYS HER TEA -

Stunned by Lady Isabella's words, I forced myself to slowly take another strawberry cream puff from the serving plate and bring it to my lips. But before I actually tasted it, I paused. "Help you? With the UnDead? Why on earth would I help *you?*"

Her mouth curved into a feline smile. Her eyes glinted like granite. "But is that not your duty, lovely Evaline? To rid the world—insofar as you are able—of vampires? I'd decided I must contact you about the problem before your wedding—for, after all, once you're Mrs. Ned Oligary, you won't be doing that sort of thing any longer, will you?"

I almost choked on the puff, but I managed to swallow it down. I was sure my eyes were goggling as wide as a dinner plate. "Oh, *I* see," I drawled. "Your work trying to control vampires with those little battery devices hasn't been going as well as you'd like, then, hmm?"

"You needn't be so bloody arrogant," she said waspishly. "You need my help just as much as I need yours."

This time I snorted instead of merely scoffing as I scooped up three more puffs. They really were beyond divine. "*Your* help?

What on earth would I need your help for? As it happens, I want to remain alive."

"You're soon to have an unwanted husband—and, as you know, I have some expertise in dealing with such a predicament." Her catlike smile was back and her eyes gleamed as she lifted her cup to sip.

This time I really did choke. It was only by taking a large gulp of tea that I was able to dislodge the small pastry that caught in my throat. (That would have been humiliating: a vampire hunter meeting her demise by choking on a cream puff while having tea with a murderer...)

"Did you just offer to murder my future husband?" I managed to say. "And were you thinking of doing it after we're married, or before?"

Lady Isabella leveled a cool stare at me. "Must you resort to such inflammatory vernacular, Evaline? And certainly afterward —so that you get the full benefit of being his widow."

I had to take another gulp of tea to stifle my response. I felt as if I were in some sort of mad dream. Was I really sitting here having this conversation *over tea*?

"Right then. Well, if not murder, what would you call it, then, Isabella?" Delicately, I picked up one of the cocoa pyramids and bit off its glazed top.

"It doesn't matter what word one uses," she said sharply. "The problem can be attended to. As mine was."

Apparently I was getting under her skin. Either her problem with the UnDead was serious enough that she was truly in trouble, or...or I was just being irritating. Which I have been known to do.

"Do stop circling around the subject, Evaline. Shall we discuss my proposition or not? I have no intention of doing business with someone who can't stay on topic."

Apparently I was merely being irritating.

And enjoying the tea pastries too much, for her glacial stare went from me to the nearly depleted plate and back again, and her brows lifted.

Blooming *fish*, she reminded me of Mina Holmes at that moment.

Then Lady Isabella seemed to calm herself. It was as if she were a mechanism gone wrong, and turned herself off and then turned back on again and was now functioning correctly. "I apologize, Miss Stoker. I've handled this badly. I merely thought... Well, perhaps I was wrong. I was under the impression you weren't particularly overjoyed about your impending wedding. I'd always been under the impression you were the sort of woman who didn't need a husband to tell her what to do. Or didn't want anyone or anything to restrict her behavior or actions." She smiled ruefully. "Apparently, I misread the situation. I do hope you'll forgive me. You must be very happy indeed to be marrying Ned Oligary. You'll be the toast of London as his bride."

Until that moment, I'd rather been enjoying our conversation. The sparring, the having a sort of upper hand, the luxurious surroundings, the pastries. Of course I found Lady Isabella fascinating—even if she was a criminal. Probably *because* she was a criminal.

But after her little apology, I felt myself deflate. Blast it, but she was *right* about me. Of course I didn't want to get married. And I certainly didn't want to give up my life as a vampire hunter.

"More tea?" she asked in that smooth voice. "The weather doesn't seem to be turning any more favorable."

She glanced toward the windows, which were still being splattered with tiny ice particles. The wind was no less contained than it had been; in fact, it seemed to have whipped up even more. "You're welcome to stay as long as you like—there's no need to go out in that, my dear. And, of course, there are plenty of empty bedchambers in this place. Shall I have one of the maids make one up for you? I promise not to bring up any sordid topics again."

"Oh, I couldn't impose," I replied automatically. But there was a small part of me that was still curious. And yet another part of me that really wanted to be away from Grantworth House and all talk of wedding plans for as long as possible. It seemed like forever since I'd been with another woman who wanted to talk about something other than flowers, gowns, and seating arrangements.

"Of course not." My hostess seemed genuinely disappointed. "It wouldn't be seemly, considering my situation." She sighed, glancing down at the black of her dress.

"But I don't need to rush off quite yet," I said, putting my cup on the platform nearest the teapot's spout. The cupholder was warm, explaining why the saucer had been heated as well.

"Perhaps you'd like to send your carriage home? I'm happy to arrange for one of my grooms to take you when you're ready to leave."

A little prickle of nerves caught me by surprise. She seemed overly eager for me to stay.

But what could happen? I was fully armed beneath my clothing. Isabella certainly couldn't overpower me, and it would take at least two or three grown men to do so. I'd sense in an instant if an UnDead were near, and I'd have plenty of opportunity to escape. I could break out of a room in which I might be locked through sheer force. I could even jump through a window with minimal injury if it came to that. I was certain I hadn't been poisoned or drugged—I didn't feel any different. My mind was clear and my physical self felt normal.

Yet I was still wary. After all, hadn't she just offered to kill my future husband?

"Thank you very much, Isabella, but there's no need. Middy doesn't mind waiting, and the Oligarys have given my brother and sister-in-law another carriage to use for the time being." I smiled innocently.

Did I imagine it, or was the quick twitch of her lips an accolade of my parry to her sword thrust?

Or was there really nothing going on beneath our conversation other than the fact that she truly was bored and didn't want to be left alone to amuse herself?

I almost wished Mina was here so we could compare notes. She'd been an expert at sending me silent messages with her eyes and facial expressions.

Not that I needed her help.

"Very well, then, Evaline. I shall simply have to enjoy whatever gracious bit of your company you choose to give me." She lifted her teacup and sipped delicately. "I daresay Mr. Oligary the younger is a vast improvement over that slippery little pickpocket with whom you seemed to be consorting. The uncommon wastrel with the odd name. What *was* it? Stix? No... I daresay grief over my dear Belmont has confuddled my memory." Her lips curled in a cool smile that looked nothing like grief or humor. "Prix, was it?"

"Pix." I didn't know why I bothered. She knew very well what his name was. After all, she'd tried to kill him. In fact, she *had* killed him.

"Oh, yes. But that's not his real name, is it? Of course not. Who would name their child something so ridiculous?" She leaned forward and plucked up one of the sugar roses for her tea. She dropped it into her cup with a little plop, then stirred with one of the tiny spoons. "I read about his arrest in the *Times*—the same day your wedding announcement was posted. And just in the nick of time, wasn't it, Evaline? How awkward that would have been if you'd been seen consorting with the likes of him on the same day your engagement to Mr. Oligary was formalized. It would have been quite a scandal. The society pages would have had a great day with that!"

How awkward indeed.

I hadn't seen Pix—whose real name was apparently Edison Smith—since that night at The Carnelian Crow. And when I woke up the next morning, it was to my excited sister-in-law's knocking on my bedchamber door. She'd been ecstatic to show me the notices of my engagement in all of the newspapers. Not just the *Times,* but *all* of the papers.

And by then, it was too late for me to do anything about any of it. But it would have been a horrible scandal if things had gone differently. If Pix hadn't been arrested, and if he'd seen or heard about the engagement, or—

I realized my fingers were digging into my palms, leaving nail imprints in my favorite forest-green gloves.

I forced myself to relax. Isabella was trying to goad me, and I wasn't going to let her. True, this sort of cat-and-mouse dialogue was more of Mina's forte—I much preferred action to words—but I was more than able to hold my own.

So, I looked up at her with a feline smile of my own. "I hardly think it would have been any more of a scandal than your husband dancing on the railing of his balcony before jumping to his death at the Yule Fête. How did you manage to arrange it, Isabella?" I reached for another of the cocoa pyramids.

"Looking for advice on how to deal with your own husband, Evaline? I've already offered to help you." She gave an obviously manufactured sigh of affront and settled back into her chair. The upholstered sapphire-blue wings seemed to embrace her. For a moment, Lady Isabella appeared almost queenly, sitting on a throne. Her long eyes glinted silver as she looked at me thoughtfully. It was a reminder of how intelligent, cunning, and powerful she was.

"Strangely enough, that was one thing Miss Holmes and I didn't discuss during our little *tête-à-tête.*"

I couldn't keep the shock from my face. I forced it to go blank as quickly as possible. Maybe she hadn't noticed. "You and Mina?" If she hadn't read my expression, the tension in my voice would have given away my incredulity.

My hostess's eyes widened and her brows lifted. I couldn't tell whether her bewilderment was genuine. "Do you mean Miss

Holmes didn't tell you about it? We had a rather intimate, extended conversation—just the two of us, of course. I daresay we both came away with quite a bit of increased admiration for the other." She looked at me from over the brim of her teacup. "I simply assumed she'd told you about our discussion regarding creating a partnership."

"A partnership?" I felt like one of those mechanical birds at Cloyster's that kept repeating phrases spoken to it.

Impossible. Mina wouldn't partner with the Ankh.

Would she?

Of course not. No matter how tempting it might be. Besides, it wasn't as if *she* were being forced into getting married.

If anyone might be tempted to align with the Ankh, it would be someone in my position.

"It's no wonder you were so taken aback by my proposal that we should work together, Evaline. Please forgive me. I believed you and Miss Holmes were so very close and loyal to each other—as my friends were, those days we lived in Paris— that I was certain she'd told you about it, and that you would have been expecting me to contact you." She sighed and folded her hands neatly in her lap. "I do seem to be apologizing to you far too much today, don't I? I supposed one must chalk it up to this horrible exile of mourning. I've lost all sense of civility."

"Not at all," I said automatically. "When did you and Mina... um...talk?"

"Oh. Well." She grimaced delicately. "It was that night at The Carnelian Crow. I really must beg your pardon—this is quite awkward, Evaline."

"What did you talk about—in regards to a partnership?" I couldn't seem to stop myself from talking, from asking, from feeling lost and confused. I probably sounded like a petulant child, but I was so taken aback by the thought that Mina had had an *intimate, extended* conversation with the villainess we had been trying to stop since we'd first begun working together—and she had never even told me about it!—that I couldn't think about anything but *why hadn't I known?*

And what had they talked about?

"Why, I simply told her how much I admired her—and everything she'd done—and that it was obvious we would make a brilliant alliance." Lady Isabella lifted her teacup again, those intense eyes watching me over the brim.

"Right." Suddenly, I was no longer interested in the teacakes. In fact, my stomach felt as if a wide steel band had tightened around it—other than my corset, I mean—and I felt a little lightheaded.

"There is no one else in the world to whom I would have suggested such a partnership, Evaline," said my hostess. "With the obvious exception of yourself. The three of us together would be unstoppable."

"I see." I couldn't seem to find the words. I rose abruptly, and realized my lightheadedness was becoming more of an ache in the back of my skull. And the tightness in my stomach hurt.

Wait.

No.

"You said you weren't going to poison me," I snarled, pulling to my feet so quickly that I lost my breath.

"I didn't poison you, my darling Evaline," said Isabella with feigned surprise.

"What did you do? What did you put in the tea?" My heart was pounding so hard that I felt ill. No—it was whatever she'd done to the food that made me ill.

"Why, Evaline, you wound me. I did nothing to the tea. Perhaps you've merely had too much to eat?"

I dug for the derringer Pepper had helped me tuck into a hidden pocket and retrieved it quickly. It felt solid and safe in my grip. "Show me out to my carriage."

"There's no need to threaten violence, Miss Stoker." She rose to her feet. "If you wish to leave, all you need do is ask."

"Well, I'm asking. Show me out." With slightly wobbly knees

and a muzzy head, I started carefully toward the door, still gripping the tiny gun.

I had no idea whether I could manage the vast hallways, let alone all the stairs to the first floor—or whether Lady Isabella would even allow me to try. But I wouldn't give up without a fight.

To my surprise, Isabella took it upon herself to escort me down the stairs and to the front hall instead of calling for a servant to do so. I was shocked and relieved when we made it to the front door without incident.

I'd never been so happy to walk out into freezing, pelting rain and winds than I was at that moment—and to find Middy waiting for me in my carriage. A footman dashed up with an umbrella, but I was already clambering into the carriage—into safety, with the help of a Middy bewildered by my rush—before the footman even had the brolly open. (Those mechanized ones *never* work properly.)

It wasn't until I settled back into the squabs of the carriage and the vehicle began to ease down the drive that I realized something.

I was fully awake, aware, and no longer feeling lightheaded or ill.

Um...

Hmmm.

I reviewed my insides, checked my limbs, and realized I felt normal.

Huh.

So she *hadn't* poisoned or drugged me?

Perhaps it *had* been too many teacakes after all.

I grimaced. That had been a horribly rude way for me to take my leave of Lady Cosgrove-Pitt. I stopped myself from wincing when I remembered there was no reason for me to feel bad. After all, the woman had tried to electrofy me. And she'd offered to murder my future husband. Surely that meant we could dispense with any sort of formality.

My thoughts were interrupted when I noticed a fancy horse-less vehicle turning into the drive of Cosgrove Terrace just as Middy eased our carriage out onto the street.

Turning in my seat to look out the rear window, I peered through the ugly gray sleet. The vehicle looked like Mr. Oligary's steam-car. Mr. Oligary the elder, I mean—Sir Emmett (who'd just recently been knighted), not Ned, my betrothed. I was certain it was his; I'd only ever seen two of them, including the one that belonged to the Oligarys.

This one definitely looked familiar: it was painted a sleek blue that was so dark it was nearly black. The size of a landau, it would only hold the driver and one passenger next to him. The wheels had fancy copper arcs over them, and the decorative swoop of metal came around to a curve in the rear where there were two stovepipe sorts of things jutting out the back. Smoke puffed out in regular clouds as the vehicle puttered along. It reminded me of Grayling's steam-cycle—but legal, of course. I couldn't tell whether there were two people inside, or only one, for the glass windows enclosing it were tinted pale blue and the world was so dark and wet.

With a little *whumpf*, I settled back, facing forward once more. I gnawed on that bit of information. Sir Emmett Oligary was paying a call on Lady Isabella. And if I had not fled Cosgrove Terrace, I would have been there as well.

Was it an unexpected call? Or had he known I was invited to tea? Had Isabella expected him to come while I was there? Had she planned it?

As my horse-drawn carriage rumbled along over the cobble-stones and winter's fury pelted the roof and windows, I mulled over my next step.

It didn't take much thought.

I had no choice. I needed to have words with Miss Mina Holmes.

MISS HOLMES

- IN WHICH OUR HEROINE TAKES ON THE MANTLE OF CRIMINALITY -

U pon arriving at my destination, I discovered I was just as hesitant to climb out of the hackney cab that had taken me far too long to find as I'd been to climb *into* it—for different reasons, of course.

The condition of the vehicle's interior was nearly unbearable, but alighting from its relative safety (if not pungency and the horrifying squishiness of some unidentifiable, decaying item on the floor) into Whitechapel was cause for apprehension. However, I had no other choice, and I steeled myself to step carefully down onto what passed for a street, but was more like a refuse-strewn alley that was currently soaking from the icy precipitation. The last thing I needed was to trip on Mrs. Raskill's too-large boots and land on my knees—or worse, in the icy muck.

I delivered myself safely onto the ground with no help from the driver, I need not add—for anyone who would conduct a business with a vehicle in that condition clearly has no sense of civility.

I also need not mention that I declined to offer the driver a tip for excellent service.

And then I looked around.

During the carriage ride, I had removed the majority of my disguise—the wig, the stovepipe bonnet, the spirit gum and fog-tinted glasses, as well as the two small wads of cotton I'd stuffed into my cheeks in order to change the shape of my face. I was, however, still garbed in the several layers of clothing that gave me the added bulk of my housekeeper and hid the fashion-conscious frock I wore. Unfortunately, because I'd been inter-rupted by those uncouth Scotland Yard officers, I was still wearing the frock on which my mechanized umbrella had poured a stream of icy rain. It was chilly and heavy, and my fingers (still gloved, of course) were cold.

During the ride, I'd taken care not to allow my market bag—which was stuffed with items I expected I'd need if, as I antici-pated, I was on an extended exile from home—to rest on the carriage's garbage-strewn floor, and now I stood on a dim, narrow corner in the part of London that was famous for the Ripper murders. (I purposely choose not to bestow any honorific on the loathsome creature who did such horrible deeds.)

Normally when I was forced to travel to this area, I was accompanied by Evaline, who had no fear and who was, I admit freely, an excellent protector. And the other times I'd visited this particular neighborhood, it had been at night. Thus, I confess, I was rather trepidatious about being in that particular locale alone, with only my wits (and the miniature steam-stream gun I'd tucked into my cloak) to protect me.

Although it was only four o'clock in the afternoon, the weather was so dreary and the clouds so heavy that it might as well have been midnight. There was nothing to suggest that anyone had even attempted to install a gas street lamp in this area, and even the nearby buildings had little or no illumination oozing from within. The only benefit to the abhorrent weather was that it was so miserable the streets were empty and the corner was deserted. That meant, I told myself as I marched across the narrow throughway to a particular public house, I was far less likely to be accosted, pickpocketed, or otherwise bothered.

Fenman's End was a dingy, dark, disgusting pub frequented by Mr. Pix—at least, until he'd been arrested for murdering Emmett Oligary's business partner. Despite Evaline's seeming attraction to the place, I had no desire to set foot in that establishment ever again. But I was desperate. Although there were several exits, the only way I knew how to access Pix's underground hide-away was through the pub. I only hoped no one would try to stop me.

Or, worse, expect me to imbibe anything poured from behind the bar counter.

I drew in a deep breath of (relatively) clean air—my last for some time, I was certain—and pushed through the door into Fenman's End.

(I had often thought to myself how well named the place was. Although I had no idea who or what Fenman was, the decrepit establishment certainly evoked the concept of a terminus of some sort—either that of any gentility, cleanliness, or refinement —or, more likely, all of the above.)

A layer of wood smoke filled the top half of the room; it seemed whoever had built up the much-needed fire against the terrible weather had neglected to check the chimney for block-ages. Nonetheless, the interior was almost pleasant relative to its temperature and lack of precipitation, and I stepped in, eager for my frozen fingers to move again.

There were six patrons inside, three sitting at a table in the corner and two placed at a distant interval along the bar counter. When I saw the man behind the stand, I grimaced in disappoint-ment. Bilbo was his name, and I venture to say he was the least sanitary person I'd ever encountered. (Up to that point, anyway. Since then, I have, unfortunately, come into contact with others who could easily wrest the title from him.)

I strode purposefully across the room to the bar counter. Fortunately, the two patrons were sitting closer to the opposite end of where I needed to go, for the entrance to Pix's lair was near the left end of the stretch. Unfortunately, Bilbo noticed me.

"Wotcher about, there, Sally-Sue?" he said loudly.

Drat. Now everyone would notice me.

But as I continued my path across the way, I realized none of the patrons had bothered to look up from their tankards. Thank Heaven for small favors.

I edged up to the counter, speaking purposefully but in an unusually low voice. "I've been sent by Mr. Pix to retrieve an item from his—er—apartments."

Bilbo, who was a man of indeterminate age—though probably well past forty—had fingers that were so dark with dirt and soot that they probably hadn't seen a splash of water for months. His sparse, graying beard and sideburns were a tangle around his mouth, and thanks to the crumbs and other detritus adhering to the growth, I could easily ascertain what he'd eaten for his last several meals. I preferred not to know this information, and stifled a shudder as I forced myself to draw closer.

"'Ave a seat there," he ordered me, pointing sharply to a stool at the farthest end of the counter, then turned to refill a tankard for the customer on the other end.

The last thing I wanted to do was place my posterior on a seat that had been dirtied by Providence knew what, but then I realized it was Mrs. Raskill's skirts that would take the brunt of whatever sticky, smelly, crunchy remnants were left there. And aside from that, Bilbo didn't seem to be in the mood for arguments.

So, taking care not to touch the counter or the stool with my gloved hands, I managed to slide myself onto the seat. I plunked my market bag onto the stool next to me and looked at Bilbo, who'd returned from his task. His lips were pursed in an irritated and, dare I say, judgmental expression.

What on *earth* had I done to deserve such a look?

Before I could decide how to approach the situation, he

leaned closer to me and said, "Bloody demmed well took ye long enough."

My eyes stung from the pungency that accompanied his movement, and I instantly ceased breathing, hoping he would quickly return to his side of the counter. Thus assaulted, I nearly missed his actual words—and the fact that they were an accusation.

"Pardon me?" I managed to say, still breathing shallowly, for he'd not yet returned to a complete upright position.

"Bloody 'ell, Sally-Sue, I been expecting ye fer months now t'get it." He glanced behind me. "Where's t'other one?"

"The other one?" One must understand that I was battling not only his personal perfume (I use that term sarcastically) as well as his incomprehensible words.

"T'other one o' ye. Molly-Sue—the one what broke Big Marv's fingers. Whaddaya think?" He spewed out a frustrated breath, and I nearly fainted.

"Right." I fought to corral my scattered thoughts and leaned back slightly on my stool. With that relative relief, I was able to discern what was happening. "If you're speaking of Miss Stoker, she is not currently assisting me. However, I am here, as antici-pated. Now, if you could please—"

"Well, wot's wrong wi' 'er, then?" he growled. "Molly-Sue fergit abou' 'im now she gots a fancy bloke on 'er arm?"

"Er...um..." Although, to some extent, his words echoed my own thoughts, I couldn't bring myself to join him in disparaging Evaline. Instead, I took an assertive position and a gamble that I'd properly read the meaning between his words. "Mr. Bilbo, if you please. Clearly you've been expecting me—hasn't enough time been wasted? Now, if you'll provide me access to Mr. Pix's—erm—apartments, I'll be able to attend to things."

He gave me a jaundiced look from his beady eyes, and the spiderlike gray and black hair of his brows seemed to punctuate his skepticism. But, to my surprise, he jerked his head toward the wall next to the bar counter. "Go on, then, wit' ye."

I wasted no time in sliding off the stool and gathering my bag. I considered myself quite fortunate in having completed a conversation with the bartender without being required to order a beverage.

I'd only been through this particular door to Pix's lair once before, and that had been in Evaline's presence—and with Bilbo's blessing. I knew I'd be walking through a dim, dark, narrow tunnel that went beneath the streets of London.

However, since taking on the responsibility of working with Miss Adler and Princess Alix, I'd had more than my share of experiences in such dismal places. Although I admittedly have an intense dislike of dim, dark, narrow underground places, one must carry on and do one's duty.

And so I did, with damp palms, weak knees, and the resolve of Her Majesty.

Having been here before made it easier for me to take the steps down, down, down to the passage, but being without Evaline made it all the more difficult. Still, someone (Pix) had thoughtfully strung up (illegal) electrical light bulbs that, though they needed to be cleaned of the grime that tends to cling in such below-ground environs, nonetheless cast small, helpful circles of light.

By the time I reached the door to the reprobate's hideaway, I was slightly out of breath—not from my exertions, but from the clamminess and nervousness that grips me when I am required to be in dark underground places. However, once I arrived at the door, which was fitted with three rows of locks in a code that I had deciphered during The Carnelian Crow Incident, I felt steadier.

Fortunately, Pix (I supposed I should begin to think of him as Mr. Smith, but old habits die hard) had not made any changes to the locks, and it took me only a moment to set the door ajar.

I all but burst into the space, knowing that at last I was safe —at least for the time being.

The hideaway was much the way I remembered it being,

which was unsurprising, since the previous time I'd been here was only days before Pix was arrested. Presumably, no one else knew how to access the place, and therefore nothing had been disturbed since he was last there.

As well appointed as any gentleman's study in the mansions of St. James Park, the large space lacked only the luxury of windows. However, I'd previously observed a number of electrical light bulbs in the room. I pushed a button near the door, and a string of lights on each of the two walls along the sides of the chamber came to life. They cast a clean white light over the space—so very different than the golden glaze that gas lamps gave to everything they illuminated. I would have been delighted to have such incandescence in my laboratory. Not for the first time, I bemoaned the fact that "the generation, utilization, and storage of electrical or electromagnetic power" was illegal, thanks to the Moseley-Haft Act.

I set my bag down and closed the door behind me. Thick, expensive rugs from Persia or Egypt covered the stone floor. Comfortable furnishings were arranged in a pleasing manner: a large brocade sofa with two generous side chairs upholstered in leather, and a low table between them. There was an eating table as well as an area that acted as an office. A massive fireplace, whose chimney presumably piped up through Fenman's End or some other building so as to maintain its secrecy, covered most of one wall and would provide plenty of heat—once I got the fire going, although the room was dry and already surprisingly comfortable in temperature, considering the blustery, ugly weather outside.

On my previous visit, I'd been both amazed and delighted to discover bookshelves filled with tomes of all subjects and fiction lining the walls of this thief's den of iniquity. It was through my careful examination of said shelves that I had been able to discern the message (of sorts) that Pix had left for me. And for Evaline, I suppose.

His sleeping area, with a thick feather mattress and pillows, was tucked behind a partition wall. He had a large wardrobe—large enough for me to walk inside. There was even, I discovered to my great astonishment, a bathing area—with a *bathing tub*—discreetly adjoining the makeshift bedchamber. I hadn't noticed it during my last visit, mainly because Evaline and I had been interrupted by an invasion of UnDead.

At the memory, I looked around, suddenly nervous. I would be vulnerable to any sort of attack by the fanged ones without Evaline here to sense them and fight them off. Although I had managed to stake a vampire myself—once—it's not nearly as simple as it seems. I would be sorely outmatched if even one UnDead made an appearance.

I checked the door and made certain it had locked behind me, and then I found the other two exits and ensured they were secured as well. It was the only thing I could do, aside from positioning garlic and holy items across the doorways. Of course, I had had the foresight to pack several vials of salted holy water, as well as a cross and a wooden stake in my bag. Considering the number of times I'd berated Evaline for not being prepared for all circumstances, I couldn't risk the same myself. Especially since I was on my own.

On my own.

It struck me, then, with the force of an anvil to the head: I was literally and figuratively alone.

I had no one with whom I could share this horrendous predicament—which was not of my own making—and no one to help me.

And now that the actual activity of fleeing had ceased and I was safe in my sanctuary, I found myself at a loss.

What should I do?

I was well hidden and no longer at a disadvantage, and there was nothing to keep me from mulling over the situation that had been so violently and unfairly thrust upon me. I had plenty of uninterrupted time to ascertain what had brought Scotland Yard to my home—with such a preposterous accusation.

Why would anyone think I'd murdered someone named Frederick Boggs? I didn't even know the individual. I'd never even heard his name.

Was it simply a mistake? Or was there some other, more pernicious reason for the misunderstanding?

I tried to focus on the problem, but for some reason, I couldn't sit. I couldn't *think*. I hadn't brought my knitting—which was something I liked to do to keep my hands busy when my brain was mulling over a puzzle.

I found it impossible to keep from pacing, from wandering about the chamber, from touching Pix's possessions and rearranging them.

All right, then, I decided. I'd put my mind to some other engagement for a while—something that had lodged in the back of my mind during my desperation to get to safety—and to avoid ingesting anything at Fenman's End.

I'd fibbed, of course, when I told Bilbo that I'd come to retrieve something for Pix from his hideaway. But the fascinating thing was that the proprietor had foreseen my arrival (I venture to say, he'd only been being polite when asking about Evaline). His unexplained anticipation of my arrival was a far easier riddle to contemplate than the other one that loomed large in my mind.

Why had Bilbo been expecting me? What was I supposedly retrieving, and *why* would he expect *me* to come? Had Pix told him I would?

I couldn't ask Bilbo about it, for that would expose my falsehood. Instead, I'd have to cogitate on the problem...perhaps by investigating Pix's hideaway.

The fact was that Pix—Edison Smith, I mean—was in jail because he was the major suspect in the murder of Hiram Bartholomew, who'd been the business partner of Mr.—now Sir—Emmett Oligary.

Inspector Grayling had been the one to arrest him, and I'm certain I wasn't the only person present to be stunned by his announcement after the end of the wild melee with the Ankh, Princess Lurelia of Betrovia, and the UnDead that had occurred at The Carnelian Crow.

Nor had Pix—drat it, *Smith*—seemed surprised by the turn of events. He almost seemed to have been expecting it. I pursed my lips, remembering something odd that had happened during the Affair of the Chess Queen. Upon seeing Pix—who'd just been resurrected (quite literally) with the help of Dylan Eckhert— Grayling had looked at him and asked whether they'd met previously. He thought he recognized him.

At the time, I assumed Grayling had perhaps seen the sly pickpocket on the periphery of one of our activities or events— but upon further contemplation, I realized that might not have been the case. Pix (I suppose I shall succumb to the ease of writing the shorter name herein) had a tendency to remain in shadow whenever possible, and he was always wearing some sort of disguise. The first and only time Grayling would have seen him without either of those obstructions was that evening in the old monastery below Fleet Street, where the Ankh had set up her experimental laboratory and had killed Pix.

Thus, Grayling might very well have recognized him because he knew of Edison Smith, the American businessman wanted for Mr. Bartholomew's murder. After all, the death was one of the inspector's unsolved cases. And it wasn't until we were fighting off UnDead at The Carnelian Crow that Grayling saw Pix once more—sans disguise—and was able to apprehend him (even as the Ankh and Princess Lurelia made their escape).

One might find it troubling that Grayling had turned around and arrested the very man who had risked his life and assisted us to escape from the vampires. However, I thought I understood his perspective, for Ambrose Grayling is a man of high integrity and principle. He would never allow a criminal to walk away freely.

Which brought my thoughts around to the situation at hand. *Had* Pix—Edison Smith—murdered Hiram Bartholomew?

Was there any doubt?

While he certainly wasn't a Holmes, Inspector Grayling was considerably accomplished in criminal investigations. Not only did he have an array of fascinating and useful devices that assisted him in the process, but he was nearly as quick-witted as I. The two of us had worked remarkably well in tandem the few times our responsibilities and cases had converged. In fact, I'd almost thought we might have become friends. Perhaps even more than friends.

Especially after a particular...erm...intimate interlude when we were at The Crow.

Apparently I had misread the—er—activity that had occurred during that event, for I'd not seen nor been contacted by the inspector since that night.

Yet another reason we of the Holmes family tend to avoid personal engagements with others and familiarity with the opposite gender.

I was shocked when I realized my eyes were stinging, and I blinked rapidly.

Bloody fool, I told myself quite harshly. I had no reason to dwell on the events of that evening. Instead, I would focus on the mystery of what I was supposed to be retrieving from this hideaway.

There were two obvious answers. One, perhaps Pix meant for me to take away something that was dangerous, that he wanted no one else—such as the Ankh—to possess. Perhaps I was to obtain one of those devices called a "battery" that the villainess had been using to try to control the UnDead, as well as people like her husband.

The other possibility was even more obvious: perhaps Pix meant for me to retrieve something that would prove his innocence—or at least cast doubt on his guilt. If, in fact, he *was* innocent.

Innocent was not a word I would ever have attributed to the scoundrel, but I must confess that over the course of the last nine months, I had come to appreciate some of his qualities. He was rather helpful in tenuous, dangerous situations. He knew quite a lot of what was going on in London in relation to the criminal activity. He'd even saved my life on one occasion, carrying me out of a burning building over his shoulder.

And he had cared for Evaline, at least in some fashion.

And, just as inconceivably, she'd seemed to care for him.

I blinked rapidly again. Why were my eyes stinging? Was there something here in this dusty underground place that was making them tear up?

Whatever affections might have been between Evaline and Pix didn't matter in the least. He was in jail, Evaline was getting married, and I hadn't spoken to either of them for months.

I sighed and ignored the heavy weight that sank inside my belly, focusing my attention on the matter at hand: what had I been meant to retrieve from this place?

During my musings, I'd wandered along the perimeter of the chamber, absently fingering the upholstery on the chairs and divan, brushing over the smooth wood of the eating table and desk. It was the desk to which I gave my attention now.

The obvious place an individual would store something of importance would be in his desk. At least, that was where most people would hide such a thing.

But Pix was canny and sly, and surprisingly intelligent. He rarely did the expected—which was perhaps why I didn't find him as attractive as Evaline obviously did. She much preferred a life of impetuosity and excitement.

I wondered how she would do, being married to the very proper and conventional Ned Oligary.

Why oh *why* had she ever agreed to it?

I gritted my teeth. I had much more pressing concerns—concerns that directly affected me and my own well-being. I didn't have time to worry over Evaline, who would soon be living in the lap of luxury.

I stepped back from the desk without having given it more

than a cursory look. As it would be the first place anyone would look for something important, I conjectured that Pix wouldn't have hidden it—whatever it was—there.

So I looked around the apartment with fresh eyes. His living quarters showed no indication that he'd left in a hurry, and clear evidence that he'd expected to return.

I studied the row of bookshelves. The last time I'd retrieved a message from him, it had been hidden inside an obvious (to me) tome. Would the same be true in this case?

Now that I knew Pix was really Edison Smith, I no longer found it quite as shocking that he—a pickpocket and criminal—would be well read. The same was true of my uncle's greatest adversary, Professor Moriarty.

I was still staring at the shelves, my eyes running over titles by Poe, Twain, Verne, when I heard a faint rattle.

At the door.

Someone was coming in.

MISS STOKER

- A STARTLING AND UNEXPECTED
ENCOUNTER -

No one was home at Mina's house. Not even the housekeeper Mrs. Raskill. I rang the bell three times.

Maybe Mina was caught up in one of her experiments in the laboratory. She was just as likely to ignore the bell as not even hear it.

I could go around to the back of the house and look. My hat was dripping and my shoes were soaked. My fingers were freezing inside their fine gloves. I didn't care. It was a far better option than returning to Grantworth House and all of the wedding talk.

Which brought my thoughts around to...

What had Mr. Oligary been doing at Lady Isabella's?

Just as I launched myself over the courtyard fence (why simply walk through a gate when you can have a little fun?), I remembered something Lady Isabella had told me during the funeral for Richard Dancy.

She and Mr. Oligary had known each other years ago, back when she and Miss Adler and Siri—the woman who was my mentor and who was also known as Desirée Holmes, Mina's mother—had lived in Paris.

I was standing there in the slippery, cold courtyard behind Mina's house thinking about this when a shadow emerged from the overhang by the back door.

Before I could react (attack), I recognized the figure as a Scotland Yard constable. The upside-down bucket-shaped hat made it obvious.

The constable shined a light in my face. "Who's there?"

"Turn that away." I squinted and held up my hand. "You're blinding me."

The light lowered a little. "Who are you?"

"I am Miss Evaline Stoker. Who are *you*, and what are you doing skulking around here?" It occurred to me that anything could have happened to Mina over the last two months. Maybe she wasn't even living here anymore—although I was certain I would have heard something about it in the papers. (Not that I actually read the papers.)

"I'm waitin'."

"Waiting for *what*?"

"Not what. *Who*."

Was it "who" or "whom"?

Mina's voice nattered in my head, so it was probably "whom." Not that I cared.

"Whom are you waiting for?" I demanded. (That didn't sound right.)

He came forward, and I had a moment of pity for the man. He was drenched. His hat dripped. He wasn't wearing gloves. And I swore there was a fringe of icicles on his mustache. "I've an arrest warrant for one Miss Alvermina Holmes. Do you know where she is?"

"A *what*?"

"An arrest warrant."

"For *what*?" I jolted back in surprise so sharply that I nearly slipped backward.

"The murder of Frederick Boggs."

I gaped at him. What on *earth* had Mina been up to in the last two months? And who was Frederick Boggs?

"D'ye know where she is? It's your head too if'n yer helpin' a criminal escape." He leaned forward menacingly. I didn't give him the satisfaction of reacting to this pronouncement.

"What is your name?" I demanded. I stepped closer to him. He moved backward, eyeing me warily as he realized I wasn't easily cowed.

"Constable Riddle," he replied in a sullen tone.

"Well, then, Constable Riddle, you'd best take care about throwing around accusations and threatening people."

He hmphed, then peered at me from beneath his dripping hat. But he didn't say anything. He just stood there and shivered. I wondered how long he had to stay here, waiting for Mina. (Which, if I knew her, would be a very long time.)

"How long have you been here?" I asked.

"Coupla hours. Told me to wait for when she gets home. Was walking round to see if she was sneaking in the back way. That's how she got out, first time. Walked out—right in front of Sergeant Blaketon—all dressed up as an old lady." His mustache twitched as he suppressed a smile.

I didn't bother. I laughed outright. That sounded exactly like Mina Holmes.

Then I sobered. I was sorry for any of Mina's troubles, but I had important things to talk to her about and I needed to find her. Still. *Murder?*

I left Constable Riddle huddled under the overhang of the roof. I didn't feel the least bit guilty about it.

Arresting Mina Holmes for murder—or, rather, *trying to*— was one of the most ridiculous things I'd ever heard.

And who was Frederick Boggs, anyway?

I settled back in the carriage, wishing I had taken the one Ned had given us to use. It had a little mechanism that warmed the seats. There was also a small, ovenlike container beneath each bench that likewise was heated and contained a blanket.

Right now, I would have liked a warm wrap to put over my icy feet.

Instead, I trundled along in a carriage that had a tiny leak at the left window. The sleet dripped down the inside, making me think fancifully of tears.

I'd already told Middy where I wanted to go. It was late, and the sun—not that we could see it today—was setting soon. I didn't know whether Inspector Grayling would be in his office, but he was the person I needed to speak to.

As we drove down Old Bailey-street, approaching Newgate Prison, I averted my eyes. I didn't want to look over there.

Newgate was an evil-looking structure, made completely from bricks blackened by soot and age. A sheer, ominous wall enclosed the building. This barrier was topped by a long, slowly revolving horizontal cylinder that boasted huge spikes. As if that wasn't enough of a deterrent, at each corner was a tall tower bursting with flames at the top.

The prison building itself was barely one story tall. That was because the cells were all underground in many levels. There were no windows to be seen except on the central tower, which jutted several feet above the dark, forbidding building. The British flag flew atop the tower. Today, it whipped in the ferocious wind. Its Union Jack was dull in the gray light.

Newgate was notorious for being dark, dirty, and horribly dangerous. It was often said that once a man—or woman—was put inside, they never saw the light of day again. Often prisoners died from disease or malnutrition, or were killed by other prisoners even before they went to trial.

Pix was in there, somewhere.

My throat burned. I tried to ignore the way my stomach tightened unpleasantly. I tried not to imagine what he was living through in there.

Of course I hadn't gone to see him after his arrest. How could I? I felt betrayed by the secret identity he'd kept from me.

And besides, the day after his arrest, all of the wedding announcements had been published.

Everyone knew I was engaged to Ned Oligary. And Pix—Edison Smith, I thought with a sneer—was an accused murderer. It would have been a scandal had I been seen visiting Newgate. And as the fiancée of one of the wealthiest men in the city, I would certainly have been noticed. Even if I'd tried to keep a visit a secret. I knew this for a fact, for there had been many *on dits* in the papers about me, my shopping, and other social activities since. Sometimes there were even people following me from place to place in the hopes of seeing some sort of gossipy event.

It simply was impossible for me to visit Pix, even if I'd wanted to.

As luck would have it (and I mean that sarcastically), my carriage was forced to stop next to the tall, black iron gate of the prison. I forced myself to look out the opposite window, where the rain continued to streak down inside. I couldn't worry about Pix. I couldn't care about him.

I'd always known he was a criminal. I'd suspected he'd done unsavory things. He was a pickpocket, he ran an underground business dealing in electrical devices, and he slunk around the city like someone up to no good.

And blast it, I'd allowed him to kiss me. Multiple times.

And yes, his kisses had been quite excellent. I even felt a stab of warmth, right then, thinking about them.

But that was due to the forbidden nature of the kiss. I knew that. Those moments had always been stolen, during times of great emotion or activity. Of course they'd been excellent.

Ned's kisses were nice. That was because they were proper. Because he was a gentleman. He wasn't a thief or a murderer. He wasn't dangerous. He was going to be my husband.

Bloody hell. Why wasn't the carriage moving? Why did we have to sit here in the shadow of Newgate?

The blasted place loomed over me like the hand of guilt.

I resolutely stared out the opposite window, willing the vehicle to *move* again.

Because if it didn't, I might just open the door.

I might just open the door, slip out, and find my way inside Newgate.

And *that*, I couldn't do.

❦

IT SEEMED LIKE FOREVER, but I finally arrived at Scotland Yard. I vaulted from the carriage as if I'd been sprung from prison myself. Middy, who was used to this unladylike activity, merely adjusted his hat and watched me as I hurried to the building. He hadn't even bothered to try to climb down from his perch to hand me out.

I'd only been inside the Met once before. I'd been with Mina, of course. Fortunately, we'd been going to the same place I was going now: to Inspector Grayling's office.

However, I wasn't certain I remembered exactly how to find his office. I got inside and strode past the front desk (which was vacant). No one else was in the vicinity. After a hesitation, I took the right arm at a Y intersection of three corridors. Moments later, I realized I was lost. Blast it.

I was in a long hallway. It wasn't lined with the offices I'd expected. Instead, darkened rooms with barred windows faced the hall. There were some lights here, but they gave off only a dim, oozing golden light. I went halfway down the hall before I realized there were people—prisoners—in some of the rooms.

I discovered this because, as I passed by, a hand snaked out from between the bars. Dirty fingers grabbed my arm and yanked me so hard that I slammed into the metal.

I stifled a shriek and yanked out of the grip with a decisive, twisting movement. The man howled with surprise and pain (surely not expecting a woman to be so strong) and withdrew his hand as if I'd bitten him.

"Try that again and I'll break it," I told him, managing to keep my voice taut and steady. Inside, my heart was pounding from shock at the sudden attack.

He glared at me from a few steps back, nursing his arm—which was enclosed in filthy clothing. "Didn't 'ave to—"

"He's mad," cried someone.

In the next cell, a man lunged from the shadows, his eyes wide and glistening with fury. "Lemme outta *'ereeeee*." His voice rose in a spiral of madness. "*Lemmeeee gooooo*."

He slammed against the bars, sending a shock of power against iron reverberating down the hall. Ogling me, he shouted profanities and continued to bang on the metal bars of his prison. His eyes rolled and darted, showing a frightening amount of white.

I'm not easily spooked. But the sudden loud fury and madness had me spinning away. Now the others in the cages had awakened. They came from the dark shadows of their confines, shouting, banging, and making all sorts of animalistic noises. I felt as if I were in one of the asylums for the mad. My heart was pounding as the clanging wildness echoed down the corridor.

Yet I refused to let them see. I even refused to turn around, to let them think they'd gotten to me.

Adding to the horrific tune of metal clanging and desperate profanity, piercing whistles shrieked down the passage, echoing sharply in my ears. Nevertheless, I continued down the corridor, safely out of arm's reach. There was a door at the end, and I was certain it led back to the main wing.

I was near the end of the hall when I glanced inside a cell, simply because it was ominously quiet.

Two dark eyes stared at me from the depths of darkness.

I froze.

As the shouts and clangs continued, I found myself moving to the cage. I couldn't have stopped myself if I'd tried. I wrapped my hands around the bars, caught by the cold, dark gaze from within.

"I thought you were at Newgate," I blurted out. The iron studs burned cold and hard into my hot cheeks.

"Don't tell me ye've spent the last two months lookin' for me there," Pix replied. His voice was as cold and flat as his eyes. "I know better'n that."

He hadn't lifted himself from the pallet on the floor of his cell. He couldn't be bothered to rise to speak to me. Yet his words penetrated cleanly, as though the continued horrific cacophony of his prison mates had gone silent. Which they hadn't.

"I..." I didn't know what to say. I felt as if the ground was dissolving beneath my feet—that I was on the edge of some crumbling cliff. I gripped the bars as if they were going to save me from tumbling.

"Although that could explain why I haven't received my wedding invitation. Did you send it to Newgate, then?"

I closed my eyes and shook my head against his jail cell.

"What are you doing here, Evaline?"

Cold. So cold. His tones sliced through me more harshly than the sleet had done.

"I'm..." I searched the darkness. I could only see his eyes and a hint of nose.

"Not here to see me, I know. An unhappy accident, isn't it, that you should've come this way? Well, no need to worry about it, luv. I won't tell anyone if you don't."

Luv.

The loathing in that single syllable shocked me breathless.

"Go away, Evaline. Your secret's safe with me."

He closed his eyes and melted into the shadows.

"Pix." I shook the bars experimentally. They actually moved.

One eye opened. It glittered with malice. "*My name is Smith.* Go away."

MISS STOKER

- IN WHICH THE AIRSHIP AT LAST MAKES AN APPEARANCE -

Miss Stoker! What are you doing down here?"

At the sound of a familiar Scottish brogue, I turned. I had to blink rapidly in order to clear the angry tears that were obscuring my vision.

"Inspector Grayling, you're just the man I was looking for." I pitched my voice toward the open doorway through which I'd just passed, leaving behind the hall of cells and the wild madness of their occupants. I hoped that blasted *Mr. Smith* heard the blithe pleasure in my voice.

"Och, well, isn't that a fine thing," Grayling replied gallantly. If he noticed the furious color in my cheeks or the glistening in my eyes, he was too much of a gentleman to mention it. He offered me his arm. "You're—er—here alone, then?"

To his credit, he didn't actually look around to see whether my usual companion was with me. I felt a little pang of sympathy for the man.

"I am, Inspector. And that's part of the reason. Is there somewhere we could speak privately?"

If he was surprised or taken aback by my informal request, again, he didn't show it. I suppose that, being a police inspector, very little surprised him.

He brought me to the office he shared with Inspector Luck-worth, who was as opposite from Grayling as possible (except that they were both men). Where the younger Grayling was a cog-noggin of the first degree and was always trying newfangled gadgets, Luckworth was very set in his ways—which meant he was more of a medieveler like me. He was also older and slightly stouter than his partner, so his mechanized leg creaked a little when he walked. He usually wore clothing that was years out of date, and because he had a young child at home, his trousers sometimes had jelly stains below the knee. He was greatly skeptical about Grayling's penchant for fancy devices and modern crime-solving techniques, and they often argued about such things.

Fortunately, Luckworth wasn't in the office. However, Grayling's three-legged beagle Angus was. He was feasting on the crumbs scattered on Luckworth's chair, which implied that the other man had only recently left. The overturned rubbish bin told even someone with my lack of observation skills that Angus had found something to nibble on therein before moving on to the chair and its crumbs.

"What can I help you with, Miss Stoker?" Grayling asked, gesturing for me to take the seat at his desk as he turned it around.

I sat, glancing at the wall where he kept all of the informa-tion about the cases he was working on. Mina said it was his Case-Wall. There were photographs and drawings of crime scenes, as well as sketches with measurements and notations. There were pictures of people—possibly suspects, or even victims—scattered about.

I gave it only a cursory glance; the investigation of crimes wasn't really my idea of fun. If there weren't any UnDead to slay, I preferred the apprehension and fighting part. Not the thinking.

"There's an arrest warrant for Mina. For the murder of someone named Frederick Boggs. I was hoping—"

"*What?*" Grayling's face went white. And since he had fairly pale skin to begin with—though it was covered liberally with freckles—the fact that it was noticeable says a lot about how much color he lost. "Pardon me. I must have misunderstood, Miss Stoker. What did you say?"

"They—some constables—are trying to arrest Mina for the murder of someone named Frederick Boggs."

Grayling stared at me for so long that I thought he'd fallen asleep with his eyes open. After a moment, he said, "Who told you this? How did you find out about this?"

"There's a Constable Riddle lurking about at Mina's house, waiting for her to come home so he can arrest her. Apparently, they tried to do so earlier, but she escaped by wearing a disguise. She walked out right under their noses. Or so he told me."

Grayling's mouth twitched. "I see." He seemed to relax a little. "Miss Holmes isn't at home, then."

"Not unless she sneaked back in and is hiding. Which, I suppose, is a possibility." I frowned. Maybe I should have gone inside to make certain.

"She's safe, then. For the moment. Riddle, did you say?" He frowned. "I don't believe I know a constable by that name."

"There was also the mention of a Sergeant Blaketon. Apparently he was the man in charge."

Grayling's brow furrowed more deeply. "Blaketon? Hm." He stared at his Case-Wall for a long moment, but I had the impression he wasn't really looking at it. "Frederick Boggs? It's not my case, but I should be able to find out more about it."

"And why Mina's a suspect," I added.

"Yes."

He frowned. "But surely Sir Mycroft or Mr. Holmes would be informed of this— Och, then. I'd forgotten. Sir Mycroft is...away. Out of the country, on some Home Office business. It's been kept out of the papers, but we were given notification of that earlier this week." His frown deepened. "But Mr. Holmes—"

Angus barked sharply, startling both of us. He was looking up at me with hopeful brown eyes, his too-long black and brown ears trailing on the ground. I supposed he was remembering the fact that the last time I'd seen him, I'd been carrying a snack in my reticule. I'd shared it with him as a way to distract Grayling so I could snatch something off his desk. (I put it back.)

"I'm sorry, old boy, but I don't have a bit of anything with me. I ate most of the teacakes at Cosgrove Terrace, and—"

"Cosgrove Terrace?" Grayling looked sharply at me.

"Yes. Uhm...Lady Isabella invited me to tea today." I tried to sound casual. I was fairly certain Grayling didn't know that the woman who was his distant relative was also the Ankh.

"She did?" He frowned again. "In this weather? While she is in mourning?"

"Yes."

He began to rub his chin. "What did Miss Holmes say about this incident with Frederick Boggs?"

I bit my lip. This was where things became a little uncomfortable. "I haven't spoken to her. About it."

"Aye, I see. Well, I trust she's...er...doing well." He seemed to be staring at the Case-Wall with great interest.

I heaved a sigh. "I have no idea. I haven't spoken to her since —since that night at The Carnelian Crow."

"Ye haven't?" His brogue had gone thick, even with those few words. "Nae at all?"

"No."

Why did I feel so guilty? *She* hadn't contacted me either. And *I* was the one who was getting married. Whose life was going to radically change in a month.

"Did... Well, blast it, Miss Stoker, the two of you have been underfoot and meddling in murder investigations and robbery cases for nearly a year now." He sighed and rubbed the bridge of his nose between two freckled fingers. "Och, well, I suppose I ken who—er—what's keeping her busy, then."

"You do?" I'd known for a long time that Grayling had a penchant for Mina. It was very obvious. But for being such a brilliant detective (her words, not mine), however, she didn't seem to have the faintest idea about his admiration.

But now that Dylan Eckhert had returned from the future, poor Grayling obviously felt discarded. He likely assumed Mina had been keeping company with Dylan. That might be the case; I honestly didn't know. I grimaced inside.

You should *know*, a nasty little voice said in my head.

"I'll look into the Frederick Boggs situation right away, Miss Stoker," he said. "May I call you a carriage home? The weather is ferocious. That's part of the reason I haven't left yet, and why no one else is here." He gave a rueful smile.

"No, thank you. I have Middy waiting for me." I started for the door of his office, then paused. "About Pi—Edison Smith."

"Yes, Miss Stoker?" His expression was studiously blank.

"Oh...nothing."

"Very well, then." He offered me his arm and escorted me back to the front entrance. This time, we avoided going down the corridor with the jail cells. "Erm...Miss Stoker, I know that you haven't spoken to Miss Holmes. But where do you think she would be—er—hiding out while—erm—evading arrest?"

I'd given that some thought myself, to be honest. "Nowhere obvious."

"Of course not." He hesitated as we reached the front door. "If you do happen to have contact with Miss Holmes, please tell her that if she is in need of help, she can come to me... I mean to say, of course, that while I must abide by the law, I am also well versed in it, and if there is anything I can do..." He grimaced. "Right, then. Miss Holmes is quite able to take care of herself, isn't she?"

"Of course I'll tell her, Inspector. If I see her. That's exactly why I came to you here." I smiled at him and patted his arm. I could see the worry in his eyes. "I knew you would help."

I took my leave then. Since Mina wasn't available, Grayling was, in my mind, the next best person to approach with a problem.

The scoundrel named Pix didn't even come to mind.

I settled back into the carriage, pleased with myself. I'd managed to squander nearly the entire day away from Grantworth House. Big Ben was striking half-eight as Middy eased the carriage into the street. Due to the weather, the throughway was relatively empty. Most everyone was huddled in at home, out of the sleet and whipping wind.

That was probably why I saw it.

I caught my breath, craning my neck to look up and over. Through the freezing rain and dark, dreary evening, I saw it in the distance, sliding silently through the sky like a creeping figure: a long, slender black airship.

I blinked, then opened my eyes. It was still there, hidden among the steam clouds and the snowy fog, above the leaning rooftops and sky-anchors where no one would look up during such ugly weather. This was the first time I'd spotted it when it wasn't very late at night.

Pix had pulled me into the shadows each time we'd seen the sleek zeppelin. It was as if he was afraid it would notice him—as if it were a living being that threatened him. Or us.

Although I didn't know why, I found myself moving away from the carriage window, out of sight.

MISS HOLMES

~ IN WHICH "EXCESSIVE CLEVERNESS" PROVES VALUABLE ~

I was momentarily paralyzed by indecision. Should I attempt to hide from whomever was attempting to gain access to Pix's (now my) hideaway, or should I announce my presence and demand to know what the individual wanted while being prepared to fight and defend myself?

The door's more insistent rattle jolted me to life. I was no Evaline Stoker, and therefore I was in no way equipped to defend myself (especially if it was an UnDead who was on the threshold) except with the mini-steam-stream gun...which was in the depths of my market bag on the other side of the chamber and would be useless against a vampire.

The obvious choice was for me to hide and watch. Thus I could determine who else was attempting to use the underground lair—or whatever purpose they had in coming inside.

The decision made, my mind snapped back into its normal lightning-quick agility. I ducked behind the partition door that separated the sleeping area from the rest of the apartments. I could slip into the wardrobe and hide deep amongst Pix's extensive clothing collection (which likely held a variety of disguise elements—a possibility that I would investigate at my earliest convenience). But first, I wanted to see who was here.

The door rattled once more, violently. And then it stopped. Something slammed against it—to my trained ear, it sounded like an angry fist—and I was certain I heard a muffled exclamation of frustration.

I cautiously eased from my hiding place. Whoever it was obviously didn't know how to get through the locks. I smiled to myself and hurried to the door, hoping to catch a glimpse of whoever it was. Presumably, Pix had some sort of visual mechanism that would allow him to see if anyone— Ah, yes. There was a small opening in the wall next to the door.

When I looked inside, I could see that a clever arrangement of angled mirrors in an irregular tube projected an image from the top of the door's exterior. I dismissed the fact that I hadn't noticed it myself during this or previous visits; I'd had no reason to look around for such an apparatus at the time.

But by now, whoever was there had disappeared back into the tunnel that led to Fenman's End. I caught only the glimpse of a retreating shadow, which gave no indication of even the gender of the person who'd been pummeling at the door.

I would wait for a short time to ensure they had gone, then open the door and examine the area. Perhaps he or she had left some clue as to their identity.

Now that my heart rate had returned to normal and my palms were no longer damp (I am no coward, but the thought of facing an UnDead—or a few of them—alone had turned my blood cold), I turned my attention back to the matter at hand: what was in here that was important to Pix?

I turned slowly in a circle from the center of the room, hoping something would strike me visually. If nothing did, I'd have to do a painstaking, hands-and-knees examination of the entire place—something that is far more difficult for a woman in petticoats and a corset than a man in trousers.

And then I saw it. *How clever.*

One had to be standing in front of the mirror he had so carefully positioned so as to see not only oneself, but the entirety of the chamber behind, and it was only by looking in the mirror and seeing an image in reverse that one could discover the obvious—yet not so obvious—hiding place.

There was, now noticeable, a short verse that could only be discerned if one were looking at it through the mirror's reflection and seeing it in reverse. Otherwise, the writing had been cleverly disguised to look like part of the pattern of the black and brown wallpaper.

The words read: *Nihil sapientiae odiosius acumine nimio.*

Of course, not only can I comprehend Latin, but I was also immediately aware of the most famous use of that verse: in the epigraph of Edgar Allan Poe's brilliant story "The Purloined Letter."

(For those who aren't well versed in Latin, I translate herewith: *Nothing is more hateful to wisdom than excessive cleverness.*)

Pix's clue was therefore telling me—for who else would he expect to enter his hideaway and find whatever it was he wanted to be found?—that the information was hidden just as it was in the Poe story: somewhere slightly disguised, but nonetheless in plain sight.

Indeed—I had suspected something of a well-crafted hiding place; Pix is not the sort to secret important papers behind wall-coverings or inside cushions, and certainly not behind paintings or portraits. And false drawers and secret partitions are far too obvious for someone as cunning as that particular knave.

And thus armed with this clue, it took me only a moment to find what he'd hidden.

On his bookshelf, he had a slender, bound copy of "The Purloined Letter." But did I pull that out and extricate his secrets from therein, as I had done only months ago when Miss Adler used the very same book for a hiding place?

No, I did not—for only a few short spaces down on the shelf from that seemingly obvious book was the actual hiding place: inside a bound leather tome titled *The Gift*, which is, of course, the volume in which "The Purloined Letter" *first* appeared. How obvious could one be? And yet...clever as a whip, for how many people would recall that the story was previously published in a collection?

He had removed many of the pages of the original matter and inserted his own information, binding it as if part of the book. One would have had to look very closely to realize that the pages were Pix's own story, if you will, rather than that of Poe and the other readings in that particular volume.

I assumed that he would expect me to remove those inserted papers for further inspection, and so I carefully cut them free from their bindings.

I spread all of it out on the eating table and decided to make tea to have whilst examining it. (Had I been with Evaline, she would have demanded sustenance much earlier on. As it was, I had just realized I hadn't eaten anything all day except for a burned piece of toast because the Flippers Fryer & Toaster had malfunctioned again.)

With a cup of bracing Darjeeling in hand (which always reminded me of Miss Adler), I settled at the table to peruse the secrets of Edison Smith.

There were newspaper clippings, correspondence, a few photographs, and even a contract. This last item drew my attention immediately, and as I read through it, I forgot my tea.

By the time I finished my examination, I had a much better understanding of Mr. Edison Smith, what he was doing here in London, why he'd been hiding out in Whitechapel, and how he was involved in the murder of Hiram Bartholomew.

It wasn't until I was prepared to slip the documents back inside the book that I noticed a photograph that had been tucked inside much farther back. I withdrew it, and as I looked down, my breath caught. I goggled at the five people captured on the sepia-toned image.

They were Emmett Oligary, Hiram Bartholomew, Edison Smith, a male individual whose face was partly obscured and whom I didn't recognize...and *my mother*.

MISS HOLMES

- DR. WATSON IS TAKEN ABACK BY ANOTHER HOLMES -

W hy was my mother in a photograph with Hiram Bartholomew, Emmett Oligary, *and Pix?*

It wasn't entirely shocking that she was with Sir Emmett, for I knew that she, Miss Adler, and Lady Isabella had all been friends in Paris many years ago—and that Emmett Oligary had occasionally spent time with them. But this was a recent photograph—before Bartholomew died, but after Edison Smith had come to London.

And, of course, before my mother disappeared—which was now nearly two years ago.

But exactly when had the photograph been taken? I had scrutinized it for clues to the date—or at least the season—but there were no convenient calendar pages or newspapers to offer a clue. The window in the background offered little information; the rectangle showed only a medium gray color which could be any day or evening in London.

I thought about everything I knew in relation to Edison Smith—who was the most surprising occupant (aside from my mother) of the photograph: he was American, he was the nephew of Mr. Thomas Edison, and he'd been in London acting as a business representative of the Edison family. The

Edisons and the Oligary-Bartholomew partnership had been about to execute a contract to manufacture electrical current equipment.

Obviously, the photograph had been taken before the business arrangement between Bartholomew, Oligary, and the Edisons had gone sour—*but what was my mother doing in the picture?* And who was the other person? Try as I might, I couldn't see his face well enough to identify him.

Despite the comfortable bed in the underground lair, I hardly slept that night, tossing and turning as I conjectured and mulled and, eventually, dreamt badly.

The image of the photograph was imprinted on my mind, and in my dream, the figures within came alive: Sir Emmett, Mr. Bartholomew, Edison Smith, and my mother, along with the fifth individual who simply faded into the background.

In both the photograph and in my dreams, the group of people were in a location that was vaguely familiar to me—a chamber with high ceilings and an open space. It wasn't until I was submerged in nocturnal ratiocination (under the guise of slumber) that I realized where I'd seen that place before: it was in a photograph in the file Grayling kept on the murder of Bartholomew.

It was the very room where he'd died, in his office in the Oligary Building.

In the dream, my mother, Bartholomew, Sir Emmett, and Edison Smith, along with the fifth person, a man, were looking at a large mechanical conglomeration. They talked about it (although in my dream, I couldn't understand what they were saying) and gestured to it. My mother mostly observed, but I noticed she stood near Sir Emmett most of the time.

The large machine was in the background of the photograph, but in my dream, the figures moved about casually, thus allowing it to come into view so I could see it fully. I expect that was because in the photographs of Hiram Bartholomew's murder scene, the complicated machinery was unobstructed by people standing in front of it, so my dreaming mind knew what it looked like.

In the file photographs, Bartholomew's dead body lay crumpled on the floor in the shadow of the electric device—which had ultimately killed him when he was allegedly pushed by Edison Smith into the bare wires of the electrical device during an altercation.

Emmett Oligary had heard his partner being electrofied (as I myself had witnessed a young lady being electrofied, I was well aware of how horrible the sound was: like a large, tortured fish, flopping about helplessly), and had attempted to save him. In the process, Sir Emmett had become burned by a bare wire—an injury that left him with a pronounced limp.

At last, I had no choice but to drag myself out of bed, for the day was nigh, and despite this new and shocking information, I had other problems to which I must attend. Namely, taking the steps to prove my innocence of murder.

As I had the opportunity, I took advantage of the very large bathing tub filled with steaming water. I'd never enjoyed such a luxurious interval, and I confess I was in no hurry to vacate. Who would have thought the criminal lair of a pickpocket would have hot, running water and a tub the size of a divan? Not to mention a special kind of liquid soap that created frothy white bubbles of pink, blue, and lavender. It smelled divine.

Of course, Edison Smith was an American, after all, and it's well known that theirs is a nation of excesses. Still, I couldn't fault him for this one.

To my surprise and delight, I'd discovered that the tub was continuously heated by the metal pipes that ran beneath it. Thus, the water stayed warm even after an hour. It was only the insistent scraping of my stomach's insides that urged me out of the water.

Not that I was soaking for an hour. Fifty minutes was long enough. (We British are much more restrained than our American friends.)

Since I wasn't about to eat anything prepared in or near Fenman's End, and the totality of my meals for the last twenty-four hours had included yesterday's sad, burned-toast breakfast, two cups of Darjeeling (which I'd had to reheat), and the few things I'd snatched while in flight from Mrs. Raskill's kitchen (an apple, a heel of bread, and half a tin of slightly stale lemon-thyme biscuits), I had no choice but to leave the lair.

Though I'd poked around, Pix had only a very limited number of foodstuffs stashed away—one being a completely green hunk of cheese (I considered bringing it to Dylan, thinking perhaps he could use the mold for his "antibiotics," and then immediately rejected the idea. Dylan and I weren't exactly... speaking) and something that might have been bread at one point but certainly no longer resembled anything edible.

Of course, I'd been correct in my surmise that Pix/Smith had an abundance of theatrical supplies that he used for disguises. By the time I was ready to leave, no one—even Uncle Sherlock —would have recognized me. Between the slight darkening of my complexion, along with the skillful application of stage makeup to subtly change the appearance of the contours of my face and an extremely high-quality false mustache that hid the shape of my upper lip, I looked like a completely different person. Even my brows were different (bushier and longer), and I wore the same pair of gray-tinted spectacles I'd donned the day before.

Naturally, I remembered to darken the skin of my hands to match my face and throat, but that was just a precaution, because I'd discovered a cunning pair of gloves that made my fingers and wrists look thicker and larger. I had to admit, Pix was rather a genius when it came to disguises.

Of course, I didn't leave his hideaway by the way I'd entered. As I've previously mentioned, there are at least two other exits from the place, and I elected to use one of them. Before I did so, however, I remembered to open the door through which I'd come last night. I'd become so absorbed in reviewing the documents Pix had hidden that I'd forgotten to look for clues as to who had tried to get in.

Footprints in the dust indicated a shoe size much larger than my own, and likely of the male persuasion—unless the individual was wearing a disguise. Nothing else was obviously disturbed, but in the dim light and closeness, I confess even I couldn't discern any other identifying factors.

I went back inside and locked the door, then after making a number of other arrangements in the apartment, I donned a large greatcoat (thankful that it was winter and I could bundle up to hide my figure) and placed a brushed-wool bowler on my head.

Fortunately, the weather was not as ill-tempered as it had been yesterday. Of course, that meant there were more people on the streets of Whitechapel. However, as it was barely nine o'clock in the morning, most of the residents of this decrepit area had not yet risen to see the light of day.

I hadn't expected to find a hackney in the borough, and I was required to walk far too many blocks before I reached an Underground station. I'm not terribly fond of the subterranean transportation tube for obvious reasons, but I hadn't brought an unlimited amount of money with me, so I had to conserve until I could safely replenish. Yesterday's lengthy hackney ride had depleted far too much of my funds.

After navigating between several trains and omnibuses, I reached the busy streets of Haymarket. The first thing I did was purchase a meat and cheddar pie and cup of tea. The pie had an unusual, spicy sauce on it that I'd never had before, but it immediately became a favorite. The tea was strong, hot, and sweetened with honey. Very bracing. Once I'd finished my small meal, I felt far more clearheaded and went in search of a paper and a hack—in that order.

While in the cab, I perused the *Times*, *News*, and *Daily Cog*, searching for a mention of Frederick Boggs. When I found it, a little prickle skittered over my shoulders. Coincidentally, Mr.

Boggs lived on a street not far from my own house. There were no photographs or drawings in the articles to give any clue to the crime scene or the victim.

The hack stopped at the address I'd given to the driver, and I alighted and paid. Then, confident in my disguise, I walked across the street.

"Dr. Watson," I said, entering that gentleman's office. He glanced up at me, lifting a finger as he continued to pound on the mechanical typing machine in front of him. As he was quite likely writing an account of another of Uncle Sherlock's cases, I took a seat to wait.

"Sorry about that, sir," he said at last, whipping a paper from the machine with a flourish. "Didn't want to lose my thoughts. Are you here for the doctor, or for the writer?" he asked with a grin that displayed two pleasant dimples parenthetical to his mustache.

As there was no one else here but the two of us—and I'd ascertained that no one was loitering outside as if in wait for me —I came to sit directly in front of him at the desk. "I need to speak to Uncle Sherlock," I said in a low voice, removing my spectacles so he could see my eyes.

"Good *gad*!" he exclaimed, his own eyes flying wide open behind his own spectacles. "Is that really you, Alver—I mean, Mina?" He squinted closely at me, his dimples reappearing as he scrunched up his face in an apparent attempt to recognize me. "Good *gad*!"

I resisted the urge to preen over the stunning effects of my disguise. After all, dear John Watson hadn't recognized his closest friend and colleague numerous times during the course of their partnership. Thanks in part to the tiny inserts that changed the shape of my nostrils, my voice came out slightly more nasally than usual. "Thank you, Doctor. I apologize for startling you, and I won't go into the details about the reasons for my current visible characterization. I do need to speak with my uncle as soon as possible. Could you send word to him?"

But Dr. Watson was already shaking his head. "I'm sorry, Mina, but Sherlock's not in the city. He's not even in the country."

Drat.

"Do you know when he'll be back? Is there a way to contact him?"

"I'm afraid not. He's on some sort of case about that Professor Moriarty. Last I heard, he was on the scoundrel's trail to somewhere in Germany. Reichenbach, I believe it was."

"Very well." I rose, my mind already making adjustments. So I couldn't count on the two male members of my family to help. And when had I ever, really?

I'd have to rely on myself—something I was fully capable of doing. In fact, I'd anticipated such a conclusion and was already prepared.

"Mina, is there something I can do?" Dr. Watson pulled himself up out of the chair. Quite frankly, there was nothing he could do for me that I couldn't do myself. I was far more resourceful than the good doctor in every way—except perhaps medical surgery. Although, as I'd recently spent a good amount of time dissecting a human hand, I anticipated soon being able to surpass him in that skill as well.

"No thank you, Dr. Watson. I have things well in hand." I gathered up the stack of newspapers I'd carried in with me and took my leave, belatedly realizing I should have asked if he'd loan me some money. That would have saved me the time and effort of having to obtain it myself.

But by then, I was several blocks from his office, riding in the steam-powered omnibus toward the residence of Mr. Frederick Boggs—the scene of the murder I had purportedly committed.

The papers had been quite helpful in this regard, and I knew the basics of what had happened. Mr. Boggs had been found very early yesterday morning, dead in his kitchen. The article didn't give the cause of death; however, it did indicate that he'd been deceased since the night before. He lived alone, and had recently moved back to London after being abroad for more than a year.

Fortunately, I hadn't been mentioned in the papers relative to being a suspect—at least so far. But I couldn't count on that being the case for much longer. What a journalistic scoop it would be to report that Sir Mycroft's daughter and Mr. Holmes's niece was to be arrested for murder!

I ground my teeth as I pushed my way off the crowded omnibus and onto the street. As previously mentioned, Mr. Boggs lived in a residential area not far from my own home. In fact, I'd been on his very street only last week.

My steps slowed as I looked around, an unpleasant feeling settling over me. I *had* been here. There'd been a letter that had accidentally been delivered to our house last week. It had been marked *URGENT*, and as the courier had already left on his bicycle, I'd taken it upon myself to deliver it to the correct address.

Which turned out to be that of Frederick Boggs, despite the fact that his name wasn't the addressee listed on the envelope.

How curious.

How coincidental.

I didn't believe in coincidences, and neither did my uncle.

Feeling as though I were walking through a heavy, unpleasant bog (the pun is certainly intentional), I nonetheless continued along the very walkway I'd traversed only a week ago. Brandishing my walking stick, I approached a pair of men who were standing in front of Boggs's address.

"Good avternoon, there, sirs," I said, adopting the accent I'd used when in disguise as a princess of Vovinga, but in a much lower register, of course. "Perhaps you can be ahv assistance. I am looking vor the residence ahv Mr. Vederick Boggs."

One of them gestured casually. "Right there, sir. But you're bound to be disappointed if you came to see him. Bloke was killed two days ago."

"Killed?" I widened my eyes. "Und how vahz that?"

"Hit over the head."

Hit over the head?

I barely controlled my reaction.

How could anyone think I would kill someone in such a vulgar, haphazard manner—let alone be strong enough to fell a man with a single blow? I scoffed deep inside, but kept my expression neutral.

"Fehrry well, zhen. I zahnk you for zee warningk. But I shall knock on zee dohr none-zee-less." I tipped my hat and started up the walkway.

Feeling far more optimistic (not that I had ever worried I'd ultimately be able to prove my innocence), I walked toward the door with manly strides. Having relatively long legs assists in such subterfuge.

I was nearly through the small gate that led to the steps when my walking stick landed on a small patch of ice and slipped. Fortunately, I wasn't leaning much of my weight on it, so I didn't actually tumble to the ground, but it was a near thing.

I managed to maintain a relatively vertical position despite a flurry of long, awkward limbs that knocked into a bush and caused clumps of snow to rain down on me, followed by a heel that landed on another patch of ice and nearly sent me to the ground *that* time.

Just then, the door to the house opened.

Gripping the small gate to help my balance, I looked up as Inspector Ambrose Grayling strode out, carrying a large attaché case that contained his crime-solving devices.

Drat.

Of course, he saw me immediately and stopped on the path next to me. I was thankful my foggy, gray-tinted glasses were still in place, as well as the other accoutrements of my disguise.

"May I help you, sir?" Grayling asked. He'd paused on the walkway in such a position that I could move in neither direction.

"Ah, no, zahnk you sir," I said quickly, adjusting my hat so its brim was low over my forehead. *Drat, drat,* drat. "I vahz loogingk for Meester Boggs. And zohse men helped me."

"I regret to inform you that Mr. Boggs—Mr. Frederick Boggs —is deceased."

"Ah, yes, zoh zhey haff said." I knew I was fumbling the accent, mixing a Betrovian affect with the Vovingan one I'd adopted before—along with Providence knew what else was in my nervous mishmash. I only hoped he didn't notice.

"Unfortunately, Mr. Boggs's home is a crime scene, sir, and I cannot allow you to go any further." He gestured in the direction from which I'd come. I would be only too happy to turn around and be on my way, but his case was jutting into the path in that direction. The space between it and the heavy gate was too narrow for me to walk, especially, as I'd discovered, it was patchy with ice. "The Met is investigating his death as suspicious."

"Yes, sir, uff course," I said, keeping my head slightly down-turned to obstruct his view of my face. Since he was so dratted tall, and I was wearing a hat with a decent brim, it was a sound strategy.

"But if you have a message, I can see that it is delivered to Mr. Boggs's next of kin," Grayling continued. He seemed to be waiting for me to turn and leave, which I was more than happy to do if he'd just scoot a little more to the side or turn his case. His large feet were also taking up too much space on the dry walkway.

I didn't really want to risk trying to slip past him between the gate, the case, and his feet, knowing how prone I was to losing my balance or mis-stepping—even when not in skirts.

"I'll be on my vay, zhen," I said, and, having no choice, thwacked him in the shin with my walking stick. Grayling muffled a yelp and stepped back, and that was all I needed to skirt past him and start down the walk.

"Ach, no, und I am zho zhorry! Zhe apologies I must make," I cried as I walked away, trying not to hurry. "It is many pardons for injuring you, sir."

I kept waiting to hear a shout, or for the sound of running feet behind me, but nothing happened.

As I turned the corner at the end of the block, I glanced back covertly.

Grayling was nowhere in sight.

MISS STOKER

~ OF CRYING, SHRIEKING, AND GENERAL
UPSET ~

My eyes were dry and gritty when I opened them next morning. I blamed that on the angry tears I'd cried well into the night. But the reason for opening them at all was because Florence was shrieking my name from downstairs.

She sounded even more irate than she'd been last night.

That was not good.

It started when I returned home after my visit to Scotland Yard. Yes, it was well after dinner. Yes, I'd been gone for more than five hours. Yes, I'd left word where I was going.

But that didn't matter, because Ned's carriage was parked in front of the house when I finally returned after nine. Apparently, he'd been waiting for me for almost an hour.

It didn't help that I was mildly bedraggled due to the weather and various trips in and out of my carriage, around Mina's house, and over her back gate. Florence swooped down on me the moment I set foot on the threshold of the house.

"*Where* have you been?" She fairly yanked me into the vestibule then began to propel me upstairs.

I couldn't ever remember seeing her that angry, at least with me. "I was having tea with Lady Cosgrove-Pi—"

"I know that you weren't," she hissed, glancing over her shoulder toward the parlor as she marched up the stairs behind me. I assumed that was where Ned was waiting. "Look at you. You're filthy and your hair is falling down..." She bit out the words as if she were chopping them—violently. Pepper was already in my bedchamber, preparing to set me to rights.

"I certainly was," I replied. But my indignation was muffled as my maid and my sister-in-law began to drag off my day dress and unpin my hair.

"I sent word, Evaline," Florence snapped. "To Cosgrove Terrace, when Mr. Oligary arrived to see you. Lady Cosgrove-Pitt wasn't at home."

I struggled to remain upright as the two women "set me to rights" in a very ungentle manner. I didn't even notice what frock Florence had chosen for me, let alone have a choice in it. Pepper met my eyes sympathetically in the mirror when Flo knelt to straighten my petticoats.

"Don't have time to change them," she muttered, obviously seeing the damp, dirty hems. "Blast it, Evaline, if you ruin this engagement, I'll—" She stood abruptly, snapping off the words as she looked at me. Her color was high and her eyes flashed as she surveyed me. "Good. You look presentable. We will talk about your lie later. To the parlor. *Now.*"

My eyes stung with fury as I descended the stairs. I fought to keep the tears from coming by blinking rapidly. I held my breath in the old trick to help a blush dissipate quickly—I knew my face was red with emotion.

How dare she treat me like I was a child? How dare she speak to me that way? I was doing this wedding thing for *her* and *Bram*, wasn't I?

I paused outside the door of the parlor, composed myself, then went in.

"Evaline." Ned rose and immediately came to me. He took my hands, which were gloved, of course, and drew me to him for a kiss on the cheek. This had become his usual way to greet me: a chaste kiss on the cheek.

That didn't mean we hadn't shared other kisses in more private settings.

As I said: they were nice, those other kisses.

At twenty-seven, Ned was nearly a decade older than me. He had brown hair and a trimmed mustache and sideburns. He was always dressed at the height of fashion in expensive, well-tailored clothing. Today he sported a coat of luxurious mahogany velvet with a gold and mahogany paisley waistcoat beneath it. A complicated expanding timepiece made from bronze, gold, and copper was tucked into the pocket of his vest, and its chain hung in a casual, glittering arc from there to where it was attached to his clothing.

"I'm so sorry to have kept you waiting," I said, still feeling stiff and out of sorts.

"I wasn't aware that you had an engagement today." His voice sounded stiff and out of sorts.

"I was asked to tea at Cosgrove Terrace," I replied. "It was an unexpected invitation. As a matter of fact, when I was leaving, I saw your brother arrive."

Ned looked at me skeptically. "You think Emmett was visiting Cosgrove Terrace? Impossible. He told me he was leaving for Paris this evening."

I hesitated. I was certain it had been the elder Oligary's steam-car, but I might have been wrong. And I hadn't had a good look at the occupant. "I thought it was him."

"He was on his way to Paris." Ned settled back into his seat, still looking at me doubtfully. "You were mistaken. Did you have a nice time at tea with Lady Cosgrove-Pitt? You seemed to be there for an exceptionally long while."

I felt my cheeks warm, and I didn't know why. I *had* been at Cosgrove Terrace. It wasn't a lie. But clearly Ned was fishing for other information. Could he believe I'd gone somewhere else?

Was he suspicious about me? Even if he was, he didn't have anything to be suspicious about.

"It was a lovely tea." Except when she invited me to join her murderous "alliance." "But Lady Isabella seems to be very bored, being confined to her house while in mourning."

He lifted his brows. "Deep mourning is only appropriate in her situation, Evaline. Don't you agree?"

"Of course. But I can certainly understand why she might... well, get bored. Especially someone like Lady Isabella, with all of her normal social obligations."

"Everyone understands that she is required to avoid social occasions right now," Ned said. I felt like he was patting me on the head as he spoke. "And I don't think it's quite proper for you to refer to her as Lady Isabella, Evaline."

I clamped my jaw closed. In fact, the woman had once told me to address her as Lady Bella. It took every ounce of control I had for me not to respond.

"Her year of mourning will be over before she realizes it," he continued. "Until then, everyone understands the need for her to be cloistered away."

"I don't suppose that makes it any easier for her, whether other people understand or not. Being shut away in one's house for a year would be very trying."

Why was I defending Lady Isabella? I didn't even like the woman. She was a criminal. A murderer.

My stomach suddenly flipped as I realized I liked another person who was (probably) (possibly) a murderer. What was wrong with me?

"It's the way things are. Ladies must follow the example of Her Majesty. It's the proper thing to do." He narrowed his eyes, looking carefully at me. "Surely you agree."

"It just seems that when you're grieving over someone, it might be more difficult to be left alone. Because then all you can do is think about it." I gave a little smile and tilted my head. "I think it would be very lonely."

In spite of what I'd thought (hoped) was compassion and a little bit of charm, it didn't affect Ned the way I'd intended. "Evaline, when someone dies—especially a close family member —*a person mourns*. It's required."

I looked at him, my brows drawing together. I'd tried to remain prudent and ladylike, but now my patience was frayed. "Required? By whom?"

His eyes flared with irritation. "By society, of course. And the model of Her Majesty. Evaline, I'm not certain I approve of the way this conversation is going. Is there something you're trying to tell me?"

I'm not certain what had gotten into me, but I did *not* feel like being circumspect. "I simply don't understand why 'society' gets to tell a person how to mourn, or what to wear, or—or what they can do. Or can't do. It's not fair."

His annoyance turned to bemusement, which was worse. "Oh, darling Evaline, you are quite adorable." The corners of his eyes crinkled in a way that I often thought was charming, but did *not* find it so at that moment. "If we didn't have societal strictures, what sort of civilization would we be?" He took my hand. "Now, enough of this banal topic of conversation. You were quite long at Cosgrove Terrace—surely you had more than merely tea? Were there other people there as well?"

"It was only Lady Isabella and myself," I told him, stubbornly using the more casual form of address. "And it was fine. The tea was just fine." I didn't feel like talking about that either, so I changed the subject. "What did you do today?"

Ned seemed mildly surprised by my question, but that didn't stop him from launching into an explanation that was so detailed it would have put Mina and her lectures to shame. He began with how his valet had awakened him at half-eleven with the newspapers and a small pot of coffee (the beans had just arrived from Brazil and had been very expensive), and went on to describe how they'd selected his waistcoat (did I not like it?) and what he'd had for breakfast (kippers, eggs, and headcheese, along with a tomato muffin).

I must have dozed off, for it was the mention of "that Edison Smith fellow" that had me jolting to attention.

"...present for an initial court hearing." Ned didn't seem to notice I'd not been listening. "The trial will begin next week. Probably be over in a day or two. Won't be too soon to see the bloke hanged for his crime, I vow."

My fingers suddenly felt cold and numb. My head felt as if it were separating from my body.

Hanged? Pix?

I hadn't really thought about that. Until now.

"Cold-blooded murderer," Ned continued, his mouth twisting unpleasantly. "Deserves the noose—unless they implement the steam-injection process before then. Supposedly more humane." He didn't seem happy about that.

"But there *will* be a trial," I managed to say. I tucked my icy hands into the folds of my skirts. "Maybe he didn't do it."

Ned laughed and reached to pat my hand. "I'm sorry, darling Evaline. I know I shouldn't mention such uncivil topics. I can imagine how upsetting it must be to you to think of Edison Smith hanging."

I caught my breath and my body went shockingly cold. The room tilted a little and my vision darkened.

Did he know? Could he know? How could he?

Of course he didn't.

Blooming Pete, I *hoped* he didn't. Surely he couldn't know how I felt—used to feel—about Pix.

"Women shouldn't be exposed to such unpleasantries, and I apologize for even raising the topic. I'm certain you must still be having nightmares over the death of Lord Cosgrove-Pitt." He reached to pat my hand again, but I moved it away. "I remember how overset you were, being a witness to that horrible event. Remember how you were so horrified you stumbled into that man? Knocked him to the ground?"

Saved his life, you mean?

"Never fear—you're not the only one, my darling. Mrs. Bennington says her daughters still wake up in the night, screaming over it."

I was still trying to breathe normally again, but these last comments made me want to roll my eyes. The Benningtons were ninnies of the highest order. I fixed my gaze demurely on the froth of skirts in my lap.

"Well, soon enough I'll be there if you awaken, terrified in the night," Ned said brightly. "Only three more weeks, Evaline."

Blooming fish. My lungs stopped working again.

He changed topics, and none too soon. "I suppose it's too late for us to go for a drive and to dinner, as I'd intended when I arrived more than an hour ago." There was a hint of petulance in his voice. "Perhaps tomorrow night—unless you have another engagement with the lonely Lady Cosgrove-Pitt?" He gave a short, teasing laugh that didn't really sound teasing.

"No, of course not," I replied. What else could I say?

I would go to dinner with him tomorrow night. And in less than a month, I'd be dining with him every night. Living in his house. Sharing adjoining bedchambers.

Sharing a bed.

※

BUT IT WASN'T that conversation with Ned that made me sob into the night and awaken with dry, gritty eyes.

It was Florence's talk with me after that did it.

And when I say "talk with," I actually mean "talk *at*."

Mina Holmes has nothing on Florence Stoker when she's in the mood to lecture.

"You *simply can't* ruin this," my sister-in-law said for at least the dozenth time *after* she'd railed at me for being gone all afternoon. "Marrying into the Oligary family is the most important thing you'll ever do."

I nearly shouted back at her, to tell her all of the *other* more important things I'd already done—like saving a few lives by killing vampires and stopping evil villainesses like the Ankh—and that there were a lot more *other* important things I could still do if I weren't going to be hampered by a *husband*...but I didn't.

All I could do was stare down at my fingers, flexing, flexing, flexing, and force myself to remember that Florence loved me. That she was worried. And frightened.

But it really didn't help. Not when she kept going and going and going...

"Look at what happened to that Landers girl—there were all those *on dits* about her in the society pages, and she had to retire to the country and become an old maid. Those gossip journalists are bloodthirsty, and they don't care who they ruin!" Her breath heaved with emotion as I wondered how a person would "become" an old maid. Was it something that happened overnight? One day you were a marriage prospect and the next you were an old maid?

"Now tell me where you really were, Evaline. And I want the truth."

When I looked up, Florence was glittering and wavery because of the angry tears in my eyes. Somehow I managed to keep my voice steady. "I went to tea at Cosgrove Terrace. I was there for quite a while. After that, I asked Middy to drive past Scotland Yard and the British Museum. There was a carriage accident and it caused a big delay. The weather was awfully bad as well. It took much longer than I thought."

"You should have come straight home," Florence said. "Driving around in this weather. What if you catch a fever? Or pneumonia? Then what will happen to your wedding?"

That was it. I snapped.

"I don't *bloody care* what happens to my wedding!" I erupted from the divan on which I'd been sitting. "I don't want to get married in the first place!" I'd snatched up a decorative pillow with me. I was so angry that I pulled at it with both hands. The cushion tore, its stuffing exploding into the parlor.

I tossed it aside, heedless of Florence's shocked face as I raged on. "I'm only doing this for you and Bram. And if I get a chill or a fever, I bloody well hope it's my *health* you're worried about, not whether my blooming wedding will happen!"

"*Evaline Eustacia Stoker!*" Florence shrieked at me. She was standing in the midst of floating cushion stuffing, some of which had settled in her hair. Her face was beet-red and her eyes bulged. "I'll not have you talk to me in that tone! How dare you!"

"You won't listen to me any other time I talk," I shot back. "If this is the only way I can get you to listen—"

"*Go to your room.*" Her voice was terrible. "Go to your room, or by heaven, I vow I'll—I'll— *Just go to your room.*"

I fled. Not because she frightened me, but because all I wanted was to be away from her, from the topic of my wedding, from *everything*.

Everything.

Why did I have to sacrifice myself—my life—for them? Why did I have to save them from their problems? No, I didn't want to be tossed out of Grantworth House, but surely there were other options besides selling me off like a horse.

And why did Ned Oligary want to marry *me*, anyway? He hardly knew me. I was no great beauty, and we Stokers were hardly the crème of society.

I didn't understand how this had all happened so blasted quickly—and without my agreement.

I threw myself onto the bed and sobbed furiously. The pillow was perfect to muffle the sound and wipe up my tears and snot.

I must have fallen asleep that way, facedown into the pillow, for when I was awakened the next morning by Florence's furious shouting, I was still dressed. Pepper had either been too frightened to come in, or had been ordered otherwise.

I dragged myself upright as Florence's pounding feet raged

up the stairs. I caught a glimpse of myself in the dressing table mirror and almost didn't recognize my face.

Creases from the pillow, puffy eyes, straggly hair, and my normal dusky complexion now off-color and sallow made me look hideous.

Maybe if Ned saw me this way, he wouldn't want to marry me.

I didn't have the opportunity to ponder this, for my bedchamber door flew open and smacked into the wall.

"This. *This.*" Florence all but threw the newspaper at me, and I had a moment of gratitude that it wasn't on a mechanical reader. That would have hurt. "*I knew you were lying. I* knew *it!*"

She was hysterical. If anyone had seen her at the moment, they would have carted her off to the nearest asylum. "You're going to ruin us all, Evaline!"

I picked up the paper. What had gotten her so upset—

Oh. *Blast it.*

The headline jumped out at me: *A Matter for the Police? Oligary Fiancée Secretly Visits the Met.*

There was a photograph of me walking into Scotland Yard. I didn't look secretive at all. And I had no idea how they'd managed to get such a clear, unmistakable picture of me on a dreary day filled with sleet. That is one of the reasons I dislike and distrust modern technology.

Florence raged, stomping around my room. She wailed about what would people think, why was I consorting with prisoners (how would she even know that?) (because I hadn't been) (not really), what would Mr. Oligary (I wasn't certain if she meant Ned or Sir Emmett) think, how would she ever show her face in public again, and what would happen to them.

Them, meaning her and Bram and their son Noel.

I read the article—barely three lines long—which, in my mind, was nothing to be concerned about. Yes, it was on the society page, tucked in the back, where all the *on dits* usually were—but what did it matter? The headline was meant to attract attention, but all the article said was that I'd walked into Scotland Yard and exited more than thirty minutes later. Someone had glimpsed a policeman (Grayling, of course) bidding me farewell at the door, but they gave no identifying characteristics of him.

Why that was such an interesting, *scandalous* fact was a mystery.

I was, however, swooningly relieved I'd never visited Newgate Prison. That would have been so much more difficult to explain.

"You're going to have to apologize to Mr. Oligary immediately," Florence said, once she'd exhausted all of her lamentations. Her expression was tight with fear. "Perhaps he'll see the humor in it—although I'm not sure how— *Whatever were you doing there, Evaline? How could you do such a thing?*"

I gaped at her. "It's not like I was visiting an opium den!" (Thank Pete she'd never learned about *that* incident.)

"Why is it such a scandal that I went into Scotland Yard?" I snapped.

For a moment, I thought she was going to strike me. I reared back a little, suddenly wary, but she didn't raise her hand to me.

"I don't know what's gotten into you, Evaline, but I don't like this recent manner you've adopted. It's that Mina Holmes, isn't it? You've been consorting with her—"

"I haven't seen Mina since my engagement was published," I said from between gritted teeth. "An announcement that was published without my knowledge or permission, might I remind you. So don't blame Mina."

I wanted to say, *Blame yourself*, but I managed to hold my tongue.

"Young women simply don't go to the Metropolitan Police," Florence said in a slightly calmer voice. But her teeth were clamped together. "It's not proper."

I shook my head. I didn't understand why, but I knew she wasn't going to explain it. I wasn't even certain *she* knew why it wasn't proper.

"*Well*," she cried suddenly, "what are you waiting for? Get up and make yourself presentable. You'll have to send a message to Mr. Oligary straightaway."

I don't know why, but I let her bully me into getting out of bed and ringing for Pepper. I sat sullenly while, in a repeat of yesterday but over a much longer span of time, the two of them fussed over me.

During a short interlude when Pepper went to get my best silk petticoat from the laundry, Florence shoved a paper and mechanical ink-pen in front of me and insisted I write a note asking Ned to call soonest.

"We need a telephone," she muttered. "For times like this. As soon as you're married, we'll have one installed."

I wrote the blasted note.

But when Florence swept from the room to have Brentwood find a messenger to deliver it, I looked down at the extra note card she'd brought in case of mistakes.

And before I quite knew what I was doing, I was writing another message.

To Lady Cosgrove-Pitt.

MISS HOLMES

- WHEREIN WE QUESTION THE WISDOM OF THE BARD -

I couldn't believe Grayling hadn't stopped me. It was both a shock and relief that he hadn't recognized me, even with my disguise.

And also—how unfortunate that he'd managed to insert himself into my investigation at a most inopportune moment! I hadn't even been able to get into Mr. Boggs's house to examine the crime scene, and I didn't know when I'd have the chance to return if he was going to be lurking about. And what had Grayling been doing there anyhow?

I maintained a masculine stride as I walked down the block, turning in the direction of my own house. I was curious as to whether more constables were waiting for my return, and hoped that they weren't so I'd be able to slip inside and retrieve some important items—in particular, more funds and clothing.

I frowned as I went on, carefully avoiding icy patches and using my walking stick to assist me when I had no choice but to step on something slippery. I'd never realized how useful such an appliance could be.

We females have nothing similar in our accessories—although perhaps a parasol would be an appropriate substitute. I thought there might be a female Egyptologist who employed one on a regular basis; I would have to investigate that matter further. Perhaps she'd even outfitted it as a weapon. I could imagine many ways in which a good, solid parasol handle would be quite useful.

How could Grayling *not* have known me? We'd very nearly bumped into each other, and my glasses and hat had gone askew.

However, I *had* donned an impervious disguise. It was impossible for anyone to see the real Mina Holmes beneath it.

I supposed Shakespeare was incorrect in his assessment that love looks not with the eyes but with the mind—but I exaggerate, of course, as not for a moment did I suppose Grayling harbored that particular sentiment toward me.

Certainly he didn't.

It was ludicrous to think so, and the fact that he *hadn't* recognized me only further validated that fact.

My frown grew deeper as I turned onto the street where I lived. I had no idea why that ridiculous Shakespearean passage had lodged in my head—except for the fact that it merely substantiated any affection—or, rather, lack thereof—the inspector might have entertained toward me.

I gave myself a severe mental talking-to about allowing my thoughts to keep running around the same cogwheel and turned my attention to my environment. I couldn't take the chance of being caught off guard, despite being so well disguised.

As usual, chimneys burped steam and black smoke into the air, and in the distance, I could see the shape of sky-anchors wafting above pitched rooftops in the more crowded parts of London.

The street on which I was traversing was empty of waiting carriages, and there was a messenger boy approaching a residence two houses down from mine and across the street. Other than that, I saw no sign of life but for a few pigeons casting about for meager sustenance during this winter month and a cat eyeing me from the window of our neighbor's house.

Nonetheless, I walked past my home and down the street. I

couldn't see much of the small courtyard behind the house, but the gate through which I'd blithely walked during my escape was closed, and there weren't any recent footprints in the crusty snow. That meant no one had been there since yesterday, for there'd been a bit of snow last night. That was a good sign.

I was just turning around so I could slip into the rear courtyard when I heard a loud mechanical roar approaching very quickly. It startled me—not only because it was so loud and it cut through a relatively peaceful moment, but also because I was certain I recognized it.

Drat!

Before I could decide what to do, a ferocious-looking steam-cycle zoomed up the street and paused next to me with a smooth rumble. My instinct was to ignore it, but no one would believe that a random passerby wouldn't look at such a monstrosity, and so I deigned to turn my head—all the while still in the character of my various-accented gentleman.

"Get on," Grayling shouted over the roar. I couldn't hear him over the noise, but I could see his mouth form the very specific words. Nor could I see his eyes behind the goggles he wore, but I suspected they were the cool gray hue they usually were when he was annoyed with me. (Although why he should be annoyed with me in this case was an excellent question.)

I debated internally for only an instant, then acquiesced. Better not to draw attention, and the sleek bronze steam-cycle— which I was certain didn't actually run on steam, but something more illicit—was certainly conspicuous as it sat there, gleaming in the street. It sent up curls of white and black smoke from the collection of bronze tailpipes that jutted from beneath its rear.

As I prepared to climb onto the vehicle—a transport I both admired and despised—I realized I was wearing trousers. That made everything *so much simpler.*

And, at the same time, all the more awkward.

After all, I had to throw my nether limb (even now as I write this, I fairly blush to think about it) over the seat of the cycle, and then to settle my posterior on the cushioned seat behind the inspector. On the previous occasions during which I'd climbed aboard the loud, fast monstrosity, I had been garbed in layers of petticoats and, once, split skirts—which had cloaked my lower limbs and obscured the shape thereof as well as dulled the vibration of the machine itself.

But now, as I settled behind him, riding astride in a very unladylike—but truly convenient—manner, I felt far more stable than I had during the other journeys on the cycle. No sooner had I placed my feet on the handy steps on either side of the machine and wrapped my arms around his waist than the cycle gave a little jerk and we were off. My fingers were a bit clumsy inside the special gloves that obscured their shape, but I managed to hold on to his heavy coat.

However, my hat was gone in an instant and his muffler flapped in my face. I took to burying my eyes in Grayling's broad, warm back in order to protect it from the bitingly cold wind. Along with that of chill and damp wool, I inhaled the pleasant and familiar scents of lemon and peppermint that usually clung to the inspector, and closed my eyes.

But they popped open when we roared around a corner and jounced wildly over a curb. As we screeched onto another street with a sharp turn, I lost the walking stick I'd lodged under my arm. I was grateful I'd tucked my small satchel under the long greatcoat I wore, so it was protected from the extreme speed and jolting turns we were bound to continue to make. Grayling was not what one would call a circumspect driver.

I had no idea where he was taking me, and after a brief moment of hope that it *wasn't* to the Met, I had another, more diverting thought.

Apparently Grayling had recognized me after all.

At last, the steam-cycle came to a halt on a block not far from

Glaston Mews. It was a residential area, with two street levels above us accessed by slender mechanized lifts. The lifts appeared functional and relatively safe, as long as one didn't crowd too many people inside. But for simple protective grids, the sides were open—unlike the street-lifts in the more expensive areas of the city, which were completely enclosed and boasted elegant copper and brass decor.

Narrow row houses crushed up against each other, crowding each block in every direction. The houses were made from dull, creamy brick that were dusted gray from decades of smoke, but each entrance was neat and devoid of debris or refuse. Curling bronze and copper railings enclosed their small porches, and small curved metal roofs over each door offered some protection from the elements. Someone had even shoveled the snow from the walkways and up most of the steps.

A Street-Agitator trundled down one side of the narrow street, sweeping up trash that hadn't fallen into the small canals on either side of the throughway. The walkways on the higher levels were narrow but appeared solid, and I could see that there were more single-story flats accessed by each bridgelike passage above. Cross-bridges attached the opposite sides of the air canals at approximately every other block, and were situated conveniently next to the street-lifts.

Grayling did something, and the steam-cycle purred into silence. I climbed off with great difficulty—for my nether limbs were unsteady and a little numb from the great vibrations of the vehicle—and I certainly wasn't accustomed to (nor overjoyed about) the vulgarity of lifting a leg high up over the seat of a vehicle. Thus, I nearly lost my balance while dismounting, and it was only the inspector's quick reaction that kept me from stumbling on my shaking knees.

He steadied me and I stepped away, suddenly feeling shy and unsettled. Grayling didn't seem to notice, for he'd turned his attention back to the monstrous cycle. With the push of a button, the conveyance seemed to collapse in and onto itself—

taking on the appearance of nothing more than a useless jumble of metal. That apparently wasn't enough, for next the inspector tossed a canvas over the mess of pipes and brass pieces. Somehow the canvas adhered to the pile—strong magnetization, I concluded, possibly electrical (which would be illegal, of course)—and when he turned from it, the formerly gleaming, sleek cycle now resembled a nondescript lump of stone. He'd parked just inside a narrow alley, which also contributed to the camouflage.

"This way, then," Grayling said, and gestured to the street-lift.

I hesitated, but stepped inside. He turned to push a lever on the inside wall—I noted with surprise that there didn't seem to be a fee to ascend—and that was when I saw my mustache clinging to the back of his coat.

I choked on a gasp that was both horror and giggle and snatched it back. He saw me and shook his head. I *thought* a smile might have tickled the corners of his mouth, but if so, it was quickly suppressed.

The street-lift stopped at the top level, where the houses were slightly less blackened from smoke and where there was a bit more sunshine—relatively speaking. No sooner had we taken a step off the lift, I heard ecstatic barking and wild howling from several doors away.

Angus.

I'd recognize his voice anywhere.

Until then, I'd suspected but hadn't known for certain that Grayling had taken me to his home.

One must understand that, despite the fact that I am most certainly what they call a *feministe*, and that I generally do my best to adhere to society's *logical* etiquette and prohibitions, it was quite an unsettling idea to think that I'd be visiting the home of a single young man *by myself.*

Still, I certainly couldn't direct Grayling to take me to Pix's hideaway, and I was in dire straits—being wanted for murder and having nowhere else to go—and so I had no option other than to follow him up the three steps that led to what was presumably his door.

Angus was beside himself when Grayling opened said door. He (the canine) spilled out onto the narrow walkway, tumbling over his ears with his mechanical leg clattering all the while as he jumped, rolled, squirmed, and otherwise made himself appear ridiculous in his excitement. He bounced and bounded so violently that he slammed into the railing of the raised walkway that looked down over two levels to the ground. The force of impact didn't dull Angus's enthusiasm in the least.

"Erm...uh..." Grayling seemed hesitant to invite me inside, so of course I took matters into my own hands and stepped across the threshold.

The place was small but neat—although there was evidence that Angus had been bored, for a shredded cushion decorated the floor in a corner of the two-room apartment. The flat was sparsely furnished, as one might expect for a bachelor employed by the stingy Met. There were two armchairs around a small table in the main room, tucked near a fat, mechanized wood stove of a very recent design that served a dual purpose: for heat as well as food preparation, without all of the ash and mess of most stoves. There was even a warming drawer, which I thought would be most convenient—one could place one's tea water and a small egg cake inside before bed, and in the morning, it would be perfectly heated.

A small pantry and cupboard with a tiny eating table seemed the extent of his kitchen area. I noted a door that was partially open through which I discerned the foot of a neatly made bed (I immediately averted my eyes), and a second door that likely led to what one would call a gentleman's lounge. I most certainly didn't find it necessary to look too closely in that direction either.

Two windows allowed some light, and the other two walls were covered with bookshelves. In the corner was a large table cluttered with mechanical parts and pieces, as well as tools I recognized as useful in the investigation of crimes: ocular magnifyers, fancy thermometers, expanding measurement devices that seemed to calculate all on their own, and other gadgets I couldn't put a purpose to.

I realized Grayling hadn't followed me inside; a glance onto the walkway told me he'd waited out there for Angus to do his personal business under a nearby tree that grew in a gigantic suspended pot on this street level. Since I didn't find it necessary to supervise, I closed the door.

Now safely within the confined place, I smelled lemon and peppermint, as well as the faint scents of beef stew and wood smoke. The cushions on the chairs were comfortably worn, but the quality of their brocade was obvious. The rug on the floor was only a few weeks old. I deduced that Angus had contributed to the necessity of that recent purchase.

Since there was no longer any need to keep up the pretense, I was only too happy to remove the most uncomfortable elements of my disguise: the clumsy gloves, the facial hair, the pads inside my cheeks (which had the disadvantage of making my mouth very dry, as the cotton absorbed every bit of moisture), the tiny wooden pegs that I'd inserted horizontally into my nostrils to change their shape, and the wig.

I was far more comfortable when Grayling and Angus (not in that order) erupted through the door. The latter immediately launched himself at me to sniff and paw at my trousered legs and masculine footwear. He seemed to be questioning my choice of attire, looking up at me with a short yip every so often during his examination.

"Yes, yes, it is I." I found to my delight that I was actually able to *bend over* to pat the little beast on his bony head. He swiped at me with his long, agile tongue, unerringly finding the single sliver of bare skin between glove and coat. I subdued a shudder, but didn't yank my arm away. The little beast could have no idea how disgusting such an action was, and I recognized he was merely showing affection.

When I returned fully upright, I saw that Grayling was watching me with an inscrutable expression. He'd removed his hat and hung it, as well as his coat, on a rack that—to my surprise—seemed non-mechanized.

"I suppose you want an explanation," I said briskly in an attempt to forestall any sort of lecture or interrogation. "And before you say anything about me and a proliferation of dead bodies, may I point out that there wasn't actually a dead body in today's situation."

He shook his head, and I swore his lips twitched again. "I suggest you not mention that to Mr. Boggs, Miss Holmes," he said sternly. "For, to the contrary, there is, in fact, a dead body in this situation."

"Surely you don't think I had anything to do with it!" I realized my voice had pitched high and tight, and I struggled to bring it back to a normal level. "Ambrose!"

His name slipped out before I could stop it, and I don't know who was more shocked—Grayling or myself. Angus, of course, was oblivious to my consternation, for he'd discovered a loose piece of trim on my shoe.

"Miss Holmes," Grayling said after a pronounced, awkward moment of silence. "Perhaps you should take a seat so we can discuss the case against you." He gestured to a straight-backed chair pushed up to the tiny table where he obviously ate his meals.

Feeling as though I'd been slapped, I extricated my footwear from Angus's teeth and sat. *The case against me?*

"So you're investigating the murder of Frederick Boggs," I said evenly.

"Unofficially. It's Blaketon's case. But I..." He sighed, scrubbing his forehead with a freckled hand. "Och, Mina—Miss Holmes—you were obviously there. People saw you, saw you arguing with Boggs, and then five days later, he turns up dead. Your footprints are all over the place, and—"

"*What are you talking about?*" I bolted up, and Angus stumbled back with a pained yelp as I trod on his paw. "What are you saying, Inspector? That's— Why, absolutely *none* of that is true!" My mouth, which had been dry before, felt utterly parched. And my brain, which normally ran swift and smooth, was clunking like a cogwheel whose teeth had gone completely out of sync. "How do you know they're my footprints—what is the meaning of all of this?"

He was watching me carefully with those steady gray eyes— as if he were assessing me. Analyzing me. Then his expression changed to something more like concern. "If you didn't murder Frederick Boggs—"

"Of course I didn't. It's absurd to think I did. Why, there are a number of very good reasons why accusing me is ludicrous— first and foremost is because if I were going to murder someone, I certainly wouldn't do it in such a haphazard, unwieldy manner.

"Hitting someone over the back of the head? That is a very foolhardy fashion in which to attempt to murder someone. There are so many ways that could go wrong—he could move at the last minute and then the culprit would be caught out, the plan foiled.

"Or if he managed it, the blow might not be strong enough— do you know how hard a single blow is required to be in order to kill someone immediately? And in just the right place on the head? Why on earth anyone would resort to such an imperfect, bungling tactic, I can't imagine. I assure you, Inspector Grayling —if I were going to murder someone, it would be in a manner with much more elegance, finesse, and certainty—*and* no one would know I'd done it. They wouldn't even know it was murder."

I'd gotten up without realizing it, gesticulating and pointing as I held forth with my position.

"Right, then." His voice shook a little. "You—erm—make excellent points."

"And I have not finished making excellent points," I told him, whirling around to pace back in the opposite direction (easier to do in trousers, but not nearly as satisfying as feeling the swirl of skirts and petticoats emphasizing the sudden movement). "You said my footprints were there? You think *I* would leave *footprints* at a crime scene? *I*, the daughter of Sir Mycroft and the niece of Sherlock?"

"N-no," he replied, muffling a cough behind his hand. "I don't believe you would."

"*Indeed.*" I was out of breath by this point, and desperately in need of something to drink, thanks to the cotton that had been in my mouth. I plunked myself back into the chair and looked around hopefully for a jug that might contain water.

He must have read my mind, for he strode over on those long legs to the mechanized water pump over a minuscule sink. After a short hum, followed by a splashing stream, he presented me with a cup of water. "Your voice sounds rough. I wouldn't want anything to—er—inhibit your speech, Miss Holmes."

There was a glint in his eyes that indicated he was having a moment of levity, possibly at my expense, but I much preferred that to the cool assessing look of moments ago. I drank gratefully.

"Thank you," I said calmly when I had finished. "Now, tell me what exactly is 'the case' against me, Inspector Grayling."

"Right, then." He scratched his nose. "As I said previously, there are witnesses who saw you arguing with Frederick Boggs five days ago—"

"That's impossible. I've never met the man before."

Grayling gave me a tight smile. "Did you want to actually hear the case against you, or shall I subside and allow you to continue ranting?"

I glared at him, but said nothing.

"Right, then. Witnesses put you at his house. They saw you

—or *someone*"—he held up his hands to forestall my furious denial—"arguing with Boggs on his doorstep. Or at least speaking vehemently. Four days later, yesterday morning, he was found dead from a blow to the back of his head. There are footprints that match a pair of your shoes—"

"How on *earth* do they know the footprints match my shoes? Oh, I see. They must have retrieved them when they went into my house yesterday, after I left. The *blackguards*!"

Grayling's expression was serious. "There was also your calling card, Miss Holmes. It was found crumpled beneath the body."

"That means nothing, of course."

He pursed his lips then seemed to change his mind about what to say. "It's obvious that while you're clearly innocent of the crime"—I nodded regally at this acknowledgment of my previous excellent arguments—"the evidence at the scene makes it plain that you should be considered a suspect—the only suspect. Which means that someone has gone out of their way to frame you up for a crime you didn't commit."

My insides tightened. He'd uttered the very conclusion at which I'd already arrived—and, for once, hoped that I was wrong.

"That means someone wants me in jail. Or—or worse." *Hanged.* I swallowed hard and immediately put the thought from my mind. I was innocent.

Grayling nodded grimly. "Someone certainly wants you out of the way or otherwise occupied, Miss Holmes. And quite desperately—for whoever it is has gone to significant trouble to create a scene that clearly implicates you."

"Not to mention committing a murder in the process," I said. "Abhorrent."

"Indeed." His eyes searched mine, and I found it difficult to pull my gaze away as he spoke gently. "Who would do such a thing, Mina? And why?"

I couldn't answer the latter question, but I had a very good idea about the answer to the first.

The Ankh.

The Ankh was up to her old tricks—and doing her best to keep away the only person she knew could stop her. *Me.*

The only real question that remained was why.

MISS STOKER

- THE DIFFERENCE BETWEEN EARLY & LATE
MORNING EDITIONS -

My conversation with Ned went far better than I'd hoped.

He arrived just after noon. I'd been chafing and pacing for two hours, waiting for his message. It wasn't *my* nerves that caused my pacing in the front parlor. It was *Florence*.

I wanted to shout at her to sit down and do some auto-embroidery or something like that, but I kept my mouth shut and waited. I wondered how long it would take Lady Isabella to respond to my message—and what she would think when she received it.

I mulled over where Mina had gone, and whether it was possible she *had* murdered this Frederick Boggs person. While I couldn't imagine a scenario where she *had*, that didn't mean it was impossible. And if she *had* murdered Boggs, surely she'd had a good reason to do so. Even though I was annoyed with her, I could admit that.

One thing was certain: if my sister-in-law didn't stop pacing and lecturing me and wailing over things she couldn't control, *I* was going to be facing a murder charge.

Ned, who never rose before eleven, did finally arrive—just in time to keep Florence from going completely mad. He didn't seem to be in any disgruntled state of mind, and I thought perhaps (and I know Florence had *hoped*) that he hadn't seen the papers.

But after his regular kiss-on-the-cheek greeting, he waited for me to sit. Then he tossed a packet of newspaper onto the table in front of me. It was the *Times*, open to the society page. And there was the headline about me, screaming from the paper.

I winced and gritted my teeth.

"I see you had a bit of a detour yesterday, then, Evaline? After tea at Cosgrove Terrace?" He gave me a small smile as he flipped up the hems of his coat so they wouldn't wrinkle when he sat next to me. "Scotland Yard? What on earth would have taken you there?"

Florence had fled the parlor as soon as Ned arrived, but I knew she was listening at the keyhole. Surely she was relieved by the nonchalant tone of voice and his easy expression.

I had had plenty of time to formulate what I thought was a reasonable explanation. I leaned closer and made a point of glancing conspiratorially at the parlor door. "I didn't want Florence to know, but I stopped in to report a thief. While Middy was driving me home, I saw a boy break the side window in a watch shop. He got away with a handful of timepieces, and since *I* couldn't chase him"—I smiled demurely—"I thought I *must* do the right thing and report the scoundrel."

"What a very smart thing to do, Evaline." Ned smiled. "I'm very proud of you."

Why did I feel as if he were patting me on the head again?

"I should hope anyone would have done the same, had they witnessed such a crime."

"Indeed. But what an odd thing for a person to do in broad daylight," Ned commented. "Such a risk."

But I was ready for him. "I thought exactly the same thing. But it was on a narrow side street, and I suppose since the weather was so terrible, and it was dark and stormy, the thief thought he was safe in taking the chance. I didn't see any constables about—probably they were staying out of the bad weather too—and so I thought I'd best go directly to the Met."

"Well, again, I'm very relieved to know that my future wife inconvenienced herself in order to do the right thing. I'm certain the shop owner will be pleased to know that someone cared enough to help."

I braced myself, for the next obvious question would be "what was the name of the shop?" or at least "where was the shop, then, Evaline?" but, to my surprise, Ned didn't pursue the topic any further.

Instead, he gave me a rueful look. "And now I must apologize to you, my dear, for I'd intended to take you to dinner tonight at Fenciful's, but I'd forgotten about a business engagement that will keep me occupied all evening."

All evening? What a terrible shame.

"I'm very sorry, and I hope you understand," he continued.

"Of course I understand—business must come first. I was looking forward to trying Fenciful's—I've heard wonderful things about a dish of fried olives they serve. Miss Southerby, I believe it was, had been telling me about it. But surely there will be another evening." I tried to sound appropriately disappointed without appearing petulant. Since I wasn't feeling either emotion, I'm not certain how believable I was.

"I promise it," he said with a smile. "As soon as possible. Now, my dear, I must be on my way. I wasn't expecting to make a detour to your side of town this morning, but of course I had to answer your summons. It's not all that often that you deign to send for me." His smile curved into teasing, affectionate one. "Never say I'm not an attentive fiancé—or husband. I'm looking forward to seeing you on Friday night."

I blinked. Oh, right. *My birthday masquerade.* "It should be interesting," I replied vaguely.

"I hope you recognize me," he said, then, rising, he kissed me on the mouth (since no one was around to witness it) and took his leave.

The fact that the meeting was done and over so quickly—and without any of the high emotion Florence had anticipated—was so surprising that I sat in the parlor for a few moments.

Then my sister-in-law burst into the room. She looked absolutely radiant. Tears of relief were actually glistening in her eyes. "Oh, Evaline, well done," she said. "Well *done*."

As I was still feeling rather stiff and annoyed with her, I merely nodded.

She didn't seem to notice, for she'd gone off on a rambling tangent about lace napkins for the wedding supper.

As usual, I wasn't listening.

But this time I had a good excuse.

When Ned left, he'd knocked the *Times* to the floor. I reached to pick it up and saw that not only had he left the Early Edition, but a single page Late Morning Edition was also in the sheaf. It was the headline on the latter that jumped out at me: *Prisoner Escapes!*

My heart surged into my throat as I read the second part of the headline below it: *Suspect in Bartholomew Murder Leaves the Met in a Bind.*

I stared at the words for a long time before they, and the accompanying article, actually sank in.

Pix had escaped from jail sometime late last night.

Only a short while after I'd been at Scotland Yard.

MISS HOLMES

- OUR HEROINE PONTIFICATES FURTHER -

You are as familiar with the workings of the criminal mind as I am, Inspector. Surely it's not necessary for me to enumerate all the possible ways the villain could have obtained a pair of my shoes in order to create false evidence," I said calmly.

"Indeed not," Grayling replied.

"As well as one of my calling cards."

"Of course."

"And I need not mention that anyone could don a disguise that, at a distance, might appear to be me." I had already explained the innocent reason I'd been in the vicinity of Boggs's home last week, which had obviously been part of the grand scheme of the Ankh—although, of course, I could never have known that at the time.

"Certainly."

"Therefore it behooves us to focus on the why, rather than the how. I am already quite certain of the *who*."

He lifted a brow, but I decided to be reticent in naming the Ankh at this early stage.

"I suppose you are speaking of the individual known as the Ankh," he said.

I managed to hide my surprise. "Who else?" I responded coolly.

"I happen to concur with your surmise, Miss Holmes. Ever since the—er—incident at The Carnelian Crow—well, since the Theophanine Chess Queen debacle—there's been no doubt in my mind as to the cunning perfidy of that woman."

I eyed him, searching for evidence that he might actually be aware of her true identity, but there was nothing in his expression that indicated he did. Or didn't. I was still considering whether to broach the subject when a strange click-clattering sound came from the large desk in the corner.

Grayling immediately went to the table, whose surface, as I've previously mentioned, was cluttered with a jumble of devices and mechanical parts. Apparently, however, a portion of the disorder was an actual gadget that had turned on—seemingly of its own accord.

Not a gadget, but some sort of communication machine, I realized after I sidled over to peek around his shoulder. But not a telegram machine.

It was a typing device, but Grayling wasn't pressing the keys. No one was. Instead, letters appeared one by one on a strip of paper as if someone was using one of those typing machines to write out a message but no one was there. I realized that somehow the information was coming across—perhaps via a telegraph wire—and causing the machine to type a message all on its own.

Fascinating! I wondered if all of the homicide inspectors had such a device in their homes, then thought of Inspector Luckworth and immediately rejected the idea.

To my frustration, Grayling stepped in front of the device and blocked my view—purposely, I knew.

"What is it?" I asked when he hissed under his breath.

He snatched the paper from the machine with a sharp rip and glared at it. "Edison Smith—the individual also known as Pix —has escaped from the Met." He transferred his attention back to me. "I apologize, Miss Holmes, but I must take my leave immediately. This is quite disastrous."

"Yes, of course." My mind was already working in many different directions. "I'd offer to accompany you—to offer my assistance in examining for clues as to how he managed to liberate himself—but of course it wouldn't be prudent for me to be seen at Scotland Yard. Despite the efficacy of my disguise."

Grayling made a strangled sort of noise. "Most certainly not, Miss Holmes. But—er—where will you go?"

I smiled mysteriously. "'Tis none of your concern, Inspector."

"But Miss Holmes, I must insist—I mean to say, you cannot stay *here*, of course, but I am certain—"

"Not at all, Inspector. I assure you, I will be quite safe." I breezed over to scoop up my coat, hat, and the satchel I'd put aside. My false mustache and the other underpinnings of my disguise I'd stuffed inside the pockets. I could don them whilst riding in a hack.

"Where are you staying?" he said in a voice that was quite insistent and could almost be described as strident.

I shook my head, still smiling. "That information I will not divulge, Inspector Grayling. Simply know that I am safe at the home of a friend." (Identifying Pix as a friend was quite a stretch, I admit, but that vernacular was an attempt to mislead the inspector of course.)

"A *friend?*" he snapped, and I got the impression that I'd done something to anger or upset him. "Right, then. I should have guessed it."

Bewildered by this mercurial change of mood, I slowly pulled on my coat and hat. "Inspector, I am grateful for your time and the information you've given me about the case against me. Particularly since you aren't the one investigating it—although I venture to say if you had been, you'd have contacted me in a much less vulgar manner than sending six constables to arrest me."

If I thought that wry statement might coax a glimmer of

humor into his eyes, I was disappointed. Instead, he said, "I must leave straightaway, Miss Holmes. I beg your pardon."

"Oh." Feeling even more confused, I followed him to the door, casting one last look at Angus—who'd been uncharacteristically quiet for some time. As I stepped toward the threshold, I saw the beast in the corner.

He was gleefully chewing on the edge of the new rug.

THE ADVANTAGE of Grayling's sudden need to leave along with his coolness toward me was that it left me the freedom to do what I had meant to do earlier: examine the scene of the crime at Frederick Boggs's home.

Despite my protestations, the inspector saw me safely (and efficiently, yet with a bare minimum of conversation) into a taxi. The last thing I saw as the hack rolled off was him removing the special magnetic canvas from his steam cycle.

I settled back into the seat of the carriage and reapplied my costume while contemplating what had caused him to become so short with me. Then I realized that of course it had nothing to ·do with me—for Pix had escaped from jail.

I knew that the murder of Hiram Bartholomew was one of Grayling's only unsolved cases. Surely he'd been looking forward to closing that one, and now, with that slippery miscreant's escape, he'd been dealt an unpleasant turn of fate. That would dampen anyone's mood.

Still, what had he meant when he responded to my teasing jest that I was staying at a friend's house? What was it he'd said... *A friend? Right, then. I should have known.*

This sort of pique was very uncharacteristic of the steady, even-tempered Scot (despite his gingery hair, which in some individuals is an indication of short temper).

I set those thoughts aside as the hack approached Boggs's house. It would take only a few moments for me to examine the crime scene to determine whether the real murderer had left any clues to his—rather, *her*—identity.

Although I was convinced the Ankh was behind this entire debacle, I wasn't certain that she herself had actually done the deed. In fact, if I wasn't convinced it was she who'd ensured I'd be named as the culprit, I would have dismissed it as impossible that the elegant, measured villainess would have resorted to conducting such a clumsy method of murder herself for the same reasons *I* would never do the same.

As much as I am loath to admit it even now, Isabella Cosgrove-Pitt and I were very much alike. We possessed many of the same admirable characteristics, we thought similarly, we were intensely quick-witted, vastly intelligent, and superior in our reasoning and deductive skills. That was, of course, why she'd entreated me to become her ally and partner that night at The Carnelian Crow.

And she'd been correct. Together, Isabella and I would be not only formidable, but, I believed, utterly unstoppable in any endeavor we undertook. We could, quite literally, rule the world. (Or at least the civilized part of it.)

It was a shame she'd elected to utilize her skills and intelligence for evildoing—although, to be fair, I suppose *she* didn't think of herself as doing evil. No great villain ever does.

I wasn't long at Frederick Boggs's house. It wasn't difficult to gain entry; no one was in attendance at the crime scene.

(That is the sort of lapse that causes Uncle Sherlock to rage and harrumph about, for he is of the mind—and now that I've conducted several of my own investigations, I wholly concur with his position—that the crime scene must be preserved for several days, if not weeks, so that all bits of evidence can be collected from it. Allowing all and sundry to wander through within days or even hours of a murder taking place only ensures that whatever tracks the criminal might have left would be obliterated or otherwise disturbed.)

I was mildly disappointed that no one was there, for I'd been prepared to explain that I was a journalist from the *Betrovian Standard* and the fiction of Mr. Boggs being a well-known purveyor and exporter of Betrovian water-silk (which, of course, is quite rare and astronomically expensive; thus there would be public interest in such a man's demise). As it was, I was able to walk inside with the same ease of entering my own home.

The first thing I noticed was a photograph of a man and woman in formal dress. At the bottom was printed: *Mr. and Mrs. Frederick Boggs.*

So now I knew what Mr. Boggs—the man I supposedly murdered—looked like. And he seemed vaguely familiar. In fact...it was possible he was the man in the photograph with my mother and Emmett Oligary and Pix.

But I couldn't be certain.

I moved on to the kitchen, where the scene of the crime was evident, for Scotland Yard had at least marked off part of the area with bright orange ribbon, and some enterprising individual had drawn out the position and location of the body in bright blue chalk.

I had just crouched to examine the floor when I heard voices approaching.

Drat!

I bolted to my feet just in time to see Sergeant Blaketon and another of the constables strolling along the block toward the house.

I had no choice but to make a premature exit. I slipped out the back door and around to the front of the house, passing Blaketon just as he turned to approach the Boggs residence. I had no fear he would recognize me in my disguise, but I was still quite frustrated, for I had barely looked at the crime scene.

I hailed another hack—reluctantly, for I was now down to my last bit of money. I didn't dare attempt to broach the entrance of my own home to replenish my funds, for it had become a sunny day (relatively speaking) and there were too many people about. Though I wouldn't be recognized, it would certainly cause comment if a strange man was seen entering the Holmes residence.

Thus I was forced to contemplate returning immediately to the safety of Pix's lair, which, as I'm certain the astute reader would have figured out by now, was an excellent plan.

For if he'd escaped from jail, surely that was the first place he'd go.

MISS STOKER

- OUR HEROINE'S DESIRE IS STYMIED -

Florence was so relieved to learn that Ned wasn't upset about the news article that she left me alone for the rest of the day. I think she was reviewing lace samples for the ribbons that were to festoon the chairs at the wedding feast, but I didn't care to ask.

I was far too distracted by the warring emotions and wild thoughts battling through me.

Instead, I tried to take a nap so I would be fresh for the night. (I don't think I actually slept.)

Florence was to accompany Bram to a dinner party with some of the Lyceum Theater's sponsors—a number which had swelled noticeably since my engagement was announced—so she was spending her afternoon preparing for that. Thus, she wasn't around to harass me.

Tonight would be the first time I sneaked out of the house since my engagement was announced, and Pepper would make certain I was fully equipped. I knew exactly where to find Pix, and I intended to confront him—and bring him back into custody if he didn't go willingly. Didn't he realize things would be much worse for him if he didn't? My hands were icy, and there was a heavy, solid rock inside my stomach.

What a fool he was!

I was so distracted that it wasn't until early in the evening when I realized I'd never received a response from Lady Isabella. Unless it had come while I was taking a nap (trying to), and Brentwood had decided not to bother me.

The clock struck seven as I hurried down from my bedchamber to see whether a message had been left for me on the salver in the front hall. I wasn't intending to visit Lady Isabella this late, for it was approaching suppertime, but I didn't want to be rude and not respond.

The salver, a gleaming, ornate silver tray, was empty. Hmm. I opened the drawer in the table. It was empty of everything but stationery and a mechanized ink-pen. I frowned. How strange that she hadn't sent word back from my message. She'd seemed so desperate for social interactions yesterday. And surely she would have been intrigued by my note.

Her message hadn't fallen on the floor; I checked. The table stood on four elegant, curving legs, and the area beneath it was clear of any envelopes. But there were cobwebs and a little clump of dust behind one of the legs, along with a string that I recognized was from my nephew Noel's pony pull toy.

I frowned. That was what happened when a place the size of Grantworth House was making do with a very small staff of servants. Our housekeeper Mrs. Gernum was stretched to manage with only one chambermaid and the cook, along with Pepper.

Because I had bent slightly to look beneath the table, I noticed a tiny corner of white poking down from behind the top of it. An envelope had fallen down between the table and the wall and lodged there.

Aha. I slipped it out, expecting to see the seal from Cosgrove Terrace. Instead, I recognized the firm, no-nonsense penmanship of Mina Holmes.

I caught my breath and stared at it for a moment. Then I tore it open.

I gasped again when I realized it was from *two months ago.* The morning after The Carnelian Crow.

Evaline:
I cannot adequately express my regrets over the unexpected conclusion of our activities last night. I'm certain it must have been quite a shock to you for your friend to have been ~~arres~~ taken away so abruptly.
I've also seen the announcement in today's papers, and I confess I was rather shocked that you hadn't mentioned the imminence of such an important event when we were together. Despite my surprise at your choice to resolve your conundrum in this manner, please know that you have my complete understanding and support as you embark on this new adventure.
I expect you'll be quite busy, but I hope you'll call as soon as you are able. We have much to discuss.

—Mina

I sank into an armless chair in the foyer, staring at the note. It changed everything.

After a moment, I rose slowly, still staring at the message. Everything I'd thought and believed in the last two months was suddenly different. Upside down.

Still stunned, I pulled the table away from the wall to make certain nothing else had become lodged back there. A pen clattered to the floor, but no other envelopes.

I sighed. Now what was I going to do? Mina was in hiding somewhere, and I realized I wanted—no, I *needed*—to talk to her.

A sudden, strong knocking at the door pulled me from my thoughts. In a more formal (and well-staffed) household, I would have waited for Brentwood to answer it, even though I was right there. But I don't stand on formality, and so I opened it myself.

"Inspector Grayling!" I couldn't have been more shocked. I started to wonder what on earth he'd be doing here, then I realized he was probably coming to tell me what he'd learned about the case against Mina. "Come in."

"Miss Stoker." He seemed very businesslike and not at all friendly. "May I have a—er—private word with you?"

"Of course. The parlor is this way."

Brentwood had appeared from the butler's pantry, and his eyes were wide with disbelief at my dismissal of propriety by actually opening the door myself. I waved at him to go away, and he did—reluctantly.

Grayling didn't waste any time. As soon as I'd taken a seat on the divan, he said, "The individual known as Pix has escaped from police custody."

"Yes, I know." What on earth did this have to do with Mina and the murder of Frederick Boggs?

"You were there yesterday. You spoke with him—and then, only hours later, he was gone. Miss Stoker, I am fully aware of your—er—connection to the man, as well as your rather—er—unconventional skills. Did you have anything to do with his escape?"

"No!" I was outraged. "Of course not! Why would I help a murderer escape?" I realized too late that my voice had risen and was likely carrying through the house. Fortunately, Florence was already gone.

Grayling looked at me suspiciously. "Miss Stoker, do you understand that aiding and abetting a criminal can land you in prison as well? If you had anything to do with it, I enjoin you to tell me now, rather than later."

I was so shocked that my mouth moved silently like that of a fish out of water. It took a moment before I could speak. "Inspector Grayling, I assure you, I had nothing to do with that loathsome man's escape. As far as I'm concerned, he should be in jail."

He still seemed skeptical, but he nodded. "Very well, Miss Stoker. Thank you for your time." He hadn't sat down, and now he turned to leave.

I bolted from the sofa. "Inspector, wait. Can you tell me anything about the—the problem with Mina? The case against her? Did you learn anything? Have you spoken to her?"

He paused at the parlor door. "It's not my case, but I have done some investigation. I'm confident Miss Holmes is innocent of the charges, and I'll be speaking with Sergeant Blaketon about it as soon as possible."

"Is she back at home, then?"

His face stiffened. "I don't believe Miss Holmes has returned to her home. And at the moment, I'm in search of a more dangerous criminal, so if you'll excuse me, I'll be on my way."

❧

I WAS STILL unsettled by Grayling's visit and accusation when I left the house three hours later. Normally, I would climb out the window of my bedchamber and down the large oak that grew there. But since Florence was gone, there was no need to do that. Besides, I was wearing a heavy cloak against the cold night, and that would have gotten tangled in the branches.

There was no need to expect—*hope*—that a secretive figure might detach itself from the shadows beneath that tree and greet me as I stepped onto the ground.

Oh, Pix, you fool.

I thrust those sappy thoughts from my mind. Edison Smith was an accused murderer, and I had to face the fact that it was very likely he was the culprit.

After all, why else would he be slinking around the city wearing disguises all the time?

The street was empty, for it was quite cold. Everyone must be tucked away somewhere warm. Other than the rustle of the trees in the breeze above and the yip of a nearby dog, the night was quiet and still.

Because I had, as Grayling put it, unconventional skills, I chose to walk to Whitechapel. I daresay I'm the only person in

London—male or female—who could be perfectly safe doing so, even at night.

I was in a strange, prickly, angry mood.

I needed to use all of the fury and frustration that had built up in me over the last two months. I felt tight as a cog with a splinter of wood in its teeth—grinding helplessly, unable to move. My breath came out in sharp white bursts in the frigid night.

I walked confidently, *daring* the dangers that lurked in the dark to accost me. Rapists, muggers, murderers—I was ready for all of them.

Even more than that, I itched to encounter an UnDead. I paid close attention to the back of my neck, waiting to feel that eerie, telltale prickle that indicated one was nearby. But it was unlikely.

There simply weren't any vampires in London anymore—other than the few Lady Cosgrove-Pitt had found and taken under her wing. And, with the help of Grayling, Pix, and even Mina, I'd slain most—if not all of them—at The Carnelian Crow.

I wondered again why Lady Isabella had asked for my assistance with the UnDead. Were there any left? Were they truly out of control? Or was she only trying to trick me?

From what Mina and I had been able to piece together, Lady Isabella—as the Ankh—had been using the little devices called batteries to attempt to control the UnDead by using small wires to connect the small mechanisms to their bodies. She had done the same with Lord Belmont. We had seen the result of that when he jumped from the balcony at Cosgrove Terrace during the Yule Fête, so obviously she'd made some progress.

But since Mina and I hadn't spoken after that night at The Carnelian Crow, we hadn't had the opportunity to share our experiences and talk about *why* the Ankh was doing this. I knew the villainess despised the way women were treated in our society—upper-class ladies like herself, particularly. I'd heard the speech she gave to the members of the Society of Sekhmet—all young women my age—meant to rouse their anger and to encourage them to join her cause.

Little did they know, her "cause" meant that one or more of them would die during the process.

Although her arguments and complaints rang true, at the time I dismissed her thoughts and ideas because I knew I was different. I had those "unconventional skills" that would protect me and enable me to move about in this world in a manner no one else could. I wasn't going to be repressed and restricted like those other young ladies. I would never marry.

Ha.

My laugh was bitter and audible in the cold night.

Who was the fool now?

By now, I'd found my way to Whitechapel. Fenman's End squatted like an ugly toad there at the intersection of two dark, cluttered roads whose street signs were long gone—if they'd ever existed.

How was it that I'd come all this way and no one had accosted me? It was infuriating.

I strode into Fenman's End. At least there, I could stir up something that would allow me to expend some of the pent-up energy inside me.

Inside, I looked around for a likely victim. Someone whose chair I could take, or a person who might be in a mood as feisty as my own and willing to start an argument. Or someone that I could insult and otherwise provoke into a fight. Or challenge to an arm wrestle.

There was no one inside. No one except Bilbo, at the bar counter, who merely lifted a brow when he saw me. This was the first time I'd ever come into Fenman's End when no one was here. How was that possible?

Was the entirety of London conspiring against me tonight?

Where were all the lowlifes? The criminals? The angry,

dangerous men who had nothing better to do than to cause trouble—or to sit around and drink?

Where was that blasted Jack the Ripper?

My feet pounded angrily as I walked across the room, the heavy cloak swishing about like a sail caught in heavy wind.

"'Bout bloody time ye made yer way 'ere, Molly-Sue," growled Bilbo.

I eyed him for a moment, then dismissed the idea of starting something with him. He was tough and wiry, but I didn't actually want to get that close to him, let alone touch him. Even though I was wearing gloves, I had enough exposed skin that something slimy or smelly would probably attach itself to me.

I'd save my fury for Pix.

Without another word, I strode to the secret door that led to the underground lair.

"Go on down, then, Molly-Sue," the barkeep said as I disappeared through the door. As if I needed his permission.

I steamed my way through the tunnel, pushing through cobwebs and avoiding skittering mice and rats without hesitation. I couldn't *wait* to get my hands on Pix.

The door, with its special three-lock combination, brought me up short. It almost made my anger with the rogue soften. After all, the combination was made up of three sets of numbers that were specific to me: my birthday, the date of the first time I met Pix, and the address of Grantworth House.

Unless he'd changed them.

Which, I soon discovered, he hadn't. That fact might also have eased some of my ire toward him, but not much.

The locks clicked pleasantly and the trio of bolts shot open. I gathered up my fury and pushed through the doorway, erupting into the room in another great swirl of cloak.

"Well it's about time," came a familiar, snippy voice. "I've been wait— *Evaline?*"

MISS HOLMES

- WHEREIN THINGS DO NOT HAPPEN AT ALL
AS ANTICIPATED -

I could only gape at Evaline and she back at me for the first moment of our unexpected reunion. It was one of the rare times I could remember being taken completely by surprise.

"Where's Pix?" she demanded at last, looking around. "And why are you dressed in trousers?"

The only way to describe her expression was that fire blazed in her eyes. It might sound clichéd, but common phrases are common for a reason. Clearly, Evaline was incensed—and just as obviously, she was aware the miscreant had escaped from jail.

I found my voice. "He's not here. *I* thought *you* were *him*." My tone was cool and frosty. After all, the reason she and I hadn't seen each other for months was because of *her*.

"He's not here?" This seemed to calm her a trifle. One might say, if one were prone to continuing the hackneyed description, that the fire in her gaze was banked.

"No." I eyed her, wondering how to proceed.

I *wanted* to demand answers from her, to expose my own anger and frustration—and perhaps a bit of hurt, but that was only a small portion of the emotion I was experiencing—due to her rude silence over the last two months. But I feared that I might...well, that I might say too much. My emotions were rather high and out of control, not at all Holmesian at the moment. I needed to bank my own fire.

"And, to answer your question, as I've been wearing a number of disguises over the past several days, I've discovered how incredibly comfortable trousers are," I informed her.

Once convinced that I had spoken the truth that Pix wasn't present, Evaline returned her attention to me. The fury in her eyes was merely smoldering now, and she was biting her lower lip. I'd never seen her do such a thing before, and I could only conjecture that she was uncertain or upset about something.

Well, that made two of us.

And, as it happened, we both spoke at the same time.

"I never got your message until today."

"I can only imagine what would bring— *What?*" For the second time in a matter of moments, I was taken by surprise. "You didn't?"

"No, Mina. I'm sorry. I'm *truly* sorry—it had fallen down behind the table in the front hallway. No one noticed it. I only just discovered it a few hours ago." Not only was the last of the flame gone from her eyes, it had clearly been extinguished by the dampness glittering there.

(I believe it's no longer necessary to continue with the fire metaphor; as a literary device, it is becoming rather tiresome.)

"I see." All at once, I felt remarkably lighter.

"And I didn't write to you because— Well, at first I was so caught off guard by the engagement announcement—and then I didn't hear anything from *you*, or so I thought—that I...I got mad." Her voice was very nearly pleading. "I suppose I was sulking a bit."

"Never mind that, Evaline," I said briskly. My throat was suddenly scratchy, and there must have been a dust speck in my eye, for I found I needed to blink rapidly. "We have many things to discuss, some of which are long overdue."

"Yes we do—including how quickly you can put together a

costume for my birthday masquerade on Friday." She smiled, and I knew the rift between us had gone quite a distance toward healing. I confess, I was grateful for its quick repair, for I'm not one to cogitate over apologies and hurt feelings and imagined slights, especially when there is work to be done.

Including, apparently, devising attire for a masquerade fête in three days. Of course I was up for the challenge.

There were so many other topics I wanted to raise, but one phrase she'd uttered had lodged in my head. "Did you say you were caught off guard by the engagement announcement?"

Her expression tightened. "Yes. Bram, Florence, Ned, and Sir Emmett all knew about it—but I didn't. Not until the next morning, after all the—after The Crow—when Florence showed me the papers."

"How *extraordinary*," I said, outraged. "How extraordinarily *terrible* of them." My mouth was tight, and I suspected my own eyes were now blazing.

Evaline's face softened. "Oh, Mina," she said, and I thought she was about to burst into tears. But, fortunately, she managed to contain herself. "Thank you for saying that. I had no one—no one I could talk to."

"I should have written again," I told her. "I should have suspected something wasn't right. It was my fault as much as it was yours." With those words, the heavy weight inside me eased even more. Then I realized something else—something that horrified me. "Did you mean to say that you didn't know the announcement was going to be published—or that you hadn't agreed to an announcement at all?"

Her eyes were wide and dark, brimming with emotion. "I don't believe I actually ever agreed to marry Ned. I just got sort of swept up in things, and the next thing I knew, the news was in the papers."

"That's despicable. How *dare* they do that to you, Evaline!"

She shrugged. "I don't see that I had any other choice, things as they are. And Ned is a nice man. I'll never have to worry about being evicted from my house ever again. Now, let us talk about what you're doing here. I should have known this is where you would hide out." Her smile was a little forced. "What's all this about a murder charge?"

"Of course I didn't murder anyone," I said unnecessarily. "Although someone has gone out of their way to make it appear that I have. The Ankh, of course." I went on to explain all of the evidence that had been manufactured to point to me as guilty. "But Grayling agrees that it's ludicrous to think I had anything to do with—"

"Grayling? You've spoken to him? When I saw him yesterday, he said you hadn't seen him for months either."

"You spoke to Grayling as well?" My heart gave a little thump and I wasn't certain what it meant.

"Of course. When I learned about the constables trying to arrest you, I went to see him right away to find out what on earth was happening. I knew something was wrong."

"That was very kind of you, Evaline." I was truly touched. "What did he—er—say?"

"He didn't know anything about it, and he was quite upset to learn that you'd been accused. He and I both had a bit of a chuckle, imagining you walking out of your house right in front of the constables." She tilted her head, looking at me carefully. "I was surprised that you hadn't told him about it, and that you hadn't spoken to him in months."

I looked away, the corners of my mouth tightening. "It seems to be a recurring event that once he kisses me, a man...er... doesn't appear eager to do so again. To be fair, *I* don't particularly want to kiss Dylan again either—"

"Are you saying *you've kissed Grayling?*"

I felt my face go very hot. "Never mind that, Evaline, we—"

"Oh no," she said. Her eyes were positively dancing. "You and Grayling *kissed?* And then what happened?"

"Why are you so gleeful about it?" I snapped. "Just like it was with Dylan—the man kissed me once, and then...it was as if nothing happened." My throat felt scratchy again. "It doesn't matter in the least. We have a far larger problem to attend to—"

But Evaline was not to be put off. She talked right over me. "When did you kiss him? How did you like it? I've been waiting for this to happen for months!"

"What on earth are you talking about?"

"Mina, *tell me what happened.*"

I examined my fingers as I spoke. My nails needed attending. "It was the night at The Carnelian Crow. There was a moment when it appeared—to him, anyway—that I was in danger. When it turned out that I was perfectly fine, he seemed rather... emotional...about the event, and the next thing I knew, he was embracing me. And then..." My cheeks burned again.

"And then he kissed you."

I glanced up at the chortle in her voice. Evaline was positively *beaming*, and I wanted to slap her.

Why was she so thrilled about my humiliation? Perhaps it was better that we weren't partners any longer. I'd forgotten how impetuous and silly she could be at times.

"Indeed," I said in a firm, brook-no-nonsense tone. "And that was the extent of it, Evaline. Clearly, I didn't do it correctly or meet his expectations, or—or something."

Evaline was shaking her head during this speech, that gleeful, annoying smile twitching her lips. "Oh, no, Mina. It had nothing to do with you. It was Dylan."

"*Dylan?* What on earth does Dylan have to do with anything?"

She sighed, rolling her eyes. "Sometimes you are utterly cog-headed, Mina. Grayling thinks you're in love with Dylan, and so when he saw that Dylan was back from the future—and after you threw yourself into his arms, might I remind you—he stepped aside. Literally and figuratively."

I stared at her. "That is utterly— Why, I've never heard anything so... Well. Evaline. I confess, that's one of the most interesting theories I've ever heard. But it's utter rubbish."

"So you've been seeing quite a bit of Dylan, then, I suppose," Evaline said, watching me closely. "And Miss Adler."

"A bit," I replied, choosing to focus on her second implied question. "Miss Adler has been keeping me quite busy with—well, with silly, rather boring tasks. Of course, I accept the challenges—if one can call them *challenges*—but they're rather mundane. I can't help but suspect she is merely trying to keep me occupied—but to what end, I cannot imagine. Do you know she actually engaged me to hunt down the pet ferret of one of the troubadours at court?"

Evaline stifled a gasp of laughter, but, to her credit, she kept her expression fairly serious. "I'm certain you were quite up to the task. But surely you spoke with her after the night at The Crow. About why she and Dylan had been there, and what they were doing. Weren't they attempting to identify the Ankh?"

My lips tightened. "Only a bit. She was very closed-mouthed over it, and refused to give me any details other than—what did she say...that it was best to keep things quiet for a while. She used the term 'possible international incident' but declined to explain what she meant—although I could surmise it might have something to do with the Betrovians, since Lurelia was there. I found it quite frustrating, especially when Miss Adler claimed she never saw Lady Isabella while she was at The Carnelian Crow, nor anyone she could have identified as the Ankh."

Evaline's expression seemed as skeptical as I felt. "But she at least has been keeping you busy with work for Princess Alix. The only contact I've received from her was a congratulatory note about my wedding and an acceptance for my birthday masquerade." She sighed. "And what about Dylan? Surely you've been seeing him quite a bit now that he's returned."

I drew back a little. "I've not been in touch with him recently."

"You haven't? But you did talk to him after that night—that night when you realized he was at The Crow."

"I did. But I was rather put off by the fact that he'd been

back in London—back in *our time*—for weeks without even attempting to contact me. And I had a severe talking-to with him about that lapse in judgment."

"I'm certain you did." Evaline cleared her throat, but that arch smile was still playing about her lips. My hand itched to wipe it off her face. "So what did he say? Why didn't he contact you once he returned?"

"He claims he didn't want to—what was the phrase he used? —'blow his cover,' I believe it was. He didn't want to take the chance that someone would recognize him, or that I would somehow expose him when he was working at The Carnelian Crow with Miss Adler. She needed a partner to help her while she was working there secretly, and he doesn't have any other connections in London—except for me."

"But he was so sad to leave you, Mina. He asked you to go with him. How could he *not* tell you he was back?"

"I don't regret for one moment deciding not to accompany him, as much as I would have loved to see the future, considering all the things he's told me about it. I've come to realize that he and I don't—wouldn't—actually suit. Even if he did stay here in our time. The fact that he didn't think to contact me made me realize that perhaps he didn't care quite enough. And I confess, once he was gone, I missed him, but I most certainly didn't pine for him. He—reminded me of my father. So caught up in his *own* business that he cannot attend to anyone or anything else around him." I could hardly believe these blunt words, this information from deep inside me, was coming out so easily. I'd never had such an intimate conversation with anyone before. Except my mother, and even those conversations had been few.

"The last time we spoke, he indicated that he would contact me the next day," I continued. "But I've not heard from him— it's been several weeks—and to be quite honest, I am simply unconcerned about the entire situation. I mean to say, I wish the best for Dylan, but clearly he has other things to attend to and I don't believe I have the *tendre* for him that I originally thought I had."

"I see." That smile was playing about the corners of her mouth again. "Perhaps you ought to mention this to Grayling the next time you see him."

"Mention *what?*"

Evaline was mad. I was not about to have a conversation with the inspector about such a personal topic.

Just then, the door rattled quietly in its moorings. I realized with a start that Evaline and I had been so shocked to see the other that neither of us had secured the entrance behind her.

We looked at each other, and she mouthed, *Pix.*

But just as the door began to swing inward, I heard a familiar bark.

MISS STOKER

~ LIKE MASTER, LIKE HOUND ~

Inspector Grayling?" I stared at him. "How on earth did you—"

"I suppose you must have followed her," Mina interrupted calmly. "You and Angus— Down there, young sir, you'll muss my trousers!" (She was speaking to the beagle, not the inspector.)

"Good evening, Miss Holmes. I must confess, I did not expect to find you here." The wildly excited Angus had surged into the room, along with his master. Both of them looked around with great interest.

"You followed me?" I asked, glaring at him as I locked the door behind them. "I suppose you must have just waited, lurking outside Grantworth House after your visit. After you accused me of helping Pix to escape from jail."

"Aye, but I went to get Angus first. He might be a bit of a rakehell, but he's got a good nose on him." He bent his tall frame to pat the dog—who was looking absolutely adorable, as usual.

Angus's ears were far too large for the rest of him, and so were his paws. He settled down and began to chew on the edge of Mina's shoe. I didn't bother to point it out to her. Surely her Holmesian observation skills would tell her.

"I didn't think you'd be leaving until it got dark," Grayling admitted to me. "And I most certainly didn't expect you to *walk* the whole way. But that made it all the easier for Angus to follow your scent. You do move rather quickly, Miss Stoker."

"I heard him bark as I left the house tonight," I said, still giving Grayling a dark look. "I didn't realize it was him."

"You helped Pix to escape?" Mina took charge of the conversation. "Evaline, why on earth would you do something so—"

"I *didn't*."

"No, I don't believe she did," Grayling said, still looking about with fascination. "Och, what a setup the bloke has here. Electricity all over the bloody place, of course. So comfortable, and the light is so clean and bright. Is that running water I see back there?"

"You don't believe I helped Pix escape? But you did earlier. What changed your mind?" I demanded.

"It appears that Edison Smith—the man also known as Pix— was forcibly removed from his jail cell at Scotland Yard last night."

"Forcibly removed," Mina muttered. "And he's not returned here, to his secret hideaway, which would be the safest place for him should he be on the run. Even if someone was aware it existed, no one could find the location—except by *following* an *unwitting person*"—she gave me an exasperated look—"and even if they did, gaining access is impossible due to the special combination lock and the hidden doors." She glanced at Grayling, who was eyeing her skeptically. She sniffed. "Of course, I was able to break the code on the door simply because of my deductive reasoning."

"And my birth date," I reminded her smugly. "You wouldn't have been able to get in the first time if I hadn't been with you. It's the tenth of February, Inspector, in case you were wondering. And I'm having a masquerade ball to celebrate it on Friday—I do hope you'll attend."

"I see." Grayling was looking at me with a jaundiced expression. "Dare I ask how you even were aware such a place existed, Miss Holmes and Miss Stoker?"

"Perhaps you shouldn't," my partner replied briskly. "Instead, I suggest a better use of time would be for you to enlighten us as to the purpose of your presence, as well as why you believe Pix did not escape on his own recognizance, but was —did you say *forcibly* removed? As in, he didn't wish to be freed?"

"There are clear indications that he was removed from the cell against his will. And I'm here, obviously, because *I* deduced"—he arched a brow at Mina—"that Miss Stoker, once learning of his disappearance—something I had to make certain she was aware of; thus the real purpose of my visit and the suggestion that she might have been involved—would attempt to find him. Of course I knew he must have a secret lair, and I concluded if anyone knew where it was, it would be Miss Stoker. And possibly yourself, Miss Holmes."

"Of course," Mina replied absently. "So someone *took* Pix out of his jail cell or otherwise made him leave. At Scotland Yard, did you say? Why was he there and not at Newgate?"

"There was a preliminary court hearing, and so he was moved to the Met for the convenience of the personnel involved," Grayling replied. "Och, then. How long have you been here, Miss Holmes? Is it possible he's come and gone without your knowledge?"

"Other than this morning, I've been here since those fools attempted to arrest me for murder," she replied. "And I would know whether someone had been here in my absence. He has not."

"You've been here? All along? So *this* is the home of a friend...?" Grayling seemed to catch himself, and though I didn't quite follow the reason why, I noticed his demeanor eased slightly. If I had to put a word to it, I'd say he was relieved.

Angus barked sharply, and I jumped. "What is it?"

"He merely wants attention, or, more likely, something to

eat," Grayling said, shaking his head affectionately. "He seems to ken as though it's his due—particularly from Miss Holmes."

Mina's cheeks were slightly pink as she bent to pat the dog on his head. "I suppose it's because I've spoiled him with those Stuffin' Muffins that Mrs. Raskill makes. I'm sorry, young sir, but I haven't any with me today. You'll have to be patient."

To my surprise, Angus seemed to understand. He sat, landing his bum on Mina's foot, and panted happily at her. If I didn't know better, I'd think he was smiling.

Clearly, both hound and master were besotted with my friend.

This was all fine and good, this little domestic scene, but I had something more important on my mind. "Inspector, when you say Pix was forcibly removed from his cell, well, what exactly do you mean?"

"I venture to say it's nothing good," Mina replied. "Unless he was clever enough to stage it to *appear* that he didn't want to leave in order to throw us off. I must admit...he *is* cunning enough to do such a thing. But if that were the case, surely he would have at least made an appearance here. Since he has not, one must surmise that he is not free to do so."

"What are you saying?" I asked, feeling increasingly nervous.

"I'm saying that the most likely explanation for his disappearance is that Pix has been abducted."

"Now, Miss Holmes, I'm not certain I'd go so far as to say that—"

She was shaking her head, barreling on in her customary manner. "And I suspect the purpose of his abduction is either to elicit some information from him, or to silence him before he divulges the fact that he, Edison Smith, is innocent of the murder of Hiram Bartholomew—and goes on to identify the real murderer. After all, he was only put in jail in order to keep him safe. Protective custody, as it were."

Instead of echoing my gasp of shock, Grayling looked at

Mina and sighed in exasperation. Yet there was a glint of admiration in his eyes. "How long have you known, Miss Holmes?"

She opened her mouth, and I could already anticipate the words that would tumble out, explaining in far too many syllables how brilliant she was and how it was *elementary* if one *observed* and *deduced* and if one were a Holmes and so on and so on...

And then she closed her mouth. A sheepish expression crossed her face—something I'd *never* seen on Mina Holmes before. "I confess I didn't actually know until just this moment when you confirmed it, Inspector. Although I have long *suspected*," she added a trifle too loudly.

But Grayling was chuckling, and Angus had begun to bark and weave his way between the two of them as if trying to decide who was the more likely to give him attention. Or food.

I, on the other hand, was far more than merely confused. "What are you talking about? Protective custody? *Innocence?*" I demanded in a voice designed to be heard over the yapping of the beagle. "And more importantly, if Pix is in danger, why are the two of you *laughing?*"

They sobered and looked at me.

"You're quite right, Evaline. This is not the time to be overcome with levity. Pix is quite possibly in considerable danger, and I venture to say that Inspector Grayling is here because he wishes to see to the matter in the most expedient way possible." She transferred her attention to him. "It would be very helpful if I could examine the cell from which he was taken. Perhaps there are clues as to who has abducted him."

Grayling lifted a brow. "Surely you don't need to examine the scene in order to surmise who it was, Miss Holmes. It's rather obvious, is it not? However, if you're in need of proof, perhaps you might like to know that this was found on the floor of the cell, amidst the signs of struggle I described previously." He withdrew a small paper packet from his pocket and handed it to Mina, who carefully opened it.

"A wire." She withdrew it from inside the envelope with careful, ungloved hands and looked up at Grayling.

"Look closely. Perhaps this will help." He handed her a small ocular-magnifyer, and she fitted it over her eyes.

"Hair. And...is that a bit of skin and blood on the end?" Mina looked up, her hazel eyes magnified and glowing catlike green behind the lenses. "This wire appears to have been inserted into someone's flesh. The other end—surely it was connected to one of those controlling battery devices! *The Ankh*," she whispered. "*I knew it.*"

"Who else?" Grayling replied, taking the wire back from her. He tucked it away in its packet.

"Indeed. Who else?" Mina began to pace, the ocular-magnifyer swinging in her hand. Her long legs swished against each other inside the woolen trousers she still wore. I couldn't help but notice how Grayling's eyes followed her figure as she stalked to and fro across the room. I might have found it amusing if the situation hadn't been so dire. "She had Pix captive before, did she not? Down in the underground cavern, where she had her laboratory. And now we have *two* instances of innocent victims being set up—*framed*—for murders they didn't commit. Myself and Edison Smith. Despite the time lapse between the two crimes, with the Ankh involved, it's no coincidence."

"No, of course not. Although I wouldn't go so far as to call Smith innocent. The bloke has certainly bent—if not outright broken—a number of statutes," Grayling said dryly.

"Yes, yes, but that's not important at the moment."

Mina was still pacing. Grayling was still watching her. Angus had taken to gnawing on a table leg.

I might just as well have not even been present.

All at once, I remembered something. "The airship!"

Whether it was my strident tone or the fact that they'd completely forgotten my presence, I don't know, but all three of their heads swiveled in my direction.

"What are you talking about, Evaline?" Mina asked.

I shook my head as I patted Angus, who'd come over to investigate me. "I don't know if it means anything, but I saw the airship. The night Pix escaped—I mean was kidnapped. I saw it sliding through the sky, not far from the Met. The sleek black zeppelin—remember, Mina, we saw it last autumn? The wicked-looking one."

"The one you were *hiding* from?"

I nodded. She could make fun of me all she wanted, but the sight of that vessel slipping through the dark like a wraith had made every hair on my body stand on end. And I knew it had done the same to Pix.

What I didn't know was *why*.

"Please explain, Miss Stoker."

I did, thankful it was my tale to tell Grayling and not Mina's, or we would have been listening for an hour. "Since the very first night I met Pix, every time he saw the airship, he ducked into the shadows as if he was afraid it would spot him. He warned me about it, but—of course—he never told me why. He just made a lot of vague warnings. Could it be a coincidence that I saw it the same night he disappeared? And much earlier in the evening than I've ever seen it before."

"I don't believe in coincidences," Mina announced (as if this was news). "But in this case...I don't see that it could be anything but chance. We have no reason to connect the airship with the Ankh."

Grayling, on the other hand, appeared quite fascinated. "Describe it to me in more detail, if you please, Miss Stoker. I'm quite versed in all types of vehicular transport, and I don't recall seeing anything of that nature. And all vehicles are to be registered and licensed."

"Even illicit steam-cycles?" Mina muttered. Grayling ignored her.

I said, "It's long and it usually flies rather low—even down some of the air canals and past the sky-anchors. Once I actually saw it navigate between buildings."

"So it must be quite slender. And silent," he mused. "In order for it not to have been noticed. And if it's black, it would meld into the shadows and hardly be noticeable at all."

"Yes. And it has spiky, pointy fins at the back. It's ugly. Black, dark, and horrible." I couldn't contain a shudder. I didn't know why the zeppelin affected me so strongly. "And sometimes there's a white light beaming down toward the ground. As if it's looking for something. All I know is, Pix didn't want to be seen when that airship was around."

"Very well. Thank you for that information, Miss Stoker."

"Well, now what do we do?" I was aware that my voice sounded high and tight, but the thought of Pix being in the clutches of the Ankh made my stomach pinch and twist.

Then I realized—why was I waiting for the two of them to decide? I was a woman of action; they were intellectual pedants who traded *conclusions* and *deductions* and theories.

I started for the door, snatching up my warm cloak as I went.

"Evaline! What on earth? Where are you going?"

"To Cosgrove Terrace, of course!"

MISS HOLMES

- OF PARIS, TROUSSEAUX, AND INTERNATIONAL RELATIONS -

No!" I cried in an effort to stop Evaline from what would likely be the most foolish, impetuous, irrational action of her life.

"Cosgrove Terrace?" Grayling said, and I winced.

Drat! He didn't know the true identity of the Ankh—that it was Lady Isabella. And any moment, Evaline was going to spill the beans over that, and then what a fine mess we would be in. Such information was going to have to be imparted to Grayling in a very careful, factual manner. But not at the moment.

"Evaline," I said from between clenched jaws, blocking her from the doorway. I was fully aware that she could brush me aside like a gnat, but I was counting on my reasonable tone of voice to keep her from doing so. "I don't think now is the time to go rushing off without *thinking everything through.*" I held her eyes with mine, desperately sending her the message to *think, think,* think.·

But her eyes were wild with what I could only assume was fear for that sneaky knave Pix—which, I need not say, was completely inappropriate, considering the fact that her nuptials to a very different man were three weeks away.

"Evaline," I said again, holding up a hand in entreaty. "We have only one chance—"

"Cosgrove Terrace?" Grayling said again.

Once again, I ignored him and continued pleading with Evaline for *sense*. "We have only one chance to manage this, and if the villainess is somehow alerted and ready for us because you go haring off like a madwoman, we might lose our opportunity to—"

"Fine." She spun and whirled back, her cloak whipping dramatically about her body. I got the impression she enjoyed the flair of that movement as an underscore to her pique. "Fine. But if Pix dies because the two of you only want to *talk* and *deduce* and *plan* then I'll *never* forgive you." Her voice was still high and tight.

And—good gad—were those *tears* glistening in her eyes? Things were far worse than I'd imagined.

"Evaline," I said more calmly. "Perhaps we should allow the inspector to see what—if anything—he can learn about the black zeppelin, along with anything else about Pix's escape. Abduction, I mean," I amended swiftly when I saw the furious light blaze in her eyes again. "Recall that everything so far is merely conjecture. And I assure you, the villain is not about to—er—do away with Pix until she—or he—is satisfied he's imparted all of the information and proof he—or she—needs. Until she's certain he's no longer the least bit valuable to her."

"So instead she'll torture him? Like she did before?" Evaline cried furiously. "And that's somehow better?"

"No, no, Evaline. Please, be calm. If the villain meant only to eliminate Pix, and not to—er—keep him for some other reason—"

"Such as?"

"Such as...bait. Or leverage. Or as a hostage. Which is, I'm quite certain, what someone as cunning as the Ankh would do. For once her bargaining chip is gone, then she's left with nothing to use." I employed reasonable tones, and I saw that she began to believe me. At least a little.

"That's true," she said quietly. "She wouldn't dump the bucket of water until she was certain she had no more use for it."

"And if all she meant to do was to kill him, Evaline, that deed is surely already done, for he's been in her clutches—if indeed that's where he is—for well over twenty-four hours. And there's nothing that could be done to save him if that's the case. So we must plan and take care. We cannot let this be another Chess Queen Debacle, with the Ankh anticipating us every step of the way."

"Right."

I felt confident I'd calmed her and convinced her to wait. But there was still the matter of Grayling...

"Why would you go to Cosgrove Terrace?" he asked.

I tried to think of something reasonable to say, something that would throw him off the scent—for I feared that if he thought I believed (even though I knew for certain) that Lady Isabella was the Ankh, he would not only think me mad, he would do something noble, like warn the woman, or—or attempt to save me from myself.

I will never forget the shameful, confusing moment when Grayling and I arrived at Cosgrove Terrace on the night Evaline and I escaped from the Ankh and her opium den. I expected to be triumphant in my conclusions, and prepared to impel Grayling to close the case.

But then I realized I was wrong about Lady Isabella being the Ankh—or, rather, that she'd *made me believe I was wrong*.

I had been humiliated in front of Grayling, and I was certain he hadn't forgotten it either. I suspected he felt he'd need to save me from myself, and that was why his ears had perked up at the mention of Cosgrove Terrace—for I had said very nearly the exact same thing on that fateful night: *I must get to Cosgrove Terrace!*

As I pushed through these tangled thoughts and emotions, I realized Evaline was speaking.

"'Going to *Paris*,' I said," she told him. "Not Cosgrove Terrace." She gave him a look as if to suggest *he* was the one who had cotton in his ears.

I had to give her credit for fast thinking while under pressure. That was one thing at which Evaline had excellent technique—bluffing her way into conversations and getting people to give her information by playing the innocent ingenue, or the besotted young lady.

"Going to Paris?" Grayling seemed even more confused.

"What I *meant* to say," Evaline said rapidly and a bit loudly, "was that I learned that Sir Emmett Oligary has just gone to Paris. And that reminded me that *I* would like to go, and—and leave all of this behind me." She cast me a desperate look behind Grayling's back, and I leapt into the verbal fray.

"Well, who wouldn't want to go to Paris?" My voice was very reasonable. "I'm certain your trousseau would be all the better for it, indeed, Evaline. I understand they have the best prices on Betrovian silk on the Champs-Élysées—unless, of course, you go to Betrovia. Which is rather difficult now that relations between our two nations are horribly strained since the disappearance of Princess Lurelia."

My little speech had the hoped-for result, for the three of us exchanged glances. I suspected we, along with Pix, and perhaps Miss Adler and Dylan, were the only people in London who were aware that Lurelia had last been seen in the company of the Ankh, as well as her vampire minions, at The Carnelian Crow.

"Right, then," Grayling said. He might have gone on to speak further, but interrupted himself with a horrified cry. "*Angus, no!*"

The inspector lunged across the room, but he was too late—for the inquisitive beagle had just discovered a pair of brand-new leather boots.

Evaline and I muffled our chuckles, for Grayling seemed severely put out by the little beast's appetite. It felt good to experience some mirth, for the last days had been very trying. Which brought another topic to mind.

"Inspector, is it safe for me to return to my home? Have you put to rest the accusations against me?" I asked as he made the chastened Angus sit in front of the door, safely distant from any sort of leather or woven carpet.

"Er...perhaps not quite yet, Miss Holmes," he said. "I've not been able to convince Sergeant Blaketon to see reason. I shall be speaking to his superior tomorrow, but until then, I suggest you remain in hiding. If you get thrown in jail, it would be that much more difficult for me to get you released." He glanced around. "Not that it appears to be much of a hardship to remain here. Smith's one toff of a bloke."

"As long as one doesn't get assaulted while traveling to Whitechapel," I said grimly.

"Of course not," he replied quickly. "I meant for you to *remain here* without venturing out at all. Traveling to or in Whitechapel is— Well, Mina, you mustn't take the chance."

I wasn't so certain of that, but for once, I was too tired to debate the point. "I suppose it's for the best—that way I will be present should Pix somehow find his way back here." I looked at Evaline. "Could I impose upon you to bring me some items from my home on the morrow? Namely, the mail and some money? Using hackneys to go to and fro across the city is quite expensive, and I've exhausted my funds."

Evaline agreed, and shortly thereafter, she and Grayling (along with a happy-again Angus) took their leave.

MISS STOKER

~ WHEREIN OUR STUBBORN HEROINE GOES ON HER OWN ~

I didn't care what Mina said. I was going to find Pix.

Cosgrove Terrace was silent and mostly dark.

From two blocks away, I could make out a single light flickering at the front entrance beyond the massive iron gate. Other than that, the windows of all four stories on the street-facing side were curtained and unlit.

The black mourning banners decorating the estate fluttered and shimmied in the night air. A bit of snow was falling, but it wasn't as ugly or messy as it had been yesterday, when I visited for tea. Though it was certainly cold.

I was going inside.

And poor Grayling—he thought he'd left me safely at Grantworth House. I smothered a grin. He and Angus had insisted on seeing me back home after we left Pix's hideout.

I slipped from shadow to shadow, taking care not to step on the few patches of ice that littered the walkway and considered my plan. I was still two blocks away, but the gates to Cosgrove Terrace were directly in front of me at the end of the street.

From my previous visits, I knew the elegant home was on a rectangle of land. Though it was in town and not far from St.

James, the property was quite large. It took up half a block in width, and was two blocks deep.

The house itself was situated near the front of the plot on a small rise that allowed it to look down over the grounds. Its location left a large space in the rear for a sprawling, three-level terrace as well as lush, manicured gardens, walkways, a small pond, arbors, and a few fruit and flowering trees. Of course, it being winter, there would be little in the way of cloaking greenery except the pines and a few bushes. Though it would make my task more challenging, that fact didn't bother me in the least.

Two blocks ahead were the gated entrance and a sweeping driveway behind it. A tall stone wall overgrown with ivy enclosed the entire grounds and kept the gardens private. Beyond the copper and brass gateway, I could see the flat roof of the house with its decorative metal ornamentation. The copper and bronze decoration matched each of the ten balconies studding the sides of the building, which was constructed of dark brown brick.

I would find a way inside—either over the stone wall, or through some side door—from the darkest, most distant corner of the grounds. And then one of the balconies would surely give me access to the inside of the house.

I smiled in anticipation, my breath making a crisp white cloud.

Finally, I was *doing* something.

Then my smile faded. This wasn't a game. It wasn't an adventure.

I was about to break into the home of a murderer. Not only did I have to get in without being noticed, but I had to somehow find Pix and get him out—if he was even there—without anyone the wiser. And the house was absolutely huge.

And, knowing the Ankh, there was an excellent chance he might not be mobile. If he was even alive.

I didn't spend a lot of time wondering why I was risking my life to (possibly) rescue a pickpocket who *might* not be a murderer. Especially when I was about to marry one of the nation's most esteemed bachelors.

At the moment, my future didn't matter.

There wasn't much of a moon tonight, and though the trees and bushes were bare and didn't offer a lot of cover, I wouldn't easily be noticed. I was dressed in dark clothing—for when Grayling escorted me home, I'd followed Mina's lead and changed into more comfortable trousers and boots. I was quick and small and strong. No one would see me in the darkness.

In the distance, Big Ben chimed half past one, the warning echoed by the less melodious bells in the Oligary Tower...which, of course, reminded me that in three weeks I'd be in that very building on the Tower Penthouse at my own wedding.

The thought settled unpleasantly in my lower belly. I ruthlessly shoved away the reminder. I would worry about that later.

I stuck to the shadows of nearby houses and occasional trees, avoiding the gaslights that cast their small golden glow over the walkway. I was still more than a block from the Cosgrove-Pitt gates when a strange noise caught my attention. It was a sort of low, rumbling hum, followed by a pronounced hiss...and it caused me to look up.

My body turned to ice.

Above the rooftops, sliding through the night like an unpleasant shadow, was the sleek black airship. It was lower in the sky than I'd ever seen it, barely clearing the chimneys below.

It was coming this way.

This way.

I flattened myself against the rough bark of an oak tree and watched, my heart in my throat, as the airship cruised closer and closer...the rumbling becoming more distinct as it slid through the night...nearer and nearer.

Tonight there was no beam of white light shooting down. If I hadn't been outside and heard it, I probably wouldn't even have seen the thing. In the cloudless night sky, it was nearly invisible.

The soft hiss of steam cut through the night as the vessel slowed...

...and then came to rest, floating in midair, just above the roof of Cosgrove Terrace.

I could hardly believe my eyes.

My hands were ice-cold, and it had nothing to do with the weather. I realized I was hardly breathing, and I couldn't look away as the airship began to sink lower and lower toward the roof of the house. I was afraid it was going to crash onto the roof...but then it finally *disappeared.*

I goggled, staring, trying to make sense of what I'd just seen.

Had it been an apparition? Some sort of trick of the eye? It was there, then it was gone.

Then I realized the zeppelin had landed on top of the house. The walls of the building must be taller than the roof—creating a clever place for the airship to hide. No one would be able to see it from the ground.

This probably meant it wasn't the first time the airship had landed here.

We have no reason to connect the airship with the Ankh, Mina had said earlier tonight.

Well—*ha!* For once, *I* was right and *she* was wrong!

Now I had a second reason to get inside Cosgrove Terrace.

Keeping my eye on the mansion beyond the gates in case the airship began to rise again, I slunk closer to the grounds. Despite the landing of the zeppelin, there seemed to be no disturbance anywhere. No different sounds, no additional lights, and certainly no people.

I wondered briefly whether the occupants of Cosgrove Terrace even knew the vessel had arrived. I supposed it was *possible* they didn't—that it was some sort of surprise attack or visit...

There was only one way to find out.

Aware that the arrival of the airship could cause an alarm or otherwise awaken anyone in the vicinity, I kept to the shadows even more closely as I approached the edge of the Cosgrove-Pitt property. I stayed far from the illuminated gated entrance.

Yet the night remained silent and still as I picked my way along the perimeter of the stone wall, looking for a doorway or other entrance to the grounds. All the while, I kept my eye on the top of the house, waiting to see whether the airship would rise again or whether something else would happen.

It took me longer than expected, but I did a complete circuit of the property without finding any other means of entrance. That meant I was going to have to go up and over the wall.

Despite what Mina might think, I was fully prepared for any situation. At least tonight. I had a strong rope and a grappler hook that would (I hoped) cling to the decorative edge of the top layer of brick.

I was just looking for a good place to sling it over the wall when a creaking noise along with a gentle scraping sound drew my attention.

It was the front gate. The doors were sliding open. Sticking to the shadows and near the wall, I bolted toward the entrance as quickly as possible. This could be my chance to slip inside without being noticed...

But who was going out or coming in at this late time? There were no vehicles on the street. I paused, hiding behind a snow-covered bush.

And then I saw it: the small pool of golden light cruising down the curved drive. It was accompanied by a quiet rumble and a purring roar, very different from that of the airship.

A steam-car came into view, and I nearly swallowed my tongue. *Sir Emmett?*

I definitely recognized the vehicle. I flattened myself against the cold stone wall, shivering as ice dripped onto my head and inside the back of my coat, and edged closer. I needed to see who was inside.

The vehicle crunched out of the driveway and turned in the

opposite direction from where I was hiding. I couldn't see who was inside, thanks to its tinted windows and the darkness.

I wavered for just a minute. Then, when I realized the gates were rolling closed, I made a dash for it, uncaring that a lamp was illuminating the entrance.

I barely streaked through. I had a moment to be grateful I wasn't wearing my cloak, because I'm sure it would have gotten caught as the gates swung shut. Only a little out of breath, I backed up against the wall between a leafless tree and an arborvitae and waited to hear whether an alarm would be raised.

The house appeared quiet. The night was still except for the quiet clatter of bare branches against each other and the ever-present whoosh of steam.

No alarm. No shouts.

No one had seen me.

I waited another few minutes just to be certain, but the world remained quiet.

Now I had to figure out how to get inside. The four stories of the mansion reared above me with a smooth face interrupted only by windows that overlooked the drive. The lamp at the front door remained lit, and I could see no other movement inside the house.

That was interesting, for if someone (Sir Emmett?) had just left, wouldn't the butler or even Lady Isabella have seen him to the door?

And what was he doing here so late at night?

Or had he been inside the airship?

That thought stopped me cold.

And then I remembered what Ned had said—that his brother had left for Paris on the same day I told him I'd seen him here at Cosgrove Terrace.

If that was true, could the airship have *taken him to Paris*? And brought him back?

And if that was the case...had Lady Isabella been with him?

Was that why she hadn't responded to my message from earlier today?

Those wild, complicated, messy thoughts made my brain feel as though it was too full—and getting fuller.

Too many ideas, too many possibilities—and all of them were strange and shocking. And most of them seemed impossible.

How did Mina do it? How did she organize all those thoughts and clues and ideas and make sense of them? And was nearly always correct?

I shook my head and, in doing so, dumped an icy clump of snow from the arborvitae into the back of my coat. I should have worn a hat, drat it. At least the brim would have kept some of it from dripping down on me.

But the shock of cold had the effect of straightening me up and jolting me from the confused thoughts. I could think about what it all meant later. I had things to *do* now.

I was just creeping out from my hiding place when the back of my neck prickled. It was an eerie sensation, a familiar one.

Blast.

An UnDead was near.

I grumbled to myself but dutifully dug out the stake from my coat pocket. I really didn't have time to mess around with a vampire. I wanted to get inside, to see if Pix was there, and to take a look at that airship.

Besides, a fight with an UnDead would probably draw attention to me. At the very least, the smell of vampire ash—once I staked it—would fill the air and cling to me like a nasty odor.

By now I'd managed to approach the house itself by staying in the shadows and skirting around the edge of the front landscaping. I had the stake in my hand. The back of my neck was still cold and prickly, and my nose was as frozen as a little icicle.

I eyed the front door, wondering if there was any chance I might be able to simply open it and walk in. After all, the huge gates would keep out the riffraff and provide security. Why lock the door?

With this optimistic thought, I climbed up onto the long, wide porch from the darker side. The door, hidden behind the shivering mourning banner, seemed accessible enough.

Aware of the growing intensity of the chill at the back of my neck, I reached for the latch, the stake gripped in my hand and ready.

To my surprise and delight, the door handle moved, lifting slightly. *So much for security*.

Smiling, I unlatched the catch and pushed the door open. I was just about to step inside when a shadow fell across me.

From behind.

I spun, just in time to see the glow of red eyes before the creature lunged for me. He was a big man with a gaunt face. His fangs gleamed a dull white as I dodged, ducking beneath his outstretched arm to come up behind him.

My stake raised, I was about to plunge it down when he twisted around suddenly. I nearly fell off the porch trying to evade his grasp, but managed to catch myself at the last second by hooking an arm around the porch pillar. Using the column for leverage, I spun and whipped my foot into his torso in one smooth motion.

The vampire grunted and staggered, and it was my turn to lunge, stake in hand, as I plunged it into his chest.

He cried out once, breaking the silence of the still night, then evaporated into the foul ash that proved I'd done my job.

I wasn't terribly out of breath. It had been exhilarating, doing what I was meant to do—the first time in months—and I paused for a moment to brush off the dust that exploded onto me.

"Brilliantly done, Evaline," came a female voice behind me... just before something crashed into the back of my head.

Everything went blank.

MISS STOKER

- A RUDE AWAKENING -

I opened my eyes to find several strangers standing over me.

"Are you all right, then, sir?" one of the strangers said. Another of them, a woman, was gently patting my cheek, as if to rouse me. A third stood behind them. For some reason, he was holding two milk cans.

And apparently, I was "sir."

I was cold and stiff and wet. I was also, somehow, sitting propped against a lamppost near the street, and my head *hurt*. When I realized I still wore trousers and a man's coat, I understood why they were calling me sir.

I blinked, looking around. I wasn't certain where I was. None of the houses seemed familiar. It was no longer night, but barely light enough to be considered morning. It was lucky that snow hadn't fallen overnight, or I could have been buried in it. Or turned into a living icicle.

"Sir? Should we call you a doctor?" asked another of the strangers.

"Can ye stand up there, sir?" asked the milkman.

"Yes," I said, and batted away the woman patting me in the face. "I can stand."

"All right, then, sir... Well, bless my soul, it's a *girl*." The first stranger must have noticed my sagging bundle of hair. "Are you certain you're all right, then, miss? What happened?"

I brushed them away with a curt thank you as I struggled to contain my frustration.

I couldn't believe it. I'd been caught red-handed trying to break into the lair of a murderess, and instead of being captured and held prisoner—or worse—someone had bonked me on the head and dropped me off on the street.

I hadn't even set *foot* inside Cosgrove Terrace, and I had a bump on the back of my head.

Despite my grumbles, the cluster of strangers—they turned out to be a milkman, the baker's wife, and a cog-cutter, all on their way to work—insisted on helping me to find a hackney.

"Can't leave a young peach like yerself wandering 'bout all disgruntled like that," said the baker's wife. "Do ye remember where ye live, then, miss?"

"Yes," I replied shortly, then remembered my manners. "Thank you very much."

It turned out that whoever had dumped me in the street had gone through the trouble of taking me several blocks from Cosgrove Terrace—as if to try to confuse me about where I'd been.

More angry with myself and the situation than injured, I climbed into the horseless taxi and settled in to sulk on my way home. Thankfully, since it was just barely dawn, Florence would still be abed.

That would be the last thing I needed—for her to catch me coming in so late *and* dressed in men's clothing.

The very thought of how she'd react made my head pound more sharply. I closed my eyes, tipping back against the seat until a sharp pain reminded me that I had a knot at the back of my head. Ugh.

Because there wasn't much traffic this early, the hackney was able to rumble so fast on the cobblestone road that it jolted and jittered me, making the headache even worse.

There was one good thing about this entire situation, however.

I could contact Mina and tell her all about it instead of trying to figure it all out alone.

And even though she would surely annoy me to no end with her incessant lecturing and pontificating, at least this time I could tell her I'd been right—and she'd been wrong.

That alone was worth the disappointment.

❧

I'D FORGOTTEN I had the final fitting for my masquerade costume this morning. Mrs. Glimmerston, the designer, was very busy and very popular, and I knew there was no chance of rescheduling. Especially since the ball was the next day.

Fortunately, when I got home at dawn, I was able to wash up then get into bed (with Pepper's assistance) and sleep for a few hours before Florence was pounding on my door. Because I'm a Venator, I heal miraculously quickly, and so the lump on the back of my head was barely noticeable by then. I no longer felt anything but the faintest twinge, even when Pepper stabbed the bump with a hairpin (it was more annoying than painful).

I was about to dash off a note to Mina when I remembered that she was still in Pix's hideaway, which meant any communication had to go through Fenman's End and Bilbo. I wasn't going to trust that.

So I suffered through my fitting—the poking, the tucking, the jolting and jerking that comes with it all—and as soon as Mrs. Glimmerston and her staff left, I told Florence I had an engagement.

I don't know whether she was feeling bad about our recent arguments, or whether she was just pleased that the fitting had gone well (meaning that I didn't gripe about it), but she didn't argue with me. She didn't even ask whom I was meeting with, which only indicated how distracted she was.

"You'll need to stay in tonight, Evaline," she told me while flipping through a multi-page list of something. "No dinner parties or theater, even with Mr. Oligary. You'll want to look fresh and beautiful for the masquerade tomorrow night. On your wedding day you'll need to share the attention with your groom. But tomorrow night, it's all about you, my dear."

That was when I realized the *entire* next day was going to be spent being prepared for the blasted masquerade ball that I really had no interest in. My mood sagged.

At least Mina was going to be there—I hoped; that was something I needed to talk to her about today—along with Grayling (which I would insist upon). I expected to see Miss Adler as well.

Perhaps between the three of them, I might enjoy my own birthday party.

❦

"AND SO SOMEONE—PRESUMABLY Lady Isabella—coshed you on the head—and this was after she complimented you on your vampire staking—and then had you dumped under a lamppost three blocks away?"

I gritted my teeth. This was the third time Mina had made me confirm that, yes, I hadn't even gotten across the threshold of the house before being taken by surprise. I was beginning to reconsider my delight in being reunited with my old partner. "Yes."

"So she didn't want you inside Cosgrove Terrace," Mina mused. "And yet she didn't want to hurt you or detain you either. I wonder why."

"She didn't want me to find Pix," I retorted. "She knew once I was inside, she couldn't keep me under her control."

"But we aren't even certain that Pix is in there. I've been thinking about it more thoroughly, Evaline, and I'm not completely certain the Ankh is the one responsible for Pix's disappearance."

"Well who else would it be?" I demanded. "Do you think he's dead?"

Mina shook her head. "No. I don't think he's dead. Because if they wanted him dead, he'd not only already *be* dead, but his body would have been found."

"But why?" I tried to squash the glimmer of hope that I really had no business feeling.

"*Because* if they want him dead, they need his body to be found. He is, after all, an accused murderer. What better way to close the case than to have the accused escape from prison and be found dead, and then the case is closed because he can no longer defend himself?"

I nodded. I supposed that made sense in a roundabout way. "All right. But you *have* to admit that I was right about the Ankh being connected to the airship."

"Evaline, you've brought up that point at least a dozen times since you arrived," Mina snapped.

I smiled at her. "It just doesn't happen very often that I'm right and you're wrong—"

"I wasn't *wrong*," she retorted. "I just wasn't *convinced* that the Ankh was connected to the airship. I didn't say she *wasn't*. I don't just leap to conclusions without first employing considerable ratiocination—"

"Well, she wants me to join forces with her—like she asked you to do." I gave her a piercing look. "Apparently there are things we need to talk about that happened at The Carnelian Crow."

"Yes indeed. The woman thought she would compliment me by asking me to partner with her," Mina said with a sniff. "As if I'd fall for something so blatantly obvious. She attempted to flatter me into the idea, and of course I declined. Presumably you did the same." She looked at me with her brows arched.

"Of course I did. She was very offended that I used the term *murder* when talking about Lord Belmont."

Mina must have found that amusing, because she smiled. "Very well, then. I surmise Lady Isabella is quite threatened by the two of us. Particularly if we are in concert, which we are now, after several months of—er—a sort of hiatus. I'm certain that's why she's framed me for the murder of Frederick Boggs. Even if I'm not thrown in jail—which was clearly the intent—I'm completely distracted by the problem...or so she would hope.

"And you—Evaline, she must assume you're so busy with your wedding plans and now this masquerade ball, along with all of the other society obligations, that you don't have the time or energy to pay attention to her either. If you hadn't found my message lost in your house, I might have suspected *she'd* caused it to go astray. It's in her best interest to keep us apart."

"I suppose that makes some sense. And maybe that's why she invited me to tea—to find out whether I was busy or not."

"Indeed. She knows that only the two of us can stop her. After all, we've stymied her several times in the past."

"Right. But stop her doing *what*?" I asked in exasperation.

Mina sighed and sank back into her chair. We were, of course, still in Pix's hideaway. "I wish I knew, drat it. And I wish I wasn't locked up in this place. But that's precisely what she wants."

"I know. But *why*?"

She frowned and looked down at her hands. "If only I had asked you to bring my knitting. I need something to do with my hands so I can free up my mind to think."

"Well, what do we know? We know that the airship landed at her house, and since she accosted me at the door, then she must have been awake and about and knew about it. I think she was with Sir Emmett and that they went to Paris. It's the only thing that makes any sense."

Mina lifted a brow. "The *only* thing? I can think of at least eight other things that make just as much sense as that, Evaline. And that's without even trying very hard."

I sighed. "Well, then what do *you* think she is going to do?"

She erupted from her seat and began stalking about the chamber. "I have *no bloody idea!*"

I stifled a laugh. It was rare to see the unflappable Miss Mina Holmes in such a state. "Well," I ventured after a moment of enjoyment watching her work herself into a dither, raging back and forth at top speed, "maybe she's not going to do *anything* at all. Maybe she's given up on her—what would you call it? Villainous plot?"

"Never. Impossible. We are talking about a woman who killed young ladies in order to raise the powers of Sekhmet from the dead—" She stopped suddenly, her eyes widening. "*Evaline.* The Theophanine Chess Queen!"

"What about it?"

"We have no idea what ancient secrets or knowledge Isabella obtained from the inside of that chess table." She whirled so quickly that I felt the air move. "What if she has some powerful information—some, some *recipe* or formula or *something* that she's about to put to use to—to take over the city?"

I might have laughed to hear Miss Specific, Pedantic Mina Holmes use the word "some" so many times in one sentence if the thought wasn't so intriguing. "That's true. We don't know what she found in there, do we?"

"She's said all along—even from the first time we heard her speaking at the Society of Sekhmet—that she wants power. Especially for women, and especially power over the men who have controlled them for so long. Even beyond power. I believe she really wants revenge."

We looked at each other.

"But what about the special battery devices she was using to control Lord Belmont? I thought that was her villainous plot."

Mina shrugged and made a noise that sounded like a pained groan. It meant she didn't know the answer.

"Perhaps with Pix in jail, she no longer had a source for the battery mechanisms. Or perhaps they didn't work as well as she intended. Or perhaps since we killed all the vampires that night at The Crow—well, except for at least the one you staked last night—she has decided to do something different."

"Or maybe whatever was in the chess table was even better than the battery devices," I said.

"Good gad, I should hope not." She paused, looked at me unseeingly, then began to pace again. "But there remains the fact that there was a small piece of wire found in Pix's jail cell—just the sort that would be attached to those battery mechanisms."

A horrible thought struck me. "What if she put the controlling device onto Pix?"

"That's the obvious explanation," Mina said in an offhand manner. "Either she did, or we are meant to believe she did. Obviously." She rolled her eyes at me.

I resisted the urge to stick my tongue out at her (I hadn't done that since I was six).

"I need to find out who Frederick Boggs is. There has to be a reason the Ankh picked *him* to kill, and frame me for the crime." She was pacing again. "Speaking of which, Evaline, what do you think about me coming as Sekhmet to your fête tomorrow night? I have an appointment with the woman who took over at Mrs. Thistle's, and she's very nearly as clever and brilliant as Mrs. Thistle was. Her name is Madame Trouxeau. With an X instead of two S's."

"Madame Trouxeau? That's her name? Really?" I scoffed.

Mina flapped a hand at me. "I haven't decided yet, but if so, you'll know it's me because Sekhmet is traditionally portrayed as a woman figure with a lion's head. She wears a *ureaus*—surely you remember from our first case that a *ureaus* is the snakelike tiara sort of crown worn by the pharaohs in Egyptian—"

"Of course I remember," I snapped. I couldn't believe she was worried about masquerade costumes when there were so many other things to attend to.

Besides, I wished *I'd* thought of coming as Sekhmet or something interesting like that to my party.

Instead, I was going to be wearing a towering wig, broad pannier skirts (which would not only be impossible to dance in— a benefit, to be sure—but also inconceivable to fight in) (not that I anticipated any UnDead at my ball) and a beauty patch because Florence had insisted I dress as Marie Antoinette.

I wondered if it was too late to change my mind.

After all, it was *my* masquerade ball.

MISS HOLMES

- OF WORLD & TIME TRAVELERS -

O ch, then, Miss Holmes," said Inspector Grayling. "I never thought I'd have occasion to cross the threshold of this establishment again."

He had, as instructed by a message from me (actually, one of several over the course of the last day), arrived to pick me up for Evaline's birthday masquerade at the former Mrs. Thistle's street fashion boutique.

His comment was in reference to the fact that during The Carnelian Crow Escapade, Evaline and I had discovered the deceased proprietress inside her shop. Grayling, of course, had been the one to manage the crime scene.

"I can assure you there are no dead bodies involved this time."

"Not yet, anyway," he muttered. Then his expression changed as he got a good look at my costume. His eyes bugged out of their sockets.

Smiling to myself—for I had hoped for such a reaction from anyone who saw my attire—I swept past him from the boutique, where Madame Trouxeau (it really was a ridiculous name, but the woman was quite a genius when it came to street fashion, so I decided it would be detrimental to my appearance to hold such creative license against her) was still nattering on about a last-minute customer who'd expected her to accommodate them for the costume ball.

But apparently this last-minute customer had promised to pay her an exorbitant amount of money, and as Madame Trouxeau was quite practical—except, clearly, when it came to the matter of her professional reputation—she accepted the fee and created (in her words) "a brilliant fashion arrangement in modern street style."

As her name would suggest, Madame Trouxeau was rather flamboyant, and the direct opposite of her assistant—a quiet blond woman who wore a long, simple gown that put me in mind of a medieval chatelaine's attire. She even went by the title "Lady" instead of madam. The two of them worked in tandem, speaking hardly any words between them as they outfitted me.

Grayling joined me in the carriage he'd arranged as our transport for the evening, and I had the opportunity to admire his costume as well. While it wasn't quite as unique as mine, his achievement in concocting his ensemble was more than adequate and rather dashing.

My companion was wearing breeches of mahogany velvet tucked into knee-high black boots that laced all the way up the front using small copper cogs as the hooks. I immediately noticed the slyly hidden pockets on the inside of each boot and was intrigued by the possibilities they presented. They would be the perfect place to secret a slender dagger or some other useful implement.

Grayling wore a rather simple but dashing duster that reached past his knees and was made from dark blue wool. As he climbed into the carriage in a pleasant waft of peppermint, I observed several pockets on the inside of the coat as it flapped open with his movements, then went on to admire the array of timepieces (both modern and a bit dated) attached to the lapels. Clearly, time was an important clue to his identity; not that I had needed that hint, of course.

Beneath the duster, Grayling had donned a waistcoat of shiny fabric striped in brown and blue over a crisp cream-colored shirt with an elegant cravat. He carried his mask, which was untraditional and an integral part of his costume: slick, complicated aviator's goggles made from black leather and copper fittings to hold them in place. The eyeholes were long oval shapes and appeared to have different colored lenses which could be flipped into place as required. And was that a tiny illuminator attached to the top? I was fascinated, but didn't want to ogle too much. Grayling also carried a small expanding map and a complicated compass of brass and bronze.

"Mr. Fogg, I presume?" I said with a smile.

He seemed pleased that I had identified him as the intrepid traveler from Mr. Verne's celebrated *Around the World in Eighty Days*.

"Yes indeed, Miss Holmes. But I am at a loss as to what your costume is meant to portray. I confess, I've never...er...seen anything quite like it before."

He certainly hadn't.

No one in 1890 London had.

I'd decided at the last minute (although apparently not as last-minute as Madame Trouxeau's other, much-lamented client) to dress as something far more daring and interesting than Sekhmet.

I'd been inspired by one of my previous conversations with Dylan, during which he'd mentioned something called flapper girls. He was explaining about how in the not-so-very-distant future—within thirty years!—not only would women get the right to vote in both England and America, but they would begin to wear more comfortable, less restrictive clothing *with shorter skirts*.

And they would all cut their hair short as a man's.

Which I had actually done—not only for the sake of this costume, but also for the practicality of it all.

Yes, indeed—on the floor of Mrs. Trouxeau's shop there had

been left long, thick tresses of my brownish/chestnut-ish/auburn-ish hair when she was done. (I'd suggested she keep the bundles in order to make a wig for her clients, and she lopped off a significant percentage of the cost for my ensemble in exchange for the donation of my lopped-off hair.)

My head now felt incredibly light, and with the weight gone, shockingly, my hair had sprung up into gentle waves. The feel of those airy tresses brushing against the sides of my neck instead of feeling the heaviness of it hanging nearly to my hips was a wildly liberating feeling.

"Did you...*cut your hair?*" Grayling asked. His expression was a cross between astonishment and, I believe, admiration.

"No, of course I didn't cut my hair, Inspector," I replied with a pedantic smile. "Her assistant cut it for me. It would have been a disaster had I attempted to do so."

"Of course." His reply was grave. He was silent for a moment, then said, "It's quite unusual. But it suits an unusual woman."

Our eyes met in the dim light of the carriage, and I couldn't help but remember that emotional moment two months ago when Ambrose had fairly crushed me to his body upon learning that I was, in fact, unharmed...and then commenced to kissing me with the same expressive sentiment.

"I shall take that as a compliment," I managed to say, despite the fact that my mouth had gone dry and my stomach felt as if a flock of butterflies had been released therein. I lifted my chin a trifle in subtle challenge. Just in case.

"It was intended as one."

I smiled and settled back in my seat even though my insides were still fluttering. "I was gratified when you agreed to attend the masquerade with me tonight. I realize it was quite short of notice, but I feel certain it will be worth your time."

"As do I."

We lapsed into a companionable—if unusual—silence during the remainder of the ride.

One might find it surprising that I should have allowed myself to be distracted by such social frivolities as a masquerade ball when there were serious matters afoot, but rest assured that I had my reasons. And it was because of them that I was particularly pleased Grayling had agreed to accompany me.

However, despite my attention being focused on the evening's upcoming revelry, there were two other items that bothered at me, and were likely the cause of my silence during the carriage ride.

One was, and would continue to be, the murder of poor Mr. Boggs.

But the other was a more recent concern, for once I'd decided to embark on a "flapper girl" design for Evaline's masquerade, I knew it would behoove me to speak to Dylan about it.

As I have previously mentioned in this narrative, my futuristic friend and I had been having some difficulties relative to our association. I have no shame in admitting I felt hurt and betrayed when I learned he'd returned to 1889 London from 2016 London and had not sought me out.

I spoke to him about it in a very composed manner, but he apparently realized the depth of my distress.

"Oh, man, Mina, I know," he said, looking at me with those beautiful blue eyes. (His habit of referring to me as a man was always a bit confusing and off-putting, but I'd learned to ignore it as a particular affectation from his era.) "I really goofed"—apparently to goof meant that he acknowledged his failings—"and I'm so sorry. I just got caught up in the whole spy thing, you know? I was undercover with Miss Adler, and there was all this sneaking around and stuff and I just forgot about it. About contacting you, I mean."

"You forgot about me?"

What *was* it about myself that made people who supposedly cared to forget about me?

My father barely recognized my existence, my mother had

disappeared and hadn't had the courtesy to contact me in more than a year...and now Dylan Eckhert, a young man I'd become quite close to and had come to trust because he saw me as someone different from the other young ladies of my society... had simply "forgotten" to contact me when he returned from the most mind-boggling journey ever?

"Mina, I couldn't stop thinking about you when I got back to my own time. I really missed you. But then I came back with Miss Adler's help, and she needed me to help her—and it just got very busy. I was practicing the music and teaching her the songs... I'm so sorry. I'm such a jerk." I hoped that "jerk" was a slang term that meant fool or even something worse. "I know it."

"Thank you for the apology," I replied. And although I was very glad to see him again, I realized my affections for him had waned.

Partly because, in our case, absence had not made my heart (and presumably his as well) grow fonder, but also because I'd found myself more intrigued by my physically demonstrative encounter with Grayling.

Dylan and I attempted to return to our casual, comfortable friendship, but things were different. We met for tea several times, but those times felt slightly awkward for me, as I still felt confused about his lack of empathy toward me.

After one particular luncheon at Gateway Cafe when our conversation had trickled into the most mundane of topics, as I took my leave, Dylan indicated he would contact me in a few days (he'd returned to working at St. Bart's Hospital now that his so-called undercover work was finished). I hardly realized when a week had gone by and he hadn't done so. As I felt no great disappointment over the lapse, I gave it little thought.

I assumed Dylan had merely become distracted by his bread mold project at the hospital. And I was busy myself with all of the cases Miss Adler was sending to me.

But yesterday, more than a month after I'd expected to hear from Dylan, I went to see him at the hospital because I wanted to get more information about the flapper girls. He'd already described their appearance to me, but I had more questions that had arisen as I'd begun to imagine the costume.

Imagine my surprise when I learned that Dylan Eckhert had not been seen at St. Bart's Hospital for over a month.

He had disappeared.

MISS STOKER

- THE MASQUERADE COMMENCES -

Florence had arranged for my birthday masquerade fête to be held at the Starlight Palace, which was the same place the welcome ball for the Betrovians had been offered last summer. That evening held little but unpleasant memories for me, and if I had realized she was planning it here, I might have objected.

I suppose that was my fault for not paying attention. I simply had not been myself since the engagement had been announced.

The last time I was in this place was the same night Mina and I—and everyone else—had watched Princess Lurelia nearly fall to her death from one of the balconies above us. Miss Adler had *not* been pleased with our performance, and had dismissed us the next morning. (We had later been re-engaged, but that was because of Lurelia's personal demand.)

That evening, I'd also danced with Pix—who'd been disguised as an American known as Martin Vanderbleeth.

I knew there would not be a repeat of that particular event tonight.

Along with the Starlight Terrace's regular décor (long, silken banners in all shades of dark blue and black that were supposed to evoke the idea of night), there were long, graceful spirals of delicate lights suspended from the ceiling. They bounced gently with every movement of the air as moving stairs and open lifts transported the equally glittering guests up, down, and side to side. Old-fashioned candles were arranged in elaborate clusters of ten to twenty lights per stem, and these elegant silver candelabra were scattered throughout the room.

Glittering copper and gold swags were draped over tables and doorways, and a large fountain illuminated with blue lights sparkled in the center of the dance floor. Because it was winter, there were few floral arrangements. Instead, massive tree branches—each thicker than a man's torso—had been painted silver or gold. Countless tiny lanterns were hung from the branches, which were suspended horizontally and at different heights over the ballroom, creating a forestlike ceiling of shiny, bare branches. One long midnight-blue stretch of fabric, glittering with gold and copper embroidery, was draped artistically over some of the branches, and its end dangled gently down to the fountain.

The orchestra was set up on a small dais next to the fountain, placing the musicians in the center of the dance floor in an unusual arrangement. I thought it was ingenious, having the full view of the floor blocked. That meant it would be easier to avoid people that I wished to avoid.

Which was both simpler and more challenging than at a normal ball, for, of course, everyone was wearing masks tonight.

Florence had not been enthusiastic when I told her I'd made some changes to my costume at the last minute, but she was too busy to argue with me—probably because I didn't exactly tell her that I'd completely changed it and would no longer be going as Marie Antoinette. I figured she'd learn eventually, and the anonymity I'd have until that time would be delightful.

I was ecstatic that I was no longer reduced to wearing the wide, cumbersome panniers of an eighteenth-century French queen—not to mention a wig half as tall as I was. It was *heavy*.

I was on the lookout for a lioness-headed Sekhmet costume,

while at the same time wondering how Miss Adler would come costumed.

I learned the answer to this second question almost immediately.

"Diana the Huntress," murmured a masked woman at my elbow as she swept her gaze over my clothing, then into my eyes as if to confirm her suspicions.

I turned, recognizing Miss Adler's voice—and even then I wasn't certain it truly was her until I got a good look in her eyes.

"Ah, it *is* you," she said with a smile. "I wasn't certain. I'd heard you were coming as Marie Antoinette."

That was the only reason I tolerated masquerade parties: no one truly knew who anyone else was until midnight, when we were all unmasked. I'd insisted to Florence that we hold to that tradition, even though she'd merely wanted a costume ball.

True, oftentimes there were rumors, and hints were dropped and secrets were shared about what costumes were to be worn at masquerade balls—for how else were ladies to identify their friends or the gentlemen they wanted to dance with?—but unless you knew for certain how someone was coming dressed, it was nearly impossible to recognize them.

"Good evening, Miss Adler," I replied quietly. "I was, but I changed my mind."

"This ensemble suits you much better," she replied.

I agreed completely. Madame Trouxeau truly was a genius. She'd managed to create for me—in a ridiculously short time—the long column of a Grecian-style gown made from a stunning, glittery bronze fabric. The cloth was airy and light and shifted like the air with even the slightest movement. It draped like a dream, pooling just over my sandal-covered feet and giving a hint of what I wore under it.

There was a strapless tubelike chemise that ended just above my knees for modesty. But over that was my favorite part of the costume, which had actually been conceived by Madame Trouxeau's assistant: a street-fashion corset of some thick but flexible material that looked rather like a Roman gladiator's costume, with a knee-length skirt made from the same leather-like substance of the corset.

The gown fell in such a way so as to reveal the gladiator armor in subtle hints. The airy bronze fabric was gathered over one shoulder with a massive bronze, copper, and jet brooch in the shape of two flowers, each as large as a teacup, one above the other. The brooch was mechanical (I had to wind it up occasionally), and its soft hum was hardly noticeable as it moved gently, the flowers rotating in slow circles on tiny cogwheels. On one of the flowers was a tiny bee suspended from an invisible wire that bounced it between the two flowers.

My left shoulder was bare, and instead of gloves I wore strips of fabric—shiny copper, glittering gold, and sleek black—in a complicated weave that enclosed my hand, wrist, and arm but left my fingers bare. Small cogs covered with black glitter marched up the length of the sleevelike glove.

My right arm, partially covered by the fabric falling from where it was gathered at my shoulder, was bare except for a short version of the same glove-sleeve that ended just past my wrist.

Madame Trouxeau had bundled up my thick, dark curls onto the very top of my head, where they sprang like a fountain from their moorings: up and then down over my shoulders. She'd woven glittering strands of gold and copper braid into the curls along with tiny matching flowers.

Over my bare shoulder I'd slung a small quiver of black leather trimmed in bronze. The four arrows inside weren't long enough to hurt anyone, but they certainly looked pretty: curling copper feathers tipped the shiny black stems. I also carried a small matching bow with cogwheels that were used to stretched the string at each end.

But the best part of the costume was my mask, which was fashioned in the shape of a sort of elegant helmet that fit around the fountain of my hair. The bronze piece covered my eyes and nose, and then curved down over the sides of my face all the way to edge of my jaw. Only my mouth and the bottom portion of my ears were visible.

"It's impossible to recognize you. The fact that you were a female warrior was all what suggested your identity," Miss Adler said.

"Thank you. It's far easier to move about in than Marie's impossible skirts. But I'm sorry, Miss Adler, I don't recognize your costume."

"Annie Oakley," she said with a smile from behind her elaborate crimson and white mask. "Also known as Little Sure Shot. Perhaps you heard about her when she visited the queen with the Buffalo Bill Show."

Oh, yes, then I could see it. She wore a white dress with a bodice fashioned of ivory buckskin. The skirts, full and frothy, ended well above the floor, but still provided some modest coverage for her legs, which were encased in gorgeous crimson boots. Their heels were slender, curvy legs of gleaming black wood, and a collection of white and black tassels spilled from the laces that ran up the fronts of them. The boots themselves were shiny as a mirror, and I immediately coveted them.

Silvery fringe fell glittering from her elbow-length red gloves and from around her neckline, which cut low and straight across the front and back, from shoulder to shoulder. I suspected Annie Oakley had never worn such a deep décolletage during any of her shows, but the look was very becoming to Miss Adler and was perfect for an evening ball.

On her head perched a silver hat that was in the style of American cowboys, I think they're called, with a sassy brim that curled up on the sides. It was trimmed with red bric-a-brac and topped with a trio of airy red feathers. Her dark hair was gathered into a loose tail at the back, falling from behind the hat. A red mask hid the top of her face from a hint of scarlet lips to above her brows. She held a rifle in her hand, and I wondered whether it was loaded.

Surely not.

But then again, this *was* Miss Adler.

"Have you spoken to Mina?" she asked very quietly.

"Not since yesterday. She intends to be here tonight," I replied. "I believe she is dressing as Sekhmet. Is something wrong?"

"It's only that Dylan seems to have disappeared. I thought perhaps she might have been in touch with him. I've been rather distracted with...complications."

"What sort of complications?" There was something in the tone of her voice that had me coming to attention. The seriousness was matched by the expression in her eyes.

She hesitated, then shook her head. "Now is not the time. Tomorrow, when we can speak freely. I believe it's time you and Mina and I had a forthright conversation."

Of course, that only made me want to press her further. But before I could do so, Miss Adler slipped off into the party, using her rifle to part the crowd.

This left me alone, which was fine with me. I stood there for a moment, noticing the array of costumes: a sparkling butterfly with long, flowing sleeves and a complicated hat with antennae curving from it, a Robin Hood toting a much larger bow than mine, a Queen Victoria (there's always at least one), and a Romeo and Juliet who'd found each other either by accident or by design.

There was a Knave of Hearts, and I believe it was Mrs. Bennington who'd chosen to dress as a daisy (I could only guess it was her because she's remarkably short, and her daughter is remarkably tall). I saw a variety of other characters that I couldn't identify.

Through the crush, I spotted a towering pink and white wig studded with birds, bees, and stars. Apparently Mrs. Glimmerston had found someone else willing to wear my costume.

And from the size of the crowd of costumed partygoers clustering around Marie Antoinette, it appeared that no one realized it wasn't me. I was *elated* when I saw that one of them was even

Florence, who was dressed as a sparkling snowflake (she'd insisted Bram dress as rain—he'd wanted to come as Count Dracula from his book—and I was rather interested to see how that had come out).

Florence was speaking energetically to a man standing next to her that, from the back, I was almost certain was my fiancée. I couldn't quite make out what his costume was, but whatever he'd chosen to wear, it was shiny and complicated. And there was a sort of crown on his head, so he was probably a prince or a king.

When I caught sight of a slender, snakelike ornament at head height moving through the crowd, I stood on my tiptoes to see better. It had to be Mina in her Sekhmet costume, but I couldn't tell for certain, for most of the other guests were taller than me.

I began to weave my way between the chatting partygoers in order to catch up with her.

But just then, the orchestra began to play its first song, and all at once I was caught up in a crush of people selecting their partners and moving en masse to the dance floor.

Unlike other balls, there was no need for dance cards at a masquerade, since everyone was supposed to be anonymous. That was how I ended up being led to the dance floor by a gentleman who had dressed as an American cowboy. He was wearing a hat similar to that of Miss Adler, which was surely only coincidence, because he was not the type of gentleman that would appeal to her.

He was off-beat for the entire waltz, and propelled me into another dancer two different times during the number. At last it was over and I was able to extricate myself from the cowboy.

Besides, I had seen the tables of food and realized how hungry I was. I also wanted to find Mina and tell her what Miss Adler had said.

I brushed past the crowd that was still clamoring around Marie Antoinette, who appeared to be lapping up the attention. Whether she was purposely pretending to be me (rather unlikely; for what purpose?) or simply unaware of the misunderstanding, I didn't know.

But from the way Florence was watching over the crowd, I could tell *she* at least had realized it...and she was in search of the guest of honor.

I smiled to myself, knowing it was extremely unlikely she or anyone else would recognize me unless we came face to face. I could visit the food table and eat whatever I wanted without having to talk to anyone or without anyone criticizing me over my appetite. It felt wonderful, being so anonymous.

Florence, likely with the monetary help of the Oligarys, had outdone herself with the food. I wanted to drool at the array of edibles arranged on a long, curving table, as well as the items on platters being offered by strolling servers.

I had my eye on a footman dressed in midnight blue. He carried a large silver tray laden with bite-sized spoons filled with some delicious-looking custard. The spoon handles were curved back and under so as to keep them upright. As I pushed through the crowd and got closer, I realized the spoons themselves were *pastries*, glazed with some silvery topping to make them appear real.

They were filled with custard. Topped with tiny sprinkles.

I was nearly in reach when someone bumped into me from behind, hard enough to send me stumbling. I knocked into a cluster of people next to me as I turned to see who'd pushed me, and this set my mask askew. Someone steadied me, taking me firmly by the hand, and it took a few moments for me to adjust my mask and regain my bearings.

By that time, the footman with the pastry spoons had disappeared into the depths of the ball. Blast it!

Then I noticed I'd emerged from the crowd near a fountain of pale blue champagne. It was bubbling gently from a graceful mermaid's mouth. My annoyance eased as I accepted a tall, slender glass from the attending footman. If I couldn't have champagne on my eighteenth birthday, when could I?

The effervescent drink was refreshing and slightly sweet. I sipped again as I made my way through the crowd toward the main table of food. I was nearly there when I realized I was somehow holding a crumpled paper in my hand. I'd find a place to dispose of it in a moment—but first I was going to try the flaming beef skewers. They turned out to be salty and delicious.

I had just discovered the tower of chilled shellfish when I noticed the snake headdress making its way through the crowd. (Even though Mina has reminded me numerous times, I can never remember what the Egyptian crown is called. The name seems vaguely unpleasant.)

I snatched up another miniature crab claw (it was absolutely adorable—only the size of my thumb, completely shelled, and chilled with just a pinch of spiced fruit relish on it) from the rotating spiral tower that also offered shrimp puffs along with caviar-laden pastry scoops, and started to push my way toward Mina.

I'd taken two steps from the table when someone hissed in my ear. "What on *earth* are you doing, Evaline?"

I spun, nearly dropping the crab claw. "Mina?"

She was *not* dressed as Sekhmet.

MISS HOLMES

- IN WHICH OUR HEROINES ARE
FOREWARNED -

W ho are you?" Evaline said.

As she had just uttered my name a moment earlier, I assumed she wanted to know the identity of my costume. "I'm a flapper."

"What on earth is a *flapper*?" she asked, and stuffed yet another crab claw into her mouth. "And how did you know it was me? I was supposed to be Marie Antoinette."

I rolled my eyes behind the relative safety of my mask. It had been an elementary exercise to identify Evaline even among the throngs of masked individuals. All I needed was to watch the food table. I knew she'd eventually make her way there and stay for a time. "Her ears were all wrong," I told her.

"Her ears?"

"Evaline, have you not listened to *anything* I've tried to teach you over the last year? There are three elements of an individual's appearance that are virtually impossible to disguise. The eyes, the hands, and the ears. Not to mention a number of mannerisms of which most people are unaware—and thus rarely take the pains to change or hide—which can also be used to identify them. That is, in part, how I was so readily able to identify the Ankh even at the earliest stages of our acquaintance.

"Thus, I knew immediately that the woman dressed as Marie Antoinette was not you because her ears were wrong. Aside from that, she's been here more than an hour and she's not had even a morsel of food." I lifted my brows at the third crab claw Evaline had snatched over the last two minutes. However, because my face was obstructed by its mask, the effect was lost on my companion.

"What's a flapper?" she asked again as she nibbled on a shrimp puff.

I heaved a sigh of exasperation (an almost pleasant experience, since I was not wearing a corset). I supposed I'd better explain or we would continue in this circuitous conversation for some time.

"It's the way women dress—and, I suppose, act—in the future. In the 1920s, particularly in America. It's sort of a revolution from wearing clothing that is so restrictive. The Ankh would be most enthralled."

She seemed impressed, and her eyes roved over my attire. "It's very nearly scandalous, Mina! You're quite brave to wear such a thing."

I sniffed, though I confess I was fully aware of the scandalous nature of my costume. And I'd *almost* changed my mind about it at the last moment. In fact, I truly might have done if Inspector Grayling hadn't arrived at the former Mrs. Thistle's shop to pick me up. By that time, I no longer had the luxury of time to change my mind.

Based on the descriptions Dylan had given me about these flapper girls, I'd had Madame Trouxeau design a rather simple frock—insofar as the silhouette goes—for me to wear. The scandalous element was that it reached barely past my knees, and—although known only to me—I was wearing no corset or restrictive body wear *at all* beneath it. Merely a close-fitting chemise of a strong rust color. It laced up tightly on both sides from beneath my arm to below my hip, and sported wide straps over my shoulders.

Over that chemise, I wore a sleeveless shift of a golden hue with a faintly bronze tint. It hung straight down my body (which isn't as curvy as Evaline's), for apparently this was the appearance flapper girls aspired to: long, smooth, and lean. (How very different from the current fashions where a female's body is coerced, tied, and laced into a particular shape.)

The overdress's fabric was stunning, for it was translucent and woven of glittering threads that made it appear as iridescent as the wings of a housefly. Rows of silky, delicate fringe, one atop the other, decorated the bottom half of the shift in the same golden-bronze color. Every time I moved, the fringes filtered and swayed delightfully. (I'm not ashamed to admit that I'd spent a significant amount of time looking in the mirror, admiring the shining, dancing rows of fringe.)

I had not been courageous enough to leave my lower appendages bare but for silk stockings (which, according to Dylan, was how the real flapper girls would have dressed), so I'd consulted with Madame Trouxeau, and she'd created elegant boots that stretched up and *over* my knees! (That way, when I sat, if the short skirt shifted, my knees would still be covered. I cannot imagine the scandal it would have created had a knee been exposed.)

The boots were rust-colored to match the under-chemise, which, of course, could be seen through the translucent fabric over it. My footwear sported short heels that bulged sweetly at the top and bottom, but curved into something quite slender in the center. (Due to my propensity for tripping and slipping, I appreciated the relatively stable shape of the heel's base.)

As both chemise and overdress were sleeveless, I wore gloves in a sparkling gold fabric that fastened tightly from wrist to just past my elbow with buttons in the shape of daisies—each of which was as wide as two of my fingers. To complete the look, I had two very long ropes of copper and bronze beads that were anchored to the chemise straps to hold them in place at the tops of my shoulders. They hung down in graceful arcs all the way to my midriff and lower back, clunking gently against me with every movement.

Instead of a hat, I wore a sequined white headband that went straight across my forehead and met in the back at a cluster of airy feathers and silk daisies in white, gold, and rust. My mask coordinated, being in the Venetian Carnival style, and was white with gold decoration. It covered my forehead, eyes, and most of my very prominent nose.

"Good gad, did you *cut your hair?*" Evaline shrieked suddenly. Fortunately, it was so loud in the ballroom that no one could have noticed.

I inclined my head and felt the still-new, but pleasant, tickle of curls brushing my cheeks and the sides and back of my neck. "It was a practical as well as a fashion decision—"

"It's beautiful," she said with such awe that I couldn't help but believe she truly meant it. "The way your hair curls up so prettily around your neck. I bet it makes your nose look smaller, too, Mina, though it's hard to tell with the mask on. And now the color seems more like auburn than dark brown—"

"My hair has always had threads of chestnut and copper in it," I interrupted. Her enthusiastic commentary was making me feel a little uncomfortable. I wasn't used to having my appearance criticized—or complimented—quite so vociferously.

"And it doesn't make you look like a man at all," she continued as if I hadn't interrupted. "Has Grayling seen you? I'll bet he swallowed his tongue!" She giggled, and I could see her eyes dancing from behind the helmetlike mask that all but obliterated her identity.

"We rode in the same carriage," I replied, feeling uncomfortable with her mirth. What *was* it about Evaline that made her so interested in Grayling and his reactions? "And I must return the compliment, Evaline, for your costume is not only utterly appropriate for you, but I do believe it's the best thing I've ever seen you wear." I suspected I'd discovered the identity of Madame Trouxeau's last-minute customer.

"Thank you. Miss Adler said the same."

"Miss Adler is here? How is she costumed? Of course I could easily find her, but if you tell me it'll save some time—"

"She's dressed as Annie Oakley, but Mina, she wants to talk to us."

"And I must speak with her as well. Evaline, Dylan has gone missing!"

"I know."

I frowned. "How on earth could you know that?"

Her mouth moved between the sides of her mask, as if she were contemplating how to respond, and then she said, "Well, Miss Adler told me. But it's not as if I couldn't have somehow discovered it myself—"

"Then Miss Adler knows. Drat. I'd rather hoped she knew where he was. What does she want to speak with us about?"

"She wouldn't tell me. But it sounds serious. She slipped off into the crowd before I could ask her more. She said we must talk tomorrow. That there have been complications."

I frowned, feeling the mask shift against my cheeks. I had wondered for some time whether Miss Adler had been giving me ludicrously mundane tasks to keep me occupied—or distracted. But what was she trying to keep me distracted from?

And then another thought struck me. One I didn't like very much, but nonetheless, a hypothesis could not be summarily discarded simply because one didn't *like* it.

It had become clear there were two people trying to keep me occupied and distracted, unless...

Was it possible *Miss Adler* had arranged for me to be suspected in the murder of Frederick Boggs?

Surely not. Of course Irene Adler wouldn't resort to murder.

Still. Something seemed wrong. And—

Someone jostled me sharply from behind, and I turned to accept their apology. But the figure didn't even hesitate as he—or she; I couldn't tell—moved past. It was a jumble of people, complicated costumes and accessories, and movement that obstructed my view, along with a slightly askew mask. I felt someone brush even more rudely past, shoving so that a dark blond ballerina stumbled against me. I opened my mouth to express my consternation when Evaline made a sudden exclamation.

Adjusting my mask so it was in its proper position, I was about to join her in her outrage at the rudeness of certain individuals when I realized she was looking down at a crumpled paper in her hand.

"What ails you, Evaline?" I asked, rubbing the soft part of my posterior, where something dull but pointed had just prodded me during the little altercation.

"Look at this, Mina!" She thrust the bedraggled paper at me. "Someone shoved this into my hand a little while ago after they bumped into *me*."

I took it and read the words hand-printed on it.

BE READY

A prickle shot down my spine. "Where on earth—"

"And Mina, look! This fell to the ground just now when you tripped and almost fell—"

"I didn't trip. I was *pushed*. Like you," I added, suddenly realizing the significance of it all.

But Evaline was still talking. "It just now fluttered down during the confusion. I think they shoved it at you, or into your hand, and you didn't take it." She bent gracefully to scoop up a piece of paper. "*Look.*"

The writing was identical; the message was the same.

BE READY

"Someone dropped this just now?" I spun around, once more bumping into the lithe ballerina who was standing next to me. "Did you see who that was?" I demanded of her. "Someone just bumped into me, and then you, and they dropped this paper! Did you see them?"

The ballerina, whom I immediately recognized beneath her gold and white mask as Miss Bella Scott-Rondeau, gaped at me. "I didn't really see him—"

"Him? Are you certain it was a man? Or was it a *she*?" I asked, furious with myself that I hadn't seen who caused the little altercation.

"I'm not certain." She rose on her toes, which were in sequined bronze ballet shoes that laced up her legs, looking out over the crowd as if to attempt to discover who had assaulted us. Her skirt, which was fashioned of alternating and overlapping panels of gold, bronze, and copper leather, lifted and shivered gently above a froth of sparkling gold tulle. "It might have been that person with the sparkling blue cape, but I'm not sure. I didn't really see who it was. It was all rather confused."

"It certainly was," I muttered in frustration. Not with her, but with myself. How could I have been so oblivious?

"Evaline, I don't suppose *you* saw who it was." Then I sighed, because my companion had discovered a serving maid who was delivering frothy meringues via a tray.

"I wasn't paying attention," she replied—surprising me not in the least.

I huffed. "Well, there is no help for it, then. At least tell me how you came to be in possession of this note"—I gestured with the crumpled paper I still held—"and you didn't see fit to mention it until now."

"I didn't realize I was holding it until just now," my companion replied as she reached for another meringue.

"How could you not realize—"

"Someone bumped into me and my mask got pushed aside. I nearly fell myself, because it was quite a crush. I didn't see who helped steady me, but they grabbed me by the wrist. They must have stuffed the paper into my hand when they did. I didn't realize I was even holding it until a few minutes later, and then I was looking for a place to discard it—which is why I still had it in my hand. When the same thing happened to you—"

"I thought you said I tripped," I snapped.

Her lips curved behind her mask. "I just said that to tease you, Mina. And you reacted exactly as I thought you would. Anyway, when the same thing happened to you," she continued over my irritated sniff, "I saw the paper fall to the ground, and it reminded me of the one I was holding, that I'd somehow acquired. That's when I actually looked at it for the first time."

By now, we'd edged away from the food tables—and thus the worst of the crowd. I found it much easier to breathe and think now that I wasn't hemmed in on either side, and knowing Evaline, I suspected she felt the same way.

"Someone made a point of giving us both the same message. Something is going to happen tonight, Evaline."

"Do you really *think* so, Mina?"

I opened my mouth to make a sharp reply about her obtuseness before I realized she was being facetious. I lifted my nose. She really could be the most incorrigible, annoying individual.

"There's very little clue to the writer of these messages." I peered at the papers through the eyeholes of my mask. "They're written on simple paper in block letters. It could have been done here, or before the messenger arrived. The ink isn't smeared, nor is it anything unusual. There seems to be a bit of embossing at the edge of one of the papers, though—as if it were torn off to keep me from identifying the source of the stationery." I peered at it more closely, but the ballroom's dim ambience wasn't conducive to a close examination of anything. I stuffed it into my glove to look at later.

"But how did the individual know it was *us*? Well, I mean to say, *you're* rather obvious, Evaline, if anyone knows anything about you. Coming as Diana the Huntress is almost like wearing a sign, to be fair. But I'm surprised anyone could have recognized me—"

"Wait!" Evaline grabbed my arm. "I thought you were going

to be here as Sekhmet, so I was watching for that tiara with the snake on it so I could find you—"

"It's called a *ureaus*, Evaline."

"Fine. But it sounds disgusting. Anyway, I saw someone wearing it. I thought it was you, and I was trying to follow them through the crowd—"

"*The Ankh*," I whispered. "She's here. It's *got* to be her. Dressed as Sekhmet."

"But Lady Cosgrove-Pitt is in mourning! She wouldn't— *Oh*. What a *perfect* chance for her to do something social." She smiled again. "No one would even know she's here with all the masks. But why would *she* warn us to be ready?"

"Well, did she not do the same thing at the Yule Fête? Don't you remember what she said to me that night? 'I'm so very glad you're here. It's going to be a very *triumphant* evening.' That's what she said. It was very nearly the same as 'Be ready.'"

"Right, then. We need to find that Egyptian person. I'm not sure it was Sekhmet, Mina—I couldn't see whether the head was a lioness or not."

"We'll find her. And we'll do as the note suggested: be ready. How is the back of your neck, Evaline?"

"Normal," she replied after the briefest of pauses. "There are no UnDead in the vicinity."

"Well, we can be thankful for that, at least." I hesitated, then plunged on. "Evaline, do you know how Sir Emmett is costumed tonight? I want to find him as well."

"Sir Emmett? Why?"

I didn't want to tell her about the photograph that included my mother, along with Sir Emmett, Hiram Bartholomew, *and* Pix. I wasn't ready to share that information with anyone else quite yet, even though Evaline had had her own relationship with my mother.

Siri, she'd called her. Siri, apparently a derivative of Desirée— the name by which I'd known her.

Perhaps that was why I didn't want to tell my partner. It was one thing I had of my mother that she didn't. Yet. Besides, knowing Evaline, she'd go off and stir up trouble without thinking things through or making a plan. She'd probably walk up to Sir Emmett and demand to know how he knew her.

I wondered if Miss Adler would know about the picture. Yet another reason I needed to speak with her.

"I was just curious," I replied belatedly to Evaline. Then I was saved from further questions, for I noticed Grayling standing near the edge of the crowd on the opposite side of the food tables. "I see the inspector over there—he's dressed as Phileas Fogg. I'm going to tell him about the notes we received."

"Good idea," Evaline said. She was standing on tiptoes, looking over the crowd. "I'm going to see if I can find the Egyptian person."

"Don't do anything rash, Evaline," I said.

"Like what?" she said then, with a grin from behind her mask, slipped off into the crowd, her delicate Greek gown rippling like a shimmery bronze veil and the elegant quiver bumping against her scapula.

I rolled my eyes. This was precisely the sort of thing she loved: mystery and the possibility of danger. I just hoped she stayed on guard. We both had to be ready to act on a moment's notice. It was too bad we had to split up—I would have preferred to keep my eye on her to make sure she didn't do anything rash.

I plowed my way through the crowd, keeping my eyes on Grayling so as not to lose him, but at the same time watching for any hint of an Egyptian-style costume. If I could find the Ankh...

I finally reached the inspector and hurried up to him and the gentleman with whom he was in conversation. The man's back was to me, which was why it was reasonable for me not to realize that he wasn't masked until it was too late.

"Oh, there you are, Inspector. I've been looking everywhere for you," I said, breezing into their conversation. I recognized the warning in Grayling's eyes just an instant too late (my excuse is that they were partially hidden behind his mask).

Then I got a good look at the other man.

It was Sergeant Blaketon of the Met.

The man who wanted to arrest me for murder.

MISS STOKER

- UNMASKING SEKHMET -

Be *ready*.

What in the blooming Pete did that mean? Should I expect vampires? Some other danger?

If it *was* the Ankh who'd warned us—which I wasn't so certain of, even if she was at the ball—why would she bother to let us know ahead of time that something was going to happen?

Or could it have been someone else? Miss Adler, maybe? But why would she warn us anonymously? I had already spoken to her. It just didn't make any sense.

I wandered over to the food table and managed to snag another two crab claws (I'd decided they were my new favorite food item—at least, that wasn't a sweet) and then obtained a second glass of the pale blue champagne. Sipping it, I wandered through the crowd, enjoying my anonymity while poor Marie Antionette continued to manage her adoring crowd. I don't think the girl (whoever the unlucky thing was that had inherited my costume) had managed to take two steps from where she'd been when I first saw her.

I was just glad it wasn't me trapped by a cluster of people, needing to make chitchat with them. And Mina was right—the poor girl hadn't had the chance to try any of the food!

I finally caught sight of the snake tiara about halfway to the center fountain and began to shove my way through the crowd as rudely as the person (or persons) who'd delivered the messages to Mina and me.

When I got close enough to see that the costume *was* a lioness's head, my pulse jumped.

Yes.

Mina was right. Of course the Ankh would be here. And her presence was her way of telling us so—for who else would think to dress as Sekhmet (except for Mina)? It was a clear signal.

Besides, who else even knew who Sekhmet was? Well, except for the young ladies who'd been part of the Society of Sekhmet —but I would think they'd learned their lesson after three of them were murdered. Unless by wearing the costume the Ankh was quietly trying to signal the society that they should meet again...

I threaded through the crowd faster now, uncaring that I was knocking into people or causing them to trip or bump into someone else. The orchestra had taken a break, which meant no one was dancing and everyone was just standing around in clumps, talking.

I finally got close enough to reach Sekhmet. I grabbed her arm and yanked her to a stop, uncaring that I bumped into the people around me. She spun around, stumbling into me.

"Hello there, Sekhmet," I said in a steely voice. "Or should I say *Isabella?*" Ignoring the shocked look in the blue eyes behind her lioness mask, I dragged it off her head and whipped it aside.

It wasn't Lady Isabella.

It was Tarra Scott-Rondeau, the mother of the ballerina who'd been standing next to Mina a few moments ago. That was when I realized that she was shorter than Lady Cosgrove-Pitt. By several inches. *Blast it.*

"Mrs. Scott-Rondeau," I said. "Oh, dear, oh no, I am so very sorry. I—I thought you were someone else."

"My daughter, perhaps? Her name is Isabella, you know." She

didn't seem upset, but she was watching me very warily. "Though no one calls her that. Only Bella."

I desperately hoped she didn't recognize me beneath my helmet mask. It would be terrible if the hostess of the ball, the guest of honor, was discovered to have been so horribly rude.

My face was already burning with mortification, which was made even warmer by the stifling helmet. "I'm so very sorry, Mrs. Scott-Rondeau. Please accept my apologies. I hope you enjoy the rest of the evening."

I started to slip away into the crowd—the sooner I got away, the better. But then I thought of something and turned back. The idea of being interrogated by Mina then listening to her grouse because I didn't have the answers she'd try to wring from me was worse than taking the chance of being recognized.

"Um...how did you decide to wear such a unique costume? It's very lovely." I realized belatedly that her lioness head with its snake tiara was still on the floor. I picked it up and handed it back to her, noticing that the snake decoration was now bent awkwardly. At least the papier-mâché lioness head-mask hadn't been crushed.

She smiled at me, and I was relieved that she hadn't turned tail and run off. "It was so unexpected! And quite a happy occurrence. The costume arrived at our house today. You see, I had planned to come as a lady-in-waiting from Queen Elizabeth's court, but somehow my costume was ruined at Mrs. Glimmerston's and I didn't have anything else to wear. I couldn't let my daughter come tonight unchaperoned, of course, and as you can imagine, Bella was in tears at the thought of missing it—for it's *Miss Stoker's* masquerade, after all—and we just couldn't imagine staying home. But then this arrived today as a replacement for my original costume. It was a most happy solution."

"Someone sent you the Sekhmet costume to wear?" I said.

"Is that what it is? What's a Sekhmet? I thought it was an Egyptian person," she replied.

"It is." I was relieved Mina wasn't present, or the poor

woman would have been given an entire lecture about who Sekhmet was. And Mrs. Scott-Rondeau was far too nice to tell Mina to stop talking, so she probably would have been stuck until the ball was over and they were extinguishing the candles. "Was there any sort of message in with it?"

"Just a note that said, 'With compliments.' That was it. It wasn't even signed."

Very interesting. I wasn't a Holmes, and even I could put it all together. Someone—surely the Ankh—had made certain Mrs. Scott-Rondeau's costume had needed to be replaced, and then sent her a Sekhmet outfit in order to confuse Mina and me. "Do you still have the message? At home, I mean?"

Mrs. Scott-Rondeau looked at me strangely. "I suppose I do. Why? What's so important—"

All at once, someone grabbed my arm with a *very* firm grip. I spun, shocked and annoyed at being so rudely interrupted, and found myself eye to eye with Florence.

Her eyes burned through her sparkling snow-white mask. "Evaline Eustacia Stoker," she said from between clenched teeth in a tone that only I could hear. I hoped. "What on *earth* do you think you're doing?"

I smiled innocently, even though the blood flow in my arm was being cut off. "Why, I was simply talking to Mrs.—"

But Florence was already dragging me away. I think she was raging on about something regarding hostessing, but I was happy to let whatever she was saying get lost in the conversations around us.

But drat and *blast*.

Now what was I going to do?

MISS HOLMES

- AN INCONCEIVABLE PREDICAMENT -

I stared at Sergeant Blaketon, immediately grateful that I was wearing a mask. It would be impossible for him to recognize me under the most promising of circumstances, but certainly not after only seeing me through the crack of the door one time.

"Miss Holmes," he said, shocking me into paralysis and obliterating all of my previous confidence. His dark, furious eyes bored into mine. "You've been quite a slippery miss, haven't you, then? But of course you would attend your closest friend's birthday ball. I knew I would find you here."

I didn't respond. I don't think I could have, even if I'd wanted to.

How could it be that I'd been able to evade Blaketon for three days by wearing a number of disguises—including passing him on the street in front of Mr. Boggs's house—and he immediately picks me out at a *masquerade ball?* A gathering to which he clearly hadn't been invited and was in no way intending to participate.

How did he even know I was going to be here?

I managed to glance at Grayling and allow him to see the variety of emotions that were surely blazing in my eyes.

Had *he* given me away?

His eyes widened, and I saw the exasperated frown behind his mask. *Don't be silly, Miss Holmes.* I could almost read the words he would have spoken if he could have.

"Oh, look—they've put another tray of canapés out," I said blithely. "I've just got to have one. If you'll excuse me, gentlemen."

I didn't even manage a full step before Blaketon moved, blocking my way. "Miss Holmes, we can make this very simple and quiet...or we can make it an event for society to talk about for years. Sir Mycroft's daughter, dragged out of a society ball, arrested for murder. The gossips will enjoy every word of the article, won't they? Watch out—there might even be a photographer to catch the moment on film."

"I have no idea what you're talking about, sir," I said haughtily, trying desperately to find a way to escape.

And why wasn't Grayling *doing* anything?

Blaketon's hand snaked out and grabbed my wrist. "Grayling!" he growled, and I was dumfounded when *my very own escort stepped forward to take my other arm.*

Once again, I was so shocked that I couldn't react. What was happening? How could Grayling do this?

"Remove your hands from me at once," I demanded. "Both of you. *Especially you,*" I added, giving Grayling a look that would have smote him to the ground if eyes were lethal. At that moment, how I wished they were. "I'll come along graciously."

"Graciously? Pah!" Blaketon scoffed. But he released my wrist.

Fortunately for his own well-being, Grayling did the same. I did not deign to look at him as I began to move very slowly toward the exit.

How could this be happening? The demand—for it wasn't a question in my head; it was a dumfounded refrain—ran over and over through my thoughts as I scrambled to think of a way out of this impossible predicament. Being arrested at a ball? I? A *Holmes*?

Especially when something important, exciting, and possibly dangerous was about to happen!

If I wasn't here, who was going to stop the Ankh from executing whatever her villainous plot was?

I hadn't even had the chance to tell Grayling about the messages—not that I would tell him *now*, the cad!

I walked stiffly, making certain I didn't come close enough to either of my escorts to even hint of brushing against them as I picked my way through the crowd as slowly as possible.

I had to think of something.

We had reached the main entrance to the Starlight Palace, and not only had no one seemed to notice my reluctant exit, but nothing had happened. The party was going on as it had been. Evaline was probably still at the seafood tower.

I ground my teeth as Blaketon gestured for me to precede him out of the ballroom and toward the exit to the outside.

I simply couldn't believe the evening was going to end this way.

This wasn't supposed to happen!

This wasn't—

And then something did happen.

From inside the ballroom, from behind us, someone screamed. Blaketon, Grayling, and I came to a halt, and I turned as if to go back.

"No you don't, missy," said the sergeant. "There will be no—"

"Hush!" Grayling said. "*Blaketon.*" His voice was urgent, and though he wasn't looking at me, I knew something was wrong.

Then I realized what it was. The chamber we had just left behind—filled with a loud, raucous, crowded party—had gone utterly silent.

The three of us turned, and as one, we started back toward the ballroom at a near run. Whatever would make an entire room go dead quiet would have to be mortally serious.

As we approached, I could see that the entire crowd was looking in the same direction—and up.

Something lodged in my throat—fear, comprehension, horror —for the image of a dumbstruck audience watching with rapt attention at a raised location immediately brought to mind the horrific event at the Yule Fête, when Lord Belmont Cosgrove-Pitt had thrown himself off the balcony in front of his guests.

I pushed blindly past my two escorts and blundered into the ballroom, already looking in the direction that everyone else was staring.

I came to a sudden halt when I saw what they saw.

Up on the balcony—the very same one Princess Lurelia nearly fell from at her Welcome Ball—was a man.

He was wearing an elegant evening coat of unrelieved black over a brilliant white shirt and black cravat. He was sitting on the rail of the balcony, his legs hanging over the front, speaking to the crowd. For once in his life, he was the only person in the room not wearing a mask.

I recognized him immediately, although it was probably the first time I'd ever seen him without a disguise.

It was Edison Smith, also known as Pix.

And he was holding a pistol.

MISS HOLMES

- PANDEMONIUM -

Grayling's muttered curse reached me from behind. I started to edge closer to the balcony, and he grabbed my wrist firmly to hold me back.

"No, Mina," he said near my ear.

I decided to forget, for the moment at least, that I was furious with him, and turned to speak quietly and urgently. "Evaline and I were both given messages that something was going to happen tonight."

He nodded to indicate he'd heard me but kept his eyes on Edison Smith, who was talking. The pistol was visible, obvious even, but he wasn't aiming it at anyone. Yet.

I felt Grayling's hand move into the depths of his coat, and I suspected he was removing his own firearm.

Good gad, I hope he won't need it.

"Now that I have your attention..." Smith said with a wry smile, still on his high perch. "Ah, I see that I truly *do* have your attention. All of you. Especially you, young lady. It's difficult to believe a neck as slender as yours could carry the weight of such a wig. But, after all, it is *your* party, isn't it?"

I tensed, for there was something about the way he was

speaking, something about the inflection in his voice that made chills run down my spine.

He didn't sound anything like the smooth, cunning charmer that I knew as Pix.

Perhaps this was how Edison Smith actually sounded and spoke. His American accent was true, if flat and a bit nasally, but there was also something that rang false about the tone. At least to my ears.

My insides were so tight that they felt as if they were being twisted into huge, heavy knots. I could hardly breathe.

"As many of you know, the horrific death of Mr. Hiram Bartholomew was no accident. And yours truly—that would be myself, Mr. Edison Smith, originally of Menlo Park, New Jersey, but most lately of the stews of Seven Dials here in the *lovely* metropolis of London—well, *I* have been identified as the culprit. Accused of murdering Hiram Bartholomew, who was the partner of the esteemed Mr. Emmett Oligary—who, as I understand it, is now known as *Sir* Emmett. I cannot imagine whom he paid off to make *that* happen. And the Genius of Modern Times, as I believe he's also been called."

There were a few soft—very soft—murmurs at this, and several heads turned as if to look around and locate Sir Emmett. I had, of course, identified him and Mr. Ned Oligary by now. The former was costumed as an Elizabethan troubadour, complete with lute, and his younger brother as Richard the Lionheart in a glittering gold and purple costume. They were standing near the crowd in the center of the room.

Right where Marie Antoinette stood, with her tall, heavy wig. Just between the balcony and the central fountain.

In the exact center of the room.

I felt a very uneasy prickle down my spine. Where was Evaline?

"I was indeed present the night of Mr. Bartholomew's death," Smith went on.

Grayling tensed next to me. I heard him mutter an oath I

need not repeat herewith, and he started to move forward to the balcony that loomed ahead and above us.

Of course, I followed him.

"But before I get to that," Smith went on, "I want to extend my felicitations to the lovely *queen* of the masquerade ball tonight—not only on the anniversary of her birth, but also for her upcoming nuptials." Using the wall for support, he climbed gracefully to his feet on the balcony railing and offered a mocking bow to Marie Antoinette from this position. "Unfortunately, after the conclusion of tonight's activities, I suspect I'll be unable to attend that happy occasion."

He shifted and raised the gun. "If it even occurs."

The room gasped as one, and I joined them.

Good gad, Pix, what are you doing?

Grayling had moved to the edge of the room in order to, I assumed, remain as far out of sight from Smith as possible while he was making his way toward the balcony. I didn't know which lift or mechanized stair would deliver me to the balcony the fastest, but I was intent on finding one.

I didn't know or care where Sergeant Blaketon had gone, the lout.

"Which might very well be in question once the evening is over," Smith continued, examining his firearm idly. "But let me get to the point of my speech—I'm certain you're all waiting for me to get there so you can return to the revelry, no?" He swung the pistol in an arc over the top of the audience, and everyone ducked and gasped as he did so (even though I could tell it was aimed far too high to do any damage to anyone).

"The point of my speech is to tell the truth of what happened that night to Hiram Bartholomew." He paused for a moment, tilting his head as if he heard something, and then reached behind the back of his neck. He seemed to be scratching or massaging something there, then: "Ah, yes, there we are. Much better."

His hand came up and over from the back of his neck, and I

saw the glint of something metal—mechanical—in his grip just before he flung the small rectangular object to the side.

I gasped. *Good heavens.*

I actually felt faint, for up until that moment, I thought—I truly believed; I desperately *hoped*—that Edison Smith was somehow acting out a part, that he had captured everyone's attention in order to make some grand accusation or announce some startling revelation.

But now I knew better.

"*Ambrose,*" I said desperately, but he was too far away to hear me. Surely he'd seen it too. Where the devil was Evaline?

I pushed through the crowd after Grayling as Smith continued, "Now, where were we? Oh, yes, I was going to tell you all about what happened the night Hiram Bartholomew died. It truly is a sordid story." He grinned, and even from below, I could see that his eyes were a little wild. My heart thudded harder.

As he spoke, Smith gestured exuberantly with both of his hands, as if he didn't recollect that one of them held a lethal weapon. "Are you listening, there, young lady? Our masked birthday *queen?*" Everyone glanced at Marie Antoinette, and some of the crowd edged away from her a bit. "This is a story just for you, *luv.* You'll—"

A loud, clanging crash interrupted him; it sounded as if someone had knocked over several large trays at once. The sudden noise released people from their horrified stupor—or, more likely, terrified them even more. The room was suddenly filled with confusion—screams, shouts, shoves—and then I heard an ugly, definite *pop.*

I knew that sound. Good gad, *I knew what that was,* and I looked up at the balcony in terror where Pix still held his gun. The gun that had just gone off.

Everything happened very quickly and very confusedly after that.

Someone screamed, "*She's been shot!*"

"*He shot her!*"

"He's shot Miss Stoker!"

People spun and shifted, gasping and crying out. Some ran for the exits as if fearing he would shoot again. But I saw the hint of a figure moving in the center of the room, turning to face the balcony—instead of toward the person who'd been shot. I couldn't see who it was, only the suggestion of a figure and the glint of metal as it lifted from the crowd.

The next events happened so quickly, all at the same time, and yet so very slowly...the figure raised a firearm, aimed it toward Pix—who was still standing on the balcony railing—there was the blur of sparkling bronze flying through the air, the report of another gunshot, and more screams as the blur of bronze—*Evaline!?*—slammed into Edison Smith and they tumbled off the railing onto the balcony and out of sight.

MISS STOKER

- FLIGHT -

I felt the bullet strike me just as I crashed into Pix.

I must have cried out, but it was lost in the pandemonium—both below and when we hit the floor of the balcony—because it *hurt*. Bloody hell, blooming Pete, devil take it—it *hurt*.

Nevertheless, my instincts took over, and, holding on to the man whose life I'd just saved, I rolled us both to the side away from the railing.

Whoever had shot at him would likely try again.

He'd regained his breath, for I'd landed on top of him with great force, and he fairly leapt to his feet, dragging me upright with him.

"Evaline!" he breathed. "You *bloody fool!*"

Before I could reply, he caught me up under his arm and lunged for the rear of the balcony. I couldn't catch my breath from the blow and the tumble, and I sagged against him.

We burst out into the hall behind the balcony. Though my head was swimming and the back of my shoulder throbbed with a dark, raging pain, I struggled to get free of his grip. Then I saw a figure approaching.

I twisted harder, pulling from Pix's grasp as I fumbled for one of my weapons—any of them—and staggered against the wall, nearly falling again. I couldn't seem to breathe properly. Pix yanked me upright and dragged me after him, but this time he didn't try to pick me up as he ran toward the person blocking our way.

Through the murkiness of pain and confusion, I managed to drag out the small dagger I'd slipped inside my corset belt and brandished it as we ran toward the person—whoever it was wore something shapeless. It flapped and fluttered and made it impossible to tell whether it was a cloak, a gown, or some other costume.

But instead of trying to stop us, the shadow stepped aside, showing us a narrow, open door.

"Go!" the figure hissed. "There's no time to lose."

We didn't slow as we scrambled down the steps—Pix half carried me, although I would have been able to walk if he hadn't done so—and we followed the narrow, dark spiral down, down, down...

My mask was long gone, which meant I could see where I was going, though I had to take care not to trip on the frothy, pooling gown I wore. Fortunately, my boots were low-heeled and I could run in them—not that what I was doing was running. Barely stumbling would be a better description.

From a distance, we could hear the wild melee of what was left of my birthday masquerade. I blocked the thought that someone had shot Marie Antoinette—someone? No, Edison Smith, the very person I was trying to save!—and focused on moving, keeping moving, keeping breathing, ignoring the throb of pain below my shoulder blade...

At last we reached the bottom and there was another door. I shoved Pix aside (he was Pix to me, not Edison Smith; not that murderer, not that crazy-eyed man who'd taunted and lectured from the railing) and fumbled for the latch.

He shoved me back and closed his fingers around the latch,

then, as I breathed heavily down his neck, he lifted it carefully...
eased the door open...and listened.

The only sounds were our panting, labored breathing, and he
grabbed me by the wrist and darted into a dark, dingy hallway
that could only be underground.

It seemed forever, but it couldn't have been that long before
we exploded from the cellar of the Starlight Palace onto some
dark, dingy, close alley. But even then, we didn't stop.

We couldn't.

We couldn't stop, and we didn't speak. We didn't need to. All
we needed to do was get to safety, and we didn't dare try a hackney. So we were on foot, dodging and dashing in the shadows,
with Pix half dragging me most of the time.

We didn't speak even when we got to Fenman's End. Not
even to Bilbo, who barely lifted his eyebrows when we rushed
across his pub and through the door to the tunnel.

Then we reached the door to Pix's secret hideaway and he
began to see to the locks.

MISS HOLMES

~ A GATHERING OF CLUES ~

By the time I got to the balcony, Evaline and Pix had disappeared. Grayling met me as I dashed into the space after bounding up a flight of moving stairs. I was out of breath but at least not restricted in movement.

"She's dead," he said flatly.

My heart nearly stopped, but I was too out of breath to react other than a weak gasp of denial. Then I realized he was looking out over the balcony into the ballroom, where a crowd remained around the fallen Marie Antoinette.

Even from up here, I could see that he was correct. The red bloom in the center of her sparkling pale pink bodice told the story. Her towering wig had tumbled into a sad white pile next to her. The broad, ungainly skirts were a creamy froth that seemed about to swallow up the slender, lifeless body.

"Dear heaven," I whispered. "That was meant to be Evaline."

"There's little doubt." He was already crouching, looking about the floor of the balcony. "No blood here. Either the bullet missed her—"

"It didn't."

I'd seen her jerk sharply on impact. The sight was burned into my memory: her graceful arc through the air, then the sharp, ugly jolt just before she slammed against Pix and fell out of sight.

But Grayling was correct—there was no blood. Not here, anyway. I moved toward the rear of the balcony, where they must have made their exit, but the lighting was so dim that I couldn't determine whether there were any blood spatters there either.

"And this." He stood, a pistol in his hand. "On the floor."

"It was his."

"Yes." He examined it in the low light and made a thoughtful noise. I itched to do the same, but he spoke before I could offer. "I'm certain you have other things on your mind, but I'd appreciate your opinions on the crime scene, Miss Holmes." His voice was grim as he looked out at the ballroom below.

I struggled internally with the realization that Evaline and Pix were gone—quite possibly together—and then made the decision to follow Grayling. "Of course."

Sergeant Blaketon had made himself useful, at least momentarily, by enlisting a group of footmen to keep the crowd away from the poor dead woman. Apparently even he understood that the crime scene must be preserved.

I didn't deign to give him even the barest of glances as I followed Grayling through the crowd and past the sergeant. I'd removed my mask by now and had no concern that Blaketon would dare attempt to put his hands on me. He had a much more pressing problem.

I didn't see Mr. and Mrs. Stoker, but Sir Emmett and Mr. Oligary were both standing nearby with stunned expressions. Their masks, and that of most of the guests, had been removed. However, the dead Marie Antoinette's covering was still in place, obscuring her features. It wasn't clear to me whether the Oligarys had realized it wasn't Evaline who lay there with a bullet hole in her middle. But from the way they murmured in hushed voices and glanced covertly at the Oligarys, it was obvious that the others still believed it was the guest of honor who lay there.

It seemed to me that if they *had* realized it wasn't Evaline, Sir

Emmett and his brother—or at least the younger Oligary—
would be looking for her, especially considering the fact that
someone had publicly attempted to murder her. For there was
simply no way in which Mr. Oligary the younger could have
known it was his fiancée who'd launched herself at her would-be
assassin.

And so instead of watching Grayling as he knelt next to the
body, I observed the Oligary brothers when the inspector
removed Marie Antoinette's mask. I heard the gasp from the
crowd as her identity was revealed, but I was watching Ned
Oligary when it happened.

His face blanched with shock, his eyes widening with what
could only be described as disbelief. But what followed that
initial reaction was not the relief one might feel at learning one's
fiancée hadn't been murdered. Only the dumbfounded-ness
remained—an emotion he seemed to share with his brother, if
the expression on Sir Emmett's face was any indication.

"Who is it?" someone in the crowd whispered, drawing my
attention to the unmasked woman.

Good gad. I smothered my own gasp as I recognized the dead
woman as Princess Lurelia of Betrovia.

What on earth was *she* doing here? That and a hundred other
questions shot through my mind.

Grayling's eyes met mine in a silent entreaty to say nothing—
which was a quite unnecessary request. I certainly wasn't about
to announce to the entire ballroom that what had been a horrific
tragedy had instantly been elevated to an International Incident.

And then I took a closer look at the bullet wound. My breath
caught and I looked at Grayling from across the princess's lifeless body as I eased her flat onto her back once again.

The inspector nodded grimly. He'd seen it too, for the location of the exit wound indicated an astonishing development.

"I'M GOING WITH YOU, Miss Holmes," Grayling said in a tone I'd never heard him use.

It was hard and angry and very, very determined. He would brook no arguments.

I was astute enough to know that the anger wasn't directed at me, although the determination doubtlessly was. "Very well."

Big Ben was striking midnight—the very moment of the planned unmasking—as we climbed aboard his steam-cycle. I didn't ask how he'd had it delivered to the Starlight Palace on such short notice. Perhaps, knowing him, he'd actually parked it there earlier today in case of an emergency. That was the sort of thing I'd expect him to do. After all, he did have a point when he commented (often) that I had a habit of attracting dead bodies. He probably assumed something like this would happen.

Grayling removed his coat and insisted I wear it, since I had nothing else to protect me from the February night. My short flapper-girl shift rode up shamefully high when I swung my booted leg over the cycle, but I refused to dwell on it. Time was of the essence—we'd already been delayed nearly an hour behind Evaline and Pix—and besides, in less than thirty years, women would be doing it every day without batting an eyelash. At least my knees were covered by the supple leather boots. The costume really was no more revealing than wearing breeches and boots, I told myself as I slid my arms around Grayling's waist, then smothered a gasp as the steam-cycle surged forward.

My short hair, free from its headband, tossed and bounced wildly beneath the aviator cap Grayling insisted I wear. The long ropes of beads swung and slid with the force of every turn. Even with Grayling's coat, it was freezing—and I didn't have any sort of hat or even gloves to protect my fingers. I buried my face into his broad, warm back and hoped my nose wouldn't get frostbite.

Our ride was short but harrowing. Although I kept my eyes closed most of the way and shivered in the cold, this was the first time I truly appreciated the speed and maneuverability of the steam-cycle—for it could slip around and between carriages,

Refuse-Agitators, and even buildings and through mews with far more ease and speed than any other vehicle. It could bound onto low walkways, take a corner with tight proximity, and even leap over a small canal. It was a good thing I was sitting behind Grayling, for if I had seen the canal before we were airborne, I would have humiliated myself by screaming.

By the time we reached Fenman's End, I was almost enjoying myself, imagining what it would be like in thirty years to be free to dress and act like this all the time (and wearing a fur coat while doing it). I wondered if women had their own steam-cycles in the future.

And then I sobered quite suddenly, as I was reminded that I only knew about the future because of my friend Dylan—who was missing—but that my closest friend Evaline was in grave danger.

Not from Edison Smith, but from the person—or persons—who'd tried to murder her.

MISS STOKER

Pix's hands shook a little as he turned the cogs for the triple combination that would unlock the door. He still wouldn't look at me.

I didn't want to look at him. But I couldn't help it.

The door opened and he fairly shoved me inside. I just caught myself from falling. With sharp movements, he secured the locks behind us.

Then he spun and came toward me, a wild, dark light in his eyes.

For one mad moment, I thought he meant to embrace me, to kiss me, and my heart leapt—but his hands were rough as he spun me away from him.

"Where?" he said, tearing the frothy over-gown from the back of my shoulder. The mechanical flower brooch fell to the floor as the filmy fabric slid to my waist, exposing the sturdy leather gladiator-like corset and short paneled skirt beneath. "Where is it?"

I didn't have time to be shocked or embarrassed that I was so exposed, for his hands suddenly stopped. "I'll be—" He muttered an oath. "It didn't go through."

His touch gentled there on my back, brushing my shoulder

blade through the corset where the dull pain still radiated—but not as strongly. I felt his fingers as they plucked free the bullet from where it had lodged in the material. And then a featherlight sensation as his fingertips brushed over my bare skin just above the leather.

My flesh prickled where his fingers slid over it. I pulled away and turned to face him, rubbing my arms. My gloves were still intact—one long, one wrist length—but my arms were cold from the winter night and for other reasons. "No, it didn't go through the corset. That's why I wasn't bleeding all over the place. But it still hurt like—like the devil."

"You *fool*," he said, and flung the bullet aside. I heard it clatter onto the table. "What did you think you were doing, Evaline? A few inches higher and you *would* have been shot. A few inches higher and you would have been *dead*."

Though my heart thudded hard in my chest, all the way up into my throat, I shook my head. "I'm a Venator, Pix, remember?"

His expression darkened. "Even a Venator can't survive a bullet to the head. You were damned lucky. *Damned* lucky, Evaline."

He turned away. His fingers trembled as they hung at his sides, clenching and unclenching. "You need to leave now, Evaline."

It took every bit of control to keep myself from laughing crazily at his demand. "Not until I get some answers."

He sighed, his shoulders sagging as if he'd expected me to say that. "Devil take it, Evaline. You need to *go*."

"Look—I just saved your miserable *life*. If I hadn't knocked you out of the way from that bullet, *you'd* have been dead!"

"That was the idea." He said it so casually as he turned back to face me.

The blood drained from my face. Suddenly I felt weak and unsteady. I groped for a chair and sat down. "What are you saying?"

"They wanted me to shoot Marie Antoinette—*you*. I knew the moment I did that—or even attempted to, or appeared to do so—I was next. I had to be. They had to get rid of me. They've been trying for a long time."

"They put that—that battery device on you. To control you. That's how it happened." I had to believe it. My eyes burned and I blinked rapidly. "They were controlling you the whole time you were up there. Like Lord Cosgrove-Pitt."

He shook his head. "No, Evaline. I was never under their control. Not fully. Not the way you think."

"I don't understand."

Please help me to understand.

"I fought it. I was able to battle against their attempts to use that device because I knew what they were trying to do. I was prepared for it; I could fight it. But mostly, it was because what they wanted me to do was *impossible* for me to do. It was *impossible*. Do you understand?"

I nodded slowly. I thought I did. And the very idea made my eyes burn even more. "But I saw you take the device away, from the back of your neck. It was attached to you."

"Theatrics." His smile was crooked. "All of tonight was merely theatrics. The device wasn't working. Not the way they thought it did."

"But you did it. You shot—me. Marie Antoinette." *Me.*

"Do you think for one minute I actually thought that girl was you?" The intensity in his gaze made my lungs clog. "Of course I knew it wasn't you."

"How?"

He tilted his head, compressed his lips, then looked away, shaking his head. "Do you not know your own countryman Shakespeare?"

I exhaled—confused, upset, hot and cold and shaky. And frustrated. Couldn't the man ever answer a direct question? "Shakespeare? I don't know what you're talking about, Pix."

"*Edison.* The charade is over. My name is Edison. Use it."

"Fine. *Edison.* So you didn't think you were shooting at me. But you were shooting at Marie Antoinette. And now some innocent woman is probably *dead.* And everyone *saw you do it.*"

He looked at me with cold, distant eyes. "I see. Very well, then, *luv.* I suppose we have nothing else to talk about."

He turned and, without another word, strode to the door.

"Where are you going?" I demanded, blinking rapidly.

Why was *he* mad? Why was *he* angry?

I was the one who'd almost been murdered. *I* was the one who'd kissed a murderer. I should be the one who was angry and confused and sharp and *I should be the one* storming out of the room.

"I've got to get back there—"

The door rattled a little, and it wasn't because he was touching it. He hadn't gotten there yet.

We exchanged glances, and both of us moved at the same time—toward the other; instinctively, we created a united front, each jockeying to be the one in front of the other. I had my dagger in hand when the door swung open.

MISS STOKER

- THE FASHION ASSISTANT'S BRILLIANCE REVEALED -

When Mina strode into the hideaway like she owned it, I didn't know whether to be relieved or upset.

But I didn't have the chance to react, for Grayling was right behind her, and I knew that meant trouble. I stood in front of Pix—Edison—almost as if to protect him (though I have no idea why I thought he *deserved* my protection). But he shoved me aside to meet Grayling face to face.

Before I could intervene, Mina rushed over to me. "Evaline, are you quite all right? You were shot!"

"I'm fine. The bullet didn't go through."

"But that isn't possible!" She started murmuring about trajectories and force and propulsion as she spun me around to examine the back of my corset. Apparently, she didn't believe that I knew I hadn't been shot.

But that was when I realized I was still only half-dressed, with my filmy Greek gown caught at my waist. I pulled it up, and Mina assisted me to refasten it as she probed the bullet hole in the corset Madam Trouxeau's assistant had fashioned for me.

"Fascinating. I've never seen this type of material before. It actually *stopped* the bullet. It's not really leather, or else it's some sort of leather that's been specially reinforced... Good gad, is that *chain mail* woven inside it? And with panels made from metal—"

Grayling and Edison had been speaking in low, insistent voices, and I pulled away from Mina to interrupt them.

"I suppose you're going to arrest him again," I said to Grayling.

The inspector gave me a look. "No, Miss Stoker, I don't believe I'll be arresting Edison Smith tonight. Or ever."

"I don't understand." I goggled at the two of them, then Mina joined the conversation.

"Of course he's not going to arrest Pix, Evaline. Didn't you hear anything I told you previously? Pix—er, Edison Smith was in protective custody because he was being framed for the murder of Hiram Bartholomew. And the real murderer has been trying to find him and silence him for months—"

"Years," Edison said quietly. "It's been years. Two and a half, to be exact." He wasn't looking at me. "I've not had my true identity for over two years."

"All right." I was so confused. "But tonight—"

"Yes, I have *many* questions about tonight, Mr. Smith," Mina said. "Once you removed the controlling battery device, you were cognizant of your own desires and had control of your own will again, correct? But up until that time, were you *aware* of what you were doing? What they had—uh—scripted you to do? Or when you removed the device, did you—well, rather, find yourself coming out of a trancelike or dreamlike state? I find all of this very interesting—"

"Mina," Grayling said. "Perhaps we can wait to discuss the finer points of the battery devices later, for Smith tells me there's little time to waste."

"For what?"

"They won't expect me to go back there," Edison said. Still not looking at me. "Not when I've just recently escaped. I've got to get—"

"But how did you escape? They must have had you under

their control—at least physically; locked or confined or other-wise indisposed—the entire time you were there," Mina interjected.

"There was a—a chambermaid," Edison said, averting his eyes. He glanced at Grayling. "Daisy. She was...very helpful to me."

Daisy. Who would name someone after a stinky, boring flower?

I immediately despised the woman. But of course I didn't show it.

"That was very nice of her," I said brightly. "To help you."

Mina looked at me strangely and opened her mouth to speak, but Grayling interrupted. "I have my steam-cycle. It'll get us across the city in less than twenty minutes. Are you certain they won't be returning tonight?"

"They intended to leave tomorrow after dark," Edison said. "But then again, things didn't go as they planned this evening, did they? They could return at any time."

"No, things didn't go as planned." Mina looked at me. "And yet some things did. Perhaps you don't know. Or you either, Mr. Smith. Princess Lurelia is dead. She was dressed as Marie Antoinette."

"What?" I struggled to make sense of it. "Lurelia was in my costume? At my ball? But how? Why?"

"The Ankh, of course," Mina said sharply. "Haven't you put it together yet, Evaline? It all makes sense now. You were the intended victim, of course, originally. You were meant to die at your own masquerade ball—but at the last minute, you, unbe-knownst to everyone, changed your costume. Somehow the Ankh discovered this and enticed Lurelia to attend as Marie Antoinette. That is precisely the sort of thing Lurelia would find exciting and adventurous—do you recall how much she enjoyed dressing as a man when we went to Bridge & Stokes? And we've known for certain she was with the Ankh for months now, since she was at The Carnelian Crow."

"But I thought she was the Ankh's partner," I said, trying to follow all of this. "Why would the Ankh want to kill her?"

Mina opened her mouth to reply, then closed it. She seemed, for once, not to have a ready answer.

Grayling spoke before she could decide to continue. "Quite simply, most likely the Ankh was finished with her—and you, Miss Stoker, by making a last-minute change to your costume— and not telling anyone about it, including Mrs. Stoker and definitely not your fiancé, made it simple for the Ankh to substitute Lurelia so she could be eliminated."

"The Ankh sent the Sekhmet costume to Mrs. Scott-Rondeau," I told Mina, grateful that I had at least something to add to the conversation besides a question. "She'd already made certain Mrs. Scott-Rondeau's costume was ruined so she'd have to wear the Sekhmet costume. She must know someone who works at Mrs. Glimmerston's."

"It's certainly something the Ankh is quite capable of doing —making a swift and excellent, if you'll pardon me for saying so, adjustment to her plans and taking advantage of the situation in order to have someone else take care of her dirty work."

"In this case, murdering Edison Smith," I said dryly. "But who shot *me*? I mean, me for real, not the person dressed as me. And who was shooting at Pi—Edison?"

"Do you mean you haven't figure it out yet, Evaline?" Mina's arch look made me want to strangle her. "It's quite obvious—"

Grayling must have recognized the light in my eyes, because he stepped between us. "We really haven't the time to discuss this now. We— Where the *devil* did he go?"

Mina and I spun as one. "He's gone. He *left*," I said, cursing in a very unladylike manner (inside my head). "We stood here talking about theories and clues and plot—"

"The word *clue* was never mentioned, Evaline," Mina snapped, but she was on my trail to the door. "Nor was theory or—"

"Miss *Holmes*." Grayling's voice was desperate. "Please."

"But where are we going?" I demanded. "Where were they keeping Pix?"

"Why, Evaline, Cosgrove Terrace, of course. Surely you figured that—"

"Not the Oligary Building?" Grayling stopped. "Are you quite certain, Miss Holmes?"

"The Oligary Building?" I looked between them. "Why would you— Are you saying Mr. Oligary is involved?"

Then it all seemed to explode in my mind. "The black airship. Cosgrove Terrace—Sir Emmett was there. Blooming fish, *how could I not have seen it?*"

"That's quite correct, Evaline," said Mina—and I wasn't certain whether she was referring to the fact that I was correct, or that I'd been so blind.

"Sir Emmett and the Ankh. Of course. He and Lady Isabella have known each other for years! I should have put it together before. She practically told me..." I trailed off as Mina gave me a horrified look, her eyes bugging out as she looked at Grayling.

"Whatever is the matter, Miss Holmes?" he asked.

"I...well..."

"Did you think I was unaware of the identity of the Ankh?" he said with a sigh of exasperation. "What sort of an imbecile do you think I am?"

"I..."

"Bloody hell, Mina." His frustration would have been amusing had the moment not been so tense. "Can we cease the nattering and be on our way?"

"But where are we going?" I demanded.

"Evaline, you should know better than anyone else. Where is the airship moored? Who has the battery devices? Where would there be a *chambermaid* to assist Pix? Cosgrove Terrace, of course."

"Very well," Grayling said. "I hope you're correct, Miss Holmes."

"I'm always—"

"You weren't right about the Ankh and the airship being connected," I reminded her as we rushed into the tunnel below Fenman's End. "You said they weren't."

"But we can't fit all three of us onto your steam-cycle," Mina said loudly—as if to drown me out. "Evaline will have to go on her own—"

"Evaline certainly will *not*—we will have to make us fit," Grayling growled.

And neither Mina nor I said another word after that.

Bilbo glanced up as we burst into the pub. He sighed, shaking his head, and went back to spitting on the counter and polishing it as we rushed past him.

Moments later, we were outside. I was a little surprised when Grayling hurried over to a pile of rusted-out metal, but moments later, it had expanded into the sleek steam-cycle I remembered from the single time I'd been on it.

He insisted that Mina climb on the front, and he handed her an aviator cap with goggles. Then he turned to me. "Climb on behind me and hold on tight. Wear this." He handed another cap to me.

I had no idea how I was going to get it on over my high fountain of hair. "All right—"

"Miss Stoker, there's a point of information I feel you need to have before—er—before we proceed."

There was something so serious in his voice that I stopped breathing. "What is it?"

"Tonight—at the ball, on the balcony. Edison's gun was not only not fired, but it wasn't even loaded. I examined it myself. There was no possible way he could have shot Marie Antoinette —or anyone."

MISS HOLMES

- INTO THE DEN OF THE LIONESS -

Cosgrove Terrace loomed behind tall stone walls, its mourning banners of black giving it an even more forbidding appearance than merely the shadows of night.

"How did you get in the last time?" I demanded of Evaline, whose demeanor had turned unaccountably quiet and sedate. Perhaps the breakneck steam-cycle ride had frightened her into submission. "Did you go over the walls?"

"The gates opened and I just walked in."

In a bold disregard for propriety, she'd discarded the shimmery over-gown from her costume and was clad only in a sort of Street Fashion Combined with Roman Gladiator attire, with tall boots. The sight of her brought to mind the Amazon women of legend. Although Evaline isn't tall or muscular as I picture those legends to be, she carries herself like one. That night, her garb was perfect for a female warrior.

I'd never seen her look so suited for her vocation as a vampire hunter. The intense expression on her face added to the potency of her appearance.

"But this time I'll go over the wall—"

"This way," Grayling said in his matter-of-fact manner, then started off into the shadows along the west wall of the property.

Moments later, he was demonstrating how helpful it was that his extended family tree included Lord Cosgrove-Pitt, for he brought us to a secret entrance in the stone wall. I started to ask how he'd known to slip behind the wall fountain that burbled charmingly (in the summer; of course it was frozen now) to find a hidden door, but decided it was best to keep conversation to a minimum.

It was short work for the three of us to get inside and sneak from shadow to shadow toward the house. Despite the sheen of white from the snow on the ground, there were enough trees, hedges, benches, statues, and arbors to provide cover for us.

The house itself was dark but for two palely lit windows— one on the ground floor near the front of the east side (servants, most likely), and one on the top, third floor, at the back. I kept my attention on that window, for it faced us as we made our progress across the grounds, and I was watching for any evidence of a figure outlined in the light, peering down at us.

I admit that at that point in the evening, despite my ratiocinations and observations, theories and conclusions, I had only a suspicion of what we might find inside and what Edison Smith's purpose was in coming back here. There was unfinished business that couldn't wait, and I suspected it had to do with the enigmatic zeppelin.

Obviously, Lady Isabella and Sir Emmett had been planning to use the airship for their escape—to where, I wasn't certain, although I had a strong suspicion about that as well—tomorrow.

But I didn't know, at that early stage, why Edison had been desperate to come back here tonight when we could have brought Scotland Yard here tomorrow to stop the fugitives.

At last we were at the wall of the house itself, and as I crept along with Grayling and Evaline (behind them, for obvious reasons), I was struck by a sudden fear.

What if I *was* wrong?

What if Edison had gone to Oligary Tower instead? What if we were here, and missing our opportunity to help him in whatever endeavor he was undertaking?

For surely, as clever and slippery and dangerous as he was, even Pix wasn't a match for two...or three (I wasn't certain about the third one yet) villainous masterminds.

Grayling, who I must admit had been with me—and perhaps even ahead of me, although I sincerely doubt it—every step of the way during this entire debacle had expected Pix to go to Oligary Tower.

If he was correct and I was...under the wrong impression... then the worst could come to pass: war with Betrovia. At the very least.

Thus, as we inched our way along the foundation of the house (to what end, I didn't know; I was merely following the two adventurers—or, at least, the adventurer and the relative of the Cosgrove-Pitts), my stomach tied itself into tight, ugly knots.

I couldn't afford to be wrong. Not tonight.

And then I saw it. On the ground near the servants' door.

A daisy.

I smiled. I'd been correct. Of course.

I didn't need to point out the sign to the others; Grayling and Evaline had already given their separate indications that they'd recognized it themselves.

The door, as one would expect from such a blatant signature, was unlatched and unguarded.

We slipped inside, three shadows. I closed the door carefully behind us, and we listened.

Nothing. Nothing but the soft *sssshhhhh* of steam impelling the mechanics of the house to do their business. Nothing more.

If we hadn't seen the fresh daisy sitting in the crusty snow, I might have thought we were wrong. Everything was so still. Surely no one was here.

But, thanks to Evaline, we knew where we had to go: up.

Up to the roof, where the airship was, I surmised, still moored.

I allowed Grayling to lead the way only because he was obviously more familiar with the layout of the house. Evaline followed me, and I paused several times to silently ask her whether she sensed any UnDead.

She either didn't see my signal, or ignored me each time I did so. But I noticed she had a stake in one hand and a dagger in the other.

Grayling took us up the main staircases instead of the servants' stairs, a decision I applauded silently. There was only one resident of the house and numerous servants, and so avoiding the servants' halls and steps was an obvious choice.

At last, we reached the highest point of the house and a door that would open into what had to be the last set of stairs—a stretch that could only lead to the attic or the roof.

Grayling reached for the latch just as Evaline came to sharp attention behind me. Her eyes widened and she spun, stake raised.

"Good evening, Miss Stoker. Miss Holmes...and...Ambrose? Is that you? I confess I'd expected someone else, but what a pleasant surprise nonetheless."

The speaker was, obviously, Lady Isabella. She'd come from one of the chambers on the same corridor. She was flanked by four UnDead—fangs gleaming, eyes burning, long-nailed hands curling—as well as two substantial mortal beings that I recognized as Bastet and Amunet from her Society of Sekhmet days.

"Please," the Ankh said smoothly, and showed us the wicked-looking steam-stream shooter she held. "Don't let me stop you now. Go on." She gestured to the stairs that led to the roof. "We'll be right behind you."

MISS STOKER

- IN WHICH THE JOURNEY BEGINS -

I was furious with myself.

Four vampires, creeping up on us without me knowing until it was too late? How was that possible? For now, the back of my neck was as cold as if a clump of snow sat on it.

"Oh, darling Evaline, no worries," Lady Isabella said in a soothing voice. It was as if she read my mind. "We were waiting for you—just inside that chamber there. Its walls are lined in lead, which, as I'd anticipated, kept you from sensing the presence of the UnDead." She gestured for me to precede her up the steps. "You passed the initial test quite handily when I invited you for tea earlier this week."

Ugh. So that was why! Blast it. She'd completely taken me in with her sad, lonely persona and her compliments. Well, she hadn't completely taken me in. I'd suspected she was up to something. I just didn't know what.

But she hadn't lied. Her reason for inviting me to tea *had* had to do with the UnDead.

We reached the top step and found ourselves not on the roof but in what could only be described as a laboratory. However, I could tell that it only took up part of that floor. I expected one of the side doors would open to the flat roof where the airship was moored.

The workshop was similar to her other ones in The Carnelian Crow and underground near the old monastery, with chairs and wires and other implements that probably drew blood and would make me ill and lightheaded if I saw them in action. I suppressed a shudder. There were no other people in the room.

Not even Pix.

My stomach knotted. Was he even here? Had he arrived yet? Had he gone somewhere else?

Had he simply fled London, now that he was free?

No. I didn't believe that for a minute. If he wasn't already here, he was on his way.

Unless he'd gone to Oligary Tower...

I still hadn't had the chance to absorb what I'd learned back in Pix's hideout. Sir Emmett Oligary and Lady Cosgrove-Pitt were in this—whatever *this* was—together?

And what about Ned? I didn't even want to consider whether he was involved in it, whether he knew about it. I felt ill.

"You're going to need to leave that stake and all of your weapons right here, Evaline. And you as well, Mina. Ambrose, I'm sorry to say that since you've taken up with these two young women, I've had to reconsider your position as my favorite nephew by marriage. Fortunately, I was able to convince Belmont to make certain changes to his will to reflect that adjustment before he, tragically, passed on. Otherwise, perhaps, you'd be living in a much nicer neighborhood than you do." She gave a genteel laugh but held the steam-stream gun pointed at us.

"Now. Disarm yourselves. Or I'll use this." Her eyes glinted coldly, and I dropped my stake and dagger onto the table she indicated. "All of them, Evaline. I'll be confirming that you are completely unarmed. And it won't be pleasant."

At that moment, all I felt was anger. Pure, deep, boiling fury. About so many things—including my own stupidity, and Edison's as well. I didn't care whether the villainess put her hands on me, or even whether one of her goons did either. I was spoiling for a fight.

While she watched, I pulled another blade from one of my boots. There was a slender vial of salted holy water tucked into the center of the high knot of my hair, and I left that one there, but withdrew another one from a tiny pocket on the side of my corset.

"That's all of it."

Lady Isabella looked at me. "I don't believe you."

I spread my hands, fingers tickling the air, and gestured to my person. "Take a look, then. It's not as if I have a long, flowing gown to hide anything in."

"In which to hide anything," I heard Mina murmur.

Really?

"Very well, then. Ambrose. You as well. And Mina, of course."

She watched as my companions dropped their weapons on the table.

We had just finished doing so when the door to the chamber opened and Sir Emmett Oligary strode in.

"Oh my," he said when he saw us. He'd removed whatever costume he'd been wearing at the ball (I never did see it) and was wearing normal clothing. "I didn't expect you quite so soon. In fact, I didn't expect you to get here before we left."

Lady Isabella gave him a look that reminded me of Mina when she was annoyed. "I told you they weren't to be underestimated, Emmett. Why do you think I was so insistent that Ned marry the girl? We need to keep a close eye on them—at the very least."

I stiffened. "What do you mean, *you* insisted?"

She looked at me with those glittering silvery eyes. "While I find you delightful, resourceful, and quite unique—in all of the best ways, of course—I'm afraid neither Emmett nor Ned fully appreciate your finer qualities, Evaline. It was only due to

Emmett's influence on Ned—that is to say, his restriction of his purse strings—that we convinced Ned to marry you. I've tried to convince Emmett of the necessity having your activities restricted—or at least under my watchful eye—but apparently until now he's been unconvinced of how dangerous you really are to our plans."

I was both relieved and insulted (relieved that if I got out of this alive, I wouldn't have to marry Ned—or break his heart, and insulted for, as Mina would say, obvious reasons).

"Your plan to assassinate the princess of Betrovia?" I said, making a wild guess, since I had no idea what the plans that I was supposedly obstructing actually were.

Lady Isabella smiled. "Princess Lurelia's untimely death at the hand of the same man who murdered Hiram Bartholomew—and who *meant* to murder Ned Oligary's fiancée—was merely a side benefit to our ultimate intentions. By the by, Evaline, I must compliment you on your deviousness in changing your costume at the last minute—and keeping it quite under wraps. Poor Emmett and Ned had no idea until Marie Antoinette was unmasked. I, of course, learned that you hadn't come for your costume at Mrs. Glimmerston's and seized the opportunity to make a slight adjustment to the evening's festivities."

"As I deduced," said Mina. "And then you further warned us with the messages to 'be ready.'"

Isabella lifted her brows. "Hmm. No, in fact I did not warn you with such a message. I assumed you'd already be prepared for any eventuality—as you always have been, with the exception of the very first night we made our acquaintance."

If Mina was taken aback by the fact that she'd been *wrong* about something, she didn't let on. "You speak of the night Evaline and I attended your Society of Sekhmet meeting beneath the Thames. The night of the Roses Ball, when we were investigating the scarab affair. When we returned to Cosgrove Terrace after making our escape, you appeared to still be present at the festivities. But that person was a stand-in for you, wasn't it? You made certain to be seen from the balcony at your home —far enough away that the deception wouldn't be recognized."

The villainess smiled. "Of course. I confess I was rather shocked you saw through that sleight of hand so easily and were able to discern the true identity of the Ankh so soon after our first meeting. But that fact only instilled the great admiration and respect I have for you both. It has been a delight sparring with the two of you. Is it any wonder I wished for you to join me in my work instead of combating it?"

"But if it wasn't to kill Lurelia, what is this great plan?" I demanded.

"Ah, Evaline. Always the decisive action and rarely the mind work. But that is why the two of you are so well suited to be partners, and I must commend Irene for suggesting it.

"As for my plan? It's really quite simple, although it has been far too long in the planning and execution. I loathe England and all of its restrictions and societal etiquette, and its suppression of the feminine person, from everything to the very clothing we wear, to the inability to have a say in our government by voting, to even being able to own our own property—well, you've heard my speech before, haven't you?

"And while I despise England, I love Betrovia and everything about it. I *should* have been on the Betrovian throne, married to the mindless prat of a man who will be king—but instead, my father insisted I wed Belmont. And so here I was exiled, to this cold, gray, suppressive place with unpalatable food ruled by a woman—and yet is *not* ruled by her at all. Instead, England shows herself as the antithesis of a nation with a female leader by allowing her to be a figurehead only, and controlling and restricting the females herein."

"And so your plan is to disrupt the relationship between England and Betrovia so decisively that it eventually escalates to war," Mina said. "And presumably, you've planned this so that the ultimate benefit will be you on the throne of Betrovia."

I gawked at her. Where on *earth* had she come up with that

ridiculous deduction? I glanced at Grayling, but he didn't seem surprised or amused.

"Succinctly put, Mina—but without all of the details of the nuances and finessing that are involved in such a long-term, complicated plot. Of which, of course, there are many. And, of course, I couldn't have done it without the assistance—the funds, the resources, the criminal enterprise—of my dear Emmett." Lady Isabella turned a smile on Sir Emmett that was so blinding in its warmth that it appeared simpering. "He's quite conniving and cunning beneath all of his gentility—and philanthropy."

He looked down at her, reaching over to tuck a wayward curl behind her ear. "Indeed, Bella—we make an impressive and devious duo, do we not?"

Beneath Sir Emmett's head, Lady Isabella slyly slid her gaze back to Mina and me and allowed us to see the truth laughing in her eyes.

Good gad, she was playing Emmett Oligary for a fool as well!

"If you wanted me under your control," I said, diverting the conversation back to the topic I was most interested in, "why didn't you just trap me when I came to tea? Or when I was here the other night—instead of conking me on the head and leaving me in the street?"

"Conking you on the head?" Isabella was obviously taken by surprise. "You were here the other night?"

"That wasn't you?" I was confused. It had been a woman who'd murmured, *Brilliantly done, Evaline*, after I'd staked the vampire—and before she coshed me—hadn't it?

"I'm afraid not. Does this mean you have another villainous admirer I'm not aware of?" Her laugh tinkled out as she gazed up at Sir Emmett, continuing the charade of being besotted with him.

The poor man had no idea what he was up against.

And it served him right, as far as I was concerned. I glanced at Grayling again to see if he was aware of this even more subtle example of Isabella's chicanery, but I couldn't tell.

"To answer your question, of course I wouldn't simply kidnap you, Evaline. You'd have been missed and it wouldn't have taken Mina long to find you. No, I thought it best to have you married in a public event and then ensconced in the household where you could be watched carefully, restricted, and controlled—physically or by pharmaceutical means—as needed." She smiled coolly, and I was reminded of the fact that she was a cold-blooded murderer.

"And as for you, Mina, darling...fortunately, you'd been quite busy chasing simplistic, mind-numbing cases that my dear Irene kept putting in your way—I really ought to write her a thank-you letter for that once we're gone. She has no idea how much I appreciate her unwitting assistance. Nonetheless, despite her attempts, I knew such things wouldn't occupy your facile mind for long, and so I decided the best way to keep you busy was to have you permanently out of the way."

"The ultimate plan was for me to hang for the murder of Frederick Boggs," Mina said in the same cool tone as Isabella. "But having me incarcerated at least for a time, while you made your escape, was helpful as well."

"Of course. And, in fact, once you were in prison, I would have certainly given you one last opportunity to ally yourself with me—and if you'd accepted my offer, I would have liberated you from Newgate—"

"As you did Edison Smith," Mina said.

Lady Isabelle's mouth tightened at the reminder of what she could only consider a failure. "Yes. That slippery sneak nearly ruined everything tonight. If Emmett here hadn't come prepared, it all would have been for naught."

"So it was Emmett, then," Mina said. "I wondered. His lute was an excellent way to hide a rifle until he was required to use it. The only problem is that the angle of the bullet wound—particularly the exit wound—indicates that Lurelia was shot not by someone high up on the balcony, but someone at closer proximity—and at the same elevation she was."

"Oh dear," Isabella said, her eyes wide. "I hadn't quite thought of that, Emmett. But surely there's no way to trace the actual bullet to the firearm that fired it."

"On the contrary," Mina said grandly. "It's becoming quite the accepted practice to match the markings on the bullet to the interior of the gun's barrel and match them." She trailed off in her pompous explanation when she recognized the same glint in Isabella's eye that I saw. She quickly changed the course of her speech. "I've known for some time that Mr. Smith wasn't who murdered Mr. Bartholomew, but why did you find it necessary to do so, Sir Emmett?"

"Couldn't have electricity come to England, is all," Sir Emmett replied. "Hiram wanted to make a partnership with the Edison Company and I didn't—it would ruin our monopoly on the manufacture of steam-works products, of course. The day we were to sign the agreement with Smith, I confronted Hiram in his office and told him I wouldn't do it. He argued with me, and I did what I had to do—pushed him into the electrical mechanism we'd been testing out. He pulled me with him, the bas—the fool, and I barely got away from being electrofied myself. I told everyone I tried to save him and that was how I injured my leg."

"And then you made it look as if Edison Smith had actually done the deed—and that he'd killed Mr. Bartholomew for trying to back out of the deal."

"I knew Smith was coming for the signing of the contract, and so I waited for him to arrive and find Hiram—and while he was there at the scene, I appeared and then called for several other witnesses. They arrived to find me attempting to subdue him while disengaging Hiram from the electrical wires. Smith slipped away in the confusion, the rotter, but it was very simple to accuse him of doing the deed. And no one present would say anything different."

"Including Frederick Boggs," Mina said. "That was why you

had to have him killed, wasn't it? I found a photograph of him in your office with Mr. Bartholomew, and—and some other people. You were afraid Edison Smith was going to tell the truth of what happened, and now that Boggs had returned to London after being abroad for several years—you probably even arranged for him to be gone, didn't you?—you knew that Boggs could contradict your story."

"No one would believe it of Emmett Oligary," Sir Emmett said, speaking of himself. "I'm so beloved by this city for everything I've done for it. New Vauxhall Gardens is quite a success, isn't it? I could go out on the street and drive a team of horses to trample over a man and they'd look the other way. Why do you think I've just recently been knighted? And now that Bella has her secret weapon—"

"That will be the crowning glory, so to speak, of everything," Isabella said. "If only you had gotten to the Theophanine Chess Table sooner, Mina." She smiled at us with feigned regret, then turned back to Sir Emmett and said, "Surely they're finished loading by now. I suppose we'd best take these two young ladies with us. They could come in handy."

He grunted in reply, but Isabella hadn't waited for his agreement. She gave a sharp gesture to her goons, who'd been waiting silently during this entire conversation.

The next thing I knew, we'd each been taken in hand—one of the UnDead grabbed my arms and jerked them behind me, and the mortals took Mina and Grayling—and we were being ushered to the side door.

I was right. The door opened onto a flat area of the roof, which was completely enclosed by tall walls that hid the airship from the ground and nearby windows.

The zeppelin seemed much smaller now that I was up close to it, and it took me a moment to realize the balloon part of it was only partially deflated. That made sense, because it would be too big not to be noticed on the roof during the day. I could hear a low, roaring *boooshhh* and realized the balloon was in the process of being inflated. The gondola or cabin or whatever the part below the balloon was called, where I guessed the driver rode, was as large as a train car.

Isabella's goons forced us up two steps into one end of the cabin on the bottom level. We found ourselves in something like a cargo hold. It was dark, windowless, and low-ceilinged. There were shapes and lumps cluttering the space.

"Make yourselves comfortable," she said. "On second thought...don't."

And the next thing I knew, something crashed into the back of my head. Everything went dark.

❦

When I awoke, the first thing I realized was that we were moving. It was hardly noticeable, but I could feel the slightest wafting movement, almost as if we were floating on still water.

The second thing I realized was that my wrists and ankles were tied.

And third, I sensed that the UnDead were still in the proximity. But not, thankfully, nearby.

I pulled experimentally on the bonds around my wrists, which were helpfully tied in front so that my hands rested in my lap. The ties were rope, and there was some give, but not enough to work free.

"Mina? Grayling?"

I heard a moaning sort of mumble that could only be Mina.

Grayling, however, responded. "Miss Stoker. I'm over he—"

"Blooming fish, Grayling, you can call me Evaline. I think we've moved beyond that sort of propriety."

I thought I heard a snort of laughter, but it was drowned out by my partner, who'd apparently found her voice. "It's the same number of syllables, Evaline, so it really doesn't make it any more efficient—"

"Then he can call me Evvie. Or Ev. All right?" I was speaking from between clenched teeth.

I supposed the fact that Mina was being her normal exacting self meant that she was uninjured. But she was the most annoying person I had ever met. I couldn't understand why Grayling was so besotted with her.

Well, I suppose I could. She *was* fantastic and interesting and kind in her own way—and if she would just keep her mouth shut, it would be so much easier to like her.

"I don't suppose anyone has an illuminator," I said.

"Of course I do," Mina replied at the same time as Grayling said, "I do."

I should have known. Two cognoggins.

"But it's tucked inside the sole of my boot," Mina said. "I need some assistance getting to it." She was making a grunting noise, and I guessed she was trying to move around.

There was a quiet click, then a soft light flared in the space, illuminating Grayling's face.

"Oh, excellent, Inspector," she said as he set the tiny device on the floor with his bound hands. It cast a small but useful glow. "Where did you have that hi—"

"Never mind, Mina. You can discuss secret pockets later. Let's get free. I don't suppose you have a hidden knife, do you, Grayling?"

"That I don't—"

"You do, Evaline."

"No, I gave them all up."

"I didn't see you remove the one in your corset."

"In my corset?"

I could hear her sigh in the dim light. "There's a slender blade right in the back where the center busk would be—I would surmise there is one down the front as well. It's very cleverly obscured by the decoration on the corset. I thought it was a metal stay, but it's got a small handle fastened by one of the leatherwork details. Whoever designed it was quite brilliant. One moment. I'll...get...it."

She grunted some more, scooting across the floor to me. Grayling helpfully lifted the light, and I remained still as Mina maneuvered her way behind me. "It's much easier to scuttle about in a short skirt," she commented. "Not so much fabric to get caught up. And no petticoats!"

I tried not to think about my blundering friend using bound hands to remove a knife from the tight stays so near my bare skin and vital organs. She grunted and strained, and I could feel my corset shift and jolt as she worked it loose. I winced and held my breath, imagining what would happen if she unexpectedly jerked the blade free.

With a triumphant exclamation, she pulled it loose—much like I imagined the boy Arthur had pulled Excalibur free from the stone—and without stabbing me.

I slid around to face her, once again a little nervous about her using the blade to cut me loose, but she did so without actually cutting *me*. (There was a point when she stabbed the soft flesh on the side of my thumb deep enough to draw a pinprick of blood, but that was all.) Thus, I was unscathed when the ropes fell away.

My fingers tingled as the feeling rushed back into them, and I immediately sucked at the drops of blood on my thumb so the UnDead wouldn't sense it. I cut Mina free, and then Grayling.

We all stood, rubbing our wrists, and looked around our prison for the first time. Grayling held the illuminator high enough for us to see the crates that littered the area. There was a slender, barely discernible square of light that outlined the single door. I saw a broom and a pile of rags or blankets in the corner and several lumps that were chairs or other furniture, covered in sheets. On the far side, I noticed a round handle in the floor. Probably a door for unloading the cargo. Other than that, the hold was dark and empty.

"They're definitely not coming back to London," Mina said,

surveying the crates and swathed furniture. "They've brought everything they need. Edison was correct."

"Speaking of Edison, where is he?" My insides were a bundle of nerves.

"More importantly, where are *we*?"

"Most certainly airborne," Grayling said. "Though not for very long, I don't believe."

Just then, we heard something at the door. The pinprick of light around it narrowed to darkness, then began to widen.

Grayling snapped off his illuminator, and we fell into silence as the door eased open to reveal a shadowy figure who slipped quickly inside.

"Well, speak of the devil," Mina said as he closed the door behind him.

It was, indeed, Edison Smith.

MISS HOLMES

~ OUR HEROES IN ACTION ~

H ow'd you get here?"

That was Evaline, of course. The woman was brilliant at asking the most obvious, mundane questions.

"Stowed away." He flipped on an illuminator of his own. "I
watched them bring you on board, then sneaked on when they
were getting ready to launch. You should know they left explo-
sives at Cosgrove Terrace." This last was directed at Grayling.
"For total destruction."

"Good gad. I hope the servants get out safely," the inspector
replied grimly.

"They have no intention of coming back, then," I said. "Or
letting us do so."

"But does anyone have any idea where we are *going*?" Evaline
again.

"Betrovia," Edison, Grayling, and I replied in unison.

Evaline stared at us, then blinked. "Oh." She frowned, and I
could almost hear her wondering how we'd all known and she
hadn't.

The answer was, of course, elementary. But even I didn't have
the energy to get into the details at the moment.

"Is Daisy here too?" Evaline asked in a snippy voice.

We all looked at her, and she glowered back as if she were the one who was offended.

"No." Edison's response was curt. "But there are two other prisoners. We should free them first."

"First? And then what?" Evaline demanded. She was obviously not thinking clearly. Or something else was bothering her.

I suppose if I knew my fiancée and/or his brother had tried to arrange for someone to kill me, I'd be a tad upset as well. Especially if the man I— Well, obviously she cared for Edison Smith a great deal; far more than she should have done, in my opinion, considering the entire time she'd known him he'd been skirting the law and acting in a criminal manner—and since he'd shown up talking about some far-too-helpful chambermaid, I suppose I could understand why she might be a bit disgruntled.

"And then we take over the airship and bring it back to London," Grayling said far more patiently than I would have done. "And Isabella and Oligary go to prison."

"Where are the others?" Evaline said as she rose and walked across the small room. Her fountain of hair, long, dark, curling, swung with alacrity from where it was moored at the top of her head. She picked up the broom I'd noticed earlier and snapped it into three pieces as if it were a twig, then handed Grayling and me each a sharp-pointed piece. "I assume *you're* already armed." She glanced at Edison.

I caught a glint of longing in his eyes when they were focused on Evaline in her gladiator attire, but it was quickly masked into a bland expression. "Yes. I managed to acquire some of the weapons she made you leave behind."

He offered her the dagger that was larger and more dangerous than the one I'd liberated from her corset, then gave Grayling his pistol and me a dagger as well. (I had no idea what I would do with a dagger—or a stake, for that matter. I preferred a steam-stream gun because I could defend myself from a healthy distance.)

Evaline nodded in thanks. "You know where the prisoners are? How are they guarded? Anything else?"

"Only that they are in another room where they've been doing their work. Two guards. Easily disposed of." He flashed a smile. "As long as we're quiet."

"What sort of work—"

But Evaline interrupted me. "Let's go. We should stay together." She had taken control like the warrior she was, and at that moment I was ashamed by my earlier snide thoughts.

Her forte was action, protection, battle. Mine was ratiocination, observation, and memory. Neither of us were competent in the professions of the other. But there was no one else I'd rather be with if I had to face an UnDead, or any other sort of murderous villain.

With all of the revelations tonight—sudden and unexpected to her, at least—she could only be confused and unsettled. I reached over and touched her hand, squeezing it with my fingers. Evaline looked at me in surprise, then away suddenly, and I'm certain I saw her blinking rapidly as if to subdue some strong emotional response.

"Let's go, then," Edison said. He too seemed more than willing to trust his safety—and possibly more—to Evaline. "Evaline and I in front. You two follow."

"Don't trip," Evaline muttered to me as she passed by. "And don't talk."

I was too annoyed to make a retort of the nature that I was obviously aware of the necessity to be as quiet as possible.

The area directly outside the cargo hold was filled with helium tanks and engines. I could see the inner workings of the airship's external fins and the other machinery thanks to small gaslights that illuminated the space and also enabled me to keep watch for anything that might catch my toe or heel. Once again, I was grateful that my short, scandalous attire left nothing to be tripped over or snagged.

Grayling remained close by my side (as much to catch me if I stumbled as any other reason, I'm certain) as we followed Edison and then Evaline.

The engine room was long and narrow, and I surmised that it ran along the entire bottom of the gondola-like cabin, with only the cargo hold taking up space down here as well. The passengers would be on an upper, more comfortable level.

Thus when Edison led us to a metal spiral staircase midway down the length of the room, I was prepared. It was a challenge to keep my boots from clanging on the steps, but I believe I managed to ascend without making any sounds that would be heard over the rather loud hum of the engines.

My pulse had increased and my breathing became shallower, for when we emerged from the ceiling hatch at the top of the steps, who knew what would be waiting for us?

To my relief, Edison and then Evaline disappeared without hesitation up into the second level. Grayling followed and offered a hand to assist me through. We were in a dim, narrow channel that stretched a short distance in both directions. At each end, there was a door that I assumed led to traveling chambers, and also the driver's lookout.

Edison led us to the door on the left leg of the hall. I noticed Evaline had touched the back of her neck, and I concluded she was feeling the presence of UnDead nearby. I gripped my stake more tightly and concentrated on keeping my footsteps soundless (difficult when one is trouncing on a metal floor in heavy, thick-soled boots).

Edison and Evaline exchanged looks when they reached the door, then he murmured something to Grayling. I was too far back to hear, but I adjusted my grip on the stake and dagger, preparing myself to use them.

To my surprise, Edison knocked on the door.

When it slid open, I caught a glimpse of a pale blond man an instant before Evaline's arm arced through the doorway and plunged the stake into his chest.

Grayling ducked around her and surged into the chamber,

followed by Edison and myself. Although I had my weapon at the ready, by the time I stepped inside and (prudently) closed the door behind me, the air was filled with the dank smell of UnDead ash and the battle, if you permit the use of the term, was done.

I estimated the Ankh was now at least two vampires the less, and in addition, one of her mortal goons was unconscious on the floor. Tucking his pistol away, Grayling stepped over the man and went about securing our new captive's limbs. The constant rumbling of the engines below would have helped to muffle the brief but violent sounds, and I was optimistic we hadn't been noticed.

Assured that the chamber was clear of danger and that no alarm had been raised, I turned my attention to the corner of the room where Edison and Evaline had gone to attend to the prisoners, who, one must assume, had been quite startled by the unexpected entrance of myself and my partners.

Rushing over to add my assurances to the people we had come to save, I finally caught sight of one of them—a female's white-blond hair. Another step closer to see around Edison and I recognized her, jolting in shock.

"Miss Babbage!" I forgot to keep my voice down, which earned me a violent *hush* from Evaline. "What are you..." Then my voice simply stopped. I felt my lips move, my mouth wanted to speak, but nothing would come out.

Dylan. The person next to her was Dylan Eckhert.

I could hardly believe my eyes as I walked toward him. It was a little bit of a *déjà vu* from the night at The Carnelian Crow, but not quite as much of a shock as it had been then when I thought he was living in the year 2016.

"I wondered where you'd gotten off to," I managed to say as many pieces of yet another puzzle clunked into place. "Presumably the Ankh—I mean to say, Lady Isabella—lured you away or otherwise kidnapped you."

"That's right. She tricked me—sent a message that was supposedly from you. I should have known better than to fall for it!" He had a black eye and a purpling bruise on his jaw. There were healing cuts on his chin and on his hand as well. Clearly he hadn't gone quietly.

I was also concerned that Dylan's handsome face was drawn and much thinner than before, but was relieved that his eyes displayed pleasure at seeing me. "I knew you'd find me."

"Well, I didn't precisely find you," I said, still confused and dumbfounded. "Edison's really the one..."

"Right, but I'm sure you would have found me—me and Olympia—eventually."

"Of course." Even as I winced at his grammatical abuse, I felt ashamed that I hadn't even realized he was missing until yesterday.

"Well, *this* certainly complicates things," Olympia Babbage interjected with a frown. She looked up from the sheaf of papers on which she'd been scribbling, her eyes wide and owllike. "*Four* more people? Dylan, I don't see how—"

"We'll figure it out," he said, and patted her arm. "We were just about to execute our escape plan by distracting the guards—"

"And now you're here, and that causes *immense* complications. I had all of the computations—" All at once, Miss Babbage tilted her head sharply as if she'd just discerned something only she could hear, then quietly hummed and began to scratch more numbers on her paper. She held her hand out blindly, and Dylan automatically slipped a clean paper into it and she scribbled some more.

The several times I'd met her before, I'd found the grand-daughter of Charles Babbage—the man who had designed the Analytic Machine—to be a resourceful yet terribly frustrating and exasperating individual.

The young woman had an inventor's brain, and that meant

that she was usually deep inside her thoughts building whatever it was she was constructing instead of attending to things going on around her. One could hardly have a conversation with Miss Babbage, for she always seemed more interested in what was on her paper or what she was calculating than what was being said to her. It was no surprise the Ankh had managed to kidnap *her*.

"Edison—er, Pix—said you're doing some work," I said to Dylan.

At this reminder, his face turned sober and even frightened as he glanced around nervously. "Yes, she's been making us work on a special project. She kidnapped us specially for it. She needed the guy from the future and the inventor. It's because of the secrets inside the Theophanine Chess Set, Mina. Olympia and I have been trying to hold her off, but I don't know how long she'll fall for it. She'll need more people, and a bigger space —so that's why they're leaving—but—"

I was trying to follow his rambling, choppy speech, but it was the mention of the chess set that caught and held my attention. "She has you working on the secret from the chess set?"

"Yes. It's something horrible. You have no idea how bad it is," Dylan said. "That's why she needed me, because—"

All at once, the airship gave a strange, great shudder, and everyone hushed, looking around alertly.

"It worked!" Olympia crowed. "I told you it would." She rustled to her feet, skirt, petticoats, and papers, and began to stuff things into a satchel. In the hall outside, I could hear shouts and the sounds of people running and clanging up metal stairs. *Up?* To the balloon, of course.

"What's going on?" I said, listening for an indication that the others—presumably Isabella and Oligary—were coming in here.

"But it's too soon!" Dylan exclaimed to Olympia. He rushed over to her, looking stricken. "I don't have the sc—"

"I don't know what happened," she said, peering at her papers as if they held the answer. "I intended to make certain we were out of London—"

Dylan was looking out a window. "But we're not! Look—there's the Oligary Building, and we're heading for the Tower of London. And the river is right there!"

"The wind might have changed—or it must be the extra persons." She looked at the four of us (Evaline, Edison, Grayling, and me) balefully. "I didn't expect the additional ballast."

"*What* is going on?" I demanded again.

"The balloon," Edison said. He'd been looking out of a different curtained window. "It's sprung a leak." His voice was remarkably calm.

Not so Evaline's. "A *leak*? How does an airship *spring a leak*?" She looked considerably worried, which made me feel considerably worried.

"I suspect it had some assistance," Grayling said, looking at Olympia and Dylan. "It's a slow leak, fortunately. I assume you punctured it somehow."

"I calculated it to the last kilogram—the weight, the location of the puncture, the size of the hole, even the timing—and of course I took into account the wind direction," Olympia said, pulling a pencil from the bundle of moonbeam hair that sagged at the back of her head. "Something went wrong. It's not supposed to deflate this rapidly." She frowned at us again, then returned to scratching her computations. "It's the extra ballast, I'm sure of it. We haven't time to lose," Olympia said, glancing up as if she were ordering milk for her tea. "Stage Two, Dylan. *Now.*"

"But I have to get the scarab," he cried. "I can't get back home without it."

The zeppelin gave another great shudder, and I'm not too proud to admit that my heart surged into my throat. I stifled a scream.

Good gad...were we going to our death in a deflating airship? The entire room was listing to the left. One of the chairs began to slide.

"What's Stage Two?" I was perspiring quite heavily beneath my flapper dress, and no one seemed to be *doing* anything.

More heavy footsteps down the hall, more shouts. Clomping feet above us, presumably attempting to repair the slowly deflating zeppelin. I expected someone to burst into the room at any moment, but they went on by. I heard a feminine shout of rage from beyond, and recognized it as Isabella.

Clearly she was otherwise occupied. If only I could instill the same urgency in my own companions!

"What is Stage Two?" I demanded a second time.

"The escape hatch, of course, and its life-basket." Olympia said, shoving more papers and items into her satchel. She glanced at me as if I were dimwitted.

"In the engine room," Edison added.

"My, you have been busy, haven't you?" Evaline said with an edge to her voice.

"Always locate the exits first," Edison replied.

"Where's the scarab?" Grayling asked as he moved to the door. He peeked out, then turned back to us. "Dylan, do you know where it is?"

"She keeps it with her things. I don't know exactly where."

I was almost certain there were tears of frustration and fear glistening in Dylan's eyes. He had cause, for if the zeppelin went down—with or without us—the scarab would be lost and he would be stuck in my time forever.

"How much time do we have, Miss Babbage?" Grayling asked.

"Time? Until what?" She peered owlishly at him.

"Until it's too late to evacuate the ship." He, too, was remarkably calm. I wanted to scream.

Miss Babbage glanced out the window, raised her eyes vacantly (presumably to calculate), and said, "Twenty minutes. No...mmm...seventeen."

"Let's go." Grayling was grim but determined. He looked at his timepiece. "Eckhert."

"I'm going with you," I was shocked to hear myself say.

"Don't be ridiculous," said Evaline as Grayling and Dylan both roared similar negative responses.

I merely lifted my nose and sailed toward the door.

That was one way to get people moving.

MISS STOKER

- SEVENTEEN SECONDS -

Blast *it!* Trust Mina Holmes to choose the most inopportune time to become rash and impetuous.

I glanced at Edison, whose sober expression gave me little hope.

"We'll secure the escape hatch. Inspector, you have less than ten minutes to return," said Edison, taking Miss Babbage by the arm and leading her through the door even as she perused her papers.

Leaving me to fend for myself.

Not that I needed any assistance.

Or wanted any.

Especially from *him*.

He'd always had a fondness for Olympia Babbage. He'd called *her* "luv" too.

When we eased into the small, hallway-like vestibule, I saw the backsides of Mina, Grayling, and Dylan rushing in the opposite direction down the hallway, which was slanted upward due to the deflating balloon. They were heading to the chamber at the other end of the cabin. Above, I could hear the sounds of shouts and the pounding of running feet.

I felt only the barest of chills at the back of my neck, since

I'd disposed of the two UnDead in this room. That meant the other two vampires were no imminent threat.

As we were climbing down the metal staircase back into the engine room, the zeppelin gave a violent shudder. The entire cabin fell sharply on one end, causing us to lose our footing and swing off the steps. In the distance, I heard shouts and a scream. I held on to the stair railing, but Miss Babbage lost her grip. She was flung off the steps and landed on the floor several feet below.

"Olympia!" Edison shouted, crawling down the tilted steps as quickly as he could. "Are you hurt?" He sounded very concerned.

The cabin had not righted itself, nor, I thought, would it. The floor remained sharply angled. The cargo hold was on the lower end. Things were getting desperate.

I released the metal railing and let myself drop the rest of the way. I landed on top of a helium tank next to Olympia as she said, "I'm all right but for my wrist." Her voice was taut with pain, and her eyes were a little glassy.

Edison and I helped her to stand on the inclining floor, and, using the mechanics and helium tanks for leverage, we began to make our way to the opposite end of the cabin—the higher end. It was like climbing a hill, and every so often we'd slide back a little bit because the floor was smooth metal and there was little for our shoes to grip. As we made our way up, the cabin continued to tilt more and more sharply.

I wondered if Miss Babbage wanted to adjust her seventeen seconds estimate. I decided not to ask.

I spotted the escape hatch as soon as we got closer. It was obvious: a round door on the low part of the wall right where it curved into the floor. The handle was a slender cross of metal. The opening would be wide enough for a person to crawl through easily.

But what was on the other side?

"Stay here and hold on," Edison told Miss Babbage, who was cradling her wrist. Her face was tight with pain and effort. He tucked her and the satchel she still wore against a large tank so she wouldn't slip back to the other end of the room. Then he looked at me. "Ready?"

"Yes."

We moved together to the hatch and began to unscrew the cover. It would have been a simple task had we not had the threat of sliding halfway across the room at any moment. I had to loop an arm around a nearby pipe while using my other hand to help turn the metal handle. I propped a foot against the edge of a tank, which helped me remain upright.

The door gave a little pop as it came free, and Edison and I let it roll away down into the cabin. It clunked wildly as it banged into tanks, pipes, and other machinery.

I hoped we didn't need to put it back.

We both pulled up at the same time to look outside. It was *cold*.

The rush of wind took my breath—and so did the sight of black nothingness.

We were suspended in the air, and there was nothing but darkness to be seen this high. In the distance, I could make out the faintest glow of dawn. Because we were on the raised end of the cabin, I wouldn't be able to see down to the ground unless I pulled myself out and looked way over.

Edison made an emphatic sound, but I began to climb out anyway. Carefully holding on to the edges of the opening, I eased my head and then torso out. My hips settled uncomfortably on the edge of the hatch opening as I leveraged myself up with a palm on the edge and the other hand gripping a metal bar on the exterior. Tiny chips of ice splattered over my face and hands.

From inside, Edison held me by the ankles with painfully tight fingers—and then the airship balked again.

This time, the jolt was so violent that we felt a sudden dip in the entire vessel as it spun and fell. I gripped the opening tighter as I bounced against the edge. The freezing, damp air rushed over my face as we swung downward. Edison held on to my legs as the vessel bumped sharply, twisting on some violent breeze, then somehow leveled out...still afloat on a significantly deflated balloon.

My heart was in my throat. My face was damp but my lungs finally started to work again.

I'd seen enough.

But before I even tried to disengage, Edison yanked hard on my ankles and I tumbled back inside. His face was white, his lips nearly colorless. "Evaline."

I shook my head, unable to speak for a moment. He said my name again, then made a move to climb out himself. I pulled him back. There was no need for both of us to risk ourselves.

I found my voice. "There's a small life-basket, like she said— the size of a hot air balloon gondola. It's got a parachute. It'll hold the six of us at least. The trick will be getting to it."

"How close are we?"

I knew he meant to the ground, not to the escape basket, but I don't think either of us wanted to speak the obvious. "Still above the rooftops."

We were. But sinking. Especially the bottom end of the cabin. I wondered what would happen if it bumped into a building or a tree.

Would that stop our free fall? Would it catch on fire? Would it smash into pieces?

"The mooring rope is tangled, so we can't draw the basket close enough to board. I'll have to climb out and bring it closer."

"No," he said. "I'll do it—"

I shook my head. "*No*. I'm stronger, Edison, *and I'm lighter.*" I held his gaze and saw the struggle in his eyes as he argued internally. "And I—I heal faster."

He swore, a short, vulgar oath—and he didn't even try to stifle it. "But you're not *immortal*, dammit. *Evaline.* You keep acting like you're *bloody immortal.*"

I just looked at him, and for a moment the world—everything around us—stopped. My breath clogged. His eyes were so beautiful. I had so many things I needed to tell him.

"I—" I bit off whatever I was going to say—I didn't even want to think about what would have come out of my mouth.

I looked away, forcing the moment to shatter. "Someone has to do it, and I'm the best person. We're running out of time, Edison."

He gave me a look—so dark, so intense, so *angry*—then nodded curtly. "We need a rope. You're not going out there without a bloody rope around your waist."

It was easier said than done, but we managed it. Miss Babbage wasn't much help; she was still redoing calculations to see whether we had five or four minutes before we crashed to our death.

But she did have a length of rope in her satchel, and that was helpful. Edison tied it around my waist, checked the knot thrice, then secured it to the most stable metal piece we could find. And he checked that too. Then he handed me his coat and I shrugged into it gratefully.

And then it was time for me to go.

I avoided looking at him again. I just couldn't. I started out of the hatch door, this time backward so I could sit on the edge and reach up.

My palms were a little slick as I lifted myself by the handles around the outside of the escape hatch. The rim of the opening cut into the backs of my legs as I eased out farther. Avoiding tangling in the rope that tied me to safety, I pulled to my feet and, turning carefully, stood on the outside of the hatch.

Then I just stood there. It was the most frightening and exhilarating moment I'd ever experienced. The night surrounded me and the injured airship. The air was crisp and frigid, and sleet pelted me. Edison's long coat flapped about my knees. I was alone in the sky, and it was infinite, vast, *wild*.

A subtle jolt from the airship reminded me I had no time to waste. And I had to take into account the possibility of slipping due to the ice, so I moved carefully along the outside of the cabin using the large metal bolts that held it together as footholds, and mooring ropes or and metal rods as handles.

Above me was the spectator rail where passengers could stand outside and view the scenery—a place I'd not even known existed until now.

Tonight, the view would have been that of a silent and dark landscape. Above the rail, I could hear the eerie whistling sound of air rushing through the puncture in the balloon. The ugly flapping sort of noise its deflated self made was an unpleasant reminder of our predicament.

Far below—but not far enough—were fuzzy lights that were street lamps. I could make out the shapes of some roofs and chimneys as they appeared on the horizon we were slipping toward. It glowed with the promise of dawn. I wondered if I'd live to see it.

Now that I had my bearings, I turned to my task. The basket wasn't too far away, and I realized that it was probably positioned so that it could be raised to the spectator deck if necessary. The mooring rope would draw it to either the hatch I was using, or up to the passenger level.

A sudden gust of wind set the cabin swinging sharply. I smothered a yelp and held on as one foot slipped off the massive bolt-head on which it was perched. The balloon above gave a ripping snort as it expelled a large burp of helium, and we sank even more.

I didn't think about that. I grabbed for the mooring rope and wrapped it around my arm, because my fingers were getting cold and I didn't trust them to hold on. Someone shouted behind me —Edison—and I felt the rope around my waist go taut.

He wanted me back inside, and I was ready to go. I inched back, closing my eyes against the icy wind, moving ever so carefully. My ears, fingers, and legs were frozen and my eyelashes fringed with icicles.

I didn't breathe again until I stepped onto the edge of the

hatch doorway. I passed the mooring rope inside. Someone yanked so hard at the rope around my waist that I lost my balance and tumbled back through the hole, rolling down the incline until I caught myself on an iron bar.

Annoyed by the abrupt movement, I looked up to where I'd fallen inside and saw that Edison and Miss Babbage were no longer the only people there.

"Thank you very much, Evaline, for retrieving the life-basket," said Isabella. She was smiling.

Oh, and she had a gun, of course.

MISS HOLMES

- A SINKING SHIP -

To this day, I do not know what possessed me to barge out of that chamber and lead the way in search of the scarab when we were quite literally falling to our death, but the fact remains that I did.

Despite my boldness, I was wildly relieved that Grayling and Dylan were immediately on my trail. We didn't know where we were going or where we might find the scarab, and in that case, three heads (and sets of eyes and hands) were better than one.

As we started down the short corridor, the airship gave a horrifying shudder, and the next thing I knew, I was tumbling down the hall as the chamber I'd just left *dropped*.

I managed to stifle a shriek as the slightly slanted floor turned into a significant incline. Grayling caught my hand, stopping me from going all the way to the bottom, as he, Dylan, and I used the wall to right ourselves.

I glanced at Dylan hopefully, though I already knew he wouldn't want to turn back and head to the escape hatch. I truly understood, but I wasn't happy about it. I knew the seconds were ticking away, and they would soon turn into the minutes that counted down our doom. (I believe, under the circumstances, I am allowed a bit of dramatic license in telling this tale.)

I pushed those thoughts (and other, even more horrifying ones) from my mind and commenced to making my way *up* the incline of a corridor. At the same time, I expected to see Lady Isabella and Sir Emmett appear at any moment, which would complicate matters even more significantly. Above us were the sounds of panic and running feet. I hoped they would just stay topside, trying to fix the balloon's leak, because for once I wasn't eager to face down the villainess at the moment. I didn't think I could continue my interrogation of her, considering our current imbroglio.

Because Grayling was assisting me, Dylan reached the door to the cabin at the top of the slanted hallway first. He pushed it open with difficulty—trying to balance himself while working against the gravity of the door wanting to stay closed—and finally worked it open enough to slide inside. A moment later, the door opened and was secured when Dylan pushed a chair to hold it against the wall.

Thus I got a clear view inside before Grayling and I, doing a sort of creeping half-crawl, arrived at the entrance. The furnishings had tumbled and slid down against the wall where the door was, explaining why it had been so difficult for Dylan to open it. Chairs, tables, clothing, rugs, and other items, like utensils, plates, and food, were strewn about.

But the thing that caught my attention, the vision that made my heart surge into my throat, was the view.

This chamber was at the end of the cabin, and there were two massive windows that joined together in a pointed seam at what was obviously the front of the airship.

There was black night stretching as far as I could see on both sides and forward. It was broad and dark and unrelieved *infinity*.

I could see nothing below.

It was terrifying.

For a moment, I couldn't breathe. I certainly couldn't move.

It was worse than being in a dark place underground, this...*frontier* of *nothing* that stretched out in front of us like an inky desert or the black pool of the sea. Because we were tilted so high up, the ground was out of sight from our vantage point. There was nothing to see but cloudless, moonless night sky.

I didn't know whether it was good or bad that I couldn't see the proximity of the ground.

"Mina." Grayling's quiet voice snapped me out of my paralysis.

"Yes," I replied without thinking, and began to look around the disarrayed chamber. "Right."

The pilot's stall must be directly above us—and the noises I could hear on the ceiling supported this conclusion.

"When is the last time you saw it?" I asked Dylan, who'd already begun rummaging through a tipped desk drawer.

"It was in a box. A small wooden box—it had Egyptian symbols on it. Mahogany. She showed it to me. She said once I was finished with the project, she'd send me back to my time and destroy the scarab so I couldn't tell anyone about it." He didn't even look up; his voice was taut and desperate.

Instead of jumping into a search that might yield nothing but a waste of time we didn't have, I looked around the chamber, thinking of Isabella. Thinking *like* her.

Grayling, who didn't have my extensive acquaintanceship with his distant relative (at least insofar as her villainous tendencies), had forced open a trunk by employing some tool attached to his person. He was scattering the chest's contents all over the floor.

I surveyed the chamber, my attention settling on the overturned desk, the upset trunk, and a spilled satchel and eliminating each one in turn. Then I saw it: crushed up against the wall in the corner, beneath a chair that had tumbled onto it—a small wooden box. As I'd suspected. Isabella wouldn't have packed away something that important. She would have had it out where she could see it or ensure its safety at any moment.

It was probably on a table or the desk when everything scattered.

I surged toward the corner where the mahogany box was wedged just as the zeppelin shivered wildly, then banked suddenly to the left. I was in mid-step, and this sudden movement threw me into a heap as furnishings slid into me, slamming me against the wall.

Something heavy caught me in the back of the head, and a wooden chair smashed my hand against the floor. I cried out, struggling valiantly to my feet even as pain roared through my body. I could be hurt later.

"There," I cried, flexing the fingers of my crushed hand. "The box is over there! Hurry, Dylan. *Hurry.*"

Grayling helped me up as Dylan dove for the box. The airship hadn't ceased its wild shuddering, and I knew we were out of time.

"We have to go," Grayling said, echoing my thoughts, dragging me toward the door. "*Now,* Eckhert."

Dylan, who'd played a sport called hockey back in his time, slid down the floor as if he were on ice skates to the box where it was wedged, and, using a broom, he smacked the box out from beneath the pile of furniture.

It skittered across the room, and I managed to snatch it up with my uninjured hand as Grayling pushed me out of the chamber.

Going back was far easier than going up, and we ran so fast down the increasing incline that I nearly lost my balance and fell on my face. If it weren't for Grayling and Dylan on either side of me, I know I would never have made it to the metal staircase that led to the engine room.

"It's like I'm living in the freaking *Titanic* movie," Dylan huffed—making no sense to me. "But in the sky."

Just as we reached the stairway, a different door opened in the wall. Someone surged through it—several someones.

"Miss Holmes!" exclaimed Sir Emmett. I couldn't tell

whether he was shocked to see me liberated, or simply shocked that I was present on the airship.

It didn't matter, for Grayling reacted immediately, pulling the pistol from his coat and pointing it at Sir Emmett. "Down the stairs, now. We've got to get off this ship before it goes down."

As I'd implied, Sir Emmett wasn't alone. His younger brother Ned was with him, and I felt a pang of remorse for Evaline as he too followed Grayling's instructions to descend the spiral steps. I was certain she'd held out hope that her fiancé wasn't actually involved in the treachery of the Ankh, but any optimism she'd harbored was about to be crushed.

Grayling descended first down the steps—which were now more horizontal than vertical—then trained the pistol up at the Oligary brothers as they followed suit. Dylan held his dagger at the ready and went behind Ned, prepared to shove him down into his brother should either attempt any shenanigans.

I was just getting myself into the strangely situated opening for the steps to the engine room when I felt a presence approaching from behind me.

I looked over and gasped.

It was an UnDead, red glowing eyes and gleaming fangs and all. He did not appear pleased—likely because he'd realized he was being left behind as all the mortals attempted to evacuate the airship.

Hanging on to the metal stair railing halfway through the hole, I fumbled the mahogany box into my other hand as I tried to grab my stake, which I'd stuck in my boot. The small wooden chest slipped from my fingers.

I cried out as it tumbled to the ground in the engine room, bouncing against a helium tank and off into gad knew where.

Someone shouted my name from below, but I was digging around for my stake and had finally grasped its handle. I pulled it free from my boot and swung it up—just as I realized I was holding a *dagger*, not the broken broomstick!

No! A dagger was hardly any use at all. The vampire leered down at me—I had the sense he wasn't fully aware of our predicament, or surely he wouldn't have wasted time making faces, but would have shoved past me to go down to the engine room.

His booted feet were right there next to me on the floor—which, might I remind you, was tilted at a sharp angle—and I suddenly had an idea. I slammed the dagger straight down into his foot as hard as I could.

He shrieked and stumbled back, but his foot was pinned to the ground and he had to tear it free. That gave me enough time to yank the hatch door closed over my head and fasten the metal latch, all the while holding on with one hand.

I considered it a miracle that I managed not only to lock the vampire out, but kept myself from falling down the curling, tipped-over stairs in the process.

I fairly slid the rest of the way down, energized by my success and driven by the desperation to get to the escape hatch in time.

When I reached the ground, I looked around for my companions.

They weren't there.

I spun, suddenly terrified, and that was when I saw them: up (literally, *up* to what was now the top of the engine room) where an opening revealed a circle of night and allowed wind and sleet inside...

All five of my companions were there—but Grayling was no longer holding the Oligarys at gunpoint.

The tables had turned and it appeared that Lady Isabella was now in control once again.

"There's no rush, Mina," she called. "The life-basket will only hold a select few of us."

I began to crawl my way up the incline toward my friends. What else was I going to do? There might be something I could do to help them.

"She's coming with us," Sir Emmett said, surprising me when I realized he was speaking about me.

"Now, Emmett, I'm not certain—" she began.

"*Isabella*. I'm bringing her. Let's go." Sir Emmett's voice was hard and flat, and very different from the simpering man he'd been earlier during my interrogation of the pair of them. He reached down and grabbed my arm, yanking me up the last bit of distance.

"What about her?" Ned said, looking at Evaline. "She can fit as well."

I yanked my arm out of Sir Emmett's grip. My efforts nearly sent me sliding back down the slanted floor, but I grabbed at a metal bracket and held. "I'd rather die than go with you and leave my friends here."

Sir Emmett's eyes flashed, and he swung me up with an arm around my waist. "Be still. You should thank me for saving your bloody life."

As he swung me around, I nearly collided with Isabella. And that was when I saw the pendant she was wearing.

The time-travel scarab.

It was with her the whole time. As I'd suspected, she hadn't locked it away at all.

I had to get it. But how? If I could bump into her...

As if reading my mind, the airship gave a great heave, and there was a sudden loud cracking noise. Someone cried out (it wasn't me, I don't think) and the lot of us were thrown into a great heap.

I slammed into Isabella and felt the hard, round curve of the scarab against me. In the confusion, I closed my fingers around it and yanked it from the chain around her neck.

But my triumph was short-lived, as the zeppelin began to shake and the weight seemed to drop out of the bottom.

Our seventeen minutes were up.

MISS STOKER

- MISS STOKER PROVES WORTHY OF HER VOCATION -

I t was chaos. And noise. Lots of noise.

I already knew we weren't getting into that life-basket. Isabella wouldn't allow it, and quite frankly, I didn't want to be in close proximity to her anyway.

Or to my fiancé.

In fact, Isabella was already scrambling to her feet, her eyes on the escape hatch. She obviously didn't care whether the Oligarys followed her or not.

I made an instant decision. "Let them go!" I grabbed Edison and yanked at Grayling. "We have to go down, back to the cargo hold. There's another hatch."

Fortunately, they both understood immediately, and as Isabella (with her pistol) disappeared into the life-basket, I saw Mina struggling to her feet. She was holding something in her hand. Ned lunged for the escape hatch in Isabella's wake, but Sir Emmett reached for Mina again.

I punched him. Right in the face.

Nothing ever felt so good.

He crashed against the wall, but I didn't wait to see whether he recovered in time to join Isabella and Ned. I was *going*.

Grayling, Edison, and Dylan were already helping Olympia

and Mina down the long, steep incline as quickly as possible. It was nearly as difficult as going up, for it was far too easy to over-balance and fall into something heavy and hard.

I hurried past them, bounding from tank to tank, dodging the pipes and huge clasps that bolted the fixtures to the floor and walls. Someone shouted, but I didn't wait. I had to get to the door.

The zeppelin hadn't ceased shaking, and I was terrified we wouldn't make it in time. I burst into the cargo hold and went immediately to the small loading door in the floor I'd seen earlier.

With one yank, I had the latch undone just as Grayling and Mina stumbled inside.

"I need a rope. A chain. Something."

I was almost afraid to look out through the opening, to see how close we were to crashing, but I did.

My heart stuttered in my chest. The river was right there. Good gad—if we fell in there, we'd die from the cold even before we drowned.

The roofs of buildings were close enough that I could jump onto them—but no one else could and survive. Air-anchors bounced gently on the skyscape ahead of us, moored to the tops of some of the highest buildings.

I had a horrible vision of colliding with one of them. Surely that would cause a spark, and then we'd go up in flames—our zeppelin and the sky-anchor both.

I closed my eyes for a moment, took a deep breath, and got back to work.

Someone thrust a rope into my hand, and there were shouts, arguments, and a lot of jockeying behind me. A moment later, Edison was there, his face grim but determined as he helped me to fasten a second rope to a metal hasp in the wall.

We had two ropes and that was it. Our only chance was to get out and down them—landing who knew where—before the airship crashed into the river. Or worse.

"Evaline. There!" Edison pointed, and I saw a flat roof, obstructed only by a single chimney and without sky-anchors. We were heading toward it—we would either crash into it or scuttle just over the top of it. I estimated we had less than three minutes before we were there.

"That's our landing spot," Grayling said, pushing in to look between us. "And the wind will take us that way. We have to go. I'm the tallest and heaviest. I'll get down and—and try to guide it in that direction. Then help the rest of you." He hesitated, then turned, his eyes searching for Mina. Then he spun and grabbed the rope.

It was a fair distance to the rooftop, and I found myself clutching Edison's hand as Grayling disappeared through the opening. He scuttled down the rope, dangling from the sagging, twisting airship high above the ground.

Mina was behind me, peering over my shoulder, and her fingers were digging painfully into my shoulders. I could feel her breath huffing over my bare neck.

Dylan shoved between us. "I'm tall too." He grabbed the second rope, and, after spinning to plant a kiss on Mina's shocked mouth, he slipped out the hole and slid down the rope.

The roof was approaching, and I gaped as the inspector dragged something from his pocket. A long, slender device suddenly extended from his hand, glinting in the burgeoning dawn.

Grayling somehow hooked the metal device over the edge of a chimney. I could see what he was doing—trying to direct our flight, and to help bring the rooftop closer for us to jump down.

I could have jumped anytime. But I knew that I'd have to be the last one off the airship. It made sense. I was more able to survive anything that went wrong. Plus I was the lightest person.

And Venators made sacrifices.

The zeppelin jolted a little, and I realized that Grayling had somehow used the long, slender device to moor the ship to the chimney. That would keep us from floating past, but it wouldn't stop the vessel from crashing to the ground.

Dylan and Grayling landed on the roof at the same time, jumping the last ten feet. They scrambled to grab the ends of the ropes, and I saw Grayling shouting directions to Dylan.

Miss Babbage was next, but she was in no condition to climb down a rope. Edison looked at me as he straddled the line, easing Miss Babbage into position in front of him.

As they disappeared down the rope, the last thing I saw were his steady, dark eyes looking at me as he helped to save Miss Babbage.

The airship suddenly pitched, throwing Mina and me to the floor.

"Go," I said, feeling a sudden eerie chill at the back of my neck. "Mina, you have to go." I pulled a stake from my boot.

"Evaline, I just want you to know," she said—of course she would be talking as she climbed onto the other rope and began to ease herself out of the opening—"I admire you greatly, and there is no one else I'd ever want to— Good gad!"

She screamed as the UnDead leapt into view—although I'm not sure if she screamed because of that, or because she was suddenly dangling from a rope over a London roof because I'd given her a push.

I had to trust that Grayling and the others would see to her safety, because I was now engaged in battle with an angry vampire.

I thrust the stake toward his chest, but missed and stumbled to the side. An inch closer, and I would have fallen through the door.

Instead, he yanked me to my feet and slammed me against the wall. I hit my head and fell, landing near his feet—one of which was a bloody (literally) mess. I gagged at the sight and averted my eyes as the airship tipped even more acutely. The sudden force sent him off balance and threw me back to the ground.

I had to get out the opening. I didn't even care if I managed to stake the creature.

I crawled across the floor, but a strong hand yanked me back by the ankle, my bare knees and fingers scraping across the floor. I twisted and swung up and out with my weapon, and he blocked my blow with a powerful arm. The strike sent the stake spinning from my hand into the depths of the cargo hold...

And that was when I knew I was going to die.

His eyes burned red as he lunged for me, tearing Edison's coat from my shoulder as my mind slid into a soupy mess. The floor beneath me rumbled and shuddered, but I was hardly aware of it as two sharp fangs plunged into my throat.

I might have cried out; it was probably more of a gurgle than a scream as the blood spewed free, surging into his hot, greedy mouth. I felt the warm rush flowing and my limbs going soft... my eyes closed as the world gave a huge, horrific jolt.

I didn't even have the energy to open them as I felt everything falling.

Or maybe it was just me...falling.

Was this what death was like?

A soft, lulling falling...

"Evaline!"

I twisted my head, turning away from the urgent voice. *No*, I thought. *This is nice. I don't want to wake up.*

"*Evaline!*"

I had no choice but to hear him—someone was lifting me, dragging me away. I didn't like it. I kicked out. I wanted to be lulled.

Then I felt nothing beneath me, and I began to struggle violently—

"Stop!" he shouted, and I nearly tumbled free of his grip. "Stop bloody *fighting*. Evaline."

And then, suddenly, I was airborne.

MISS HOLMES

- THE END OF THE ANKH -

Of course Evaline and Edison (that does have a nice ring to it, doesn't it?) landed safely on the roof.

But that doesn't mean I wasn't watching the failing airship and their acrobatic leap with my heart in my throat, gripping Grayling's arm as if that would somehow make a difference to the result.

But it was close. Very close.

Even now, I occasionally have a dream where things don't work out so well—where Evaline and Edison jump, but land in lifeless heaps on the roof, or where the airship tumbles down behind them, crashing atop all of us waiting on the rooftop—instead of shunting off into the air.

The vessel eventually ended up in the frigid river (as Miss Babbage predicted loudly once she was safely on the rooftop and was able to adjust her infernal computations). No one was injured from an airship's fiery crash. It didn't even catch on fire, landing in the Thames as it did then sinking like a black behemoth into the deep.

However, as we stood, gasping for breath, still terrified and yet energized that all six of us had made it to safety, Dylan grabbed my arm and pointed up.

"There!"

In the dawn-lightening sky, we saw the life-basket with its parachute.

It was bouncing wildly through the air. Something had gone wrong, for the protective canvas that arced above the gondola wasn't stretched properly over whatever ribbing was meant to keep it in shape. The parachute was malfunctioning horribly.

As it tumbled from the sky, wafting and gliding out of control, I could see three figures battling to save themselves. Isabella, Emmett, and Ned.

The basket tipped and swayed due to their desperate actions —or maybe it was just the inevitable result of a damaged para-chute—and finally, in a horrific moment, dumped them all free. Suddenly the trio was plummeting to the earth.

With a gasp, I closed my eyes and buried my face in the object closest to me—Grayling's chest. His arm stole tight around my waist, and I allowed myself to release the pent-up emotions that had wound up so tightly inside. I shuddered, breathing in the comforting scents of lemon and mint and the solidness of his stature. When I pulled away, I'm not ashamed to admit that my face was a little damp. And probably flushed as well.

Mine was not the only countenance that betrayed strong emotions.

Everyone was silent for a long while after that, standing on the roof beneath a dawning sky, shivering from cold and agita-tion. It was quiet for London and I knew it would be the only peace we would have for the next little while once we found our way off this roof.

There were many things to which we must attend, questions to answer, and people to see. Including my father, whom, I presumed, had been called back to London by now.

I had to tamp down my frustration that, with the Ankh now certainly dead—along with her henchmen the Oligarys—I may never have confirmation of some of my conclusions and deductions. Of course, I knew I was correct in them, but there's a matter of personal satisfaction in hearing the villain brag about how clever they are—and having already been clever enough to figure it out on my own.

As we walked off the roof, Dylan came up next to me where I was walking with Grayling and said, "I've got to ask you something, Mina."

"What's that?" I replied, expecting to at last be able to explain all of my conclusions and observations—including how I'd come to possess the time-travel scarab after all. Although I was exhausted, of course I would manage.

"Why are you dressed like a flapper?"

MISS HOLMES

- OF CALCULATIONS & COMPUTATIONS -

T hat was an exceptionally long seventeen minutes," I
said, looking down my nose at Miss Babbage. "On the
airship."

"Sixteen minutes and fifteen seconds," she replied in a tone
that implied she was *correcting* me.

"I *beg* your pardon?" I responded.

"I miscalculated. It was sixteen minutes and fifteen seconds
before the airship actually crashed—"

"But it seemed so much longer," Evaline interrupted. "So
many things happened."

Miss Babbage gave her a quelling look. "One cannot argue
with fact. Or scientific calculations. My timepiece is perfectly
accurate, and it measured sixteen minutes and fifteen seconds
from the time I looked at it until the airship touched the
Thames." And then she went on, *ad nauseam*, about how she'd
done those computations and what factors she'd included, giving
us *far* more information than anyone needed.

I sniffed and adjusted the bustle beneath my seat. I was back
to wearing a froth of petticoats and skirts, along with a street-
fashion corset. While my attire was certainly warmer than the
flapper-girl costume, it wasn't terribly comfortable. However,

when one is called to a meeting at the Parliamentary Offices, one dresses appropriately.

It was later on the same day we'd landed on the roof during our daring escape. The three of us were droopy-eyed and exhausted, and I, for one, was sore in areas I had not even realized could *be* sore. I had numerous scrapes and bruises and a lump at the back of my head. It was difficult to believe so many things had happened since I'd arrived at Evaline's masquerade ball the evening before.

We were seated in a chamber with a large table and a dozen chairs. Evaline had fancifully commented that it brought to mind the Knights of the Round Table, and I couldn't fault her for that comparison, as the arrangement reminded me of the sort of meeting room for an advisory council or planning meeting.

The door to the chamber opened and Dylan came in, along with Miss Adler, Inspector Grayling, and Edison Smith.

I was embarrassingly pleased when Grayling took the seat next to me, but Edison sat as far from Evaline as possible. I noticed it was in a seat where he could easily view her, but she would not be able to see him without turning to look.

Miss Adler came into the room just as we were getting settled, and I noticed her attention went directly to Dylan before sliding over the rest of us. "I'm so relieved you're all safe," she said.

"Presumably there is no longer a need for the 'forthright' conversation you meant for us to have," I said meaningfully to Miss Adler.

She smiled—a little bashfully, I thought—and said, "Despite the events of last evening, there are still some things we should discuss."

"I agree, and the first is an acknowledgement on my part that I was fully aware that you were attempting to keep me otherwise occupied over the last two months with simplistic, plebeian investigations. I didn't object, but rest assured I was aware of your intent. Presumably it was because you feared the Ankh—

Lady Isabella—was about to make her move and that Evaline and I could be caught in the crossfire, so to speak."

"Indeed," Miss Adler replied. "I had become well aware of her fascination—and perhaps even obsession—with you two, and I simply didn't want either of you to be hurt—or worse."

"Or enticed to join her," I added with a castigating look.

"I never thought you would join forces with the Ankh!" Miss Adler said flatly. "Not even once."

I was very pleased to hear the stark vehemence in her voice. "I am relieved to hear that. Thank you for that confidence."

"However, I would never have approached you and Evaline a year ago about the clockwork scarab problem had I known Isabella Cosgrove-Pitt was the culprit. She was—as you've no doubt realized—a cunning, evil woman."

I confess I felt a little strange about Miss Adler's use of the word "evil" to describe the Ankh. Of course she was a murderous woman with the bodies of more than five individuals (that I knew of) on her conscience—but at the same time, I could almost empathize with her opinions about our great nation and the way our female gender is treated. She could understand Evaline's disgust at (nearly) being forced to marry against her will —and Lurelia's as well.

But I suppose anyone who blithely kills others, no matter what the reasoning, must be regarded as evil.

"Indeed." I was about to continue speaking when I recognized that Miss Adler was attempting to formulate her next sentence. I sensed there was something important she wanted— or needed—to tell us, and so I waited.

"There's something you should know, Mina. And Evaline," she added, although her next words told me why my partner had been a sort of afterthought. "I know that you were quite unsettled when Dylan returned and didn't contact you."

I felt Grayling shift next to me, and my cheeks warmed with a touch of heat, but I merely nodded. There are times when silence is the most appropriate response.

"It was mostly because of my encouragement that he didn't contact you. Partly because we were working—undercover is the word, yes?" she asked, glancing at him. He nodded, and I noticed that he seemed to have some great emotion stamped on his face.

A shocking, unexpected thought erupted in my mind, and I stiffened. I had a sense I knew what she was about to say—and I didn't know how I was going to react when she did.

Miss Adler and Dylan? No, no, no. I simply couldn't countenance it. He was twenty-one, and she had to be at least in her late thirties...

I remained silent, steeling myself for her announcement. Rest assured, my mixed emotions weren't because I was envious of any sort of relationship Dylan might have with Miss Adler—or any other woman—but because it seemed like such a foreign, strange concept.

"But it was also because I wanted to spend as much time with him as possible," Miss Adler went on, giving me a slightly sick feeling. "Because...well...because Dylan is my great-great-grandson."

I stared at her as the words penetrated my brain and their meaning settled there.

"Your great-great-grandson?" Evaline exclaimed. "Why, that's wonderful!"

"We thought so as well, once we figured it out," Miss Adler replied. "It was only by chance that we did."

But Evaline was looking at her closely now. "But you don't have any children. So...well, does that mean you're...er...going to be in a family way?"

Miss Adler gave her a funny smile. "As a matter of fact...it may happen sooner than you think."

I looked over to see that Dylan was beaming, and I realized I was as well. I was genuinely happy for both of them—and for myself, for now I better understood (and excused) his lapse in judgment by not contacting me upon his return.

"That is happy news," I said to Dylan once the felicitations from my companions became less effusive. "But that reminds me of one of the important questions to which I must have an answer. You indicated that Isabella specifically wanted you—the man from the future—and Miss Babbage to work on a project. She called it her secret weapon, I believe, and referenced the Theophanine Chess Table. Am I to surmise that this information she obtained from the chess table is, in fact, related to some future event?"

I heard Evaline's sound of interest and surprise. "Are you saying that whatever was in the chess table was from the future? How is that possible?"

"Presumably the same way Dylan himself has traveled to and from the future now several times," I replied coolly. "The scarab is of Egyptian origin, is it not? My suspicion is that someone from that era—at least one, perhaps more—have used this scarab"—I placed it on the table—"to travel. And they brought something back with them."

Dylan was looking at me, nodding and smiling as I spoke. "That's what she said—Isabella. The thing was, she didn't know what it was—what the documents were, what they meant. And I'm guessing no one else over the centuries knew what it was either—it wouldn't have made any sense to them at the time, because it's all about the theory of relativity and quantum physics." Then he sobered. "It's the plans for the worst, most destructive weapon in the history of the world. It's called a nuclear bomb."

"But she knew you were from the future, and she thought you'd be able to make this bomb?" Evaline said.

Dylan laughed. "Well, *I* couldn't make it. But Olympia has the smarts to do it—although she'd need some help. The thing was, the Ankh—Isabella—needed me to tell her what it was, and to help sort of translate the information. And she wanted me to work with Olympia to make it."

"What does this bomb do?" Grayling asked.

Dylan's expression turned grim. "It could flatten all of

London. And then destroy miles and miles around it, and even beyond that, it sort of...it affects people and animals. It's devastating."

"And this bomb—has it ever been used?"

Dylan nodded. "Twice. In 1945. It was horrible. And it will never, hopefully, be used again. And," he added quickly, "the plans—the documents—all went down with the airship. So no one else here will get them."

"Until 1945, at least," Edison said quietly.

Dylan sighed. "Yeah."

Just then, the door opened and my father strode in.

I automatically sat up straighter. He glanced at me. "Alvermina. You look well. Good afternoon, Miss Adler. Inspector Grayling. Mr. Smith, is it?" His gaze—sharp and intelligent as always—surveyed our other companions. He gave them each a businesslike nod then took a seat in the chair at the spot of the round table that would have been noon on a timepiece.

"Anything that is discussed in this chamber cannot be repeated, implied, hinted at, or otherwise confirmed after today's meeting. Is that understood?"

We all nodded, and he continued, "We are waiting for one more individual."

At that, the door opened and in walked a woman.

"Daisy?"

"Siri!"

"*Mother?*"

MISS HOLMES

- A FINAL, SHOCKING ENTRANCE -

I t was, indeed, my maternal parent, Desirée Holmes, who'd joined us. I could hardly breathe, and my thoughts collapsed into a wild jumble.

To my great mortification, tears sprang to my eyes as I struggled to control my emotions.

Then she made it worse, for instead of simply taking a seat and allowing me to come to terms with the fact that not only had my mother returned, but she had apparently been a *chambermaid at Cosgrove Terrace* (for how long? why? had she been there the several times I was there? *why?*) she came directly to me. I looked up at her through blurry vision, still without words or coherent thoughts.

"*Mina*," she said in a strange, tight voice, and, taking my hands, drew me to my feet.

Sir Mycroft made a harrumphing sound, and she turned to him. "I'll have a moment with my daughter, Myc." Her tone was firm and even arrogant. "Your bloody speech can wait."

Mother embraced me with tight arms and whispered in my ear, "I'm so very sorry, Mina. I hope you can forgive me for all of the secrecy—for abandoning you with hardly a word. And I'm very proud of you—of everything you've accomplished in relation to this case. *Thank you*."

Although I didn't understand at that moment why she was thanking me, I held her tightly and tried in vain to keep from dripping tears all over the shoulder of her fine shirtwaist. "I'm glad you've returned," I said, pulling back at last. Someone stuffed a handkerchief into my hand—Grayling—and I took it gratefully.

Mother leaned closer again. "Your short hair is beautiful. And so very unique and bold. Just like my daughter."

And drat it—I had to dab my eyes again with the handkerchief.

"If we can begin?" Sir Mycroft said.

But Mother ignored him and went to Evaline to embrace her as well. "Well done," she said, clasping her hands and looking down at her student. "*Brilliantly done*. Victoria Gardella could have done no better."

Brilliantly done? Evaline and I exchanged glances as we realized that was exactly what someone had said to her before coshing her on the head outside of Cosgrove Terrace. It had been my mother who'd done so, not Isabella!

Mother turned to Miss Adler, who'd been watching all of this. The tip of Miss Adler's nose was slightly pink from the suppression of her own emotions, but her eyes were dark and filled with censure.

"Desirée. I had no idea you were here. The whole time? If only I had *known*..." Despite her angry words and tone, she embraced my mother tightly. When I saw Miss Adler's dark head next to my mother's taller chestnut one, it reminded me, suddenly, of my partnership with Evaline. "You should have told me, Desirée." Her voice was bitter.

"I'm so sorry, Irene. He didn't want to take the chance, but I—I should have found a way to tell you. You deserved to know."

I knew—and I suspect everyone in the chamber did as well—that the "he" she referred to was Sir Mycroft.

As she and Miss Adler parted, Mother displayed her ungloved hands. They were no longer the fine hands of a lady, but showed evidence of her position as a chambermaid. "It was a difficult two years," she said with a wry smile. Then, instead of allowing my father to speak, she went on.

At first, I confess, I hardly listened, for I was filling up my eyes with the woman I hadn't seen for so long. Despite her work-worn hands, she appeared every inch a lady. Her dark honey-colored hair was coiffed in a complicated twist settled high at the back of her head with a few random wisps to frame her lovely face. Her eyes were the same changeable light brown-to-green as mine, but her nose was much smaller and more delicate. She wore a beautiful day dress of mustard yellow with a subtle paisley pattern in navy. The sleeves, hems, and gathers were trimmed in orange and navy bric-a-brac and white lace.

As always, she carried herself with the elegance and grace I've forever admired and never quite achieved.

"The first thing you should know, Mina, Evaline, Inspector—is it Grayling?—Mr. Smith, and Mr.—er— Eckhert?—is that Sir Emmett is not the philanthropist and pleasant man most Londoners believe he is. Or was, I should say. From my understanding, he, his brother, and Isabella are all quite deceased."

She glanced at my father, who nodded. And then, of course, he picked up the thread. "Yes. They're dead. And a twenty-year project has now come to an end."

"Twenty years?" I repeated. "Since you knew Isabella and Emmett Oligary in Paris?"

Mother inclined her head. "Yes—nearly as long. We were friends first, before— Well, it was during that time that I first began to work, along with Sir Mycroft, with the Home Office. I have...certain skills, as some of you are aware...that are valuable to the Crown and this country for obvious reasons. That is part of the reason Irene approached the two of you"—she smiled warmly at Evaline and me—"to ask for your assistance, originally with the scarab problem, which of course I was aware of but could do nothing about, as I was working in an assumed position under an assumed name. Undercover, as you say," she added, looking at Dylan.

He nodded.

Mother continued. "Suffice to say that whilst Irene has done her duty to her own nation as well as lending her assistance to the Crown here in England, I've also been involved. That is how Sir Mycroft and I came to be Mr. and Mrs. Holmes." She gave my father a brief smile, then turned to me. There was something in her eyes that told me there was more to the story. And a silent assurance that she would tell me later.

"To put it bluntly, Oligary built his business illegally, and continued to grow it via illegal means," said my father. "Smuggling, counterfeiting money, and other illicit trades that need not be described for—er—the delicate ears of young—"

"Oh, bloody hell, Myc, the girls have nearly died over the last year—not to mention seen and experienced more than most men. I would venture to say their ears—and the rest of them—can hardly be described as *delicate*."

I stifled a delighted gasp at my mother's blunt words and exchanged looks with Evaline, who appeared ready to burst into applause at any moment. Grayling shifted next to me, and I glanced at him to see his mouth quirking in a smile of what I hoped was agreement and not shock.

Sir Mycroft gave Mother a look of censure, but continued. "Without going into details, we—the Home Office and our Imperial Security Department—have been aware of Emmett Oligary's criminal tendencies for two decades. But it's been impossible to prove. Still, we've had him under our surveillance and have been gathering evidence in order to build a case."

"But twenty years?" I said again. It seemed like a very long time.

"As Sir Mycroft said, Emmett was very, very careful. And Isabella took advantage of her friendship with him and knowledge of his less-than-legal means of doing business as she began to develop her plans to disrupt the relationship with Betrovia."

"The relationship between England and Betrovia, as you are aware, has not been very friendly over the last fifty years," said Sir Mycroft. "Since the last state visit—aside from the recent one with Princess Lurelia—"

"Which also ended badly by her disappearing," Miss Adler said. "And taking up with Isabella in her persona as the Ankh."

"Indeed," Sir Mycroft continued. "In short, and without going into too many confidential details—national security matters, you understand—Isabella Cosgrove-Pitt was determined to disrupt the relationship even further in order to promote Betrovia's strength over our fair England's. She had been feeding national secrets, gleaned from her husband, back to the Betrovians for at least the last three years."

"Not to mention trying to raise an Egyptian goddess and use her powers to acquire immortality," I said dryly.

"Yes, well," Sir Mycroft said, "while that was certainly a bold and dangerous thing to do, it wasn't as much of a threat as when she began controlling her husband Belmont and attempting to utterly destroy relations with Betrovia on a national level. With her chess table shenanigans and luring Lurelia to her side, she nearly brought us to the brink of *war*."

"That was her intention," I said. "She told us that was the case, and in fact she has been developing a very dangerous, far-reaching weapon that would have destroyed all of London."

Sir Mycroft's eyes bulged a little, and I wasn't entirely certain whether it was because I'd interrupted him, spoken at all, or given him information he didn't have. "Yes. Right, then, Alvermina."

"I can only assume the concerns over our relationship with Betrovia are the reason you were out of the country secretly this past week," I said, silently adding *when I needed you to keep me out of jail.*

He speared me with his eyes. "And how did you know about that? It was supposed to be a state secret."

I lifted my chin and looked at him. *Delicate ears, my eye!*

"This is all much too confusing," Evaline complained. "I have some questions, and if you keep bogging us down with all of these international details, it'll be next week before I get the answers."

"All right, then. What do you want to know, Evaline?" Mother asked.

"I want to know *how* you managed to be under Isabella Cosgrove-Pitt's nose for two years, in her house, without her knowing!"

Mother smiled. "A lady like Isabella Cosgrove-Pitt never notices her servants. Especially the chambermaids and scullery maids. She hardly looked at me on the rare occasion we were in the same room, and I took care to ensure she didn't get a good look any way. I also adjusted my appearance very slightly while I was there—wearing glasses that made my eyes look bigger, and allowing my eyebrows to grow quite thick and bushy, things of that nature."

Apparently, my mother was well aware of the subtleties of disguise. I nodded approvingly, and she gave me a smile. "Mr. Smith here was quite adept at disguising himself as well."

"The first time I met Daisy—as she was called—when she was undercover was during the Yule Fête," Edison said. "We were both dressed as chambermaids and we were both sneaking around Lady Isabella's study. At the time, I didn't realize she was the same woman I'd met in Oligary's office."

"And then, when Isabella had Edison abducted from the jail, I had occasion to see him. He remembered me, and that was how we began to help each other."

"You helped *me*," he said. "The first day when you made certain the wires on the battery device came loose on me was the beginning of helping me to resist the control."

"Isabella and Emmett planned for everything to go as it did

at the masquerade ball, except they didn't realize Edison wasn't under the control of the device," Mother explained.

"But he pretended to be for obvious reasons, because if anyone else had been holding that gun in the balcony, Evaline would be dead," I said flatly.

Edison gave me a look of gratitude and continued. "I intended to announce what truly happened the night Hiram Bartholomew was killed, but I needed to make them think I was under their control for a while. They realized almost too late that something had gone wrong, and that's when Isabella made the distraction—she tripped a server; I saw her do it—so Emmett could—uh—shoot Marie Antoinette."

The entire time he was speaking, Edison was not looking at Evaline, or even acknowledging her. He spoke smoothly and confidently, but his hands were curled in his lap so tightly that the knuckles were white.

"And instead of killing Evaline—I don't know why Isabella actually intended for that to happen; perhaps she thought it would be enough if she was shot *at* in public by the murderer of Hiram Bartholomew—"

"Or she assumed I would survive a gunshot," Evaline said. "And then she would have the benefit of a public assassination attempt *and* me, recovering, in her clutches—"

"And Edison Smith, who could expose Emmett Oligary during the murder trial for Hiram Bartholomew, would be dead, himself shot after he opened fire at the ball," I said. "Isabella nearly got everything she wanted. If it weren't for that special corset you were wearing—who did you say fashioned it?"

"It was Madame Trouxeau's assistant. Her name was Lady Warren or Wayren or something like that."

"Ah, Wayren," Mother murmured with a quiet smile.

"Yes, well, as it happened, everything turned out fine," Sir Mycroft said in a trifle too-loud voice. "And thanks to Desirée and the last two years she spent—er—what is it? Undercover?— we have a significant amount of information related to Isabella as well as Oligary and other of their cohorts both in England and in Betrovia. The only unexpected and untimely event was the death of Princess Lurelia. Now, Desirée, I realize you need to speak with Alvermina, so perhaps you might go into my office and commence with that."

He gestured to a side door. Mother gave me a look that could only be described as uneasy, which of course made *me* feel nauseated.

But I rose and followed her from the room. What on earth could she need to speak with me about—besides, I supposed, everything?

I expelled a long breath as I walked through from the meeting room to a very well-appointed office that, apparently, belonged to my father.

"So it was you who coshed Evaline on the head outside Cosgrove Terrace," I said quickly, before Mother could speak.

"Yes. I felt bad that I had to hurt her, but I couldn't let her go inside and disrupt things. We knew Isabella and Emmett were close to making their final move—and escape—and I was afraid if anything went wrong they would leave before we could get all of the evidence and information we needed."

"You must have been at the masquerade ball, then—to see how things went on. And you gave us the messages to 'be ready.' You must also have been the person who was there when they first ran off the balcony—Evaline thought it had to be Miss Adler, but it must have been you."

She nodded, smiling. Were her eyes glistening with tears? What was it that she had to tell me? Did I want to know? Was she going to leave me again—was that it?

"There's nothing that slips past you, is there, Mina? I'm so very proud of you."

"I'm a Holmes," I said.

Her lips curved into a soft smile. "Actually, Mina, you aren't."

"I'm...not... What?"

"You're not a Holmes."

MISS HOLMES

~ REVELATIONS ~

Y ou're not Mycroft Holmes's daughter?" Evaline
shrieked. Thank heavens we were in the cellar of the
British Museum and no one else could hear her. "But
whose daughter are you? How can that be?"

It was two days later—two days after the most exhausting,
tension-filled days I can remember.

I'd spent the days following our airship escape in a much
more relaxed manner than the preceding ones. I was with
Mother mostly, while Evaline spent her time soothing Florence
and Bram over the cancellation of her wedding and accepting all
of the condolences from society over the death of her fiancé and
his brother. Ned Oligary's funeral was tomorrow, and I fully
intended to be there, standing with Evaline as she pretended to
mourn for her fiancé and his murderous brother.

Today, however, we (Evaline, Miss Adler, Dylan, and myself)
were gathered in the British Museum for what would likely be
the last time. We were sending Dylan back to his proper year,
and he would never return. But it was the first opportunity I'd
had to speak to Evaline about the shocking news my mother had
given me, and of course she'd demanded to know what it was
Mother had taken me to the next room to tell me.

I could hardly believe it myself—not only that I wasn't truly a Holmes (which was both incredibly devastating and, in some ways, liberating), but because of who my father really was.

"Emmett Oligary was my father," I said.

Evaline's jaw dropped, and she goggled at me for a full thirty seconds before she closed it. I could see the thoughts and questions darting around inside her head, and I sympathized, for I had had all of the ones she could conceive—and more.

"Quite simply, my mother had a liaison with Emmett, and when she realized she was—er—in a family way, she knew she didn't want the child to be raised by such an evil person." I reflected on the fact that I found it easier to speak of my father as evil than I did Isabella Cosgrove-Pitt; I supposed because I understood her more than I ever understood him, and because the fact that he was my natural father was still very foreign to me. He was merely Emmett Oligary to me unless I reminded myself otherwise.

"Why did she have a liaison with him if he was so awful anyway?"

Trust Evaline to ask the most pressing question, and ever so bluntly.

"She didn't realize the extent of his perfidy at the time—but by the time she realized her condition, their liaison had long ended. And she knew she didn't want him to—well—be my father. And so—"

"And so Sir Mycroft came to the rescue and married her?" Evaline scoffed as Miss Adler snickered. "I can hardly imagine that."

"You aren't the only one," Miss Adler said with a smile. "The entirety of London society was flummoxed when that wedding occurred. But Desirée knew Mycroft would protect her—and you, Mina."

"Sir Mycroft knew all along, though, didn't he?" Evaline asked.

"He did. And Desirée confided in me as well," Miss Adler said.

"Apparently, Sir Emmett was also aware. That must be the reason he tried to force me to escape from the airship with them. And I suspect Isabella knew as well," I said.

Miss Adler looked at me. "She said something to you?"

I nodded. "When we were at The Crow that evening, Isabella and I spoke alone. She said, 'I never expected to be as challenged as I've been with you and Miss Stoker. The two of you make a formidable team.' And then she added, 'Though I suppose I shouldn't be surprised, knowing from whence you spring.'

"I responded, 'The Holmes mental acuity and deductive abilities are, indeed, formidable.' And she...she laughed. And sort of brushed it off. Then she said, 'Holmes? Forget what the men have told you, Mina. I was speaking of your mother.'"

Miss Adler drew in a breath and nodded. "Yes. She knew. Somehow, she knew."

"Well, I for one am glad you weren't raised by Emmett Oligary, Mina," Dylan said. He was looking sober and sad, and yet excited at the same time. I knew he was eager to return to his time, and there was no reason to delay it any longer.

This farewell, I knew, would not be the same emotionally charged goodbye as the last. At least for me—I suspected Miss Adler would be rather disconsolate to bid her great-great-grandson farewell.

"Thank you for everything, Mina," Dylan said as he embraced me. "I'll never forget you—hey, didn't we already do this once?" he asked with a watery laugh.

I appreciated his levity because I had been so emotionally wrung out over the last several days that I could hardly bear it. "I think we did. Be safe. And thank you for all you've done for me, as well. I care for you very much, you know."

As we hugged one last time, he murmured, "I'm pretty sure Grayling's going to step up now that I'm gone. So don't stomp on his heart too much."

I pulled away to look into his blue eyes, which were dancing with humor. I wasn't certain I completely understood his slang, but I got the general idea. "I don't know about that," I said dismissively.

"Oh, believe me. He will. He couldn't wait to see me go," he said with a laugh. "Why do you think he was willing to help me get the scarab when we were on the airship?"

Oh. "I thought he was just being nice," I said.

Dylan laughed heartily and kissed me on the mouth in that easy way of his. "He was, but he was also being nice to himself." He turned to Evaline, who flung herself into his arms.

"I suppose you'll miss Olympia," she said in a hopeful voice. "You two seemed very taken with each other—working on the project."

"Olympia? No, I don't think I'm her type," Dylan said with a funny smile.

Evaline's face fell. "Oh." Then she frowned. "What do you mean by your type?"

"I mean the kind of person she's—you know—attracted to."

"Oh. So I suppose she likes dark-haired men instead of blond-haired men. Mysterious cads instead of nice ones?" She tried to smile, but it wavered. I knew she was thinking about Edison.

Dylan shook his head, laughing. "No, no, I mean, I don't think she likes men at all. I mean, that way. Olympia likes females."

Oh. I tilted my head thoughtfully. Why, that did make sense. I knew (mainly from my association with the man who was no longer my Uncle Sherlock and from listening in on conversations he wasn't aware I was listening to) that there were individuals who preferred to associate intimately with members of their own gender. And apparently, Olympia Babbage was one such female.

Fascinating. I found it most curious and enlightening, and

decided I would have to have an extended conversation with her about this at the first opportunity.

In the meantime, the expression on Evaline's face was so shocked—and then pleased—that I couldn't contain a smile of my own.

How could she have thought for one minute that Edison Smith could prefer Olympia Babbage to Evaline Stoker? It was ludicrous. The man was completely enamored with her— although, I admit, it was only because I am an excellent student of human behavior and a practiced observer for even the slightest of clues that I knew this about Edison. For he certainly didn't make it obvious.

In fact, the casual observer would believe he was quite indifferent to Evaline, perhaps even felt enmity toward her.

By now, Miss Adler was kissing Dylan on both cheeks as she bade him farewell. As before, he took the blue scarab and placed it in the base of the Sekhmet statue—the one that had launched all of our adventures nearly a year ago.

There was a shimmery sort of light, a little zip of energy, and a *pop*.

And he was gone.

Miss Adler knelt to pick up the scarab, and, as Evaline and I watched, she took a hammer and smashed it into smithereens.

MISS STOKER

~ CONDOLENCES & CONFESSIONS ~

I had to attend the funeral service for Ned and Emmett Oligary. I had no choice.

It seemed as if myself and the entirety of London were there, bursting at the seams of Westminster Abbey.

If I could have avoided being there, I would have done so. I considered pretending to be prostrate with grief, but I didn't think even that would work with Florence.

The worst—the absolute *worst*—part about all of it was that now I was supposed to be in mourning! For a man I'd never wanted to marry *and his brother who'd tried to kill me!*

Was there ever a more ludicrous situation? And of course I'd have to wear *black* all the time—for at least a year—thanks to Her Majesty and her setting the standard.

How ironic that Ned and I had actually had a conversation about the appropriate way to mourn.

The only positive side to the entire predicament was that, for a blessed year, I could avoid all society events. That meant I could probably still sneak out at night and stir up trouble whenever I liked (Florence wouldn't know).

And, since the Oligarys had paid off all of Bram and

Florence's debts already, they wouldn't be harassing me about getting married in a year when the mourning period was over.

So I managed to sit through the funeral and pretend to feel grief. But it was really more like elation.

Not that I wanted Ned to die—or Emmett either, to be honest—but it wasn't my fault they had gotten themselves killed.

And so I sat through the long, drawn-out ceremony. I listened to the speeches and the eulogies about how wonderful Emmett Oligary had been, all the while knowing that none of it was true.

Mina sat next to me and we exchanged meaningful glances throughout. She was, after all, supposedly mourning the death of her natural father—which was not common knowledge, but would eventually leak out due to the fact that she was the *heiress to the Oligary fortune*.

Imagine that!

Once the service was over, I thought my escape would be nigh. I'd forgotten about the long lines of people who wanted to give me their condolences about the terrible airship crash that had taken the lives of the Oligarys. I stood with Florence and Bram—Mina having escaped this sentence due to the fact that she wasn't a (known) family member.

The faces and accompanying offers of condolence became a blur only a quarter of an hour into the receiving line—and it was another nearly two hours later before I finished speaking to the last person.

I wanted to go *home*. I wanted food. Lots of food. Roast beef and mashed potatoes and peas...

As I turned away, my hands sore from all of the people gripping them, holding them, pressing them, squeezing them, I looked over and saw him.

Edison.

My heart gave a funny lurch, and I turned away before he noticed I'd seen him. Had he been here the whole time? Why?

He was standing off to the side, lounging against the stone

wall of the church's vestibule. Was he waiting for something? For me? Surely not.

Maybe?

My hands grew clammy inside their gloves, and I was furious with myself for reacting that way.

He looked up at that moment, and our eyes met. Edison gave a little nod, held my eyes, and then, when I didn't move—I didn't know what to do!—he gave a funny shrug. Then he turned away and started for the side door.

I heard Florence calling my name, but I was already running across the vestibule to the door as Edison went through it. I ignored her.

I burst through the door and he wasn't there.

Where had he gone? The courtyard was empty of everything but a thin crust of snow. It was a mild day, and everything was dripping. Which was the *only* reason I had to wipe my eyes and nose with the handkerchief that, until now, had remained bone dry during the entire service.

"I didn't know ye cared for 'im so."

"Blast it, Pix!" I spun, furious that he'd managed to sneak up on me once again. Especially since he'd caught me sniveling.

He was there, undisguised, unfettered, unshadowed but for a narrow slash of shade from the brim of his hat. Good gad, he was handsome. The very sight of him made my stomach squishy.

"I'm sorry. I didn't mean to intrude on your grief."

He didn't even berate me for calling him Pix. There was no lingering insouciance, no subtle tease in his voice. He was—so bloody proper and gentlemanly. And distant.

I crumpled the handkerchief in my hand. "It's not him I care for, you bloody fool."

The words came out of my mouth before I knew it, before I could stop them. Blast it!

Edison was watching me warily, as if he wasn't certain whether I was going to spring into attack or run away. I couldn't think of anything else to say that wouldn't make me sound like a blithering idiot.

"You came back for me."

There it was again—my mouth working without permission. Drat and blast and devil take it!

"Up in the airship. You came back. You climbed back up...for me."

In for a penny, in for a pound, I supposed. I might just as well let my mouth run off with itself, since I'd already opened the door.

"You r-risked your life. You faced a v-vampire." Blooming Pete, couldn't my voice cooperate? Did it have to sound so bloody shaky? Why was my throat burning?

I needed to get away from here. From him. I needed—

"Ah, Evaline." The words sounded as if they were wrung from deep inside him. "*Yes*. Always."

This time when he came toward me with that dark, wild look in his eyes, he did what I hoped—what I expected: he pulled me into his arms. I went, surging into him, meeting his mouth with mine.

His lips were warm on the chill day, and he tasted just...so good. So right and familiar.

Not nice.

Not fine.

But...right.

"But why?" he asked, pulling away just long enough so I could take a breath. He gently kissed the corner of my mouth, featherlight and warm, and looked at me. "Why would ye do it?"

The Cockney sounded good on him; like the Pix I knew, not the formal, stilted American businessman.

"I didn't mean to... They just..." I told him everything—about how I got swept up into my engagement without really doing anything—except not saying no loudly enough.

It wasn't only Florence's fault. It was mine too—for not

standing up for myself. And for loving my family enough to sacrifice part of my life for them.

Venators made sacrifices.

I was fortunate that it had turned out the way it did, or...

"What is it? You're shivering, Evaline."

"No. I'm all right." I looked at him, touched the heavy, dark hair that brushed the back of his neck.

"Evaline, I never shot at you. I never shot at anyone." His voice was so insistent, so tight and hoarse, that it made my throat hurt. "I meant it when I said it would have been impossible for me to do what they wanted me to."

"I know, I know," I said, talking over him. He needed to realize that I understood, that I hadn't meant that accusation back in his hideaway, that I'd never really believed he could do something like that. "Grayling told me the gun wasn't fired, it wasn't loaded, it—"

"No," he said, and stepped back. "You don't understand."

My hands fell to my sides. I felt bereft and cold. "What?"

"They could never control me, could never make me do what they wanted because I could never...*never*...hurt you. Even in my head. Even in my thoughts. It was impossible for them to make me do it because, deep inside, I wouldn't allow it. My...well, damn it, my bloody heart wouldn't allow it. Or my head."

I have no idea what I said, but it didn't seem to matter. This time, our kisses were flavored with salt, and it wasn't due to grief but relief and happiness.

But when he pulled away again and stepped back, that barrier was there again. The remoteness.

"I have to go back, Evaline," he said. "Back to America. Back home. They've thought I was dead—gone—for two years now. And then they thought I was a murderer."

No. I blinked rapidly. No, not now. But my mouth behaved this time, and I only nodded, pinching my lips together so they wouldn't tremble.

"Evaline..." He looked away, turned back, then dropped to

one knee in front of me, there on the snow-covered lawn. "Would ye go wi' me, luv? Would ye be my trouble and strife, Evaline?"

"Trouble and stri—" I stopped, then stared down at him. "That's Cockney slang...isn't it? F-for wife? You want me to marry you? And live in America?" My heart exploded, and I burst into tears.

"Evaline, Evaline," he said, surging to his feet. "I'm sorry, don't cry—I'm sorry, I shouldn't have asked." He was holding my sore hands, looking miserable. "I just thought..."

I was laughing and crying at the same time. "Edison...yes. Yes, I'll be your trouble and strife, and you— What's Cockney slang for husband?"

He barked a laugh. "Pot and pan, luv," he said, and kissed me. Very, very, *very* well.

So well that I didn't even remember where we were until a plot of snow fell on my head.

I pulled away, brushing the icy slush from my bonnet. "Do you know the best part about me going to America to marry you?"

He looked at me warily. "I'm not certain, love." He took my hand, closing his warm fingers around it, and I realized he'd used the endearment in a completely different way. "Tell me."

Love. I had to swallow past the lump in my throat before I could tell him. "I won't have to pretend to be in mourning for a year."

That was the first time I ever saw him roar with laughter.

MISS HOLMES

- IN WHICH THE END IS JUST ANOTHER BEGINNING -

For how long did you know that Lady Isabella was the Ankh?" I said. It was my first opportunity to have such a conversation with Grayling.

The last two weeks had kept me wildly busy attending to the many changes in my life. Today was the first of March—the date of Evaline's original wedding—and in an ironic and bittersweet turn of events, we were riding in a carriage on our way to the docks to bid Evaline and Edison farewell for their move to America.

"I've ken nearly since the beginning."

I narrowed my eyes at him. "I don't believe you."

He had the grace to look a little flustered. "When ye insisted I take you to Cosgrove Terrace the night you escaped the opium den, I ken ye must have had a reason. And—well, if you could have seen your expression when Lady Isabella appeared..." He shrugged. "That caused me to look more closely at the situation. And it wasn't long before I began to suspect her as well."

"Even though there was a dead body that you and your colleagues claimed was the Ankh?" I asked frostily.

He sighed. "It was clearly meant to mislead us—and if you hadn't raised questions, I imagine no one would have ever known. But you raised questions, and I—" He shrugged. "I thought it would behoove myself to pay attention to you. Er, I mean your questions."

As I found his answer satisfactory, I refrained from making the obvious comment about why had he not chosen to share his thoughts with me. After all, I had not done the same—although I had excellent reasons for keeping the information to myself that his relative was a conniving murderess.

"Is there anything else, Miss Holmes?" he said. There was a teasing light in his eyes.

"There is the matter of you attempting to arrest me the night of the masquerade ball, Inspector. I haven't forgotten about that, you know."

He sighed and settled back into his seat across from me. "I assumed you hadn't."

"Then certainly you've had time to prepare a sufficient explanation."

His lips quirked, and I was reminded that I had recently had occasion to press my own to his during a very pleasurable—but far too brief—interlude. I had no complaints about their mobility, texture, warmth—or any of the other delightful characteristics of his mouth, in fact. I drew my gaze away, belatedly aware that I'd been staring.

The heightened ruddiness of his own cheeks indicated his awareness of my attention.

"Och, Mina, ye ken I didn't have a choice at the time. I knew I could get you out of jail if you even got that far, but I couldna make a scene then—Blaketon would have suspected my motives."

I lifted my nose and looked down its long expanse at him. (Apparently, I hadn't inherited my proboscis from Mycroft Holmes after all.) "I should hope you would never have allowed it to get so far that I was put in *jail*."

"Of course not."

Satisfied that I had made my point, I settled back in my seat and glanced out the window. We were nearly there.

"Today was the day Evaline was supposed to marry Ned Oligary," I said. "What a strange turn of fate."

"She will marry Smith, then, won't she?"

I nodded. "Yes, but not for a while. His family wants to meet her, and of course they have to plan the wedding. However, if I know Evaline, she might simply drag Edison to a judge or minister some day and get it done."

"I thought she didn't want to get married."

"She didn't want to wed *Mr. Oligary*. Fancy that—she would have been my sister-by-law if she had done so." I felt my eyes sting a bit. Evaline would have been a real sister to me. "She *wants* to marry Edison."

He was silent for a moment, then said, "If ye ever change your opinion about the travails of marriage, I'll want to know, Mina."

"And if I ever change my opinion, I'll make certain you're apprised of the situation immediately, Ambrose." My cheeks were warm.

Had that just been a marriage proposal of sorts? Not that I was ever going to marry, but it was nice to know that it was an option. Particularly with Grayling.

Most especially with Grayling.

"Make certain of that, now, then will you, Mina? After all, with all of the traveling you'll be doing with your mother and your newfound fortune, perhaps you won't ever come back to London." Although his words were provocative, there was a light of question in his eyes.

"I've always wanted to see Paris. And Egypt. But there's no doubt I'll return. The projects Sir Mycroft has asked us to attend to won't last more than a few months." I was looking forward to working with my mother on a few interesting tasks for the Home Office. Apparently, such work ran in the family, Holmes or not.

I smiled quietly at Grayling. "But you—you'll never leave London, will you?"

"Nae. I can't, Mina. I've work to do here."

I nodded. I understood, for there had been four packets of files in the drawer of his office desk. Four files of difficult, unusual, and unsolved cases. Three of them had now been satisfactorily resolved and put away: the Murder of Hiram Bartholomew, the Individual Known as the Ankh, and Evidence of Vampires in London.

But the fourth file was the one that kept him here in London, and I knew that it would until it, too, was put away. If ever. The Death of Melissa Grayling.

I wouldn't expect otherwise of the man I'd come to know and admire.

The fishy smell of the wharfs and the shouts from the sailors told me we'd arrived. Grayling handed me out of the carriage and tucked my fingers into the crook of his elbow as we walked to the great ship that would be taking Evaline and Edison to America.

I had firmly informed myself not to tear up. I wouldn't need a handkerchief, of course. This wasn't truly a farewell. It was merely an *au revoir*—an "until we meet again."

But when I came face to face with Evaline, my eyes began to sting. It was because of the pungent air, of course, and it was blowing in my face.

"Mina." She took my hands. "I don't know what to say. This last year, since we met—"

"It's not quite a year yet," I informed her. "Not until April."

She laughed and blinked rapidly. The tip of her nose was red. "Of course not. But sometimes it felt like one when you were lecturing or speechifying. Especially when you were going on and on and *on* about the Theophanine Chess Queen."

"And I'm certain I lived several lifetimes during the moments you flung us into jeopardy, when I was certain it would be my last seconds on this earth. It's a wonder my hair hasn't turned completely white from all of the harrowing experiences you've gotten us into."

We both laughed, and my eyes stung a little more. *Drat.*

"I probably should tell you that when we first met, I didn't like you very much."

"I certainly didn't want to be your partner, either," I replied. "I didn't need a brash, impetuous person ruining my plans."

"And yet..." Her voice trailed off, and I found I couldn't speak either.

We held each other's hands, swinging them a little between us as we looked at each other. For some reason, her image was blurry.

"Isabella was right," I said when I found my voice again. "Miss Adler made a great decision, pairing us to work together."

"Oh, Mina, I've learned so much from you!" She flung herself into my arms, and I embraced her tightly.

I was *not* going to cry. I was *not*.

"You've taught me many things as well." I was speaking into the side of her bonnet, as Evaline is quite a bit shorter than me. "Not about science or deductions or anything terribly pertinent, but—"

She was shaking, and I pulled free of the embrace to see what was wrong. She was laughing. I began to laugh as well, though my face was wet and I needed a handkerchief for my nose. Someone pushed one into my hand—Grayling, of course—and I used it.

Evaline and I looked at each other. "It's been the most amazing nearly year I've ever known," I forced myself to say past the lump in my throat. "Thank...you." I barely got the words out. "For making me feel like I belong—"

"Stop it or I'll be bawling all the way to New York," she said, smiling through another wave of tears. Then she took my hand and drew me away so that Grayling and Edison couldn't hear her. "Mina, I'm frightened."

My tears immediately dried up. "Why? What's wrong? Is

there an UnDead on the ship? Did you see someone carrying a body on board?"

"No, no." Evaline was as sober as I'd ever seen her. "I'm a vampire hunter. I can't be a *wife* too...I just don't see how I can be good at both. And someday a *mother*?" Tears welled in her eyes. "Maybe I shouldn't do this..." She glanced miserably at Edison.

"No. Absolutely not, Evaline, don't be ridiculous. If there is anyone on this earth who could manage to do both, it's you. Of course you can do it."

"I know you'd never lie to me—or even finesse the truth," she said. But she still didn't seem convinced.

"Evaline, you're marrying the *perfect* man to be the husband of a vampire hunter. He's known from the beginning who you are —and he's not exactly a naive innocent either."

"How *did* he know from the beginning about me?" she said. "That very first night at the British Museum, when he sneaked up on me in the shadows, he knew all about me. But how?"

"Do you mean you've never asked him?"

She flushed a little. "No. We're usually—er—doing other things."

I laughed. I glanced at Grayling. I could imagine those "other things" quite well. "Evaline, the answer to that is simple: he's known my mother since before the day in Hiram Bartholomew's office. Surely she told him."

"Why, of course. That makes perfect sense."

"Rest assured, Evaline—I haven't the *slightest* doubt in my mind that you and Edison will wreak as much havoc in America as you did here. And as you are aware, I am an excellent judge of human character. After all, I am a H—" I snapped my mouth closed.

"You can still say it, Mina," Evaline said. "*Nothing* about you has changed—you're still as brilliant as you ever were. And you don't have to blame it on that cold, intimidating fish of a father of yours! The only thing that's really changed," she said with a grin, "is that now you're filthy rich."

I laughed, and we embraced one last time. It was time to let her go—time to send my best, dearest, most impetuous and life-changing friend off on her next adventure.

And for me go on to mine.

A NOTE FROM THE AUTHOR

Is this the end of the Stoker & Holmes series?

Yes, but...probably not.

Surely Mina and Evaline have more work to do, even though they are now going to be separated by the Atlantic Ocean. (I'm sure they aren't finished having adventures.)

While you're waiting for the possibility of more tales, why not check out the story of Evaline's predecessor Victoria Gardella?

The Gardella Vampire Hunters series is available wherever books are sold—and to give you a taste for this very different, yet similar woman and the choices *she* must make as a Venator, **go here to download a free, short story** about Victoria Gardella: **cgbks.com/victoria**

I hope you enjoy the read!

༄༅༅

Please follow me on Facebook, Twitter, or Instagram for updates and news—or sign up here for my monthly newsletter which gives details and news about all my books: cgbks.com/news

Thanks for reading, and for supporting Mina & Evaline and their adventures. I'd love to hear from you—email me at books@colleengleason.com or drop me a line via my website or any of my social media accounts and tell me what you think.

—Colleen Gleason, August 2019

ABOUT THE AUTHOR

Colleen Gleason is an award-winning, New York Times and USA Today best-selling author. She's written more than forty novels in a variety of genres—truly, something for everyone!

She loves to hear from readers, so feel free to find her online.

❧

Get SMS/Text alerts for any
New Releases or **Promotions!**

Text: **COLLEEN** to **38470**

(You will only receive a single message when Colleen has a new release or title on sale. *We promise*.)

❧

If you would like SMS/Text alerts for any **Events** or book signings Colleen is attending,
Text: **MEET** to **38470**

❧

Subscribe to Colleen's non-spam newsletter for other updates, news, sneak peeks, and special offers!

http://cgbks.com/news

Connect with Colleen online:

www.colleengleason.com

books@colleengleason.com